Arrivals and Departures
from Normal

Arrivals and Departures ~ from Normal ~

LANA JEAN ROSE

Arrivals and Departures from Normal

iUniverse books may be ordered through booksellers or by contacting:

iUniverse
1663 Liberty Drive
Bloomington, IN 47403
www.iuniverse.com
1-800-Authors (1-800-288-4677)

Because of the dynamic nature of the Internet, any web addresses or links contained in this book may have changed since publication and may no longer be valid. The views expressed in this work are solely those of the author and do not necessarily reflect the views of the publisher, and the publisher hereby disclaims any responsibility for them.

Any people depicted in stock imagery provided by Thinkstock are models, and such images are being used for illustrative purposes only. Certain stock imagery © Thinkstock.

ISBN: 978-1-4917-7495-3 (sc)
ISBN: 978-1-4917-7496-0 (hc)
ISBN: 978-1-4917-7497-7 (e)

Library of Congress Control Number: 2015914072

Print information available on the last page.

iUniverse rev. date: 01/21/2016

This book is dedicated to all the people in my life that have continued to inspire me to pursue my passion of expressing myself through various forms of art and my deep desire to make a difference in other people's lives. A special thanks to my dearest friend and mentor, Scott McBride, whose continual belief in me as an artist has inspired me to discover myself in ways I'd never have known without his perceptiveness and vision.

❧ 1 ❧

"Dinner's ready!" yelled D. J., Airstream's mother. Debbie Jane was her mom's real name.

Air; her two younger brothers, Ron and Jim; and her dad, Mitchell, all sat down at the table with the usual apprehension. Dinners were the highlight of the day for D. J. since this was the time she'd announce her latest plans for her new project.

Air sat tensely and stared at her mother. She could feel the beginnings of an achy tummy accompanied with the onset of the loss of her appetite. Mitchell just sat there staring out the window with a look that said, *Jesus, here we go again.* The family could sense D. J. was just a little too happy, which was a signal of a looming announcement.

Her plans were a reminder to the kids that they dare not bring any of their friends' home from school. *No doubt, Air and her dad and brothers were about to hear all about what would be the latest in a series of creations that looked like the early works of Tim Burton, if he had lived in Texas in the fifties.* She did not create anything normal or pleasant to the eye; it was not in her nature. She said normal things were ugly and her creations were "un-use-u-elle" and true art. She was convinced everyone envied her talents.

D. J. set fried chicken and okra in the middle of the table. She sat down and smiled at everyone. "Daddy!" she squealed in a way that had way too much zealousness in it. "I think it's 'bout time we did some *re-deck-er-ate-in!*"

The family moaned in unison, and little Jimmy, who was six years old, started crying. Air tried to soothe him while she rubbed her own tummy.

In Texas, everyone knew there was a general unspoken rule that *sheep followed sheep*—as in, ever'-ba-dee's house otta look like ever'-ba-dee else's house. D. J. did everything in her power to explain to the family her deep belief they were "*u-nique*" and different from everyone else.

"Mom, what kind of redecorating are you thinking about?" Air asked, as if she was interested rather than apprehensive and about ready to throw up. "I think the house is perfect. It looks as nice as everyone else's house in the neighborhood."

"Wh-elle now, honey, that's e-zack-u-lee my point, ack-shoe-ally! Ain't no sense us tryin' ta be like ever'-ba-dee else 'cuz we're *u-nique*! How many times I gotta remind y'all *we're special* and we outta be proud!"

Air sat there staring at her plate. She thought about how her mother spent so much time "creating" instead of being a mother. Creating was not something other mothers did, and D. J. was always up to something bizarre and extremely embarrassing. D. J.'s deep Texas accent upset Air as well. It was as though she wanted more attention than she deserved, so she'd make a point of drawing out every word. Air remembered when she was barely five years old and D. J. had come to her and said, "Airstream, honey, if ya ever meet up with the devil, ya just lookie him straight in his eyes and ya tell him you ain't got no time for him! Ya just keep right on a-walkin'!

D. J. was a tiny, bird-boned woman, barely five feet tall, skinny as a rail, and with long, coal-black hair and beady, dark brown eyes. She hadn't always looked that way. When she was a little girl, she'd had beautiful blonde hair with soft curls and skin as white as pearls. When she was sixteen years old, her beautiful blonde hair started growing black roots, startling everyone who knew her. Her skin had transformed as well, her extremely fair complexion slowly becoming a dark olive. Her parents made sure pictures of D. J. as a child were displayed as prominently and profusely as possible to prove she'd come from pure German descent. Everyone in the family was fair skinned, had a freckled complexion, strawberry or blond hair, and brown eyes. The family felt tremendous pressure to make up a story about what the hell had caused D. J. to go through the inexplicable physical transition.

Of course, everyone in town whispered that she was "possessed." Some said God had simply "willed" this blessing, and they were all just to accept "his way." This may have been the beginning of D. J.'s hardheadedness about "the way."

"There ain't nobody gettin' in my way!" she would chant while creating.

She was considered the black sheep of the family. She emitted a presence that warned others, "Don'tcha even think of fuckin' with me." She was forever telling the kids, "Honey, we're *unique!*" She rebelled against everything her parents told her she should do whether it was the way she wore her hair or the way she dressed. She wanted to be different. She did not want to go to church or participate in normal family activities. She was convinced other women were evil and would stab you in the back given the chance.

Every Sunday, all the family members, aunts, uncles, and cousins, gathered at Air's parents' house for Sunday brunch. Air prayed her Mom would, for once, go into the parlor with all of her sisters and paint "purdy little roses" on thin, eggshell china plates. D. J. would have nothing to do with the useless activity. She would remark, "That ain't art! It's just wasted earth life time!"

Air's grandparents, Papaw and Mamaw, were the heads of one of the wealthiest and most prominent Texas families. They owned thousands of acres of cornfields and herds of Black Angus cattle. Papaw was a Mason and a very remote man, except when it came to any family decisions. Mamaw was always quiet, rarely uttering a word.

Sadly, the family had a big secret. Just as her hair was coming in black, D. J. had run off with her girlfriend to experience New Orleans for the weekend without permission. The very first night, she met a truck driver and fell in love with him and ended up getting herself "preggers."

Since Papaw and Mamaw's main concern was to keep the family's name from being "tainted," they told all their friends D. J. had been accepted into a famous fashion house in Paris and would study fashion design for three years. They told everyone D. J. had been preparing for this for quite a while and had the deep "feelin'" that she should pack and be prepared to fly to Paris in a moment's notice. In fact, they lied and said she'd actually already flown over to

Paris and had even met an ambassador's son she was quite fond of. Mamaw thought this story would work and D. J. would be allowed back home after the child was two years old.

Meanwhile, Papaw and Mamaw made arrangements to send D. J. to live in New Orleans with Mitchell, the truck driver, in one of Papaw's trailer properties, which he owned all over the United States. Mamaw kept telling elaborate stories of how D. J. had met the man of her dreams in Europe. She'd update the community at church each Sunday. Mamaw and Papaw would act real proud, since D. J.'s new love was supposed to be from a prominent French family, and they'd hint about their suspicions of a weddin' in the plannin'.

In reality, Air's father held down two jobs. One was as a vegetable truck driver, and the other was making sure D. J. was always busy because "idle hands were the work of the devil." It was true. D. J. *was* always up to something that would make eyes roll, whether it was the way she was dressed or the forever coming response—"My God, D. J., what in hell is that?'—to her latest fashion "dee-zign." Did she, for example, realize her pink-stained white tennis shoes didn't have any shoelaces?

"Wh-elle, of course they don't; it's the latest style!"

When Air was born, she was given the name Airstream. Papaw had allowed Mitchell and D. J. to live in a deluxe Airstream trailer in New Orleans. D. J. thought the name Airstream was "u-nique" and would be a great name for their new baby girl. Mitchell just shook his head. He was becoming used to being told how things were going to be.

Finally, the time came for D. J., Mitchell, and Airstream to move "back to the States." They were given a very lush, overabundant, Texas-style homecoming party. Everyone who was anyone was invited, including relatives who lived out of state. Of course everyone came to see the son of a diplomat and the new baby. But if truth be known, they were all really there to see if D. J. still had jet-black hair and look to see the color of the little girl's hair and skin. Mamaw almost fainted with relief when she saw Airstream's strawberry blonde hair and big brown eyes.

"Oh! Praise the Lord; she's a beautiful little girl! Look, Pa—she sure looks like her mama did when she was a little girl, doesn't she? We'll all pray she will grow up to be a beautiful, rare brown-eyed, strawberry-blonde young woman of German descent!"

Everyone started crying and glared at D. J.

D. J. just smiled back with a slight smirk, holding Mitchell's arm tightly.

Little did D. J. know, Papaw had already arranged the little family's entire future. There in Texas, D. J. and Mitchell would be treated like they were Mamaw and Papaw's own Barbie and Ken dolls. D. J. would go crazy when, after the party, she'd learn that her father had bought a huge two-story brick home in a prominent neighborhood where they would live and two Cadillac's, one for each of them to drive; had picked out the private school Airstream would attend; and had provided all three with complete attire for every occasion they might need to attend. The house was fully furnished with the latest of furniture styles; a highly prized German shepherd; and, of course, two live-in maids.

And while Papaw had arranged the family's future, Mamaw had done some arranging of her own—of the past. The welcome party hadn't been going long when Mamaw started telling everybody her tale of how the child had gotten her name.

D. J. glared at her mother. "Oh now, Mama, let's keep some stories sacred. We don't have to tell 'em all our secrets."

Papaw jumped in. "Apparently, D. J. was always tickled pink how quick the flight from one country to another seemed to be. Mitchell always reminded her of the jet airstreams the plane could catch."

Mamaw beamed at the crowd and continued her storytelling. "As I'm sure y'all kin imagine, Mitchell owns his own plane. And that's all it took! They both decided that, with all the traveling they were doing, it would be appropriate to name their firstborn Airstream! Don't you think it's a lovely and unusual name? She'll grow up to be quite the unusual, extraordinary young lady, no doubt!"

Mamaw sighed. "Oh wh-elle," she added, "y'all kin see just how much Mitchell adores her. Lookie at the way he holds her around that tiny little waist of hers."

Throughout the party, Mamaw's gushing continued. "I think he has at least three castles!" she told anyone who would listen. "Apparently, it's a way of life over there in E-your-row-pee. I just can't imagine why they go to all that fuss. And his family just loves her. You should see the beautiful new E-your-row-pee gowns she now owns. And ever' one of them was designed just for her! There ain't another gown like each of them in the world."

Thank God I was only two years old when all those lies were being told, Air thought. She knew she would have said something to the contrary as Mamaw went on and on. *I just wish to God Mother would quit repeating the stories to me over and over, word for word.*

"Airstream! Airstream!" Her mother's voice cut into her reverie. "Did ya hear *any* of my new re-deck-er-atin' ideas? Where *is* your mind? And why aren'tcha eating? Ya just asked me a question, and when I gave ya my answer, ya just stared at your plate! Wh-elle? What d'ya think of my new project ideas?"

"I'm sorry, Mom. What were you saying you were going to do? I was thinking about my homework. I really have a lot of homework tonight. May I be excused from the table?" Air asked politely.

"Not just yet, young lady. I *said* I think it's 'bout time we did some *re-deck-er-ate-in' around here*! I want the living room to just flow on in the kitchen!"

"Oh yeah, I remember now. Mom, I think the house looks great just as it is."

"Wh-elle, I think if we continue this here Japanesey kitchen design on in ta the living room, it'd look be-u-t-ful!"

"Whatcha think, Daddy?" D. J. asked impatiently.

Air looked at her father and could see his loss for words. Air remembered last week when she'd come home from school to find D. J. had painted the kitchen ceiling bright tangerine and the walls a darker tangerine. She'd already had Daddy put up some black paneling, which ran from the floor up the wall about six feet. She had hung a black, ball-shaped Japanese lamp made of paper over the kitchen table. She loved the "panellin'" so much she made Daddy continue to "run it on into the living room."

"Wh-elle, I think the panellin' in the living room would look much purdier if we were to paint it green!"

"Green! There's nothing in there that would match green!"

"Wh-elle, not yet there ain't, but I got pa-lans for that room, honey."

She left the conversation at that. Daddy didn't comment one way or the other. He knew she was on a mission, and he didn't dare ask her what she had in mind.

"Wh-elle, I've decided that ta-mar-ra I'm gonna paint that panellin' in the living room green. I've already bought the paint!"

"I thought we'd already gone over this. There is nothing in there that would match green."

"Wh-elle, yes, there is; it just ain't in there yet."

"What do you mean it ain't in there yet?"

"Oh now, honey, I just wantcha ta do me a little favor. I wantcha ta build me a waterfall! I got it all pa-land out! I got these here designs right here. Would ya like to see 'em?"

"Waterfall! What kind of waterfall, Mom?" Air asked loudly and a little too defiantly.

"You watch your language, little lady! Yeap! We're gonna have us a waterfall! We kin pick up some see-ment and maybe some of them colored aquarium pebbles. I think I'll line the bottoms of each of the bowls with 'em."

"*Each* of the bowls? What do you mean each of the bowls, Mom?"

"Wh-elle, I've designed this here Japanesey waterfall that has these here three tiers that'll be full of water, and they're gonna flow from the top and end up in the bottom bowl and then go back up to the top and start all over. Oh! It's gonna be so u-nique! And I figger we could put the couch over there next to the winda and the stuffed owls and that ole turtle your granddaddy killed right next to the waterfall! What'd ya think? Oh honey! You kin figger out some way to make the water flow from one bowl to another, can'tcha, Mitchell? Just like a real waterfall in Yosemite, California?"

Air looked at her father as he sat there trying not to choke on his food. He didn't lift his head from his plate. She prayed he'd put his foot down, but he didn't.

Air again asked to be excused. She went straight to her room. She slammed the door and threw herself onto her bed. She looked around at the beautiful furniture her mamaw had chosen for her. Her canopy bed looked like a princess bed. It was fully draped from side to side with vintage handmade pink lace, and in some areas the lace was pulled back with stunning large satin bows. Her pink handmade silk quilt had belonged to her great grandmother. The family said she was the most beautiful creature most had ever seen. D. J. had a younger sister, Jacqueline, who was as gorgeous as her great grandmother.

Air remembered her aunt once taking her out shopping to buy her a birthday present. Men would stop her and tell her how beautiful she was. D. J. was jealous of her sister. D. J. knew her parents favored her sister and her children more than they did D. J. and her family. Airstream realized her mother was right about mamaw favoring Jacqueline. She watched as mamaw doted over her and her cousins. Jacqueline had her own seamstress and all her clothes were one of a kind. She never wore an outfit twice and made sure everyone knew she donated her clothes immediately after wearing them to the local charity.

Air looked down at the pink satin sheets that matched her quilt. It was truly a princess room Air could share with no one. She stared at her many beautiful handmade German dolls that had been special ordered from Germany. She wanted to be as beautiful as the dolls someday. Air had a photograph of her great grandmother next to the German dolls and thought she was the most beautiful woman she'd ever seen. Her face looked just like the porcelain faces of all hand-painted doll's faces. They were dressed in silk brocade gowns with tiny red blossoms. The gowns had V-necks and the sleeves flowed out into wide bells. The gowns were replicas of gowns worn by German queens. They were breathtaking and extremely delicate. Air wasn't allowed to play with them but she daydreamed that when she grew up she would wear gowns like these and look as beautiful and elegant as her great grandmother did. She imagined she would be the most popular girl in town and sought after by all the boys.

Unfortunately, the dolls were to be seen and not touched. To make sure Air didn't touch them, special glass cases were built, and all had locks on them.

Air desperately wanted to share her beautiful bedroom with her friends. She longed to have pajama parties, but that was out of the question. She had to kept her beautiful room to herself and take solace in knowing she had the most beautiful bedroom of all her girlfriends but she was reminded too that the neighbors were always pulling back their curtains to peek over and see what kooky D. J. was up to. Air did not dare let any of her girl friends know how different her life was from theirs.

D. J. didn't have any friends, and she liked it that way. Air had once asked her mother if she had any girlfriends.

"I ain't got no time for nobody!" D. J. had snapped. "All they ever do is talk about their aching and a painin'. They're just a bunch of pity par-tee-ers, and that's toxic for me!"

Air was exhausted. She fell asleep on top of her bed fully clothed.

She woke up the next morning in the same shoes and dress she'd had on the day before, since her parents never came to her room to say good night to her and tuck her in with a bedtime story. She sat up and rubbed her eyes. She could already hear loud voices coming from the kitchen.

"Wh-elle, when do you think you could have it done?"

"For Christ sakes, I work all the time! I don't know when I'll have the time to build a waterfall!"

"Wh-elle, I hope it's soon, cuz I almost have ever'thing I need to finish up this here project."

Air heard the back door slam and her father drive off. Mitchell loved to build things. In a way, he enjoyed D. J.'s challenges of design.

Somehow, after a month of working on different ideas, Mitchell had managed to set up a water system that was able to recycle water from the bottom bowl back up to the top bowl. While the cement on her new waterfall was still wet, D. J. pushed polished pebbles into the surface of each bowl. As soon as it was dry and hard, she and Mitchell set the waterfall up in the corner of the living room, just like D. J. had wanted.

It was clear to Air that D. J. had immediately started planning the next phase of the project. She'd already painted the black paneling green, and yet there was still nothing in the living room that was green. One morning, D. J. watched out the window as Mitchell drove off to work. Air felt a fearful quiver run through her body as she watched her mother. She sensed D. J. was planning to do something that would send her father into a rage and that he might take it out on her and her brothers.

As soon as he was out of sight, she called for the kids to come into the kitchen. She lined Air and her two younger brothers up and said, "Wh-elle, my little honeys, taday we're gonna go on a *big* advent-chure! Y'all just falla me and stay re-eel close behind, hear?"

D. J. stood there with one arm gripping the biggest empty pickle jar Air'd ever seen. It had a can of Aqua Net hair spray and a pair of tweezers inside of it. In her other hand, was her famous pokin' stick, which she always had and was forever using to poke at stuff and say, "Wh-elle now, would ya lookie there at that! I wonder what I kin do with that, honey?"

Everything was a "po-tench-e-al project." One might say D. J. was one of the original environmental artists long before repurposing or making art from found objects was cool or any attention was even being given to the environment. Even if making art from found objects had been considered avant-garde somewhere in the 1950s, it still would not have been appreciated in Texas.

Air and her two brothers looked around to see if any neighbors' curtains were moving. They all stood in front of their house wondering what kind of trouble D. J. was going to get herself into this time. They wished they didn't have to be a part of whatever was about to happen.

The house was trimmed with bushes about two feet tall all the way around to the backyard. Daddy had told the kids to stay away from those bushes. They had no idea why—somethin' about somethin' being deadly in 'em. And since it was coming from Daddy, they never went close to those bushes, for fear of one of his brutal and constant beatings! Any reason was a good reason to beat the kids, especially if his Giants lost a baseball game.

Well, the deadly part was what the kids were about to find out. D. J. was on her final mission to make the "green Japanesey" room complete. Whatever the main draw to this Japanesey scene for the living room was, it lay hidden in the bushes.

The kids walked slowly behind her, watching her as she gently poked and moved the stems and leaves of the bushes. Suddenly, they all stopped and stared in utter terror as D. J. started screaming.

"Oh ma gads! Just lookie! There's one right there! Look at 'er."

"'Er" turned out to be a spider, and it was the hugest goddamned spider Air'd ever seen in her life. Her class had just studied insects, and she knew straightaway these were black widow spiders. Leave it to D. J. to only play in the big leagues.

Suddenly, D. J. turned to the kids, "Y'all all move back outta the way! Oh ma gads, y'all gotta get way, way back from here and just watch your mama in action!"

Air turned once again to see if any of the neighbors' curtains were moving. She thought about how her mother had never given her a hug or told her she loved her in her whole life. Air wondered what love felt like. Air knew her father didn't love her either. He was always telling her she was a worthless piece of shit that no one would ever love, especially whenever he'd had too much to drink. Then there was the never-ending "shit list" that had Air's name all over it. Air wondered how her best friend, Cindy, felt after being told how pretty she was by her parents. Air longed to just hear her parents were proud of her. Completely unable to visualize herself, Air had to go to the mirror to see what she looked like since she was never told she was pretty.

Air turned back to watch D. J. prepare to make her "first catch of the day." She had no idea what the spider was destined for or that there'd be more than "one hunt." She felt a chill run through her body. There was such greed in D. J.'s eyes. She realized her mother enjoyed catching her first spider more than she enjoyed spending time with her kids, much less cooking breakfast for her children. She'd get up to feed the dogs and then go back to bed. Perhaps if

Air and her brothers were black, shiny and had red hourglasses on their tummies, D. J. might have cooked breakfast for them too, but that wouldn't have worked either since "black" meant dirty and "the other side" of town.

D. J. quickly set the pickle jar down and got out the hair spray. She started spraying the hell of out the spider. Air was terrified. The kids stood there staring at their mother and the so-called stunned spider in disbelief. They didn't understand how hairspray could kill spiders.

D. J. continued poking through the bushes, eventually "stunning" two more spiders. Air watched in horror as her mother continued spraying until the can of hairspray was empty; leaving the spiders lying lifeless on the ground. D. J. continued to squeal with utter joy and delight. She took out her tweezers and carefully placed her kills into the jar.

"Oh ma gads! I can't believe I found myself three spiders on my first hunt! Oh sweet Jesus, there must be more out here somewhere. I need more than just three. We'll go on out to the garden shed. I betcha there's some back there. It's dark in there and lots of places they can hide."

The kids stood there as stunned as the spiders. They could not move from fear. They had just witnessed her spraying the hair spray as if she was putting out a bushfire! Air felt an overwhelming sense that something really bad could happen. It seemed to her that her mother was not in the same world where she and her brothers existed. She knew this was all really weird, really crazy, and really dangerous; and yet, there was something about the danger of all of this that was mesmerizing. She prayed as fast as she could to her guardian angels. *Please, just don't let any of the neighbors see us.*

D. J. headed toward the garden shed but stopped short when she realized she'd used up all her hair spray. "Damn. I need more hair spray," she muttered. "We're through for the day, kids. We'll go out to the shed ta-mar-ra. I gotta buy some more spray."

The kids followed D. J. back into the house, all of them wondering what their mother was going to do with the three spiders she'd caught. A couple of weeks went by, and there was no talk of any "hunts." Things seemed as normal as they could be, and Air started to relax. She told herself it had just been a onetime "escapade." The weekend was coming, and there was talk of a picnic. But things didn't turn out that way.

On Friday night, Air had a nightmare that a giant spider web was anchored from each of the corners of the ceiling in her bedroom. On one side of the web sat a giant black widow. Air had somehow gotten herself tangled in the web, and the spider, taking note, quickly ran to her and spun her into a bundle, as though she were some kind of insect that had accidently fallen into the web. Then the spider stuffed what felt like a straw into the tightly woven gossamer binding that glued her to the web. She dreamt the spider was slowly sucking all her blood but being careful to leave her body intact. Just as the spider was about to stretch Air's body out for viewing, Air woke up screaming.

She was terrified. She half expected to see one of her parents come running into her room. She quickly realized she was dreaming on both counts. One, she'd just had a nightmare. Two, no one was coming. She got dressed and went down the hall into the kitchen, where she could smell the bacon the maid was cooking for her father. Air wanted to tell him about "the hunt" and her nightmare, but she knew better. The kitchen door opened, and D. J. appeared bright-eyed and just a little too perky.

Oh God, what is she planning? Air asked herself.

"I have to run down to the grocery store for a few things, y'all. I'll be back soon."

"Daddy, do you have to go to work today? It's Saturday. I could help you wash the car," Air said.

"Sorry, Air, I have a meeting with your papaw. I'll be gone all day."

This was really bad news. Air knew D. J. had gone to the grocery store to buy more hair spray. She knew more "hunts" were on the agenda. She hoped D. J. would go alone. She wondered how many more spiders she needed to catch. And what was she planning to do with them? She knew her father had no idea what was happening.

Mitchell left just as her brothers came into the kitchen.

"Where's Mom?" asked Ron.

"The grocery store, and Daddy's not going to be home all day," Air remarked with an ominous tone of voice. "I bet we're going on another one of those spider hunts today. I don't think she's caught enough spiders for whatever she's planning. I think she's going out to the garden shed today to see what she can find."

"I'm not gonna go. I'm too scared. I could die. I'm gonna tell Daddy what she made us do with her when he gets home."

"Oh no you're not, unless you want a real bad whooping."

"I'm staying inside with Ron," said Jimmy. "I don't feel so good."

Suddenly the front door burst open, and D. J. came inside with her arms full of grocery bags.

"Oh, y'all, we're gonna have another fun day," she said, beaming. "I bought some more hair spray. We're gonna go out to that garden shed. I'm just gonna put the food away, and then we'll all go and see if there's anythin' hiding out there just waitin' for us."

"Do we have to go?" moaned Jimmy. "Cuz I don't feel good."

"Wh-elle then, you kin just go to your bedroom and we'll go without cha."

D. J. put the groceries away, except for the hair spray. She went over to the kitchen closet, grabbed the giant pickle jar, and turned around with a look that said, "Let's go!"

From what Air could remember, no one ever went into the garden shed. Maybe the gardeners who took care of the yard used the shed, but she'd never seen them in there. The grounds were full of magnolia trees, yellow roses and stone paths that led out to an elaborate patio with everything that was needed for a grand family gathering. The kid's swing set looked like something from the county fair with slides and it's own roller coaster. The gardener's shed was tucked back behind a giant weeping willow tree out of sight.

D. J. walked briskly, her poking stick in hand. When she reached the shed, she set the jar and stick down and turned to the kids. She told them they had to wait outside until she'd cleared away any webs they might have to walk through. She opened the door, and they all looked in. It was dark, but D. J. found a light switch. She turned the light on. The shed wasn't full of garden tools at all. Instead, there were shelves on the wall with jars of preserved fruit. D. J. had no idea how they'd gotten there or whose they were. She didn't give it much more thought since she was on a "hunt" for spiders, not fruit. It didn't take long before she started squealing.

"Oh, lan' sakes alive. I see at least five spiders right there in the corner! Oh, they're so big! Y'all get back so I kin spray 'em. Get back," she yelled.

Air and Ron backed up and watched. She started spraying as fast as she could. The spiders started falling to the floor, and D. J. continued to spray.

When she ran out of hair spray, she started yelling. "I ain't done yet! There's more spiders in here, and I want 'em!"

She turned to the kids with a frustrated look and told them to just stay where they were. She carefully gathered approximately ten black widow spiders and put them in her pickle jar. She took a deep breath and turned to the kids. "Okay, y'all, come on. Mommie's gonna make 'em all re-elle purdy now."

Re-elle purdy was a scary thought to Airstream. She didn't want to know what that meant, but she followed as her mother led her and Ron back into the house. D. J. set the jar on the kitchen table and went to the closet again. She brought out a piece of plywood board about two feet by two feet. It was covered with black velvet. She reached for a box of straight pins that were right beside the board and, for some reason, a bottle of clear fingernail polish. She put the plywood on the table and set the pickle jar, pins, and fingernail polish alongside it. She went back into the closet and brought out another jar of spiders, which she gently added to the giant pickle jar.

Air was horrified. *Another jar of spiders? Where did that come from?* She stood motionless and watched her mother. Using tweezers, D. J. carefully pulled a spider from the jar and placed it on the velvet board. She gently pulled the spider's curled legs out from under it, slowly and intently uncurling each spindly leg until it had been stretched to its full extent. Once she had them in a position she found "appealin'," she pinned the spider to the board. Meticulously, she repeated the process with each of the spiders one by one until the board was full. About twenty spiders covered the black surface, each

15

at least an inch in size. Next, she took the clear fingernail polish and coated each one to make them even "purdier" than they were before.

"See here, honeys. This is why ya never ever use *real* bug spray on 'em. It just hurts 'em and makes 'em jam their legs up too tight and cramps their long, beautiful legs. They don't wanna stretch out their legs again after that. They're sorta frozen in a ball. Hair spray is merciful. They don't feel a thang. It's kinda like I just put 'em to sleep."

Airstream wondered how D. J. had planned all this out without anyone knowing. She wondered where the plywood had come from and when had D. J. gone out to buy velvet. For that matter, how did she even know to cover the wood with velvet? The scariest question was where had she gotten the extra spiders?"

"Lookie there. Now they're purdy and shiny forever!" D. J. exclaimed.

"Like they weren't shiny enough to begin with," Air thought to herself.

She stood there staring at her mother and the shiny spiders all lined up across the board drying. She felt completely drained and wanted to cry. She thought back to all the strange trips she and her brothers had taken over the last few weekends and then D. J. asking for a waterfall. It all started to make sense. About a month prior to the spider hunts, she'd piled the entire family into her car and drove three hours to a plastic plant nursery. The store was huge and had every type of plant you could imagine. They were beautiful, and yet they weren't real. Air had never seen fake plants. D. J. headed straight for the endless choices of green plastic ferns. There were different varieties of ferns from all over the world, and they came in all different shades of green. Air asked about the really tall ones.

"Oh yeah, those are called tree ferns, but I'm looking for fiddle ferns in all their stages of growth! Aren't they just so exotic! I don't know how I'm gonna make up my mind about which ones to choose. I really like the lime-colored ones the most!"

Finally, she decided to buy a bunch of lime-green plastic ferns. None of the kids had any clue back then that she was planning to put them behind a three-tiered waterfall that their father would build and it would end up in the living room. *Now* Air understood why D. J. had ordered a waterfall pump, aquarium rocks, and bags of cement from a catalog long ago.

Air wondered what was next. She realized she was in a family that was basically every man and woman for him or herself and that she had to set aside all her dreams of the future and submerge herself in survival mode for the next eight years.

"Okay, listen up, y'all," D. J. said sternly. "Ya can't tell your daddy about this. It's gonna be a re-eel big sir-prize! I gotta arrange these here ferns just right! Imagine how purdy the waterfall's gonna be as the water flows from one bowl to another right there in our living room! And the spiders are gonna look like they're re-eel happy after I've arranged them on the ferns, don'tcha think?"

Now that the waterfall was completed and the spiders had dried, D. J. ran down the hall and brought out four bags of plastic lime-green ferns and arranged them behind the waterfall. She strategically positioned the "widas" on the ferns, gently gluing each shiny body until the lime-green plants were completely covered with them. It was a horrific sight!

Bringing anyone home from school was now definitely out of the question, especially since her brothers pissed in the bottom bowl anytime her parents left the house.

Later that night, when Air's father came home from work, the first thing he saw was black spiders and lime-green ferns all around the beautiful waterfall he'd made.

"Good God! Oh my God almighty! What in the hell is this, Debbie Jane?"

"See there, Daddy. I told ya there was gonna be green in this here room! What d'ya think?"

The yelling didn't stop for hours. Air wanted to tell him about the "hunts" and how D. J. had made her and her brothers go along with her. But she knew D. J. would give her the "evil eye" and that it was better to stay in her room.

"Purdy as a picture!" she heard D. J. declare brazenly.

2

One day, while the kids were at school, Mitchell came home from work early. He walked straight by D. J. and headed to the bedroom. He got out a suitcase and started to pack his clothes. He told D. J. he was leaving. He said he was not going to miss one more sports event on TV because the family forced him to go to church and then to D. J.'s parent's house for Sunday brunch.

"I also hate wearing suits, ties, and hard leather shoes; eating fried okra; wondering what the hell the neighbors are thinking about us; getting orders from your parents as to how to cut my hair; and painting the goddamn dog's nails red! For Christ sakes! It's a male dog! I'm moving back to the Bay Area in California, where my mother and sisters still live. If you want to be a real family calling our own shots and living our own lives, you're going to make the decision to stand on your own two feet and stop taking orders from your parents, Debbie Jane!"

"I can't go against my parents, Mitchell. Who'll cook for the kids? They'll cut off my inheritance! We'll lose the house and the cars. I don't know the first thing about ironing or washing clothes, much less ironing the sheets at night to keep the kids warm in the winter if we don't have the maids."

Mitchell walked straight passed her and out the front door.

D. J. stood there watching him drive away until she could not see the car anymore. Then panic crept through her. "I can't breathe," she gasped. *I don't know how to take care of myself much less the children.* She couldn't stop the thought from repeating itself.

What would she tell her parents about Mitchell's sudden decision to leave her and the kids? She sank onto the couch. She had to come up with something quickly; school was out, and the kids would be home any minute. Immediately, it dawned on her—she could tell the kids and her parents that Mitchell's momma was real sick and in the hospital. She could say he'd gotten a call from his sister asking him to come home as soon as possible. Afraid to fly on commercial airlines, Mitchell decided to drive to California. She went over to the phone and tried to think of something that would make her cry before calling her parents. Not much made her cry, except thinking about her "wida's."

"Mama? It's your daughter, Debbie Jane. I'm so upset I can't think straight!"

"Debbie Jane darlin', what's happened? Tell me right now, and don't beat around the bush. Just out with it!"

"It's Mitchell's mama! She's taken sick and is in the hospital in California, and we don't know how bad she is or what's even wrong with 'er."

D. J. kept the tears rolling, remembering how hard she'd worked to make each of those wida's perfect. She actually became hysterical remembering how Mitchell had taken each fern outside and shook the hell out of each stem. Black widow spiders were all around him like he was standing on a black rug.

"Wh-elle, why aren'tcha with him?" yelled D. J.'s mom.

"You know his family doesn't like me, Mama," D. J. cried. "They pretend I don't even exist. Once on the phone, Mitchell's sister, Barbara, told me I was self-centered," she added, her tone growing icy. "That was enough for me. I've never talked to them since. You know that," she snapped.

"But, Debbie Jane, this is different," her mother pleaded. "You're supposed to be by your husband's side, no matter what. And since when did you ever let someone tell you what to do? Good grief, child! You gotta somehow catch him before he gets too far away. Your daddy's gonna have a fit when he hears you let Mitchell go off alone to be with his family in a time of dire need."

"Mama, there's nothing I can do," D. J. said in a pouty whine. "He's already left. You know he doesn't fly alone, so he took the car. He's probably already outside Fort Worth by now."

"Listen here, Debbie Jane," Mamaw said, audibly grinding her teeth. "This is a command. Stop with your crying and hysteria. At some point, he'll pull over and call to check in on you and the kids. You gotta dee-mand he drive right back and get you. That's all I gotta say about this. You'd better hope to heaven he calls soon, Debbie Jane, before your daddy finds out! Your husband's mama's sick, and you just let him drive off without you? What in the world were you thinking?"

"I know you're right, Mama! I will get down on my knees and pray. Will you pray with me, Mama?"

"I have company right now. I'll pray later. You better get down on those knees of yours and start begging the Lord for forgiveness and for Mitchell to call soon!"

D. J.'s mom hung up the phone without even saying good-bye. D. J. stopped crying immediately. She would tell the kids the same story she'd told her mother, deleting the part about Mitchell's family not caring for her. As for the question she knew they'd ask, she'd simply tell them she had no idea when their father would be back.

Air would later learn that her father had driven to California, stopping only one night.

The phone rang, and D. J. knew it was her daddy before she answered.

"Debbie Jane, this is your daddy. How the hell could you let your husband just take off without you?"

"Daddy, there was no time for me to pack. He grabbed one suitcase and ran out the door. I begged him to let me come with him, but he said he didn't think that was such a good idea."

"I don't give a good goddamn! What will everyone at church say when you say your husband's mama is in the hospital and you're not there with him? You pack your suitcases, Debbie Jane, and catch the next flight to California," he bellowed. "I'll drive you to the airport."

"Oh, Daddy, I don't even know what city they live in. And besides, they hate me," she protested, her voice growing louder and louder.

"Well then, you and the kids will come over here and stay with us until he returns. We can just say one of the cars is in the machine shop. You will not be seen without your husband! Do you understand me, young lady? Now, as soon as my grandkids get home, you call me and I will come pick y'all up. When you get here, we'll pull around back behind to the carriage house. You and the kids will stay there. Do you understand me?"

"Yes, Daddy."

D. J. hung the phone up and stared out the window. Now what? She was in quite a pickle. She thought and thought, trying to come up with a way out of all this. She didn't dare go against her Daddy.

Air slowly walked home from school. No need to rush.

When she came through the front door, she found D. J. sitting on the couch crying.

"What's wrong?" Air asked.

"Go start your homework until your brothers get home. I'm only gonna tell the story once," her mother replied without looking up.

As soon as Air sat down on her bed, she heard Ron and Jimmy talking to D. J. Air got up and went into the living room. She watched her mother, who started crying again. Air intuitively knew everything that was going to come out of D. J.'s mouth was going to be a lie. Her mother never cried. What was going on? She began to get that achy stomach she would always get when D. J. had created a scene.

"You kids come over here and sit down. Your daddy's sister, Barbara, called him this morning after y'all left for school. She told him that your grandmother, his mother out in California, is very sick and in the hospital. Barbara asked if he would please come back there to California to be with the family. Of course, I couldn't leave you children alone so he's driving back there by himself. He left this morning."

"Why didn't you go with him?" Jimmy cried out.

"Wh-elle, like I said, I'm not comfortable with leaving y'all here without one of your parents with ya."

Air's eyes rolled. Since when did her mother even remember she had three kids? She knew there was more to this story than D. J. was telling.

"I talked to Mamaw and Papaw, and they want us to go stay with them until your daddy gets back."

"I don't want to stay there. It smells like mothballs," Jimmy yelled.

"Wh-elle, let me try and think of something so we can stay home, but it's not going to be easy. You know your papaw when he's got his mind made up about something."

"Mother, I think you should just tell them we don't want to go there because we don't feel comfortable sleeping when we're there. Say that I'm supposed to go on a school field trip with my class tomorrow. Tell them something like that," Air pleaded.

"Wh-elle, I'm doing the best I kin to come up with something."

"I think you should just fly to California and surprise Daddy," Jimmy chipped in with one of his high-pitched, edgy tones. "The maids can take care of us. They always do. What's the difference? You never take care of us!"

"What'd you say, Jimmy?" D. J. snarled. "How dare you talk to your mama like that! I've always had one eye on you kids. And don'tcha ever forget that! And don'tcha ever tell your mamaw and papaw I don't take care of you."

"I'm going to tell Papaw I'll get hives if I don't get to go on my field trip."

"Wh-elle now, that's a good idea. I'll go cut up a tomato and pour you some Coca-Cola right now. We'll wait a half an hour. I'm sure you'll break out in hives all over your face!"

"I'll get hives on top of hives all over my forehead," Air lamented.

"Okay, you go into the kitchen and do what you have to do. I'll go and pretend to pack suitcases because your papaw's on his way over here right now. When he sees your hive reaction, he just might let us stay home."

Within fifteen minutes, Air had hives all over her face. Her fingers were swollen twice their normal size. D. J. called her mom and told her about what had happened. Luckily, Papaw hadn't left the house yet. They decided to wait for Mitchell to call.

"In the meantime, Debbie Jane, we gotta come up with some excuse as to why Mitchell didn't take you with him," Mamaw said.

D. J. was in hog heaven. In the end, no one told her what she could and couldn't do. She knew she would probably have to get a job, but she loved getting out of the house. She had a girlfriend who worked as a waitress at an Italian restaurant in the next county. She would ask her if she could put in a good word for her. She knew nothing about working, but she knew she could learn quickly.

If I work in another county, no one will know, she reasoned. *I'll work in the evenings since Mother and Daddy never call in the evenings. I'll start looking for a babysitter too.*

A week had passed since Mitchell had left. He had not called. D. J. lied to her parents and said that he had called and would be in California for at least a month. Going to church had become a tremendous ordeal for Mamaw. She was distraught over having to keep up with the different lies about Mitchell's whereabouts. On top of that, the church community did not understand why D. J and the kids weren't going to church to pray for Mitchell and his mother.

Meanwhile, D. J. met with the manager of the Italian restaurant, was hired the same day and started work the next week. She was terrified someone would recognize her and tell her parents. She told the maids she'd joined an evening knitting women's group and that they would have the evenings off. She would find a teenage girl to look after the kids in the evenings.

There was a bulletin board at the local grocery store where teenage girls looking for babysitting jobs put up postings. D. J. spoke with three young girls. She decided on a young girl named Paige. Paige couldn't have been more than fifteen.

The kids really liked Paige because she let them do whatever they wanted. As soon as D. J. left for work, Paige's boyfriend would come to the house. He and Paige would spend the entire evening in Air's parents' bedroom with the door closed. Airstream knew one day Paige would get caught. She would be in big trouble, not only for having her boyfriend over but because no one was ever allowed in D. J.'s bedroom, not even the kids. The kids had no idea what Paige and her boyfriend were doing in their mom's room, but they didn't really care since Paige's absence meant they were able to do whatever they wanted.

One day, Paige's boyfriend couldn't visit her, so Paige asked Air if she wanted to try smoking a cigarette.

Air took a deep breath and said, "I guess so." She didn't want Paige to think she was a chicken, and she did want try smoking like all the teenagers did.

"Okay, tonight after I put your brothers to bed, you and I will smoke a cigarette together. I'll write you a note giving you permission to buy some cigarettes at the little corner store. Buy us a pack of Springs."

"Okay," Air said.

Air was scared to walk to the corner store because the owner had free-roaming killer dogs. He never disciplined them, and rumor had it that a little boy had run into them on his way to buy an ice cream bar, and they had chewed his leg off! Air was terrified. She walked slowly, passing each growling dog with their mouths dripping white, foamy drool, and sniffing her within inches of her ankles. She wondered if risking her life was worth smoking a cigarette, but it seemed like something exciting to do. Hell, even her parents smoked. Air walked into the store and went straight to the counter. It was a small store and had only the basics.

"I have this note to buy some cigarettes."

"Let me see that note," the man demanded. "Where did you get this note?"

"From my babysitter."

He handed the cigarettes to Air and said, "Tell her next time to come in herself!"

Air left the store and once again walked slowly by the dogs. After about a block, she ran all the way home.

"Here they are, Paige! The store owner said next time you have to go in yourself."

Later that evening, Paige put Jimmy and Ron to bed. She made sure the maids had gone home.

"Come on, let's go into your mother's bedroom. We'll watch TV and smoke."

"Oh no, I can't do that. We're not allowed to go into my parents' bedroom," Air said with fear in her voice.

"Ah, come on, she won't know," Paige insisted.

Paige went into D. J.'s room and sat down on the bed. She motioned for Air to come have a seat next to her. Air had never been in her mother's bedroom, much less sat on her bed. Paige turned on the TV and lit a couple of cigarettes. She handed one to Air. Before Air could take a puff, Paige slowly turned toward her as if in slow motion. She looked straight into Air's eyes.

"I didn't mean to kill her," she said with a completely motionless face and a voice that was as cold as a Texas winter day.

Air didn't know if she was kidding or repeating something she'd just heard on the TV. Paige stared at her for a full minute with a look of dead seriousness. Air had no idea what was happening. She became so frightened she instantly peed her panties. *Oh my God, I'm not only going to get into trouble for being in Mom's bedroom, but now I just peed on her bed.*

"What'd ya mean, ya killed somebody?" Air stuttered, still not believing her. "Killed who? Who did you kill?"

"I really didn't mean to kill her. It just sort of happened. I don't really remember her name. I only remember the last part of her first name was *Lene*."

"Oh my God! Do you mean Charlene? The girl who lives down at the end of the street?" Air said, astonished and completely horrified.

"Yeah, maybe," Paige answered with a distant voice.

"What do you mean? Yeah, maybe you killed someone or yeah, maybe you killed Charlene?" Air asked with an incredulous tone.

"Yeah, maybe," Paige answered again stoically.

"When did you kill her? I just saw her yesterday."

"Last night, after you went to bed."

Air looked around the room trying to find a way past Paige and out the door, but she also felt she should stay and try to talk to her. Maybe Paige was just trying to trick her and was going to laugh all night at her for believing such an absurd story. She tried to act casual while being terrified. Air was so naive she had no idea what to do. She was afraid if she ran next door Paige would kill her brothers. She decided to make small talk.

"How did you kill her?" Air asked in a tone she hoped was relaxed and soothing.

Paige looked around D. J.'s room and pointed to the lamp at the end of the D. J.'s dresser. "I killed her with that lamp."

Air's body started to tremble severely. She tried holding her legs still but to no avail. They began to spasm and cramp at this point. Paige seemed to be in another world and didn't even seem to notice Air at all.

"How did you take the lamp down the street, kill Charlene, and put the lamp back without anyone seeing you?" Air asked with a gentle tone.

"Like I said, I took it right after I put you to bed. I just walked up the street. No one saw me. When I got to Charlene's house, I asked some boy if he'd seen her. He told me she was playing in her backyard. I walked up behind her and just hit her real hard on the head with the lamp. I came back here and put the lamp back at the end of your mom's dresser. I left after your mom got home," she said with an irritated voice, as if she was tired of being questioned.

Still trembling, Air realized she should not challenge Paige with any more questions. Still smoking and not saying a word to Air, Paige continued to stare at the TV. Air still held the half- burned cigarette in her hand, which was shaking uncontrollably. She decided to not inhale the smoke. Out of the corner of Air's eye, she could see Paige slowly turning toward her. She pretended to continue watching the TV.

In the most chilling voice one could imagine, Paige said to Air, "You're the only one who knows. Now I'll have to kill you, too." She stared straight into Air's eyes.

Air felt the sting of a hollow and empty stare. She jumped off her mother's bed and ran down the long, left wing hallway into the kitchen. The house was huge and shaped like an L. It seemed to take forever for her to get to the phone. She stopped and listened to hear if Paige was following her. Air grabbed the phone and called her mother at her at job.

She screamed into the phone, "Mom! Paige just told me she killed Charlene, and now she's gonna kill me since I'm the only one who knows!"

"Airstream, if you ever call me at work ever again, *I'm* gonna kill ya. Now, go back to bed," D. J. snapped, slamming down the phone.

Air turned around. There stood Paige. She was standing near the kitchen sink with a gigantic butcher knife in her right hand.

"Paige! What are you doing? Have you gone crazy?" Air screamed.

"I gotta kill ya. You're the only one who knows," she told Air.

"Paige, I swear I'll never tell anyone. I promise!" Air begged.

"It's too late. I'm sorry, Airstream, but I must put you to sleep now and forever."

Paige started to chase Airstream throughout the ranch-style house with the butcher knife held straight out in front of her. They ran around the large kitchen table and into the living room, which was dominated by a very large, modern V-shaped coffee table. Air stood at one end of the table, her eyes darting from the front door to the hallway that led to her room. She didn't know what to do. Finally, she darted down the hallway toward her bedroom. She ran in, slammed the door, and locked it. She waited for Paige to try and open it, but she didn't. Air waited for what seemed an eternity, and nothing happened. No sounds. No voices. No footsteps. Nothing. Air slowly opened her door and peeked down the hall. Paige was nowhere in sight. Airstream very quietly yet quickly went back into the kitchen and called D. J. again.

"Mom, please, you have to believe me! Paige is chasing me around the house with a really big butcher knife. She says she's gonna kill me! She says she killed Charlene with your bedroom lamp—the one that's at the end of your dresser!"

"Goddamn it, Airstream! When I get home, your ass has had it!" Again, D. J. hung up the phone.

Air just stood there, numb, trembling, holding the dead receiver, and having no idea what to do—for what seemed like a lifetime. For some reason, only God knew, she decided to go back down the hall and peek into D. J.'s room. She saw Paige sitting on the edge of her mom's bed. Air couldn't believe her eyes. Paige was completely naked.

She was smoking a cigarette, which had burned down to the butt. The cigarette looked as if it was burning Paige's fingers. A very long trail of cigarette ash was somehow balancing itself in her fingers. She seemed totally oblivious to the situation, as though her world had never changed. Air couldn't see the knife.

"I hear ya, Air, and don'tcha worry, cuz I am still gonna kill ya! I'm just not in the mood right now," Paige said in a frightening voice.

Air slowly backed up and starting tiptoeing back toward her bedroom when, suddenly, six policemen burst through the front door. Air started screaming and telling them about Paige.

"Young lady! Where is the woman with the knife?" asked one of the officer's.

"Oh thank God! Paige is in my mom's bedroom at the end of the hall. Did my mother call you?" Air asked.

Three men dressed all in white appeared, charging down the hall with what looked like a bed on wheels. Air heard Paige let out a bloodcurdling scream. "I didn't mean to do it," she cried. "She told me she wanted me to come and kill her, so I did!"

Air heard the police coming up the hallway. The men dressed in white clothing followed. She looked up to see Paige, lying on the narrow bed. She was completely wrapped with sheets and tightly secured to the bed with some sort of straps. The men wheeled her straight out of the house. Air stood in the corner of the living room trembling. It seemed as though there were too many people in the house. She didn't know what to do. She was so scared she collapsed on the couch. No one noticed her nor did anyone approach her to talk about what had happened. It seemed as though she was invisible.

Almost everyone who lived on the street was now standing outside trying to see what all the commotion was about. Air could still hear Paige screaming, "I didn't want to kill 'em.

"Kill who?" Air heard her mother screaming back.

"Your boys! They wanted me to kill 'em, too! They begged me! It was what they wanted!"

"Oh ma gads!" screamed D. J.

She ran into the house, passing Air without saying a word to her, and down the opposite hallway to where her brothers' bedrooms were. She was screaming out their names as she opened the doors to their rooms. Both of the boys were alive and sound asleep.

Air sat on the couch with tears streaming down her face, still invisible. No one said a word to her. No one asked her any questions. Ever.

D. J. walked back to the front room and started to say something to Air when the policemen began to question her. She turned and looked at Air.

"Get your ass in your bedroom, young lady," D. J. said. "Everythin's gonna be okay. Paige just had a little attack of appendicitis!"

"Mrs. Johnson, can you tell us what happened here tonight?" one officer asked.

"Wh-elle, I was at work and my daughter, Airstream, started calling me and telling me this farfetched story about the babysitter tryin' to kill 'er!"

"Do you have any idea what made the babysitter lose control of herself?"

"Wh-elle, like I said, my daughter kept on a callin' me at work telling me Paige was chasing her around the house with a butcher knife and that she'd killed the girl, Charlene, up the street. That's all I know. I've always had the feelin' something wasn't right with that child!"

Not another word was ever spoken about Paige.

3

Air's father had been gone for two months when the scene with Paige had occurred. He immediately drove back to Texas. Air suspected D. J. had called him and told him all about the nightmare.

"How could you have let this happen, Debbie Jane?" Mitchell asked. "Where in the hell were you when this happened? And where the hell were the maids? You have maids so the children are taken care of, for Christ's sake!"

"Wh-elle, she was only here that one night."

"Were you out with you sister gallivanting around town? No doubt, the two of you got into some kind of trouble. Do your parents know about this?"

"No! They don't," she snapped. "And I want it kept that way!"

"Goddamn it, you haven't changed one bit! Have you made up your mind about moving to California because I'm headed back there," he hollered. "So either you're coming with me or you're on your own!"

"Mitchell, please don't do this to me," she pleaded. "I will talk to my parents and tell 'em we need to be able to have more say about our own decisions and how we live our lives."

"That'll be a cold day in hell, and you know it! I will give you one day to decide, Debbie Jane. After that, I'm leaving with or without you and the kids."

Mitchell went into the parlor and turned on the TV.

"I gotta go lay down for a while. I don't feel so well," she said to Mitchell.

"No, you're going to sit here with me and we are going to talk more!"

Air sat on her bed staring at her dolls as she listened to her parents' fight. She thought about Paige being wheeled out of the

30

house that horrible night. *Why, God? Why couldn't it have been my mother they wheeled out of the house instead of Paige? She's just as crazy as Paige!*

Again, she felt that sense intense loneliness and wondered if her father was right and she was a worthless piece of shit and no one would ever love her? She wondered what a worthless piece of shit was. How could shit be worth anything? She wondered if anyone at school suspected she was beaten daily. Air's tummy started to churn. She turned over and went to sleep, even though the yelling was getting worse.

The next morning, Mitchell made a phone call. Air heard him tell whoever was on the other end of the line to come over and get started right away. He slammed the receiver down and yelled for the kids to get out of bed and go to school.

Air suffered with an upset stomach all day. She couldn't tell anyone about what was happening in her life. Finally, the school bell rang signaling the end of the day. She was happy school was over but she was scared to go home. She was very fearful about what she might come home to. She wondered if her father would still be there.

As she approached her street, she could see a very large truck parked close to her house. She'd never seen a moving truck before. As she got closer, she could see the truck was parked in her driveway. She walked up to the truck and peered into the open back end. She saw her bedroom furniture, which had been disabled. She was sad to see her mattresses just leaned up against the wall of the truck. The kitchen table and chairs, the couch, and the coffee tables, along with her parents' bedroom set were all covered with plastic. The waterfall seemed anchored to the back wall of the truck and surrounded by lots of stacked boxes that were partially covered with blue blankets. She looked around for her parents. They were not there, and only one of the cars was in the driveway.

Feeling light-headed, she walked into the house. She was shocked to see there was almost nothing left in the house! She collapsed onto the living room floor. Her schoolbooks went flying and hit the wall. When she came to, her eyes were blurry and she was in shock. There was still no sign of her parents. The house she'd grown up in was now almost empty. Just that morning when she'd left for school, her two brothers hadn't realized they were pissing in the "Japan-knee-z" pond for the last time in Texas. Suddenly her mother's voice grew louder. Air could hear D. J. and her father arguing, but Air couldn't quite hear what they were fighting about. She looked out the living room window and saw her mom's car now parked in the driveway.

"Come on, Daddy! The trunk of the car is the only safe place for my ferns! Them's my babies! I can't letcha jus' box 'em up and put 'em in that there truck. They're gonna need me. I gotta be near 'em! They're all I have left of my art piece!"

Air's father finally decided it was easier to stuff the ferns into the trunk of the car than to continue arguing with her. He knew once she'd made her mind up, there was nothing, come hell or high water that could change it. She was one of those people who adhered to a simple, unbreakable principle—don't confuse me with the facts; my mind is made up."

Suddenly a small truck parked in front of the house and three men got out. Air overheard them telling her father they had taken a break for dinner and were going to finish loading the truck. They told him they would be about an hour more and then were planning to head out ahead of them. Air didn't understand but knew not to ask questions. Air stared at her father's new Chevy Impala. *Oh my God. It's black and shiny with a red interior just like the spiders!*

Mitchell had traded his Cadillac for the Chevy as soon as he had the opportunity. Cadillac's were not a car that he felt comfortable driving nor did he feel it was a car that reflected what kind of man he was. They left Debbie Jane's Cadillac in the driveway with the keys under the front seat floor mat. The moving truck had already left.

"Kids! It's time to move. We're heading to California!"

Air wondered about what would happen to her homework and school. She wondered if she would ever see her friends again.

"All right, Airstream, you and your brothers get in the backseat of the car."

"Aren't we going to stop and see Mamaw and Papaw, Daddy?" Air asked.

"That's where we're headed right now," he answered.

As they drove into town, Air stared out her window as if to say good-bye to the large working ranches each with hundreds of acres of pastureland. She watched the horses and cows mindlessly roaming. They approached the most prestigious boulevard in Fort Worth and turned into the long and winding circular driveway to her grandparent's house. Air looked up at the three-story brick home. It was the most prominent house on the boulevard. The front yard seemed as big as her schoolyard and the huge magnolia trees all but covered the front entrance to the house. The giant white pillars that lined the walkway from the street to the porch were as tall as the house itself.

"Kids, we're just here to say good-bye. We aren't going to be spending any time here. In fact, we aren't even getting out of the car. We're just here to say good-bye," Mitchell repeated.

Mitchell honked the horn a couple of times in front of the majestic house. Just as Daddy had said, none of them got out of the car. Air's grandparents came out and said their good-byes.

"Mitchell, don't you think it's a little late to get started driving on the freeway?" Papaw asked.

"There's nothing to hold us back now!"

"Mamaw, I don't wanna go! Can't I just live with you?" Jimmy asked.

"Aw, you know your mamaw and papaw love y'all very much," Mamaw replied. "We're really gonna miss y'all too, but you need to be with your parents."

"You'll have a good time in California! Maybe someday we'll come visit you," said Papaw.

"Here, I want to give each of ya a brand-new, crisp five-dollar bill, and you save it for as long as you can," Mamaw said.

"Wh-elle, I guess there's no changin' your mind, Debbie Jane?" asked Papaw. "You and the kids can live with us for as long as you want."

"Thank you, Daddy, but my place is with Mitchell. I love you both very much, and I will surely miss ya."

"Good luck, Mitchell, and take good care of my daughter and my grandchildren, ya hear?"

"You bet; no problem," Mitchell replied and added quickly, "Oh by the way, I left the keys to Debbie's car under the front seat floor mat. Well, we better get going."

As soon as Mitchell had driven a few blocks down the street and out of sight of Mamaw and Papaw, D. J. turned and held out her hand in the direction of the kids, demanding each of them to give her their brand new crispy five dollar bills.

The drive from hell that would last three days and two nights began. Air didn't know how she felt. She couldn't find one word to describe how she felt. She looked over at her two brothers; they both had tears running down their faces. But they knew better than to say a word. If they did, their father would just pull over and beat the shit out of them and tell them he didn't want to hear a word out of either of them until they reached California.

Air felt sorry for her dad. Her mother was so self-centered. She rarely drove, since she always had people to drive her anywhere she wanted to go. D. J. fell asleep the moment the car approached the freeway.

If I fall asleep, we might all die. I have to stay awake and talk to Daddy the whole trip, Air thought.

"Daddy, don't you think it would be a good idea to stay in a hotel on one of the nights? Driving all that way without sleep is scary."

"Air, that's what your daddy does for a living. We'll be fine. I might take a few breaks at the roadside rest stops for trucks. Don't you worry I'll be just fine," he told her reassuringly.

Air wondered what she could talk to him about.

"Daddy, will you find a new bowling alley and join a new league?"

"Already have," he declared. "We've got a great team too!"

"Oh, I bet you're the best one on the team," Air replied.

"There's some pretty good bowlers, and we have a good chance to win the season this year."

"I'll root for you, Daddy," Air declared with a sense of excitement.

Even though Daddy had reassured her he could handle the driving, she felt a sense of obligation to make sure he wouldn't fall asleep. She stayed awake by licking her fingers and rubbing the saliva over her eyes. The saliva stung, but she ignored the pain and continued to make small talk. She looked out the windows of the car. Both sides of the freeway were thick with the silhouettes of large cactus trees. Air saw a sign that read "Rest Stop Ahead" and asked her dad if he had noticed the sign.

"Yeap, I did, and I think we're going to pull in and use their bathrooms."

Air got out with him and walked around. The rest of the family was deep in sleep. The sky was clear and full of stars. She wondered if California had this many stars. She wondered what her parents had told her school about their move. She prayed that D. J. would find a new hobby besides art when they got to California.

"Daddy, do you think that maybe Mom will find a new hobby?"

"Airstream, I don't want you to worry about your mother. Things are going to be very different from here on. I can see the sun is starting to come up. We're lucky the weather is so clear. There's not a cloud in the sky. I want you to get a little rest today. Everyone will be waking up, and you'll be able to rest."

D. J. started to move a bit, and Jimmy woke up.

"Where are we? I'm hungry," Jimmy whined.

"Good morning, Mitchell," D. J. said in a weary voice.

"Where are we?" she said in echo of her son. "I could sure use a cup of coffee. Do you think we could find an exit that might have a breakfast diner?"

"Well, we're just outside of Albuquerque, and my stomach's growling too. I could use a break. Everyone keep their eyes open for signs of gas stations and food."

"There's a sign that says gas and food, Mitchell. Do we need to get gas?" D. J. asked.

"Yes, we'll find somewhere to eat and then fill up."

"Could we find a gas station that has food? I would really like to have some sunflower seeds," Air said.

"We'll see. Let's just find a place to eat for now."

They found a restaurant and parked. Everyone combed his or her hair and straightened his or her clothes. D. J. put on some lipstick and straightened her hair back into its perfect French roll style.

"Okay, kids, out of the car. I want each one of you to be on your best behavior. No arguing and stay in your chair at all times," Mitchell warned.

They stood in the waiting area to be seated.

"Good morning, everyone. How are you all this morning? If you'll follow me, I will take you to your booth," a bubbly, young waitress with her hair in a ponytail said over her shoulder.

"We're fine, thank you. Bacon and pancakes for everyone, and my wife and I would like some coffee. The kids will have milk."

"Coming right up, sir. I'll be right back with your coffee."

The waitress brought the coffee and milk. Everyone sat in silence just staring out the restaurant window.

"I hope the food comes soon. My stomach is growling," said Ron.

The waitress appeared with everyone's food as soon as Ron had finished making this remark.

"Is there anything else I can get for any of you this morning?" the waitress asked.

"Do you have any strawberries?" asked Ron.

"I want some too," Jimmy said.

"Of course. I'll bring a bowl enough for everyone. How's that?"

"That would be great. Looks like we just missed the breakfast crowd," Mitchell said to the waitress.

"You sure did. We were packed about an hour ago. You would have had to wait about a half hour to be seated. So your timing is prefect. Anything else that I can get for you?"

"Just refills on the coffee."

"You got it."

Everyone ate fast and in silence. Air hated the silence. She wanted to be a family that talked and laughed while eating, but that was never going to happen. She sighed and wiped her lips that were raw from the non-stop licking with her napkin.

"Well, I think we're done here," Mitchell announced. "Anyone need to use the bathroom?"

"Yes, I do," D. J. replied. "I'm sure the kids do, too. She turned to them and said, "I want y'all to go anyway even if you don't think you need to."

When D. J. returned to the table, she said, "You must be tired, Mitchell. I wish I could help you drive, but you know how easily I get lost."

"No, that's fine. I'm very comfortable with this drive. I've driven it a few times now. It's an easy drive until we hit the Sierra's. I'm not looking forward to that. We may have to buy some chains, but we'll wait and see."

"You said three days and two nights, so just one more night, right? The weather looks like it will be beautiful. How far do you think we'll get today?" D. J. asked.

"Oh, we'll make good time today. The roads are clear, and we haven't hit the mountains yet. We won't until late tonight. Everybody ready to go?"

"Get your jacket," Mitchell said to Ron.

The family left the restaurant and piled back into the car.

"Mitchell, I'm a little bit worried about you," D. J. said. "This is a lot of driving for one person. Maybe we should spend the night in a motel tonight."

"Oh that sounds like a great idea," Air said enthusiastically and in a tone that confirmed her mother's thought.

"No. I'll be just fine. Okay, everybody, let's get back in the car. Let's enjoy the view. Arizona is beautiful."

The kids each had a coloring book and got out their crayons.

D. J. stared out the window as they drove through the town heading back to the highway.

"Everything looks alike. It seems like a lot of these families are really poor. Hardly anyone's wearing a coat, and it's really cold outside," D. J. remarked. "Seems like nobody cares about their front yards."

There's a lot of garbage in the gutters, too," said Air.

"You're just used to living in a nice neighborhood and having too much money. You have no idea how the rest of the world lives, Debbie Jane. You've lived a life most people only dream about, and you don't even know it," Mitchell said in a snide tone.

"Ya know, I do know how to fry chicken. I wish I'd had the time to fry us up a bunch before we left."

"Things happened too fast," Mitchell said abruptly.

"I'm glad we didn't have much time to think about this. I know it was the only choice we had and I know leaving Texas was the right decision," D. J. said.

"I hope so, Debbie. Jane. You're going to be making a lot of lifestyle changes. You're a strong woman, and I do have faith in you. But I don't think you have any idea how different our lives will. It'll be different from anything you've ever known. You've never had to live on a budget," he said.

"A budget. Why in the world will I have to live on a budget?"

Mitchell didn't answer. Airstream felt a chill down her back. She sensed California might not be such a good idea after all but there was no turning back now.

The ride had become monotonous. The views were boring, and there was five people trapped in a Chevy Impala. The kids played all the car games they knew but grew bored and irritated. Mitchell was growing more and more tired and for the first time, he yelled at the kids to keep the noise down.

Airstream grew anxious. She knew D. J. would soon fall asleep and her brothers would keep arguing and would be put on restriction. Air was occasionally beginning to nod off, but she started pinching herself so hard that all she could think about was the pain. She continued to wet her eyes with her salvia to stay awake. The scenery was the same, and there was nothing to keep her attention. She nodded off.

Suddenly, the car jolted severely to the right and seemed to have left the pavement. Everyone woke up, and D. J. screamed. The car was now off the road and driving in the desert sand. The next thing Air knew; the car had slowly come to a stop. Air looked at her daddy. Mitchell was asleep.

"Holy shit! Mitchell! Mitchell! Wake up!" D. J. yelled.

Both the boys started crying, and Airstream kept trying to reassure them everything was okay. Everyone got out of the car so that Mitchell could drive the car back up alongside the road. They were lucky they didn't get stuck in the sand.

Mitchell momentarily sat there in the driver's seat, wiping his face with his handkerchief. He took out his hair comb and combed his hair out of his eyes.

"I must have closed my eyes for just a second. I'd better stop driving so fast. I'm tired. I'll take a nap at the next rest stop for half an hour," he told everyone.

They all got back into the car, and D. J. told the boys to stop their crying.

"Mitchell, we'll stay at a motel tonight," D. J. said firmly. "You're pushing yourself too hard. We're not in that big of a hurry."

"I'll see how I feel," was all he said.

At the next rest stop, the kids got out and went over to the playground equipment. Airstream just climbed into a swing and stayed there until it was time to go. She felt she'd let her father down since she had fallen asleep. She turned away from everyone and began swinging while she cried. D. J. polished her nails a blood red color that matched her lipstick. After about an hour, Mitchell woke up and told everyone to get back in the car.

"How d'ya feel?" D. J. asked.

"Much better. I'll be fine now. We'll be in California tomorrow."

They drove for hours in silence. The sun was beginning to set. *I wish mother would wake up and demand that we stop and check into a motel,* Air thought. She didn't, and Air was too afraid to wake her.

"I can see the mountains you told us about in the distance, Daddy!"

"Yeap, those are the Sierra mountain range. They're quite a sight, aren't they?" he replied.

"We were just starting to read about the settlers crossing those mountains in school."

"Yeap, that was back in the gold rush days. It truly was the Wild West. Lots of people died from the winters. They had to blaze their own trails. Sometimes, they had to completely take their covered wagons apart and lower them down the hills by ropes. It must have been hell. Can you imagine traveling across the United States without any roads? What happens when you reach a mountain and there's no other way, but up and over it?" he asked Air.

Airstream tried to imagine the world without roads and cars. She thought about people living without electricity and heat. As much as she thought she lived a tough life, it was really nothing compared to the "old days."

Finally, they approached the California border. Air saw a huge, flashing, brightly lit sign that said, "No Plants, No Fruit, No Vegetables across the California Border."

Air didn't think much about what the sign meant. It was now the middle of the night. She was extremely tired, but she continued to lick her fingers and rub her eyes. The bright lights didn't wake her brothers or her mother. Air was thankful for the lights because her father had still been nodding off from time to time. Air never stopped staring at him.

"Daddy, why is everyone stopping?"

"This is called the border line for the agricultural inspectors, sweetie. They want to make sure we're not bringing in any plants or fruits into the state. California's an agricultural state, and they have to make sure we're not bringing in any bugs that could ruin the farmers' crops."

"Oh," she said wearily.

Mitchell slowed the car down and stopped at one of the four booths.

He rolled down his window, and a man, whose face Airstream couldn't quite see from her position in the backseat, leaned in.

"Good evening, sir," the man said in a deep, friendly voice. He glanced in the backseat and Air caught a glimpse of round cheeks and a thick mustache.

"How are you and your family tonight?" he asked, looking back at her father.

"Just fine, officer. How about yourself?"

"Ah, not too bad. Do you have any plants, vegetables, or fruit with you or in the trunk, sir?" the inspector asked.

"No, sir," replied Air's father.

At that very moment, one of the state inspectors had lifted up the trunk of the car and started yelling at the top of his lungs. "Over here! Over here, quick! Look what I've found!"

Air turned around to look back at the trunk of the car. There were four state inspectors with their flashlights pointed into the trunk.

"Sir, I need to ask you to step out of the car, please."

Air was terrified. She didn't know how to help her father. This was all D. J.'s fault! She stared in disbelief as the officer pushed her father up against the side of the car door. She watched as they felt his whole body up and down for some reason.

Air shook D. J. "Mom, wake up! They're doing something to Daddy!"

D. J. opened her eyes and looked around. "What the hell's going on? Where's your daddy?"

"The policemen have your ferns, and they're going to keep them, Mom," Air said quietly, yet smugly.

When D. J. heard Air's remarks, she jumped out of the car as fast as grease lightning.

"Hey! Them's my pa-lants! You can't have 'em. Don'tcha even dare touch 'em," she hollered. "Hey, mister! Those are mine—all mine—and they need me. You have no idea how to take care of 'em. They need special care and attention. They won't listen to you. They only understand me!" squealed D. J.

"Ma'am, you need to get back in the car, please. Now!" one of the officers said, his tone firm.

"I ain't gonna go nowhere without my pa-lants! You give 'em to me now," D. J. demanded.

Air looked out the window at her father. The inspectors had finally let him go after realizing the plants were plastic. Air could see the look of pain and the memories of the past coming across his face. He looked straight through D. J.

"Ah jeez, mister," said the officer, who'd just told D. J. to get back in the car. His tone was softer now. "We're sorry," he added. "We thought … well, you're free to go. Sorry for the hassle. Here, ma'am, here's your plants."

D. J. got back in the car with her ferns and held them close to her chest like they were her children. She actually had tears in her eyes.

Daddy got back into the car. He looked over at D. J. once again before starting the car. His hands gripped the steering wheel as though they were gripping her neck. He kept squeezing tighter and tighter.

Kill her Daddy, kill her! She loves those plastic ferns more than she loves any of us!

Air's head was spinning with fear and exhaustion. Those stupid fake plants. She wished her father would just throw them out the window.

All of a sudden, Daddy turned to D. J. and said in a very frightening voice, "When we see the next rest stop, we're stopping. You. You are going to throw those fucking, fake green ferns into the garbage! Do you understand? These are my final words."

I wish Paige had killed Mother. She imagined Paige screaming, "I didn't mean to do it! She needed to be killed! She was causing her family too much pain!"

Air put her elbow on the edge of the window and rested her chin on her hand. She couldn't stop the relentless questions that were twirling in her head. *Why in the world did Daddy come back for Mother? It was his chance to be free of her. She doesn't love him. She never hugs or kisses him. She never tells him she loves him. What reason does he have for loving her? She's crazy! She's embarrassing.*

Air was afraid to be alone with her mother. She sensed she could not trust her. After all, D. J. had actually told her, "You don't love me, Airstream, and I know it. You never did. The moment you were born, you stuck your tongue out at me."

Besides creating crazy things, D. J. was always dressed up in clothes with colors that didn't match, especially orange and red. She looked so different from all the other mothers. People stared at her no matter where she was and what she was wearing.

The fact that D. J. didn't care what other people thought upset Air. She wanted her to care. When they were out together, Air tried to follow as far behind her as she could so people wouldn't think they were together. How could anybody love a woman who seemed to have no feelings except toward dogs, spiders, fake ferns, and rocks? Air felt nothing but bitterness toward her mother.

She struggled to feel love for her mother. She felt nothing. *D. J.'s never once hugged me, never once told me she loved me,* Air told herself. *She's never reassured me that everything will be okay. If she died tomorrow, I wouldn't feel anything. I know I wouldn't even cry. Why should I? I don't love her either. I don't feel like I have a mother.*

Air felt very abandoned when it came to mothers. She was so sorrowful that she didn't have a mother like her girlfriends. Their mothers were sweet and even loving toward her. She suspected they knew Air was being raised in a family that was "not blessed with family love." She had become all too familiar with taking care of herself. She knew she'd become a survivor and that was the only way she would make it out in one piece. She knew that, even though she was still a child, she'd already safely hidden her real self. She felt she'd simply disappeared among her belongings one day. She would remerge later in life when it was safe.

Finally, they came to a rest stop exit sign. Daddy pulled into the parking lot and just let go of the wheel and stared straight ahead. D. J. got out of the car and walked over to the garbage cans. She lifted one of the lids, and she dropped her ferns inside. She returned to the car. Not a word was said. They drove on into the dark of the night, in silence.

Air wondered what California would be like. She'd just turned twelve years old, and it was the beginning of the sixties.

Mitchell hadn't told D. J. he'd already bought a place to live in California. He was sure he would never return to Texas. He'd decided to buy property near his family in El Cerrito. His mother lived with his sister, Barbara, and her family. His other sister, Carol and her family, lived just down the street from Barbara.

He'd never told his family how difficult being married to D. J. had been. He'd never told them much of anything about how he and his wife had met or that D. J. had been pregnant before they married. He hadn't told them how her parents "owned" them nor did he mention why he had left Texas and his family. He kept most of his life with her and her family to himself and no one asked any questions.

He was not a highly educated man, but he did know how to save money. He'd been able to save a considerable amount since D. J.'s parents never asked how much money they had.

It hadn't even occurred to D. J. to wonder what Mitchell did with his money, since her daddy had credit accounts at all the fancy stores enabling her to buy whatever she wanted.

"Just put it on my daddy's account!" she'd shout as she skipped out of a boutique.

The drive through the mountains of California delighted D. J. The sun was just beginning to rise. She'd never seen so many trees and mountains in her whole life.

"You know, Daddy," she said firmly, "I have Indian blood in me. I ain't never told nobody about that. My mama told me when I was a little girl. She said I have supernatural powers because of the Apache blood in me. Sometimes I can tell when something is going to happen before it happens. I can even see into the future! My mama said it was called, "*the feelin*.'" She said I would know when I had it. My body feels like I am just air and a part of ever'thing. My eyes can see words floating behind words when people are a talkin'. Mitchell, I feel like I've always known these trees—like I've lived with 'em before. They're kind, and they help us to breathe.

"My mama also told me my sister didn't have the feelin'," she continued even though Mitchell didn't respond. "Only special people are blessed with the feelin'. She said to never be afraid because the feelin' would always protect me. Air has the power, too. She just doesn't know it yet."

"So, you can see the future?" Daddy remarked sarcastically.

"Yeap! I can see when certain things are gonna happen. Like I know ever'thin' in California is gonna work out just fine! I ain't worried at all. I trust ya, Mitchell."

"Well, Debbie Jane, life's sure going to be different for you. California is completely different than Texas. People live a very different lifestyle here, and their values are very different, too."

"How much farther is it?" asked Jimmy.

"Well Son, we'll be there in about four hours!"

"Oh my God, I gotta fix my face!" D. J. squealed. "Are we going straight to your mother's house?"

"Yeah, we'll stop by her house first. I want the kids to meet their other grandmother!"

"Do we have any cousins, Daddy?" asked Ron.

"Oh boy, do you ever! My two sisters each have eight kids, all close to your ages. You're going to have a lot of fun with them," Mitchell promised. "They don't live far from us either, so you'll see them a lot!"

D. J.'s blood ran cold. "What ya mean, Mitchell, they don't live far from us?" She had a sense she wasn't going to like the answers to her questions. "Where are we gonna live? We're still gonna live in the trees, aren't we?"

"No, but the trees will only be four hours away from us, and we can go camping anytime we want. There's a national forest called Yosemite Park, and there's a tree big enough for a car to drive through!"

"Can we go!" the kids all yelled.

"Yes, we will go and camp there. You'll see bears and huge waterfalls. You won't believe the amount of stars you can see at night!"

"When can we go, Daddy?" Jimmy asked. "When can we go?"

"Well, how about we go in about a month after we're settled in. How's that?"

Airstream took a deep breath and sat back in the seat. *What was camping? And were beatings allowed there?*

"Mitchell, ain'tcha gonna tell us where we're gonna live?" D. J. asked meekly.

"Well, I will tell you, I already have a job as a bus driver for the local bus company, A. C. Transit. I'm making good money now, but when I first started driving, I started at the lowest pay scale. I was given routes none of the other drivers wanted. They were dangerous routes—in the rundown parts of towns. In the beginning, I also had to work a split shift. This meant I had to get up in the middle of the night to be at work at 4:00 a.m. I was back home by 8:30 a.m. and then went back from 1:00 p.m.to 4:00 p.m. Now, I've been given safer routes, decent hours, and I got a pay raise," he told her. "I can hardly wait to see the looks on your faces when we arrive at our new home in El Cerrito, California!" he added.

"Oh my! We already have a new home? In a town called El Cerrito? How did you find us a new home, Mitchell? Can you tell us about it? How many bedrooms does it have? Does it have a big backyard?" D. J. asked.

"Well, this part is going to be a surprise. We'll be there in about an hour, so for now, just enjoy the view. Look, kids! Look straight ahead and you'll see the San Francisco-Oakland Bay Bridge! It connects the East Bay with San Francisco. And just beyond that is the ocean! We'll drive over to San Francisco in a couple of days."

Mitchell thought about how surprised D. J. was going to be when she found out he had bought a duplex while they were separated.

They arrived at the duplex just before noon. Mitchell pulled into the driveway.

"Is this it? What kinda place is this? It looks like two houses stuck together, Mitchell." D. J. said loudly.

"It's called a duplex. We live on one side, and there are tenants on the other side. They pay the rent for the whole building. We pay nothing. It's a great investment."

"Wh-elle, I ain't never lived so close to nobody before. Can they hear us talking?"

"No, not at all. We're perfectly in our own world. It might be a little smaller than what you're used to, but it's going to work out just fine!"

D. J. was in shock. Air just smiled at her mother.

Mitchell had given the movers keys to the duplex, and they were almost done unloading. D. J. had never heard of families sharing one big house with separate entries.

"I don't know if I can live like this, Mitchell," she said slowly.

"Well, get used to it because I bought it, and it's our new home now. I told you things were going to change, Debbie Jane!"

Mitchell told D. J. to walk down to the school and enroll the kids while he helped the movers. "The elementary school is only about six blocks down the street."

Air would be in the middle of fifth grade, and Ron would be in the third grade.

"They don't have to start school today, but you can enroll them. Go on, Debbie Jane. The kids have to be in school. The movers will be done sooner if I help."

"I don't even know our address. Do we have a phone yet?"

Mitchell handed D. J. a piece of paper that had their new address and phone number.

She and the kids started walking toward the school.

Air could see that her mother was still in shock, and she didn't utter a word to the kids, not even when Jimmy tugged at her arm and said, "I'm scared, Mommy."

Air looked up at her mother's face. She looked as though she was about to start crying. Her lips were trembling, and she looked like a little girl. For some reason, Air remembered when she was about four years old. Her mother had put her and her two brothers down for a nap back in Texas and then had gone to visit a neighbor. As soon as she was gone, Air had crawled out of bed and quietly walked into the kitchen.

Where did I get the idea of making a cradle for my doll at the age of four? Air asked herself.

She remembered climbing up onto the kitchen counter and opening the cabinet door. She reached for the box of Quaker Oats. She took the container into the bathroom and emptied the contents into the toilet. She tiptoed back to the kitchen and got out a serrated table knife and laid the cylinder on its side.

I remember how good it felt to stick that knife into the container and slowly cut a window in the middle about two inches by four inches. I remember going into the parlor and picking out a couple of lacy handkerchiefs. I laid one down inside the window and put my doll inside. Then I put the other handkerchief on top of the doll. I remember slowly rolling that cylinder back and forth. She giggled out loud at the memory. *I can't believe I did that and didn't get caught,* she thought with a devilish smile.

Air discovered she had the skill to see something she liked and create it out of whatever she could find, but she would not allow herself to compare that innate ability to her mother. Soon, Barbie dolls arrived on the scene. Air would get a doll for her birthday, but that was it, no extra dresses or accessories. She would have to make her own doll clothes. She took apart the only doll dress she had and used it as the foundation for all the designs she would create. Air was very good at creating the most stunning dresses for her doll. She was given small amounts of fabric remnants D. J. would find at the Goodwill store. She worked best this way. She could create something that was quite unique from very little fabric. Having access to a limited supply of fabric forced Air to be very creative. After school, she would stop by the local five and dime store and head to the infant section. When no one was looking, she would gently pull off a label. Once home, she would sew it into the little dress she'd made. She and her friends would get together on the weekends and play with their dolls. Air's dolls' dresses were very different from those of her friend's. She would trim the dresses with seam binding or yarn or glue on small rhinestones she'd found in her mother's sewing basket.

"Wow Air, where did you get that dress?" her friends would ask frequently with envy and curiosity.

"Oh, I don't know," Air would reply. "My mom goes shopping while I'm at school. If I bring home my homework with an A on it, she gives me a new dress for my doll."

"Where does she buy them? I want one for my doll, too!" they would chime in unison.

"Oh, I have no idea," Air would reply nonchalantly. "She goes to those specialty stores in San Francisco. I'll ask her where she buys them, but if you want to trade dresses, that's fine with me. I like your doll's dress. You can keep my dress overnight if you want, and we'll trade back tomorrow."

Trading doll clothes delighted her friends and gave Air a tremendous sense of acceptance. She always made a point of opening the little dresses and showing her friends the tiny labels to prove they had been manufactured. She would have simply died if anyone knew she had made the dresses herself. Handmade anything was frowned on. It meant poor, and her friends were from well-to-do families.

Fifth grade carved a shift in Air's life path. She began to form a deep sense of confidence in herself artistically. She knew she was good and that her talent came easy. She could design and sew clothes, which would eventually lead not only to her designing all her own school clothes, but to a career in the fashion world as well.

~ 4 ~

The first few years in California passed relatively quickly, and the family adjusted quickly to their new environment.

No one made a big deal about your clothes in elementary school. But when Air entered junior high, everything seemed to have changed overnight. The many years she'd spent looking at Vogue magazines gave Air reassurance she would have no problem fitting in with the other girls. She knew from looking at the couture clothing from the fifties that she could design clothes that would never go out of style. She was going be a trendsetter. She would never wear clothes that were "in style" or were a fad.

She'd made a basic pattern by taking apart a dress she had. This was all she needed to create what she saw in fashion magazines. She'd embellish outfits she already had and make them into her own designs. Her designs were quite unique. She learned to never mix and match anything. Every outfit in her closet had its own complete set of accessories. She had no inhibitions about wearing an outfit that had its own matching hat, gloves, purse, jewelry, stockings, shoes, and coat. Each outfit was a piece of art. It was as though she was into "performance art" without being aware of it.

Ninth grade was tough on her and her father. That was the year of the "commie-pinko scene," hair permanents, and experiments with her body.

At this point, Air's father hated his job as a bus driver. He'd been with the company long enough that he was now driving the high-paying routes. His schedule changed from a route that drove right through their neighborhood in El Cerrito to the number 72 route that ran right through the heart of the Berkeley—quite a scene in the sixties.

One day, while driving the bus through Berkeley, a man got on and started up a conversation. He told Mitchell he was the manager for the Oakland A's baseball league. "No shit? I used to be a pitcher for the Indiana Bulls in the minors in Louisiana," Mitchell replied. "I was headed for the majors, but the war came."

When the man got off the bus, tears rolled down Mitchell's face. His dreams—the dreams he'd had all his life were nothing more than empty dreams now. They all came flashing back to him, no longer hidden in the corners of his mind. He had been right on the verge of becoming a famous pitcher. Everyone had called him "Lucky" because he threw so many no-hitter games. His mother would often remind him she still had a scrapbook full of newspaper articles and photos she'd cut out and pasted into a family album. "It's yours anytime you want it, darling," she would tell him. Mitchell didn't want any part of the scrapbook. It was too painful.

That day, Mitchell came home in a rage that lasted for hours. The kids thought for sure they were about to get lined up at any moment and get one hell of a "whooping."

Air would learn later in the day about the baseball conversation and would discern that this was what had really upset her dad, though his rant quickly changed from baseball to the teenagers in Berkeley. She simply listened as her father went on and on about these "young, goddamn arrogant, asshole teenagers and their ugly, white girlfriends" who held hands together on his bus.

"Those dirty girls sit at the back of my bus with their dirty boyfriends and make out. Airstream! Don't you ever let me catch you or hear of you kissing a boy on a bus, do you understand me, young lady?"

"Yes, sir!"

"You know, D. J., I think they just stand there and wait for my bus because they know how much they piss me off. Someday, I'm going to tell them to fuck off!"

"Why don'tcha just drive right on by their stop, honey?"

"I did a couple of times and I think they called the supervisor on me. Out of the blue, he's been double-parked at that stop for over a week.

"Those goddamned ugly girls! They all have this long, dirty, straight hair, and they wear those goddamn, dark blue stockings.

They're just a bunch of goddamn commie-pinkos! I better not ever catch you holding hands with any boy, Airstream!"

He looked over at D. J. "Isn't there something you can do with her hair? Her hair looks just like theirs!"

"Oh now, honey, you don't got anythin' to worry about. Airstream knows she doesn't ever need any man in her life. She's way to in-tell-in-gent to ever let any man tell her what to do! She's always gonna take care of herself. Why, she's gonna be famous someday, all by herself! And as for her hair, wh-elle, it's na-chur-allie straight, honey. I think it's kinda purdy."

"I think she looks like a goddamned dog! Like a Collie! I hate Collies!"

"You mean you hate Lassie?" cried out Jimmy.

Air's father ignored him.

"Wh-elle, I guess I could give 'er a pur-men-it."

"Well, then give her one of 'em so she don't look like all them commie-pinko lovers! Don't kid yourself, D. J. Just because she was born and raised in Texas don't mean she's racist!"

~~~

"Hold still, goddammit!"

"But Mom, I'm going to look ridiculous," Air protested. "My hair isn't supposed to be curly. Everyone is going to laugh at me!"

"Airstream, I'm warning ya, hold still! If anybody says anything to you about your hair, just lookie 'em in the eye and tell them you're different and you're proud of it."

"But, I don't want to be different," Air shot back. "I just want to look like everybody else!"

"Wh-elle, I'm sorry, sweetie. You'd be a whole lot better off if you'd just accept the way things are. Just like your daddy's different, you're different. There's no way around it, Air."

Every night, D. J. would put Air's hair up in rollers. Every morning, Air would get up before everyone else and take the rollers out. Quietly, she would get out the iron and the ironing board. She'd lay her head down on the ironing board. One by one, she'd stretch out each curl and iron it straight.

It always reminded her of D. J. stretching out those goddamned, curled-up spider legs. She took the iron and pressed the very life out of her hair. She carefully put her scorched and lifeless curls back onto the rollers just how D. J. had arranged them.

"Oh! Just lookie, Air! Lookie at how straight I got this here row!"

"I guess so."

"What'd ya mean, ya guess so? Honey, this ain't easy. It's a lot of work. I have to concentrate! Oh my, just look at that row!"

"Mom, I'm going to be leaving early each morning the next semester. I have to study for French exams. I'm going to go to the library early so I'll just comb my hair out at school."

"French, huh? What about Mexican? They speak a lot of Mexican in Texas. I even know how to count to ten in Mexican!"

"Mom, it's called, Spanish."

"Wh-elle, that's what I said."

"When I grow up, I'm not planning on spending any time in Texas. I'm going to go to Paris or maybe even Monte Carlo."

"Mon-tree Carlo? Where the hell is that?"

"It's in Europe."

All the way to school, Air prayed no one would see her with rollers in her hair. She'd sneak into the school's hallways and go directly to the girl's bathroom and comb out her straight, burned hair. It was lonely in that bathroom so early in the morning. The entire school was completely silent, except for the occasional sounds of the janitor's broom. She didn't feel safe being there, and as the days passed, she started to feel as though she was the janitor's daughter.

Her hair was soon brittle and dry from the heat treatments, but she had to keep up her image. She wasn't a commie-pinko! She was a surf bunny! It didn't matter to her that she didn't know any surfers. All the fashion magazines had pictures of surfer girls hanging out with boys at the beach with their surfboards. All the surf bunnies had long, straight hair. She wanted to look like a surfer so badly. Sometimes, she'd sit entire weekends rubbing her knees back and forth on the cement sidewalk in front of her house creating those so-called "surfer bumps." She'd read real surfers had calloused knots just below their knees from endlessly sitting on their boards waiting for the perfect wave. Sometimes, at school during lunch, she'd complain about how bad her knees hurt from surfing all weekend. Air didn't even know how to swim.

The suntanned look was tough too. If you were a surfer, you were out at the beach all weekend soaking up the rays and getting a great tan. Not Airstream. Rays meant freckles. Air was white as white could be, and she had fire-engine-red hair. Ten minutes in the sun, and Air was covered with freckles all over her body.

The day came when she discovered the new instant tan crap called QT. The first time she put QT on her body, her face broke out in a horrible rash. Of course, she'd put three applications all over her body. She ended up streaked as hell, with lily-white hands and feet. Her neck and knees were almost cocoa brown, and her face was simply a disaster. She tried to use household powder cleansers to scrub it off. She was raw for two weeks and, to boot, streaked more than ever! She looked like she had some kind of disease no one had ever seen before.

She tried to convince her father she was just a surfer "pretend style." She told him surfer girls all had long, straight hair, but she couldn't get through to him. To him, long, straight hair meant one thing and one thing only—commie-pinko lover.

"Airstream, you'd better wise up or else ain't no white boy gonna wanna ever have anything to do with you. You'll end up like those ugly, fat white girls!"

That remark was really a joke, since Air was as skinny as a rail. She was ridiculed at school for being so skinny.

"Hey, Airstream," her classmates would yell during lunch. "Don't turn sideways, or you'll disappear!"

One day at school, she realized all the intellectual girls in her classes were very skinny too. She wondered why they were never made fun of. She knew these girls weren't even noticed by the popular guys at school. They were just simply labeled nerdy and left alone. Airstream decided that, if she couldn't look like a surf bunny and certainly wasn't a hippie, she might as well look like an intellectual. She decided to stop by the library on the way home from school. She wanted to look like an elitist walking around in her own world carrying very complicated books on all sorts of complex subjects. She desperately wanted to be noticed by some guy who was headed to college.

She started to recognize many students who had the same classes as she did and wondered why none of her friends were in her classes. Her counselor told her that students had a "status" according to their grade averages. If you were on the honor role, you were placed in classes that were for the college bound students. These classes were more demanding than the regular classes in the same subject. She wanted to be seen carrying the same magazines the other honor roll students read. After school, she stopped by the library and checked out *Ramparts* magazine and *The Berkeley Barb*.

When she got home, her father about died. His blood pressure shot up immediately when he saw her with a couple of issues of *Ramparts* magazines. "Good god," he screamed. "That's *exactly* what all those damned ugly girls carry around!"

He grabbed the magazines and started going "ape shit," to use one of his terms. As he whipped the magazines around, pictures of the Rolling Stones fell out.

"Why the hell don't you carry around pictures of those freaking Beatle people?" he demanded. "These Rolling Stone losers are just what all of those goddamned hippies carry around! They are communists!"

Thinking about all this, Air found herself staring back at her father. Giving into a rare moment of open defiance, she answered in a loud voice, "Everyone's into the Beatles! The Rolling Stones are different, and Mom's always said we are supposed to be *u-nique*, right?"

Supposedly, Berkeley was very different from where she lived. In Berkeley, kids looked like hippies, and there was this thing called the "free speech movement." There was a lot of yelling about something in some famous park. They called themselves "free spirits" and dressed very differently than Air did. She had no idea the hippies were changing the nation. She had no idea some of her favorite songs on the radio were by bands that actually lived and played in clubs at night right there in the Bay Area. No one Air hung out with knew this either.

Air was very cloistered, not only by her family, but also by a self-induced isolation. She was so scared someone would find out the truth about her—that her family was really crazy—and she was emotionally tortured daily.

I know everyone is making fun of me behind my back, she would tell herself. *I know they are probably saying terrible things about me like that I'm stuck-up when it's just that I'm so insecure. I'm sure everyone knows I make my own clothes and that I stuff my bra. I am sure they think the way I dress is too weird, and I bet they make fun of how my ears stick out through my thin, straight hair. I bet the guys laugh about me, too.*

She didn't laugh easily and throw her hair back casually like the other girls. She had no idea how to just walk up to a boy and start talking and laughing. She walked the halls of the schools with her head down. She appeared shy when, in actuality, she was embarrassed. Most of her friends knew she always made the honor roll and figured she preferred to be home studying after school.

During the summer months, Air spent hours in her bedroom practicing how to laugh and talk easily with other students. She would look into her dresser mirror and imagine she saw a popular pretty girl who naturally tossed her hair back as she smiled with ease and confidence.

"Oh, Jesus, she's fifteen now, D. J.," Mitchell had said more than once. "We'd better start keeping an eye on her. She's heading down a bad path, and I don't know if we have any control over her anymore!"

Keep an eye on her? Boy, was that a joke! Dating boys was out of the question. During the school year, on the weekends, she had her choice of either going to a movie during the day or spending the night with a girlfriend. During the summer months, she was not allowed to leave the house. She spent her time in her bedroom listening to D. J. smacking Juicy Fruit gum all day and the goddamn mynah bird chanting over and over, 'Pretty little Janie, pretty little Janie, you're young and alive!' She told her friends she would be spending the summer with her rich aunt.

Once, Air was put on restriction for a couple of weeks because she'd gotten caught trying to teach the bird to say something different.

"Airstream! What the hell do you think you're doing?" D. J. had screamed.

"Nothing. I was just trying to teach the bird how to say, 'Y'all drive careful.'"

"Wait'll your daddy hears this! You just don't know how to stay outta trouble, do you?" D. J. warned.

That stupid bird said, "Little D. J., little D. J., you're young and alive," over and over, all day long every day, every week. It was pure torture! Come to think of it, that poor bird was sentenced to its own sort of restriction. Air laughed.

Later in life, Airstream would invite D. J. to visit for a couple of days. They would be watching TV when a commercial about child abuse prevention would cause Air's breath to catch in her throat. She would use the moment to bring up a topic that had been on her mind for a long time.

"Mom, when we were little, how could you just sit there and let Dad beat us so horribly with that gigantic bus driver belt day after day? For Christ's sake, Mother, I can't believe how you could just sit there at the kitchen table, smacking on that goddamn Juicy Fruit chewing gum, swinging your leg back and forth to whatever song was playing on the radio and act as if nothing was happening while Dad almost beat us to death! I remember that the backs of both my legs were covered with giant black belt buckle marks for weeks. Fuck, Mother. Sometimes, out of the blue, I start crying when I remember how Dad would continue to beat Ron way after he'd passed out from pain. You didn't do anything but continue to sing along with the music!"

D. J. just sat there, exactly like she had sat there when Air was "getting it."

Air realized that her mother was hopeless and that "her river would never make it to the sea." Air knew she was wasting her time trying to get D. J. to see that her failure was the cause of much pain for all of her children—that because she'd never stood up to Mitchell, never demanded that he stop beating her children, all three now deeply suffered and were clueless as to how to lead a normal life. Air wished she could ram of a piece of Juicy Fruit gum down her mother's throat at that very moment. She watched D. J.'s eyes and face, looking for the least bit of guilt or remorse. She saw nothing. Hell, if she had it do over, she'd do the same damn thing. Air was sure of it. She saw no regrets in her mother.

"Airstream, honey, we never *abused* you!" D. J. finally said, her voice loud and her tone indignant. "No one ever stuck lit cigarettes to your body. No one ever broke any of your bones. No, Airstream, you were never *abused*—never. Whoever in the world told you that?"

"Told me that? Mother, are you out of your fucking mind? I lived it! I went to elementary school with dark black and blue belt buckle marks all down the back of my legs. I was so naive I thought all the kids had bruises down the backs of their skinny little legs, too. Mother, I'd say that was child abuse!

"I'm talking giant black marks that lasted for weeks! Mom, I had such a bird-boned body. Dad could have killed me! You did nothing to save me. Did you see my body was like a little bird's? Shit, from what I have read now, I could have had a stroke from all those broken blood vessels! Do you know that nowadays, Mom, if a schoolteacher sees a child with unexplained bruises, he or she is under legal obligation to file a report with Child Protective Services? You and dad would have been arrested, and you would have lost custody of your children, which probably wouldn't have mattered to you anyway."

"Air, honey, you're making a mountain outta a molehill! Sweetie, you were always a natural born leader. You were such a strong person until you were converted by that communist teacher you had. Do you remember him? You were just in the fifth grade, honey."

"Oh, Mother, give it up! Of course, I remember that teacher in fifth grade who made fun of the way I dressed in front of the whole class! He used to tell the class, 'Doesn't she think she's something? Just look at all those petticoats she has on. She can't even make it to the pencil sharpener without knocking everything off every student's desk.'

"I knew it was wrong, Mom, but what could I do? If you want to know the truth, I remember a lot of things from when I was very young. I remember when I was just a year old, and you locked me in a dark room while there was a terrible Texas thunderstorm going on! There was nothing in that room except my crib. I remember how the lightning and thunder were so bright and loud it lit up the room and how terrified I was. I screamed for you to come to me. You just left me in there crying my heart out. I think I knew then you didn't really care if I lived or died, much less whether Dad killed me during a beating!"

"Wh-elle, I'll be damned! You remember that? Wh-elle, I don't. I think you've seen too many of those quack head doctors, Airstream. They just love to see ya coming. They getcha ta make things up and make ya give 'em your money. There ain't nothing wrong with ya, and there ain't never been. You just like tellin' stories!"

"Oh my God, Mother. You're truly nuts! Of course, you're not going to let yourself remember those times because I bet you do feel guilty you didn't do anything to stop him. You were afraid of him! Going from riches to rags made you hate Dad. I even remember the time before Ron was born and you were changing my diaper on the floor in front of the TV. I was super-embarrassed and ashamed that all those people on TV could see me naked. I didn't understand it was just a TV. I thought they were real people in the room watching me without clothes on. Now, I wonder where the hell I got the message at that age that a naked body was not only bad but dirty and something to be ashamed of?"

"Wh-elle, I don't know unless you heard it somewhere while you were outside playing."

"*Out playing?*" Airstream practically screamed.

"Mother, I was just a year and a half old! Gee, let me think, it doesn't take a rocket scientist to figure out that maybe, just maybe, I might have already been being sexually molested by someone?"

"Sex-u-alee moe-less-teed? Oh my God, young lady! That teacher did more damage to you than I thought. I knew we shoulda gone down to that school and got him fired! He was a real nutcase. Anyway, honey, you were only in the fifth grade, and he was a

Communist teacher. Let me think, cuz I know I remember his name. His name was Darrel MacDaniel. Do you remember him, honey? Wh-elle, he brainwashed you, sweetie. You've never been the same since. Your daddy and I tried to save ya, but it was too late."

Dazed, Air realized she was wasting her time. She felt an overwhelming sense of sadness. How could you get a mother in touch with her shit about raising her kids if she didn't already feel pain in her heart? You didn't, but Air would spend forever trying. Air felt light-headed. Suddenly, she heard a voice talking to her.

"Give it up, Air," whispered a voice—a voice who, by that point, Air had come to know as Claire. "Your Mom simply doesn't have enough time left on the planet to get off that nest of bitter eggs she's sitting on. Your mom's been damaged herself, and she'll never talk about it. Her parents didn't tell her she was loved or that everything would work out. They never reassured her of anything, and she, like you, felt she had to fend for herself. Her parents let the maids take care of her and her brothers and sisters. Children were to be seen and not heard. God only knows what happened to her as a child, and you'll never know because she doesn't know how to talk about it."

"What did you say, Mom? I heard a voice talking to me. Did you hear it?"

"Wh-elle, you're the one that's doing all the talkin'. I can't even get a word in edgewise. Airstream, honey, you and your daddy were re-elle close, always. From the moment you were born, you loved him more than you loved me. Do you have any idea how much that hurt me?"

Talk about creating your own reality, Air thought. *Maybe D. J. doesn't hate me so much as I think; maybe she has bottled-up anger about running away that weekend to Louisiana in the first place, and she can't deal with the reality that a daughter was born as a result. She resents how she became bound to a life she knew nothing about and three children she had no idea how to mother. Good grief, she was just fifteen years old when she got pregnant. The only life she'd ever known was that of a child of a wealthy Texas family. Her family ranch was the largest and most prominent for miles. She was accustomed to being spoiled and doted over by the maids. They combed her hair daily and dressed her in hand-embroidered dresses made just for her. Nightly, her bed sheets were ironed so she would get into a warm bed. She was beautiful and every boy in the county was crazy for her. Maybe I've got this story all wrong,* she thought momentarily.

Air could not imagine her mother being molested as a child by her father; it was an extremely painful thought. But it was a consideration she'd examine at a much later point in her life.

Back in ninth grade, she didn't have room to consider anything but how she'd make it through the difficulties of her home life from day to day.

5

"I'll have some eggs. Sunny-side up, like my sister's tits!" Jimmy said. He turned to Air with a twisted grin. "Hey, Miss Flat Eggs, did anybody ever tell you you've got nothing but yolks for tits?"

"Shut up, you four-eyed beaver!" Air yelled back. "Mom, make him stop saying those bad things about me."

Air had never given much thought to her breasts until her brothers had begun making fun of her tits, or "yolks" as they called them. You know things are bad when your brothers make fun of your tits. She was in seventh grade when her brothers had first pointed out she didn't have any tits, and the peer pressure in seventh grade was beginning to be full of land mines.

"It's your turn, Airstream," a male classmate had said. "Stand up straight and tall. Now look down at your toes. Can you see them?"

Air thought something fabulous was about to happen to her since she could see them. Perhaps she'd become a true member of the "in crowd."

"Yeah!" she yelled "Sure! I can see them!"

"You lose! If you had any tits, you wouldn't be able to see your toes, dummy," cried one of the boys, laughing.

She was in a crisis. On the one hand, she liked her body. On the other hand, the boys relentlessly teased her about her body. They said her ears stuck out too much, she didn't have any eyebrows or eyelashes since they were white, her red hair was nerdy, she had a boy butt, and her freckles were the ultimate beauty curse.

Of course, Airstream, being the daughter of an experimenter, began laboratory experimentation with her own body. She conducted projects and experiments like "what to stuff your bra with," "how to de-frecklize," "how to get your ears to stay back," and "what color to wear to offset your fire-red hair." Her ears were a great source of pain.

It wasn't that she was born with painful ears; rather, the methods she'd come up with to get them to stay flush against her head caused her pain. Her first experiment was to take a rubber band, stretch it around her head, just barely enough to catch the tops of her ears. She'd then pull her hair over the rubber band so it wasn't noticeable. After a week, she realized she was getting an indentation about a fourth of an inch deep around her head. Being a hypochondriac, she was convinced she'd started herself down the road of having an early stroke, so she abandoned the rubber band act. She was desperate, but brain damage was just too high a price to pay.

She soon discovered the bald spot everyone has behind their ears. *Great!* She thought. And thus began "the liquid glue act." Glue? Sure. Each night, just before she was going to bed, she'd put a glob of glue behind one ear at a time and lay on that side of her head until it dried. She'd then turn over and glue the other side. This was ideal except for the times she accidently glued some of her hair to her ears. But, she was willing to give up a little hair now and then. Just no brain tumors—please, God. A part of her, the hypochondriac part, was trying to convince her glue had terrible side effects on the brain, as in tumors.

But the glue act worked perfectly. It would last until the bus ride home the next day. About half way home, each ear would pop out from the sides of her head. Thank God most of the kids on the bus were in lower grades and paid no attention to her. She always carried a sweater cap, and when "the moment of release" occurred, she'd just put on her cap.

Her freckles were also a constant cause of concern. Her mother decided to help her out. "Airstream, honey, haven't you ever heard of O. J.'s Freckle Remover? I think it ack-shoe-ally comes in a cream, if I ain't mistaken."

"No, and how would do you know about that stuff?"

"Wh-elle, one time I had two freckles right here on my arm."

"Great, you had two freckles on your arm. Big deal!" Air said. "I've got a million on my nose alone!"

The next day, Air stopped by the drug store on her way home from school. She went straight to the face section for O. J.'s Freckle

Remover, half-convinced it was extinct or would be in some Southern snake oil treatment section. She found it! She put it in her purse and left. Thank God, it was Easter vacation. After two days of using the solution, she had burned off the first five layers of her face! She hurt so badly, she couldn't talk or smile for two weeks. She looked like a burn victim.

Thank God no one ever laughs or smiles in my house, Air thought. *My skin would split wide open, and I'd be scarred for life.*

"Airstream," D. J. cried with a cackle when Air first emerged, timidly, from the bathroom, trying to hide her burned face. "You used too much! I don't know why the hell you mess around with your face, anyway," she added, refocusing on the magazine she was engrossed in. "You kin hardly see your freckles. I think they make you look unusual. Besides, they'll fade with age."

Air could have killed her! Age? Unusual? She was just fifteen! How long was "fade with age" going to take? Besides, she didn't have freckles anymore. She had burned them off. Her face was now whiter than her neck. Her skin peeled for a month. The minute she was back out in the sun, she had more freckles than ever. She had to wear twice as much makeup to hide them. Of course, she started having pimple problems. She'd never had a pimple in her life!

"Air, honey, if you're gonna wear that much makeup on your face, ya gotta learn how ta blend," D. J. said when she walked in on Air staring forlornly into the mirror.

"Blend?" Air asked, catching her mother's eye in the mirror. "What do you mean, blend?"

"Wh-elle, ya gotta gently stroke it easy-like upwards from your neck so ya don't have that color line," D. J. focused on the mirror, pressing two fingertips against her neck and moving them up and over her chin. "Like so. Have ya ever looked at yourself in the mirra sideways, honey?"

"No."

"Wh-elle, go lookie at yourself in the mirra."

Air ran to the bathroom. She stared with disbelief. Her face had a pinkish tone that ended right where her chin met her neck. It looked horrible. How long had she been going to school two-toned?"

Shit, now she could add "two-toned" to the list of "forever screwed up." Of course D. J.'s list was called "forever young." Even the mynah bird had learned to sing those words in case any of them forgot.

"Mother! Why can't I go to Blouin's and buy some makeup that really works? The cheap stuff looks so fake."

"Where, honey?" D. J. asked.

"Blouin's Beauty Boutique!"

"Wh-elle, I ain't never heard of that place, but I tell ya what. How 'bout we go down to the market tamarra cuz it's my shoppin' day and we'll lookie in the drug section and see what we kin find. How's that sound?"

A trip to the store meant one thing to Air. She would have to endure the glares of disbelief on the faces of other women shoppers when they noticed D. J.'s god awful black sweater with aquarium rock glued all around the edges. "No thanks, Mom. I still have plenty of that stuff you bought me last time."

Oh God, then there were epic tit experiments in how to look "stacked." That was the most agonizing challenge of all for Air. The questions went on forever; what would look real? What would feel real? What would stay inside and not eventually work its way up to her chin or down to her ankles? She tried stuffing everything into her AAA bra.

At first, there was the toilet paper act. This seemed simple enough, certainly in terms of excuses. If a square of toilet paper made its big escape upward toward her chin, she'd look like she was a Kleenex box with a tissue dangling—up for offering to a passing stranger in the hall who had a runny nose. She could just smile and say, "I have plenty to spare."

The nylon act caused Air the most perplexing of all her body problems. Tissues were a waste of time and nylons never stayed in place. Since she didn't have any tits, she had no idea if breasts were as soft and as mushy as nylons felt. If someone bumped into Air's boom booms, their chances of ending up in her ribcage were pretty great. She was so skinny bruised ribs became everyday common. The nylons had a way of working their way around to her shoulder blades. Sometimes they'd get stuck under her armpits, making her look like a football player since she couldn't put her arms against her body whenever this happened. She always knew when they'd made their big escape. It wasn't so much she could suddenly see her toes, as it was the looks of horror on the faces of her friends as they passed her by in the hall. Airstream, being so Pollyanna, never thought of sewing the wadded up nylons into her bra.

"Airstream! What is that?" asked a friend, passing her by in the hall one day.

Air looked down at her chest and saw a wad of nylons beginning to stick up out of her dress. "Oh, I'm not allowed to wear nylons to school," she improvised. "So, I just stuff them down my dress." Air would come up with all kinds of tall tales, but the one about her mom not letting her wear nylons to school worked the best.

Air was so skinny that you could see her rib cage and bones. Once she stuffed her brother's crew socks inside her bra. They were so thick and hard they felt like rocks against her flat chest. A fellow classmate accidently bumped into her while she was standing at her locker. He elbowed her right in the chest. She felt like she'd been hit with a baseball bat. The crew socks were so hard that they bruised her ribs and she could barely breathe for a week. If she kept up the crew socks act, she'd have to come up with a way to cushion them from her chest. She was clueless what to do--the nylons were too mushy and crew socks felt like rocks.

Air always made sure she was the first to arrive home so she could take out the nylons before any of the family saw her "overnight blossoming." But the day came when she got caught. Her father was sick and hadn't gone into work. Her mother was also at home cooking dinner for the dogs. Air walked through the front room and headed as quickly as possible to her room. As she walked by her father his eyes popped out of his head.

"Since when did our little girl blossom?" he asked her mother.

"She didn't," D. J. said in an angry tone. "Airstream, get the hell out here, right now! I want to talk to you!"

Air knew this meant one thing and one thing only—restriction.

"What the hell do you have stuffed in your bra?" Daddy asked.

"Nothing."

"Listen here, young lady, you take that crap out immediately," he barked. "You're on restriction for six weeks! Do you understand? And your mother is going to check you every morning to make sure you never pull this again. Do you understand me?"

Shit, this is right up Mother's alley. General D. J. herself. She loves "illegal search and seizures," just like she loved the spider hunts. Too bad those spiders didn't have legal representation. I wish mother would have a seizure.

After that, every morning before Air could walk out the front door, she had to go through an "inspection."

"Okay, young lady, where do ya have 'em hidden? I know there's paddin' in there somewhere. I just know it! You can't fool me. Might as well hand 'em over now, cuz you know I'll find 'em."

Air stood there while D. J. went through her purse and schoolbooks. After a meticulous search without any results, D. J. just stood staring at her with her hands on her hips.

"Maybe, ya got 'em at school. If I find out that's what you're doing, I'm gonna tell your daddy!"

Air kept a straight face and told her mother she wasn't stuffing her bra anymore. But D. J. was a natural born "hunter," and Air knew she would get caught sooner or later.

Finally, the day came when, during a routine inspection, a very deranged look came over D. J.'s face.

"Airstream, wait a minute here. Take down your panties."

"Oh my God, Mother! Are you out of your mind!"

"I said take down your panties. I know you've got that goddamned stuffing somewhere on ya, and I'm gonna find it!"

She is sadistic. You bitch, Miss flat eggs yourself. You don't have any tits, and you'll damned if I ever sprout any flower buds either!

Air slowly took down her panties. D. J. was biting her lips at that point. Air's underwear revealed nothing. D. J. looked her Air up and down. "Take off them there shoes, Airstream!"

Air, reluctantly, kicked off her shoes. D. J. grabbed 'em and shook out the nylons that were stuffed in the tips of the shoes.

D. J. started jumping up and down squealing, "Thought you were pretty smart didn't ya, little lady? I knew all along you had 'em on ya somewhere. Wh-elle, you're in trouble now."

Air had to ride the bus au naturel that morning. For the first time in a year, she didn't have to bob her body up and down to make her stationary boobs bounce like all the other girls' big tits did. Air had spent a lot of time observing big tits, and they all jiggled as the bus rode merrily along its path filled with "big headlights." She'd even learned how to walk down the halls "bobbing." Air was convinced even the bus driver noticed her suddenly deflated chest that morning. She decided to cut first class and go over to the mall and steal some nylons. She'd have to figure out a new hiding spot, too. She would not be able to get away with hiding them on her body anymore.

As Air walked through the department store, she came up with the idea of cutting out the cups of a larger bra and stuffing them into her bra. Heavens only knows why, but Air chose a bra that was neon pink. The bra sort of "stuck out" from all the other bras the way Air wanted her tits to stick out. She also stole some nylons to get her through the day until she could cut the pads out of the enormous neon pink, Size-D cup later in the school's bathroom. She decided she'd hide the slip-in cups in the bushes down the street from her house, figuring they'd be easy to just slide in and out as she was walking to and from the bus stop each day.

The giant pads barely fit into her thirty-two, triple A size bra. She looked like Miss Boom Boom La Tour herself overnight. Oh God, if only she could get felt up with the size of these tits. Air had no clue of how ridiculous she looked. No cleavage, just two huge rocks jutting out from the side of a sheer cliff.

The day came when Air's greatest terror—getting busted by her friends—came true. She was in her French class when the drama unfolded. Her French teacher called on her to recite a poem they were studying. She had to stand in front of the class. As she started to stand up, the class joker, who sat directly behind, popped her bra strap. He was a pro and never misgauged exactly where the straps met. She felt like a slot machine as though someone had pulled the lever down and hit the jackpot. Air stood up, and her bra was now undone, out fell two enormous neon pink bra pads. She was horrified. She could hear the entire class laughing. She turned and looked back at John's face with utter disdain. He was laughing so hard his face was as pink as her lost tits!

Suddenly and unconsciously, she looked down to the floor and instinctively kicked the falsies across the room. From that moment on, everything seemed to happen in slow motion. She watched as the two neon flying saucer-looking objects went flying high above everyone heads. She had kicked them so hard they slammed into the windows across the room and fell flat on top of the radiators!

"They're not mine! They're not mine!" she screamed.

She ran out of the classroom hysterically crying. She could hear the class howling with laughter, and the class joker was yelling out, "I bet she doesn't have any peach fuzz either!"

Air didn't wait around for the teacher to deal with the situation. He was a big loser himself. On the first day of her French class, everyone had noticed a puddle of water around his feet just as he stood up to welcome them to their new French class. Word was out he wore diapers.

Shit, if you didn't have Mount Shasta's and a thick curly bush down there and stand around drooling at all the cute boys during the lunchtime dance, you could forget being a part of the "in crowd." And you could just accept you would always end up dancing with your girlfriend during the lunch hour dance.

Air's "boom boom" act was over by lunchtime. By then, almost everyone had heard what had happened in her French class. For the past two years, she'd had the reputation of being the hardest girl "to get." This was only because she couldn't let any guy touch her tits and discover the truth. Her days as Miss Boom Boom La Tour were over. She was now Popeye's Olive Oyl.

The next day at school, Air's best friend told her the worst news she'd ever heard in her life. "Word's out, Air; everyone's calling you *Pinkie* now."

Shit, all her life she'd been called nicknames and not the ones of the affectionate genre. It had been Dumbo when she was in second grade because her ears stuck straight out from her head. "Dumbo, Dumbo, fly away, fly away!"

"Hey, Pinkie! "What color are your pads today?"

"Hey, Pinkie, how about a couple of Dixie Cups? There's plenty in the cafeteria!"

"Hey, Miss Boom Boom! Did you think of trying water balloons?"

Hell, she'd never thought of that—water balloons.

The lunch bell rang, and everyone headed back into the school building. Air slowly walked into her English class. Straightaway, the teacher gave the class an assignment. The class was to look around the room and write a short description of someone they did not know. The writer was to describe the person so everyone in the class would be able to identify him or her.

Air looked around the classroom. She immediately noticed James. He was well groomed and had great skin. He was quite handsome—not in the traditional sense of handsome most girls had fantasies about, but exactly the type of handsome Air had always had fantasies about. He was the picture of the future successful, family oriented man who was devoted to his wife. He had blond hair, fair skin, no freckles, and a body that looked like he played tennis a lot. In Air's mind, there was no doubt he was college bound. She loved the way he way dressed. He had on a tan, collared shirt with a gray plaid, wool sweater pulled over it that matched his corduroy pants. He was wearing the latest style in shoes called desert boots. She imagined he came from a well-to-do family and had loving parents.

She watched him for a few minutes, and suddenly she saw "it." He had a mole about half an inch long on the top of his left ear! It was quite noticeable from across the room. She decided the mole was certainly a distinguishable characteristic. She'd always had a thing for moles, since she had about nineteen moles just around the area of her left breast. She wrote about the mole, his shoes, his gray corduroy pants with his matching sweater, and how she had not seen anyone in the school as nicely dressed as him. Air wondered if he had noticed her.

"All right, class. Time is up."

The teacher collected all the papers and then randomly selected two to read out loud to the class. She began to read the first one. Air couldn't believe the teacher was reading any of the descriptions out loud, much less that she had chosen hers!

"And he has a mole at the top of his left ear that looks like a thumb trying to hitch a ride," the teacher read.

The class started laughing. Air felt terrible. She looked over at James. His face was beet red, and "the ear" looked as though he was pulsing with embarrassment. Air knew how awful he felt. She could hear the word *Pinkie* ringing in her ears. The teacher continued with the next descriptive narrative.

"She's very pretty and has long red hair. She dresses like her family has a lot of money. But she's a pirate's dream; she has a sunken treasure chest!"

Whoever wrote that obviously had no idea that she was already being made fun of by her classmates, much less that she had the nickname Pinkie. The class roared with laughter. Air got up out of her seat and ran out of the classroom after seeing everyone looking at her.

Will the "tiny titties" shit ever stop? Air asked the Tit Gods as she leaned against the hall lockers crying.

James followed her out into the empty hallway. "Gee, I'm sorry. I had no idea she'd read them out loud."

"You wrote that?"

"Yeah."

"I wrote the other one about you!"

They both started laughing and looked at each other forgivingly. In that moment, they both sensed they would be lifelong comrades.

"Just to show you how sorry I really am, I'll let you in on a secret," James said.

Air looked down as he had pulled his pants forward enough for her to see everything, including his pubic hair and his dick. She about fainted. She'd never seen an adult dick with pubic hair in her life! She'd only seen her brothers when she was young and peeing in the waterfall!

"Look, my mother didn't do the laundry! I had to come to school without any underwear on today! Don't tell anyone okay?"

Oh my god, this guy is beyond help. The fact that he has a mother who neglected to make sure he's prepared for school is in direct alignment with D. J.'s complete neglect on all levels of any kind when it comes to the needs of her kids, whether it's being prepared for school with clean clothes or making sure we have something to eat during lunchtime. My God, D. J. never even cooks breakfast for us, much less setting out clothing for school. How could I have been so wrong about him? I thought he was living a wonderful life.

"I can tell you and I are different from everyone else," James said.

Oh my God, now he's starting to sound just like D. J. I wonder if he thinks he's u-nique?

"Air, are you going to the school's 'Let's Get to Know Each Other' picnic up at Lake Anza this Saturday?" he asked.

"I haven't made up my mind yet. Are you going?" she asked, acting as though she knew all about the event, which she didn't.

"Yeah, if you want, we could go together. I have a car and could pick you up."

"That sounds great."

"Have you been up to Lake Anza in Tilden Park?" James asked.

"No."

"Have you?"

"Yeah, it's a beautiful lake up in the Berkeley hills. There's a beach, and it's great for swimming."

"Swimming? I don't know how to swim," she said, almost as if she was ashamed.

"Just don't get in the water. Anyway, there's this rumor that a huge creature lives in the lake, so most people don't swim out too far."

"Will everyone be in swimsuits?"

"Yeah sure. Why?"

"No reason, just wondering."

"We should get out the hall and go back into class."

"I can't go back in there. I'm going to the library until next period," Air remarked.

Shit! Lake! That means bikinis and major breast exposure. How in the hell am I going to manage a pair of crew socks or nylons in a bathing suit?

⁓ℛℯ⁓

Air was petrified. Nylons and crew socks were out of the question.

The only thing I can do is come up with something to push-up my tits in the bikini top. What in the world am I going to do? I need something to put under my tits that will look natural and stay put.

Air suddenly had a brilliant idea. She would use kitchen sponges. They were soft, and she could put them under her boobs once she had the bikini top on. D. J. had sponges in all shapes and sizes, and all were green—lime green, as in the lime green of her beloved plastic ferns and the green glass dragons. Air chose an enormous sponge about four inches by five inches and about one inch thick. She put on her bathing suit top. She cut the sponge in half and tucked each half under a tit. Hell, she was so "pushed up" her nipples were showing. She cut the sponges down a little bit smaller. Perfect, she looked very natural. She smiled and giggled as she looked at herself in the mirror. *I just might have fun at this picnic.*

James picked her up the following Saturday. They drove up to the lake, laughing and talking about the scene in the English class the week before. They parked and walked down toward the water. They arrived at the picnic and started talking with some of their friends. Air was standing next to James when, all of a sudden, some senior asshole grabbed Air and started running with her down to the lake.

"Hey, she doesn't know how to swim!" yelled James.

No one knew who the senior who threw her into the water was. She went down under the water and when she surfaced, gasping for air, she momentarily saw two lime-green sponges floating next to her and went under again.

"Hey, Pinkie! Your tits are now lime green! They match the algae," yelled someone from the crowd who had gathered to witness both James diving into the water to save Air from drowning and the sponges as they floated with the current.

73

James carried Air up to the beach and handed Air a towel. "Here, wrap yourself up. We're leaving now."

As they drove away from the park, James looked over at Air, "You're in really big trouble. As soon as you hit the water, I'm not kidding Air, out shot those two green sponges you had stuffed in your top. They looked like bullets! They shot up in the air at least six feet. That guy was lucky he didn't get hit by one of them. Honestly, I don't want to hurt your feelings, but it was hysterically funny. I know you're not in the mood to hear this right now, but believe me; someday you're going to appreciate how funny this is—not today, but someday. Air, I swear we're going to laugh our asses off."

6

During the mid-sixties, everything seemed to have changed overnight. Hairstyles and the styles of clothes changed drastically. Girls started wearing long "Granny Dresses" and shoes that looked like moccasins. Some now wore fresh flowers in their hair. The hangout spots changed from their homes to the local parks. Everyone was listening to Janis Joplin, The Who, Led Zeppelin, The Kinks, Steppenwolf, and Jimi Hendrix. Of course, there were The Beatles and The Rolling Stones.

Her friends' lives seemed so different than the life she lived. They were free to do what they wanted after school without checking in with their parents. They just had to be home by dinner. It was overwhelming for Air. Her life was simple: Go to school; go directly home. She was literally a prisoner. Her parents rarely watched the TV news to hear about what was happening in the Bay Area and the changes the sixties were bringing. Everything seemed chaotic and confusing to her. She didn't understand what was happening. She was still a very shy girl, desperately trying to hide her home life from her friends. She kept up the act of being a nurtured and loved young girl with overly protective parents. She told everyone she couldn't attend a lot of the parties because she had to study. Most of her friends were not in the accelerated college prep courses that she was in, but they accepted her excuses.

Most everyone knew which students they could go to get their drugs of choice. Getting what drug you liked best by the end of the day was never a problem if you got your order in early before school started. No one knew where these students went to buy the drugs. The whole thing was very secretive, and Air felt uneasy about even knowing anything at all about who was buying what. Everyone gave their money up front, and God only knew what they really received.

Some opted for LSD in different forms, "reds" or "downers"; others wanted pot or "cross tops," which made you stay up all night and party. Then there was heroin and cocaine. Air stayed as far away from the crowds who were into hard drugs as possible. All of the drugs scared her, but she wanted desperately to be accepted by her friends.

Many students mixed drugs with alcohol. This was becoming the norm. Somebody's parents were always away for the weekend, and news of a party traveled fast. Air felt strong peer pressure to at least smoke marijuana. She didn't like being on drugs. Being "stoned" scared her. She felt like she was going to die, and she felt a sense of deep mistrust, never sure what she was really ingesting. From her life experiences, Air had little trust in anything, much less drugs. Her background had taught her you never knew what was going to happen next.

She knew her classmates were all high without any fear or question as to the dangers. They were getting high and drinking during school hours. After school, they'd drive to Berkeley to find more drugs and hang out at a place called People's Park. She was invited to go along, but she knew that was completely out of the question. She was always able to gracefully decline due to homework. Air had no clue as to what was going on in Berkeley outside of what she would hear from her father. She was naive about the weekend night scene in Berkeley with all the young people getting stoned, dancing in the streets, and listening to music. Her friends never mentioned that there were many young people who were homeless living on Telegraph Ave, which was the heart of the Berkeley scene.

"Airstream, don't you let me ever find out you've been to that dirty, whacko town of Berkeley!"

"I'll never go to Berkeley, Daddy," Airstream said in a tone she hoped would reassure him. "I wouldn't even know how to get there!"

"Oh, don't give me that bullshit," he snapped. "I bet you've already been there. I bet one of your dates took you up there where all those fucking hippies and communists hang out!"

"No, I've never been to Berkeley, Daddy! I know you don't want me to go there."

"Wh-elle, you're gonna be eighteen soon, and you know we have the right to kick your ass out of this house, don't you? So you better think twice about where you go. If you lie to us, that's it! You're out of here so fast you won't know what hit cha!"

"I don't understand what the big deal is here. I don't even have any friends who hang out in Berkeley. I'm going to my room. I need to study. Good night."

Air went to her room and closed the door. She sat on her bed and wondered why the hell her life was so fucked up.

Shit, I study so hard, she thought. *I make straight A's, except for an occasional C in PE.* All she wanted was to be able to go to UC Berkeley, but her parents just didn't support her. In fact, she was sure that they wanted her out of the house. *They're crazy,* she told herself. *They think I'm a communist! This is so nuts. I can't keep living like this.* She wished the rich aunt she'd invented as an excuse for her unavailability during the summer was real or that she was with Mamaw and Papaw. *They would never let Mom and Dad treat me like this. Mom would get in big trouble. I know she's sick. She's delusional. I'm sure she'd love to kick me out. Then she could do more of her weird designs without anyone giving her crap!*

"Mitchell, she's gonna be eighteen next month ya know," she heard D. J. say.

"Yeah, and I've about had it with her attitude!" her dad snapped back.

"Wh-elle, I think we outta think about tossing her little ass out. I kin just feel she's up to something behind our backs. I kin just feel it! We have no idea where she goes when she leaves here on a Friday night. God forbid she should she get herself preggars, and then we gotta raise her child."

On Air's eighteenth birthday, she got up half expecting some sort of surprise from her parents. After all, eighteen was a big deal, and they could at least make an attempt to let her know they hoped she had a great day at school. She knew there would be no presents or cake, but maybe a Happy Birthday card would have been nice.

Her father had left for work, and D. J. stayed in bed. Air dressed herself and gathered her homework. She left the house and slowly walked down the hill to the bus stop. None of her friends were aware it was her birthday. She was too ashamed to tell anyone since she was not having a big celebration party. She was so unhappy in her first period class she almost started crying. As usual, she pinched her thigh to keep from crying. This adaptive behavior—hurting herself when she felt out of control—had become routine.

She left her last class of the day feeling quite despondent. She boarded the public transit bus unconsciously and headed home. She sat alone and stared out at her friends walking and laughing as the bus drove away from the school. She wondered if they were going to each other's houses to study together or just hang out for a couple of hours. She wondered what she was missing out on. It seemed like all her girlfriends had boyfriends walking with them. Did they hang out somewhere before going home?

The ride home that day seemed endless. It took half an hour to get home. When her stop came, she pulled the cord and got off. Glumly, she thought, *At least it's a sunny day. I'm supposed to be happy, but instead I'm so sad. I know everyone who turns eighteen has all their friends over and they get a lot of presents. Maybe they go to a pizza place and dance to music on a jukebox.*

She could see her mother's car parked in the driveway of her house. As she walked closer, she could see a bunch of boxes stacked on the front porch. Her stomach instantly started to hurt just the way it did when she was a little girl and saw the moving truck parked in her driveway in Texas. She walked up the driveway, stopped halfway, and just stared at what she saw. There were about five boxes all sealed up with tape. Air slowly opened one enough to peek in. It was full of her clothing. *Oh my god! This is all of my stuff packed in these boxes! They're trying to kick me out of the house. Holy shit, where am I supposed to go and how am I supposed to get to school. Where the fuck am I supposed to sleep and eat. Oh my God, this can't be happening.*

On top of the pile she noticed an envelope. Confused and shocked she opened it slowly and a worn dirty crumbled fifty-dollar bill fell out. The card read, "Happy Birthday. Here is fifty dollars.

Good luck." It was signed, Mom and Dad. She tried the door, but it was locked. She knocked on the door lightly. No answer. She started pounding on the door and yelling, "I know you're in there, Mother. Open the door!"

She became overwhelmingly distressed and started to hyperventilate. Extremely dizzy and faint, she felt her body dropping down onto the porch. She could hear her head hitting the step. She began sobbing uncontrollably. This time she didn't care what the neighbors thought. Hysterically, she asked herself, *Now what?*

She sobbed for what seemed an hour. Occasionally she would gather herself together and pound on the door screaming for her mother to let her in.

"Mother, you guys can't just kick me out of the house. How will I finish school? Where will I sleep at night? How can you live with yourself if I don't graduate? What if someone tries to kidnap me? Mother! Open the door. Please, I haven't done anything wrong. Why are you doing this to me?"

Distraught, she walked back down the hill and looked for a phone booth to call the only real friend she had besides James, Lyda.

"My God, Lyda, you're not going to believe this. I just came home and found all my clothes boxed up and stacked on the front porch. I know my mother is in the house, but she is refusing to answer the door! There was a birthday card with fifty bucks in it and the card simply said 'good luck.' I can't believe this. How can they do this? How the hell am I going to continue going to school and graduate? I'm totally freaked out. I have no clue what I am supposed to do. Where the hell am I supposed to go?" Air said as she stood there in the phone booth trembling and still sobbing.

"Air, I had no idea today was your birthday. Why didn't you tell me? Let me talk with my mom, Air. I'm sure my folks will let you stay with us for awhile. I'll call you back," Lyda promised. "What is the phone number you're calling from? Stay right there by the phone booth. Don't leave! I'll call you right back."

Lyda ran into her kitchen. "Mom, Airstream just got home from school and found all her clothes packed in boxes and set out on her front porch! Today is her eighteenth birthday. Her father told her that when she turned eighteen he was going to kick her out of the house. There was a birthday card on top of the boxes with fifty dollars in it. The card just said, 'Good luck.' Air said she tried to open the front door, but it was locked. She says her mom's inside, but she won't answer the door. She doesn't have anywhere to go. How will she get to school? We have to help her!"

Airstream waited and waited for the phone to ring. Sweat, mixed with tears was running down both her sides of her body. She'd never perspired. She'd never worn deodorant. She stood by the phone booth wondering what it would be like to live with Lyda and her family if they decided to take her in.

God, Lyda's family is so religious. Her father prays all the time, and there are Crosses everywhere. What if they think I'm a communist, too?

The phone rang. "Air, I talked with my mother and told her what's happened. We're coming to pick you up. Go back to your house and we'll pick you up in about twenty minutes. My brother, Ben, is coming along to help load your boxes into the car," Lyda said reassuringly. "Everything is going to be alright. My mother said that your parents are evil."

Later that night, Lyda's family and Airstream all sat down to dinner. When everyone was through eating, Mr. Benson, Lyda's father, told everyone to go into the living room so that they could talk.

Mr. Benson began the discussion. "Airstream, Mrs. Benson and I have had a long discussion regarding your situation. The Lord has brought you into our family now and we want to help you graduate," he said firmly reminding Air of her father. "We know you're a very intelligent young lady and that you study hard. Lyda has always told us you are an honor roll student. We've known you for at least two years and you seem to be a good kid. We're very sorry your parents are doing the work of the devil and you undoubtedly must be very worried about your future. We strongly feel you should stay with us—at least until you graduate," he said as if he were preaching to her. "No child should ever endure the hardships we've heard you've been through with your parents. It is not the work of God. God is good and that is why you are here with us. You are now a part of this family and we expect you to abide by the same rules as Lyda. You've been around this family long enough to know how we all get along and what is expected of each member," he continued in his firm voice. "With that said, you girls should finish your homework and go to bed. I will drive you to school in the morning as I do every morning and I will pick you two up after school."

Air sat on the couch staring in disbelief at Lyda's parents. She was a bundle of emotions. She'd gone from feeling completely abandoned to being accepted into a new family in one harrowing day. Though racked by the shame of her parents' abandonment and embarrassed to ask for help, she realized that, if she stayed with Lyda's family, she'd be able to graduate. After that, she'd get a job, and somehow, she'd figure out how to go to UC Berkeley. She would talk to her counselor at school and see what she needed to do to get the process started.

"Thank you so much for allowing me to stay with you," she finally said, her voice timid. "I've studied so hard so I can graduate and go to college. If it weren't for you caring about me, I have no idea what I would do. This is pretty crazy, and I am worried about my brothers," she added, again pinching herself so she wouldn't break down and start sobbing. "I will help out in anyway I can. Please let me know what I can do to help with the chores."

Within two weeks, Air realized living with Lyda's family was not going to be easy. Lyda's older brother, Ben, had always been sexually attracted to Air. In the past, when Air had visited Lyda, Ben would tell her how sexy she was and tease her nonstop. He wanted to have sex with Air more than he loved his motorcycle. He hassled her constantly and tried to kiss her daily.

She told Lyda about Ben trying to kiss her but she couldn't make him stop harassing her. Air told Ben time after time she was not interested in him as a boyfriend. Ben, being a very vindictive guy, had a plan that would get Air kicked out of the house instantly. Sunday nights the family watched TV together after dinner. It was a family ritual. Earlier that Sunday morning, Ben hid some marijuana down the end of the family sofa.

During a commercial, Ben reached his hand down the side of the cushion and brought out a plastic bag full of marijuana. "My God!" he said. "What is this?"

"Give that to me!" demanded Bill. "What is this and who does it belong to?"

Every family member turned and looked at Airstream.

Airstream was stunned and instantly started crying, "That's not my stuff. I have no idea how it got there, but I do know it's not mine. I don't do drugs. Lyda! Tell them I don't do drugs!"

"Mom! It's true. Air doesn't use drugs. Drugs scare her."

"I think everyone should just go to bed now," said Bill. "Your mother and I will discuss what has just happened."

Airstream and Lyda headed to the bathroom.

"Lyda, I can't believe this! You know it's your brother trying to set me up because I won't have sex with him."

"I know! But, I know my parents, and they're going to believe Ben. I don't know what to say. I can't go tell them what Ben has been doing to you. I bet my parents are going to ask you to leave. You know how religious they are."

The next morning before breakfast, Bill came into the kitchen and looked at Air.

"Airstream, we've thought this through and unfortunately we've decided you need to find somewhere else to live. We cannot have the devil's ways in our home. Do you have anyone you can call, Airstream, to come and pick you up after school today?"

"No, sir."

"You don't have any relatives you could call?" he inquired with a tilted face.

"No, sir."

"If you can find a place to stay, I'll give you a ride if you need one."

"Thank you very much, Mr. Benson. That's very kind of you," Air said, tears running down her face.

Mr. Benson was waiting out front of the school at the end of the day. The three of them rode home in silence. When they arrived at Lyda's house the two girls went straight to Lyda bedroom. Air sat on the bed. "Lyda, where will I go?"

"Air, I have no clue. I'm in total shock! I can't believe my brother would do this to you. I'm not going to sleep at all tonight knowing you're out there somewhere. There must be somewhere you can go. We have to think about this more. Did you call James?"

"Of course I did! He was just as shocked as us and said that his parents were drunk and fighting. He said there was no way I could stay there. He actually told me to go to the police and tell them what my parents had done to me. I guess I'll just have your father take me to the bus stop and take a bus back over to my old neighborhood. At least I know that area, and it's safe. I was thinking I would just wait until it gets dark and then hang out on one of my old neighbor's front porches."

"You're kidding, right?" Lyda asked in horror.

"Do you have a better idea?" Air replied.

Tragically, Air's family had absolutely no relationship with her father's two sisters. D. J. had forbidden the kids to contact any of Mitchells' family. She was still stuck with her story that they all hated her, and she didn't want any of the kids being around "toxic" people.

After dinner, Air knew she had to leave. "Air, I'm just sick about this. I am so sorry and I wish there was something I could do," Lyda said. "I'm so scared for you. That "ice pick killer" is still out there somewhere. Air and Lyda had two classmates who were recently found murdered by the "ice pick killer." Everyone knew the girls because they both were exceedingly intelligent and were known for their had long hair and dressing alike. They were never seen without each other. They co-edited the school newspaper and were known to hitch hike everywhere. "No matter what you do, don't walk around late at night for very long. Plus, do not get into anyone's car you don't know. That "ice pick killer" is still out there driving around in an ice cream truck so watch out." She hugged Air goodbye and watched as she disappeared into the darkness carrying only a small suitcase.

Air was fearless, but she was still too embarrassed to call either of her aunts out of the blue. She didn't have the slightest clue if they would be receptive to her. Air wondered if she was going to have to live on the streets like the homeless people she'd seen living in cardboard box huts down street alleys and under freeway overpasses. She had no idea where to go or where she would spend the night. She'd left most of her belongings behind at Lyda's since she could only carry one suitcase. The family had agreed to let her store most of her stuff in the garage until she found a permanent home.

Outwardly, Air seemed to be a shy, sweet, and intelligent teenage girl, on the inside she also had strong survivor skills. After all, she had survived living eighteen years with D. J. and Mitchell. As she walked the sidewalks of an unfamiliar neighborhood in the dark, she started to feel that overwhelming familiar sense of worthlessness. *Somebody knows something about me I don't know.* In her mind, all she could think of was the phrases that had long haunted her: *You don't fit in. No one will ever love you. You're a worthless piece of shit!*

Well, you certainly look like a sweet little thing to me. How in the world could your parents tell you to leave the house when you were still in school? Isn't that against the law? The questions just kept coming. *What do mean your family doesn't want you anymore? Where are you going to sleep tonight?*

Her stomach began to ache and fill with emotion. She could feel the on-coming tears beginning to burn her eyes. *Being homeless is surely proof I am worthless. What decent man would ever want to marry a woman who didn't graduate from high school and lived on the streets?* It was beyond her comprehension that her parents actually kicked her out of her house without letting her at least graduate. According to them, she was getting exactly what she had wanted.

She started thinking how lucky they were. Another teenager might have cracked under the stress and butchered them in the night while they slept. Even if she'd wanted to kill her parents, it was too late. The butchering had already been done—to Air. After the experience with Paige, she'd imagined that someone might be able to suddenly kill somebody else; and as deranged and murderous as that soul might be, he or she still could have a sense of personal dignity and be on "a mission from God."

Air didn't have a sense of personal dignity or a relationship with God. None of her close friends would be able to deal with the fact she was on living on the streets without anywhere to go. Air's mind began to deconstruct. She felt as though she could not breathe. She thought she was dying. Perhaps that might not be such a bad idea.

Airstream, having been cloistered much of her life, had no idea all she had to do was get herself to Berkeley. If she'd known there were thousands of kids, like her, sleeping in People's Park or simply on the sidewalks in Berkeley, she would have gone directly there. Airstream was unique, but she was also naive and extremely unaware of the changes that were going on around her.

Air wandered the streets until she was exhausted. She decided to walk down to the main street of town. Embarrassed and freaked out about the notion that someone she knew might see her, she hid her suitcase along side a local creek that ran through town. As she was walking, she noticed a gas station that had lots of floodlights and a sign that said it was open twenty-four hours. The streets were empty, and there was not a soul at the station getting gas. She noticed a young man inside reading the newspaper.

"Excuse me, sir," she said to the attendant. "My name is Airstream, and I am homeless. Do you happen to have a car I could sleep in for a few hours? I have no where to go."

"You've got to be kidding!" He laughed. "You're just a kid! What do you mean you're homeless?"

"I just had my eighteen birthday last month, and my parents think I am a communist, so they kicked me out of the house. I was in my senior year of high school. My best friend's family took me in for a few weeks, but that didn't work out. I'm really scared and don't know what to do."

"Don't you have some family member you can call?"

As they talked, one car drove into the station. The man got out of his car and bought some cigarettes from the attendant. The attendant motioned for Air to come into the small office.

"No, I don't have any family here in California. I was raised in Texas, and we moved to California when I was in sixth grade. My daddy was raised here, and when my mother met my dad's mother and sisters, she convinced herself they hated her. I grew up without ever getting to know any of my aunts or my eleven cousins. We all went to the same high school and just ignored each other in the hallways. So no, I have no one to call."

"Oh man, that's tough! I'm sorry for you, kid. Sure, my car is all yours. Hey, what are you doing for food?"

"Honestly, earlier tonight, I stole some cookies from the market."

"Jesus, you poor thing! Here, have a bag of chips. That's all I have."

"Thanks," Air said as she took the bag of chips. She wanted to tell him more of the story but felt uneasy. She stood there thinking, *You know, I'm not going to get to finish my senior year. All through school, I took college prep courses and made really good grades. I participated in every extracurricular activity possible to get an edge on getting into UC Berkeley. I guess I would have rather been acting like some goddamned hippie; instead, I'm homeless and about to spend my first night in the backseat of a stranger's car, a stranger who seems to care more about me than my parents.* Instead of telling him all this, she followed the attendant over to his car.

He had a brand new two-toned, blue and white Chevy. The attendant told her she could lay in the backseat. "You'll be safe and comfortable. I work until six in the morning, so you're welcome to sleep here until then. No one will bother you. I'll watch the car just to make sure."

"Thank you so much," Air said as she made her way into the backseat. She used her coat for a blanket and her purse for a pillow.

"I'll be here for the rest of the week if you need a place to sleep," he said as he walked back to his office. "By the way, my name is Dave."

The all-night gas station attendants' car became her shelter at night. Dave became very protective of Air and began bringing extra food to work with him so she could have something to eat. He told Air he was still living with his parents until he could save enough money to move down south. The parking lot was well lit, but she was still scared—too scared to sleep. She was terrified someone would try and get into the car with her. She didn't really trust the gas station attendant completely, although he never made a move on her.

Each morning over the next week, after cleaning herself in the gas station bathroom, she'd thank him for letting her sleep in his car. He'd ask if he would see her later, and she'd nod sadly. She'd pick up her small suitcase and begin her usual walk.

The only places she knew where she could hang out without getting into trouble for not being in school was the library or the El Cerrito Mall. Air loved to write and kept a journal of her daily life when she was at the library. She secretly had hopes that some day she would publish her journal and it would become a movie.

On this morning, she decided on the mall because she needed something clean to wear. It never occurred to her she could still go to school during the day and act as though nothing was any different. She could tell Lyda her parents had taken her back in until she graduated. It just didn't seem like something she could do without falling apart. She was familiar with the mall, since she and James would go there almost every weekend and hang out with the crowds of kids that weren't into drugs or the hippie lifestyle.

Of course, she knew she'd have to steal clothes and shoes from now on, but she had no choice. She was not afraid to steal since she thought she looked like the last person who would be a thief. The way she naturally carried herself, despite the fact she was homeless, still made her look as though she came from a well-to-do family. She believed no one would ever, in their wildest dreams, think she was homeless and a thief. She had a natural regal presence about her. She was unaware of it, but others could sense it.

Deep inside, she still held on to her belief that she was unique and special, and that helped her adjust to her homeless life better than she would have expected. She'd just been dealt a bad hand. In some odd way, she felt that, after living with her parents for so many years and enduring all the physical and emotional abuse and the emptiness she'd experienced there; she was prepared for this lonely journey. Air was a survivor. She would tell herself constantly, *I'm not homeless, I'm simply temporarily displaced.* When her clothes got dirty, she'd simply throw them away and steal something new. She tried to not let it get to her that she was forced to steal, but it did. It was like Snow White suddenly becoming a thief. She couldn't believe this was what she found herself being forced to do and it went against all her values. *It doesn't matter that I have to steal what I need for now; I'll just make individuality so different no one will ever question where I get my clothes. I need to find the Airstream I put away so long ago and then people will love me. This is my only chance at being accepted since I know my true self is sweet and charismatic. I have to remind myself that I am not who my parents say I am. They have no clue as to who I am. Nobody does. Right now, I am the only one who loves me.*

Hiding the suitcase along the bank of the creek and shopping became a daily routine. Once at the mall, she headed for her favorite department store to begin her own "hunt." Something like the perfect gray suit would be the prey of the day, and she would pounce on it and then casually leave. In those days, department stores would display a full pair of shoes, not just one. Air would create a completely new outfit from different model displays —a sweater from one model and a dress from another. There was always a pair of new shoes and a purse to match what she had put together. Her natural distinctive taste for couture made assembling something new easy. Air stood out in a crowd. Women would look her up and down and often asked where she bought "her outfit." She'd reply, "Oh, I just love fashion and experimenting with putting different colors and textures together." They would nod and say, "Well, you look beautiful." These remarks made Air feel happy--like she was accepted into some secret society of "the elusive and elite crowd of people who are extraordinary compared to normal folks."

She wandered around her favorite boutique store and thought, *Perhaps yellow today.*

She found a cute pale yellow dress and a pair of matching yellow sandals. She moved slowly toward the dressing room so as not to catch anyone's attention. Along the way, she noticed a purse that matched. *I'll pick that up on the way out of the store,* she thought to herself. She pulled the dress over her head and looked in the three-sided mirror.

This color is perfect and the dress fits like a glove, she thought. *Yellow looks great with my hair. The billowy sleeves and tight bodice look great on me. The waistline is tight, but I love the thin cloth belt and full circular skirt. You have to be skinny for this dress to really great. I am lucky I can dress like the models in Vogue.*

The boutique was crowded since a sale was on. She looked around to see if anyone was looking at her. Clothes were strewn everywhere, and Air almost tripped over a stack of cheap straw hats. As she walked over the clothes on the floor with the yellow dress stuffed up under her bra, she ran into a couple of her prior classmates. Suddenly, the aisles seemed to close in on Air. She began to panic.

"Air, where have you been? Everyone is asking about you! We miss you," Vickie said woefully.

Air hesitated to answer. She didn't want to bring attention to herself in the store. She had been able to move among the aisles of the clothing without being noticed. Now people were looking and listening. Air looked over at the clerk, who seemed to be busy with a customer.

"Lyda told us she hasn't even seen you in awhile. Something about you live with your aunt now? Did you and Lyda get into some big fight or something?"

"Oh no, not at all. We just live far apart now. I live with my Aunt Sarah now. She offered to send me to a private, all-girls school up in the Oakland hills."

"You're kidding!" Nancy said, with a tone of astonishment.

"No I'm not. I'm very lucky. Listen, I don't mean to be rude, but she's waiting in the car. I have to go."

"Hey, my cousin's band just got a record contract with some big-time recording company in New York City, and there's going to be a great party Friday night out in Crockett to celebrate the signing. My cousin said I could invite a few of my friends. It's going to be at that old theater. Please try to come, Air. I'm personally inviting you. The band will be playing and there's a birthday celebration for someone. It should be a lot of fun!"

"I'll try, I promise," Air said, wanting to get away as fast as she could. "I have to go. See you later."

Later that night, at the gas station, Air called James, "Hey James! How are you?"

"Air! Where the hell are you? Why haven't you called me sooner? I've been worried out of my mind. I talked to Lyda yesterday and she told me that you're sleeping in the back seat of some guy's car while he's working at an all night gas station. Is that true? She said you haven't found anywhere to live. How are you eating and what do you do all day long?"

"I'm at the gas station now. There's this guy, his name is Dave, and he let's me sleep in his car. I'm using the office phone. I've been staying here every night since I left Lyda's. I'm sorry I haven't called. I don't have any money. This guy is a real sweet. He's been really good to me. He lets me wash my hair in the bathroom. It's been really scary, James."

"Man, you're so lucky you found this guy! Do you trust him?"

"Yes. He still lives with his parents and brings extra food to work so I have something to eat. He also gives me a couple of bucks when he can. He has a younger sister and feels obligated to help me out. He tells me that he can't imagine my situation happening to his sister. He gets really angry when I talk about my parents and them kicking me out before I had a chance to graduate. He says if that ever happened to his sister he'd completely loose it. He says he wouldn't trust himself to not kick his father's ass. I think to myself how lucky his sister is to have such a loving brother."

"Which gas station are you staying at, Air?" asked James. "Is it the one where that guy, Steven Wilson, used to work?"

"Yeah, it is."

"Does he remember you dating Steven?"

"No, he said he started working here after Steven quit his job."

"Oh well that's probably a good thing. You don't want word to get out that you sleep in the guy's car!

"Well, it's been okay so far. Lyda's not going to tell anyone, but I don't know what I am going to do tomorrow night. He doesn't work on the weekends. Honestly, I just walk around all day or sit in the Richmond Library and write in my journal. Oh my God, I just ran into Vickie and Nancy at a boutique store in El Cerrito this afternoon. They said there's going to be a great party out in Crockett tomorrow night. It's going to be at the old theatre with a live band. Some guy is having a birthday party. I was thinking you and I could go out there together. I'd sure like to go. How about you, since you're the one with a car? Do you have any plans?"

"No, I don't have any plans and that sounds great. I was thinking Air; why don't we think about me picking you up after I'm through with school? We could pick some place to go and we could just hang out together until I have to go home?"

"God, James, that sounds absolutely wonderful. I am so freaked out living like this. I just go brain-dead and totally lose my common sense with the situation I'm in. I totally forgot that you have a car. I've been in such a fog."

"I can pick you up right after school tomorrow and we can hang out until it's time to go to the party. Where should I pick you up?"

"How about at Foster Freeze? Had you heard anything about this party out in Crockett?" Air asked.

"I know that Vickie's cousin is in the band and he told her she could invite a few friends. She invited me, but I didn't know she'd invited you too. There will be a bunch of rich college kids there, but we'll just stay close to Vickie and Nancy and who ever else she invited. Does that sound okay?"

"Oh God, yes!"

"I'll pick you tomorrow at Foster Freeze after school, say around three."

Air hung up the phone and headed to the backseat of Dave's car. *Wow, a party.* She couldn't help but be excited. She hadn't seen any of the old gang for what seemed like forever. *I'll go out tomorrow and find something nice to wear to the party. Maybe I'll go to that vintage store on San Pablo Ave and look for a vintage silk nightgown with lots of lace. I want to look angelic.*

Early the next morning, Air rode the bus up to the vintage store called Something Old Something New. She looked through the vintage silk nightgowns. This was what all the young hippie girls were wearing. She could always sense when she had confidence about stealing and when she might get caught. She felt confident that day. The weather was warm enough to wear something sheer for the party. She knew her body well enough that she didn't have to try clothes on to know if they would fit and look great on her. She knew she had to hurry and get back so that James would not have to wait to pick her up. Air wore sunglasses so she was able to look around and decide if it was safe to push the nightgown into her purse. She casually walked out and went straight to the bus stop. Air was wearing her pale yellow dress and sandals when James arrived. She didn't mention anything about going to the vintage store nor how she was going to dress for the party.

"Hi, James," Air said as James' car approached her.

"Wow, Air, you look great. Is that what you're wearing to the party?"

"No, I actually have this vintage silk nightgown in my purse. I thought I'd put it on later before we drive to the party. I thought you said we'd just hang out until the party so I'll change later."

"Cool. Let's drive up to Indian Rock in the El Cerrito hills and watch the sunset. We'll head out to the theatre later."

"Perfect."

Indian Rock was a well-known landmark. People hiked the dirt path to get to the outcropping of boulders. The rocks were located right in the middle of an affluent neighborhood with beautiful homes. Parents brought their children there to play and picnic. Lovers came to watch the sunsets. The view from the rocks was remarkable. You could see San Francisco and the entire Bay Area.

On a clear day, all four bridges—The San Rafael Bridge, The Golden Gate, the Oakland/San Francisco Bay Bridge, and the San Mateo Bridge—could be seen. The beauty was dramatic.

"This is the most beautiful sunset I've seen in a long time," James said.

"I agree."

"Air, let's go get something to eat, my treat. I'm really hungry. Is the House of Pancakes okay?"

"Wherever you want to go, James. Thank you, that's very kind of you."

They both ordered pancakes with strawberries and whipped cream. When they finished eating, Air turned to James and said, "I think I'll change my clothes here in their bathroom. I'll also put some makeup on and fix my hair, if you don't mind waiting a few minutes. We can head out to Crockett after that. Is that okay with you?" she asked.

"Sure, I'll just sit here and pretend I'm still eating."

Air quickly changed into the vintage cream-colored nightgown. It was in mint condition. She felt like a princess. There were no tears or stains, and the silk embroidery looked as though it had been just been sewn yesterday. The heart-shaped bodice with its T-straps was very revealing. The intricate embroidery and lace were interwoven with the silk all the way down to the floor. The bodice was created to fit her upper body like a glove, and from the waist, the skirt hung flowingly since the silk had been cut on the bias. The design of the dress accented her wide shoulders and hips. Air wore it as if she had always worn couture gowns. Wearing vintage silk nightgowns was probably the one and only time Air followed the fad of fashion.

Air quickly put a small amount of mascara on her eyes and blush on her cheeks. She pulled her long, straight golden hair to one side. She had small sterling silver hoop earrings on and a necklace with an 18 karat gold locket her grandmother had given her. It opened but there were no pictures in it. She repositioned the rings her mother had given her on her delicate hands and made sure her long fingernails were clean. One ring was an ornate design of layers of silver with an amethyst stone set to one side of the design that her mother had made, and the other was her mother's wide band of plated gold with two diamonds she'd been given as a child by her grandmother. Air was extremely careful not to loose these rings and locket. It was all she physically had to remind her of her mother. She didn't need anything to remind her of the evilness and emotional abandonment. She returned to the table where James was patiently waiting.

"Oh my God, Air, you look angelic! You look gorgeous! Where did you get that nightgown? Is it a vintage gown? What a killer outfit. Oh my God, I can hardly believe how beautiful you look. I mean you are a beautiful girl, but that gown makes you look like a goddess! A hippie goddess!"

They both started laughing and Air started to feel self-conscious.

"Let me take a piss before we get kicked out," James said. "I'll meet you in the car.

7

The town of Crockett was historical. It was located on the banks of the Sacramento River. The old C&H factory had been built there, but neither James nor Air knew if it was still in business. Air had studied the history of the town in school. She knew that Crockett was located on some Mexican land grant and was named after a judge whose name was Crockett. Another man bought the land from him and started the C&H Sugar Company. The town had been established in the middle 1800s, and it still had the character of those times. It was a small town with old Victorian homes and their original carriage houses. The quaint streets were lined with Magnolia and Weeping Willow trees that reminded Air of Texas.

As Air and James approached the theater, the music was so loud they could hear it two blocks away. Parking was difficult, so they parked a couple of blocks away and walked. As soon as they got out of the car, they began to smell marijuana. Air stood out front of the old art deco theater with James. It was a beautiful historical building that had been a theatre since the forties. Anyone in the community could now rent it to host special events.

"This party is supposed to be both a birthday party and a celebration for the band, Just Getting Started. Air, you've heard the band play, right?"

"No," Air replied.

"Jim and I saw them play one night in Berkeley last year. They're really good. It's also a party for this guy named Frank. He's supposed to be some big-time record producer. Apparently, he just signed the band with the record company he works for. God, the music's so loud. Let's go in; there's no cover charge," James said. "Oh my God, Air, you're going to blow everyone's mind with that dress."

The thought that this evening would change Air's life forever was the wildest thought she could have had, and yet, that was exactly what was about to happen. As Air walked into the theater almost every guy's head turned. She looked stunning. Her strawberry hair streaked with gold highlights lit up the dark theater, and not a person in the room could avoid staring into the headlights of her doe eyes.

"Let's dance!" James said immediately.

Air and James walked out to the dance floor and started dancing. Air looked around to see who else was dancing. She noticed a lot of her classmates. She was starting to feel anxious but quickly told herself to just tell the story about her aunt. No one would question her; no one would believe she lived on the streets—not the shy, smart, popular girl she portrayed herself to be.

The moment Air stepped onto the dance floor, Frank noticed her. Frank was the birthday boy. He was originally from the Bay Area and had known the guys in the band for years. The lead guitarist had played backup with many famous bands and also wrote and sang a lot of his own songs. Frank's intentions were to sign the group up with the record company he worked for in New York City. From conversations Air had heard about him, he had been a famous artist before becoming involved in the music business.

"I heard he's been commissioned to create pieces of art for very famous people. He's actually designed a few albums covers. Part of his job is to entertain the bands his company has signed. Most of the time he lives in New York City, but he's in Crockett to celebrate his birthday since it's his hometown. I heard he's turning thirty," James told Air as they danced.

As Air danced she had the sense of being completely naïve and out of place. Judging by the way people were dressed and the conversations she could overhear, she felt she was in a world she'd only dreamed about.

"Air, I also heard this guy rides around only in limousines and drinks only the finest French wines!" James said.

As she danced, Frank was "holding court." Everyone gathered around him to listen to his stories. She could see and hear he was quite the storyteller. He had people rolling on the floor with laughter.

He used his hands as he talked, almost like some sort of outreach program for those who didn't get the joke the first time around. Air smiled; it occurred to her that it was as if Frank thought his stories should be told in caption for the "hard-of-understanding."

Air thought he was an odd-looking character. He looked like an old hippie with long hair and a beard. He had embroidery all over his shirt. She'd never met a real hippie. No one she knew had a real hippie friend.

He was wearing a cowboy hat, and his long, blond locks seemed to be tangled and sticking out everywhere. He had a mustache and wore round glasses with thin, wire rims. He was thin and handsome in an eclectic way. She could see people were mesmerized by his stories. Her spider senses told her he harbored deep sadness within him. He seemed to be talking as fast as she was dancing.

When their eyes met, she acted demure and tried to look past him, as though she were looking at someone halfway across the room. Suddenly, she felt as though she wasn't being herself. It was as if she were acting like she was more sophisticated than she knew herself to be. The naive, shy girl was acting like a mature seductress. She was confused and a bit dizzy. She had no idea how this could be happening to her. She knew she wanted him to study her. She wanted him to realize he wanted her lips. She wanted to study his eyes. She wondered if he would ever stop talking for a moment while he gazed inquisitively at her.

When he did, everyone turned to see who was stealing his thunder. Frank was looking directly at Air, and the silence of the moment seemed to last for an eternity.

Air could see Frank leaning over to talk with Billy, who she knew from high school. He had graduated the year before. She could see Frank taking a deep breath and could hear him say to Billy, "That girl there in the cream-colored silk gown, who is she? She reminds me of a small doe, innocent and very delicate. I want her with me."

Oh my God, I'm blood in the water. Air felt trapped. *I should leave now,* she thought, looking around desperately for James. But he had disappeared. She could still hear Billy talking to Frank, and she suddenly felt like Cinderella. She knew she needed to leave immediately.

But then Billy was waving her over. "Hey, Airstream!" he called. Come here! I want you to meet someone."

James suddenly appeared. "What up, Air?"

"Sorry, James," Air said. "I think I'm destined to meet the famous guy."

"Go for it, girl!"

Billy motioned again for Air to come over to where Frank was sitting. As though in slow motion, Air found herself slowly gliding over to Frank.

"How the hell are you?" asked Billy. "I haven't seen you for a while. How have you been? I heard you are going to a private school now and you live with one of your rich aunts?"

"Yes, that's all true," said Air in a nonchalant tone.

"Have you met Frank?"

"No, we haven't been introduced," responded Air.

"Frank, I'd like you to meet Airstream. Airstream, I'd like to introduce Frank. It's his birthday. Plus, he just signed the band to a contract with the record company he works for in New York City."

As Air stared into Frank's eyes, she said coyly, "Frank, it is a pleasure to meet you."

"Billy, could you give us some time alone?" asked Frank.

Billy left.

"Airstream, don't let me frighten you away, but Billy said you are living with your aunt. Am I to believe that's by choice? Or does your aunt have custody of you? You don't appear to be happy with your life. You are a beguiling, young creature, and I'm sure you are aware of your unique qualities. I would be delighted to take you away from the misery I see in your eyes. There is such sensual sadness in your eyes. Let me introduce you to my world. I promise you will not regret it," Frank said, his voice dripping with longing.

And I'd finally have a home.

"You are astonishingly swanlike. You have a unique style all unto your own. You know you have piercing, beautiful, big brown eyes, right? Your hair is a mixture of colors I've never seen. You have reds, gold, blonds all against your pearl-white skin that makes you look eerily almost extinct or of another time period," Frank said in a very low voice.

Air was clueless as to her beauty. She had go to the mirror to see what she looked like. After the many years of abuse, she'd long ago made a deal with herself. She'd left her body in a safe place, knowing someday she would reclaim herself; until then, she wouldn't recognize herself.

"Would you like to dance with me?" he asked. "Would you like to spend the rest of your life with me?"

As long as you don't glaze me with clear nail polish, Air thought.

"I've already fallen for you, Airstream. Is that possible? Please stay the night with me?"

"I can't think of anything else I'd rather do, Frank," Air whispered, trying to restrain herself from screaming with joy.

"I'm staying in Mike's guest house," he said, explaining that Mike was the band's lead guitarist. "Do you know him?"

"Yes, I do," she responded. "He lives here in Crockett, doesn't he?"

"Yes, he does. His home is beautiful. It's right on the Sacramento River."

For the rest of the party, Air did not leave Frank's side. She looked over at James, and he gave her a "thumbs up," accompanied with a raised eyebrow of approval. She smiled at James, and turned back to Frank. If someone started to talk to her, Frank would pull her closer to him. He kept his arm around her for the rest of the evening.

As the party came to a close, Frank told Air they should exit out the back door. Air looked over at James and nodded good night. Frank took Air's hand, and together they walked out to a limousine.

As she was walking, she thought, *Oh my God, my suitcase.* But then it occurred to her that she wouldn't need anything in the suitcase, mostly clothes, anymore. She had her makeup in her purse. And Frank would likely realize that she had only what was on her body. *I don't care if I have to wear this nightgown for the rest of my life, as long as I don't have to sleep in the back of a car again*, she thought. *God, please whisper to me. Tell me I will never wonder where I'll sleep again. Tell me, I will never again experience the cold of the night as I have.*

The limo driver drove around to the back of Mike's house, to the guesthouse where Frank was staying while was in town for the week. For the rest of the evening, Air had a wonderful time listening to his stories. Before they realized it, it was dawn, and the sun shone brightly through the lacy curtains.

"Airstream, would you let me take you to out for breakfast?"

"Of course! I hope you don't mind I am still in my evening gown."

"Not at all. You look beautiful. After breakfast, we will go buy you some clothes," Frank responded.

Frank called the limo driver and asked to be picked up. Mike suggested Frank and Air have breakfast at a quaint little French restaurant along the river that served freshly baked croissants and great coffee. As they rode to the restaurant, Frank turned to Air and asked, "Airstream, do you have to go back to your aunt's house?" His eyes shone, and he held her hand as gazed at her longingly.

She smiled and gently squeezed Frank's hand and said, "No, Frank, I don't. I want to be with you, Frank."

"Then I want you to stay with me. I will take care of you. You'll never worry about anything again, I promise."

"That sounds like heaven, Frank."

The next morning, Air turned over in the bed and slowly opened her eyes to see that Frank had already gotten up. She wandered through the house looking for him. She stood at the back door that led out to one of the most beautiful gardens she'd ever seen. There were flowers blooming everywhere, along with stone paths that led out to a wooden gazebo just past a very long swimming pool. Frank was sitting in the gazebo at the far end of the garden. She could barely make out the silhouette of his body. He was drinking his morning coffee and reading the morning newspaper. She opened the door, and he looked up and glanced her way. He motioned for her to join him. She stood there in the doorway, dressed in one of his T-shirts and bare feet. She stepped outside and tiptoed along the stone path to the gazebo and sat down in one of the overstuffed garden chairs.

Air sat motionless with her knees up to her chin and the T-shirt pulled over her legs.

"Would you like to go for a swim? You don't need a suit here. We're all alone. I need to make a couple of calls, and then I'll join you."

He picked up the phone and dialed the number to the president of the Mercury Records. Air took off his T-shirt and slowly walked down the steps of the pool. Frank put his hand over the receiver of the phone and said, "You look lovey! You're one of the few women I've ever known to have such extraordinary beauty. You wake up looking effortlessly sexy and gorgeous. Ah, Air; I thoroughly enjoy hanging out with you. You are simply a delightful. You are humorous without knowing it. Did you sleep well?" he asked as he waited for the president to pick up the other end of the call.

"Yes, I slept like a baby. And you?" she asked.

"Oh, I went out like a log. Didn't wake up until six. Sorry, I wasn't there to greet you when you woke up, but I have to make some calls back East, and they are three hours ahead of us in time you know. I also need to meet with the band for a couple of hours this morning. Will you be okay here alone?"

"Of course. I'll find something to read until you get back," she answered.

Frank motioned to Air that he could no longer talk for a few moments. When the conversation was over, he took off his robe and set it on the chair and joined Air in the pool.

"Mike said someone left a suitcase for you on the front porch last night. Did you leave it in the car of the person you came with?"

Airstream, completely taken off guard, quickly said, "Oh yes, I was planning on spending the weekend with my best friend, James. I did leave my suitcase in his car. That's so sweet of him to drop it off."

"Well I hope you don't take offense, but I did open it to make sure it was your stuff. I found drawings that were signed by you. I had no idea you were so talented. Have you been studying art in school?"

"Oh no, I just enjoy drawing. I've never taken an art class in my life. I just love to draw and design clothes. I make all my own clothes."

"Oh that reminds me, there should be a delivery for you sometime this morning. I took the liberty of ordering a few things for you to lounge around in until we have the time to go shopping in the city," Frank said as he smiled at her.

At that very moment, Mike shouted out from the back door that a box addressed to Air had just been delivered. Frank excused himself and went to got the package. He returned and handed the box to Air.

"I guessed at the sizes, but try these on, and if they don't fit, we'll send them back. Air was completely taken aback and wanted to open the box immediately. She went inside and ripped into the box. She found two beautiful silk sleeveless flowered dresses, a white silk slip, two pairs of sheer nylons, a black leather purse, and a pair of black leather shoes with a small bow near the toe. She stepped into the slip and pulled one of the dresses over her head. She put the nylons on and slipped into the black shoes. She loved them. She went back out to model for Frank.

"There's nothing more sexy on a woman than a man's T-shirt, you know. But you look fabulous in that dress, and it looks like the shoes fit perfectly. We'll do more shopping this week when I'm finished up with this contract," Frank told Air.

She giggled and ran and kissed him.

"Let's go have something to eat, and then I'll drop you off back here before I run my errands. I'll give you a couple of fine point rapidiogragh pens I have in my briefcase. I'm sure we can find some drawing paper around here."

After a quick breakfast, Frank dropped Air back at Mike's. He kissed her forehead and left for a few hours. Air hung out in the gazebo and doodled the entire time Frank was gone. She drew images of everything that was around her. Her drawings made her happy. She hoped Frank would like them as well.

The rest of the week went by quickly, and before she knew it, Air and Frank were boarding a plane headed to New York City.

"Oh, Frank, I'm so excited," Air gasped. "I've never been on an airplane before! How long is the flight to New York City?"

"About five hours."

"Where do you live? I can't believe I've never asked you that. Do you live in right in the city?"

"We're going to live about forty minutes upstate from New York City in Oscar Hammerstein III's summer home. It's breathtaking! The house is a historical mansion and is nestled on five secluded acres of gardens. There's a large stone outside the front of the house that states, 'George Washington spent the night here.'"

"You're kidding!" Air gasped.

"No, you'll see. You're going to love it. The house is enormous and fully furnished. There are two wings to the house, each with its own living room, dining room and fireplaces so large you can stand inside of them. They are made out of large stones that are over two hundred years old," Frank started to tell Air as she became light-headed and had to catch her breath.

Are you okay sweetheart?"

"Yes, I am just blown away. I am trying to imagine all this."

"Let me finish. There are two wings to the house that join at the kitchen. The house has six bedrooms and eight bathrooms. There is a master bedroom in each wing and each have their own fireplace. There is a smaller fireplace in the kitchen that you can actually cook in. The original hooks for the pots are still there. Almost every room has floor-to-ceiling windows, all of which look out at the massive garden grounds. The kitchen has two twelve feet high wooden paned window doors that overlook an outdoor Olympic sized swimming pool with lots of fabulously comfortable lounge chairs and a changing room. On the outside of the wing that's located on the backside of the house there's an outdoor Italian kitchen with everything we need for entertaining; two large barbeques, a giant stove, refrigerator, sinks, dishes, wine glasses, a long wooden handmade table that seats twelve; everything, you name it and it's there just waiting for us to have our first big welcoming party.

Air gasped as she listened to Frank, "You must be kidding me? How much does all this cost?"

"You, my dear, are not to worry your pretty little head about a thing. I made you a promise that you will never have to worry about anything again, remember? I will always honor that promise.

I love you, Air. You deserve any and everything your wondrous heart desires. My hunch is had your childhood is not a story I want to hear. You will never suffer again. You have a new life now. One that will bring you nothing but joy."

Air sat back in her seat and looked out the window at the clouds. *Bless you my guardian angel. You have protected me all my life and now you have brought me a life I can live in without shame and fear.*

"Oh, there's also a workout room with both a steam and dry sauna, as well as, a Jacuzzi. The kitchen is state of the art and it's big enough for a family to live in! Air, you will have your own art studio and dressing rooms."

"What do you mean my own art studio?" Air asked breathlessly.

"You'll need a large room that is just for you to create your art. You're so very talented, and I want you to pursue your artistic side. So you will have a room filled with every type of art material you want! You'll have another room just to sew your designs in. We'll get you the best sewing machine available and have shelving built to hold the yards of fabric you'll buy. You'll have special boards to hold all the different colors of threads you'll need and a large table for laying out your patterns. And of course you'll have a dress model that's your size so you can create right on the model. I want you to have another room that is only for painting. It'll have two easels and a table of your choosing for laying out your materials. You'll have only the best handmade canvases in all different sizes and perpendicular shelving so you can slide your work in and out of. In the room that'll be for storing your art materials, I'm going to make sure you have every tube of paint available and canisters full of different varieties and sizes of paintbrushes. I want you to have the complete freedom to just throw paint around and explore what makes you happy.

I want you to have your own sacred space that is just for you. A room that is full of windows and light where you can just relax and have tea and enjoy looking at art books for inspiration. There will be shelves full of art books and handmade overstuffed velvet chairs and tables from Paris. I want vases full of freshly cut flowers daily everywhere! You'll have your own veranda, and you can entertain other artist friends that you will make. I want you to have everything you need to express yourself, Air."

Air wished she could tell Frank about her childhood; she wanted him to understand how overwhelming all of this was for her. *But, I can't,* Air told herself. *He has no clue how messed up I really am. He thinks he knows how tough life was for me. He has so much respect for me. I can't let him in on how hard my life has been. Not yet, maybe someday.*

The flight seemed to take forever. It was late evening when they landed. Frank had a limo waiting for them. The chauffeur helped Air with her coat and purse as he guided her into the back of the car. They drove off into the darkness.

"Oh I sure wish I could see the view," Air said. "But it's too dark."

"We'll go into the city in a few days, once we've settled in. I want to show you every inch of the house and the town. It is all very historical."

"That sounds great," said Air, a giant smile spreading across her face.

As they arrived at the gate around the property Air could see a very large home looming along the skyline. They drove for almost a block up the hill before they arrived at the entrance to the house. Air saw flowers as far as she could see, and she could sense there was a lot of land around the house. It was thickly forested, so she didn't really have a sense of the spaciousness of the property.

Before going into the house, Frank took Air's arm and slowly walked her over to the large rock that was etched with the announcement, "George Washington spent the night here."

"I'm so impressed, Frank." She tried very hard to act sophisticated far beyond her years or experience just to please him.

"Air, follow me and come see your new home."

Air could hardly catch her breath and thought she was on the verge of fainting.

"You're dehydrated from the flight. Let's go inside, I had the maid set out a platter with some pate and smoked Norwegian salmon. We'll have sparkling water and then drink champagne and celebrate!"

"Indeed! Let's party!" Air replied with a joyful voice.

She looked around at the house. It seemed to go on forever. There were long hallways everywhere she looked.

"This hallway leads to the original part of the house which I didn't really talk about much," Frank explained, gesturing down one of the hallways. "I wanted to surprise you. Come on, let's go check out the original rooms of this mansion."

They walked down a long hallway with rooms on either side full of beautiful, antique French furniture. Air could see enormous beds with large, hand-carved headboards and layers of soft bedding and large pillows. Each room had its own balcony overlooking the grounds. At the end of the hall, they came to a white, wooden door with small panes of glass and a very old doorknob. Frank slowly opened the door. The room was completely empty, but the bright light coming through the wooden-paned windows made it feel comfortable despite its lack of furniture.

"Smells like cherries in here," Air said. "Look at the floor. I've never seen wood planks this wide. They must be eight inches wide. Look at the nails," she added on closer inspection. "They have square heads. They must be really old."

"There's a balcony in this room as well. Let's walk out there," Frank said.

Frank opened the enormous doors, which had small, wooden-paned windows as well, and walked out slowly, carefully avoiding the missing planks. Each step was accompanied with a loud creak, as though the balcony could collapse at any moment. The view that lay out before them was astounding. As far as they could see, there were white birch trees.

"Tomorrow, these trees will be full of cardinals," Frank remarked.

Air had never seen a cardinal before, and couldn't stop commenting on how beautiful they must look. It all seemed surrealistic to her. She'd never been in such a beautiful home.

"Wait until autumn. The leaves will drop from all the trees, and the branches will ice over and look like crystal. You'll look away, and then when you look back, the trees will be solid red from all the cardinals that have suddenly landed on the branches. You'll cry. You won't be able to help yourself."

Air, a bit afraid of the creaky balcony, walked back into the empty room. "I have a funny feeling about this part of the house," she commented softly.

"Well, it is mostly for show. No one ever stays in here. It's not safe," he said.

"It's really beautiful in here. I love the walls and the designs of the wooden grain, and the large, old windows are simply stunning," she said. "But I feel like we're not alone."

They walked out of the room, slowly closing the door behind them with a sense of finality, as though they would never reenter it. They continued to explore the huge home, filled with delightful collections of books, furniture, paintings, and sculptural art. Air was numb. She had never seen such luxury. Frank had forgotten to mention there was a tennis court.

"How did you find this place?" Air asked.

"The company pays for it," Frank said. "It comes with the job."

"Wow, to think my friends at home are having a hard time paying eighty-dollar-a-month rent," Air said. "And this place must rent for a thousand dollars a month!" she shrieked.

"Air, come here and stand inside the fireplace!" Frank said, grinning at her. "Are you hungry? There's the platter of food I mentioned by the couch."

"I would love a fire and a glass of champagne. I just need a moment to just mellow out. This is all so over-whelming, Frank."

"Not a problem my love; there is plenty of wood. Be right back."

Frank built a fire, and the two of them just stared at it in silence. At one point, Air looked over at Frank, and he was staring at her.

"Frank, stop it! You're making me uncomfortable." She laughed.

"I've never seen anyone so innocent and so incredibly sensual without knowing it. You remind me of a baby fawn, Air. I have an idea! Tomorrow we'll unpack our suitcases and then go into the city. We'll go to an art store and order everything you'll need for your studio!"

"Frank, I'm not really an artist," Air protested. "All I've done is design clothes and do a few drawings."

"Yes, I have seen your fashion designs and your drawings. They're incredibly unique," he replied, his voice booming with pride. "They are you! You are gifted with natural talent, my dear. I am going to nurture that creativity of yours. First off, you must learn how to trust your intuitiveness. This 'feeling thing' you talk about, you have to run with it and see where it takes you. Don't resist. Your ability to survive in the world before we met is a bucket of gold for creativity! It took a lot of talent besides your courage."

Air wondered what he meant by that remark but didn't pry. She didn't want to know what he meant, if he knew anything about her past.

Frank had two weeks before he had to go back to work, and he and Air had spent every moment of that time together—exploring the town, the restaurants, and each other. The first day Frank went into the city, Air decided to try and paint scenes in their house on small canvases.

When Frank returned home, he couldn't believe what she had created. "Airstream, are you sure you've never taken an art class?"

"Oh God no! I don't even like to go to museums. I don't want to be influenced by anything. I don't even want to know what the primary colors are."

Frank picked up one of the canvases. "Good grief, this is incredible. It reminds me of Cocteau's work. Have you seen any of his work?"

"I've never even heard of the guy!"

"Air, the Museum of Modern Art has an exhibit of some of his drawings now. We'll go. I want you to see his work."

"No, I don't want to go to any museums," Air protested. "Please! I don't want to know what I'm supposed to do and not supposed to do! I have to protect myself, Frank. Otherwise, I know I'll never even pick up a paintbrush again."

"I just want to nurture your spontaneity," Frank explained. "I can teach you everything I know about art. I can teach you how to mix colors and how to use different brushes for different effects. Air, you're a natural born artist. You are so much better than I'll ever be and I have a Masters degree in art. I will give you my eyes. I want to show you how to 'see' the world as an artist. I can sense you have far more natural talent than I ever could have imagined. You say you've never taken an art class or studied anything about art? Your talents can't be taught. You were born with them. You'll go a long way in the art world. I'll make sure you go all the way to the top, Air! I know a lot of people who can spot talent a mile away."

He'd already shown her how to "see" the world in a different way than she'd ever known. It didn't take much to be impressed by Frank, given that she was only eighteen and given the lifestyle she'd come from—raised in a family who thought fresh vegetables came in a can.

Air did wonder about the age difference between she and Frank though.

"Let's eat something here to tide us over and then go into the city and hang out at the Bitter End," Frank suggested, one evening.

He went into the kitchen and made them a couple of sandwiches—sliced chicken breast with alfalfa sprouts and avocados on seeded, organic brown bread. He made some peppermint tea and served Airstream.

"Here you go, my dear. This should tide us over until dinner."

Air could not believe what she had just eaten. Later, she called James in California to tell him all about the plane ride, the house, and the sandwiches.

"James, listen to me. You have to find a health food store and buy something called alfalfa sprouts, tea that is made from peppermint leaves and organic, seeded brown bread. Then make a sandwich with this stuff and also put some sliced avocado and chicken breast on it. It is unbelievably delicious!"

At the Bitter End that night, Air listened to Frank talk about people and lifestyles she'd always secretly dreamed about. She thought she was going to become rich and famous somehow just by knowing Frank.

Occasionally, Air would call home to talk with her parents. She wanted them to know she'd survived the brutality of living on the streets and was now living a fairytale life. The life Air lived now was nothing in comparison to D. J.'s so-called wealth and prominence. Her lifestyle was now so much richer in so many ways than D. J. could ever imagine.

D. J. would always say, "Mar-ree him, honey."

Her parents had no idea about Air and Frank's age difference or that the music business was steeped in drugs and sex. She knew better than to say anything. Air listened to her heart, since her heart never lied except when she was having an anxiety attack. She knew Frank was her ticket "to the other side" of all the harshness she'd always known. She knew she had been whisked up by one of her high celestial spirits and taken to where she could finally feel safe—where she could rest, regroup, and prepare for a new life.

One day, the phone rang. Air set her paintbrush down and answered.

"Air, it's me. It's important that you get really dressed up right now and drive into the city immediately."

"What's up, Frank?"

"I'll tell you once you get here. Drive carefully!"

Air quickly took the black cashmere Betsey Johnson dress she'd recently bought for herself as a treat out of her closet. It was a simple dress, and yet it had that couture appearance. Her choice in clothes all accented her shoulders and long waistline. The dress had long, tight-fitting sleeves and was floor length. She loved dresses that were cut on the bias so that the skirt part of the dress was fully circular. It had the appearance of a long, fitted, collared shirt with tiny buttons an inch apart all the way to the bottom. There were thin straps on the side that tied in a bow in the back. She decided to wear her Channel, black velvet, pointed two-inch heels that had straps around the ankle. She looked in the mirror at her hair.

She'd gone to Vidal Sassoon's the week before and had his latest cutting-edge haircut. Air's previous long straight hair that was parted in the middle now had sides that were cut on a severe angle, going from very short around her eyes to slowly blending in around her shoulders. She had a face that didn't need to hide behind bangs. Her large forehead, along with her dark brown eyes; full lids and brow; high, chiseled cheekbones; and a pair of naturally puckered lips made for the perfect face for being in full view. Because she was fair skinned, one hardly noticed her eyelashes and eyebrows were almost white. She put a bit of blush on her cheeks, along with a matching color of lipstick and dashed out the door.

Air was in the city in about forty minutes. The record company was located on West 52nd Street and was on the forty-second floor of a huge building. Apple Records was just two floors up on the forty-fourth floor. The elevator doors opened directly into the company, and Air walked in. Frank was just snapping his briefcase closed when he saw Air.

"Hi, sweetie, what's going on?" Air asked.

"We're having dinner at the famous restaurant called Johnny O's with Frank Sinatra!"

"Are you fucking kidding me?"

"No, I'm not. Let's go. We're barely going to get there in time."

The idea of having dinner with Frank Sinatra was simply impossible for Air to grasp. She gave Frank a dazed, glassy-eyed glare and surmised he was experiencing the same emotions as she was. She'd become comfortable meeting and entertaining famous musicians and riding up and down the elevators with John Lennon and Yoko Ono, but Frank Sinatra? Frank would joke with John and the two would laugh, while Yoko seemed to cower from the attention the two of them received. On several occasions, Air had walked down Fifth Avenue chatting with George Harrison, chatting about everyday common events. Sometimes the two of them would stop by the Chelsea Hotel and join Leonard Cohen for lunch.

The three of them would always order their favorite dish, giant shrimp in green sauce, along with two bottles of sangria. They would laugh and sing all through lunch. Leonard loved to make George sing, "Let It Be," long before the Beatles had recorded it. George would egg Leonard on to sing "Suzanne." Air felt completely relaxed softly singing in the background.

Air had a secret she was keeping to herself—she was taking guitar lessons from a man who lived neared the house. She had a great voice and could move to falsetto easily. Her greatest asset was being able to write her own songs. Frank had a lovey classical guitar she was using to learn how to play. Her callouses were building up quickly. She was planning on surprising Frank one night with her new skills. She would play and sing her first song she'd written.

The limo pulled up in front of the restaurant, and Frank and Air went in. Frank took great pleasure in making sure Air was introduced to everyone who was of great magnitude. He was honored to have her by his side. He knew Air was modest and naive about her beauty and talent, so he was all too happy to be the one to introduce her to others who he felt were of significance. He was also becoming aware of the fact she could write really well. While Air was at the store the week before, he'd wandered around her studio to see what she'd been doing. He lifted up some of her latest drawing and come across some drawings with poems she'd written scrawled over the images. She was very expressive and could write about her emotions in a way that was raw, sacred and captured truths most people dared not even speak about to their best friends. He loved that she was oblivious to how cutting edge she was. Air always seemed to be the last one to understand just how special she was.

Having dinner with *the* Frank Sinatra was another ballgame altogether. This opportunity to spend the evening with a legend meant that they were now really playing in the big leagues.

During the dinner, Air couldn't resist relishing the notion of calling her parents (no matter how distant she'd grown from them) and casually dropping Frank's name and the fact that she was having dinner with him, just to rub in what a wonderful life she had now. She excused herself and went to the phone booth.

"Hi, Mom, it's Air. I know we haven't talked in awhile, but I'm in a really good mood and out on the town having a fabulous time," she began. "How are you and Dad?"

"Wh-elle, hi there. We're just fine. What's up?" D. J. asked suspiciously.

"Oh, I thought I'd call and tell you that Frank and I are at one of the most famous restaurants in all of New York City. It's called Johnny O's. But even better than that, you'll never guess who we're having dinner with!"

"Wh-elle, I can't imagine. Who?"

"Frank Sinatra and his girlfriend!"

"You're kiddin' me!"

"Nope. He's really nice."

"Air, is he really as handsome as he is on TV?"

"Yes, Mom, and he's with the most beautiful woman I've ever seen. I don't think I've ever seen a woman more gorgeous than she is. She has the most beautiful auburn hair and is wearing a forest green satin evening dress. Frank is dressed in a black suit with a black shirt and white tie. This whole evening has been incredible! It's like I'm dreaming."

"Whatcha wearing?"

"Oh, tonight I'm wearing a fabulous dress by the designer Betsey Johnson. I just love her line of clothes. They're very avant-garde couture. She's very famous, you know. I'm sure you've heard of her," Air remarked snidely. "The dress is floor length and made of the most exquisite black cashmere you've ever seen or felt. I'm wearing black velvet, pointed heels with straps around the ankles that are by Channel. I wish you could see me. I look beautiful!"

"What are you eating?" D. J. asked in a solemn tone.

"Well, I'm having duck, and Frank Sinatra's eating some kind of meat. I'm sure it's filet mignon. My Frank's having escargot, and Frank Sinatra's girlfriend is eating scampi."

"Hmmm. Wh-elle have a nice time, and you kin call me and tell me all about it later if you want."

Air returned to the table and continued quietly eating for the rest of the evening. She didn't feel comfortable engaging in the conversation. It seemed to be more of a business meeting between the Franks. When they weren't talking business, everyone listened to Frank Sinatra talk about his latest adventures in show business. He seemed extremely self-centered to Air, never seeming to realize he was monopolizing the entire evening with his stories. Air watched her Frank. He wasn't talking at all, which was unusual, to say the least. And she thought, *He's intimidated.* Frank S.'s girlfriend sat stoically staring at Frank S., never uttering a word until the end of the evening.

Air suddenly became mindful she was staring a hole through the woman and couldn't even remember her name. She glanced over at Air, and in a voice that sounded like a pig squealing from being thrown into hot oil said, with each word very drawn out, "Sooooo, Airrrrr-stream, what do youuuuuuu doooooo?"

Air was shattered. *Oh my God, why did she have to open her mouth? What a horrible voice she has.* The voice made the woman seem like a complete airhead, with ruining all Air's fantasies and moments of inspiration. "I've always loved to design clothes," Air replied. "I started when I was young with Barbie dolls. I also like abstract painting. I have an unbelievable art studio in our home. It's like an art store. I spend a lot of my time just hanging out there. It's very relaxing."

"Air's extremely talented," Frank remarked. "She's also a writer. She paints her poetry over her images. I'm encouraging her to write a book. I think she could easily write a novel if she wanted. Her poetry is excellent. You and Frank are welcome to come out to the house anytime you'd like. I'm sure Air would love to share her work with you. Wouldn't you, Air?"

"Absolutely! It's a beautiful drive to our home. We live in a historical town called Pearl River. It's about forty-five minutes upstate, just over the Washington Bridge. Actually, it was Oscar Hammerstein the third's country home."

"That's very kind of you, Airstream. We just might decide on taking a drive up there someday. We'll give you plenty of notice," Frank S. said in a cheery voice.

They finished eating, and Frank S. abruptly announced he needed to call it an evening. He stood up and took the arm of the unknown woman. He shook Frank's hand heartily and kissed Air on the cheek. "What a beautiful young woman you are. Frank's a lucky man," he said to Air.

Frank helped Air put on her coat and asked for the limo to be called.

"Air, we'll ride back to the parking lot, and I'll leave my car there overnight. We'll drive your car home, and I'll call for a limo in the morning to drive me back into the city. Air looked up at Frank, and he leaned forward and lifted her face with both his hands. He kissed her passionately. She felt safe and very loved. There was very little chatter on the ride home, other than Air expressing her feelings about the woman with Frank Sinatra.

"She was so beautiful, Frank. I couldn't keep my eyes off of her. Honestly, I've never seen a more gorgeous woman. But I have to say I about died when I heard her voice. She was so quiet all night, and then when she spoke, I about fell out of my chair."

"Air, she's probably lived in New York City all her life, and that's just her accent you're hearing."

"Oh my God, we just had dinner with Frank Sinatra!"

8

Over the next twelve months, Air created exceptional paintings. She also designed beautiful clothes. Her paintings and clothing designs seemed to mirror one another. She stayed with the same color palette of winter tones for both.

There was still much about Air's past she did not want Frank to know. The past was difficult for her to talk about. Too many old wounds would surface when she tried. She did have a way of telling the darkest of stories humorously. She was a good storyteller. She loved to write in her journal about her past. She would occasionally spend entire days writing if the words flowed easily and the memories weren't too painful. Sometimes she would get so distressed that she'd skip dinner; she never ate if her stomach was upset. The moment she felt tears starting to run down her face, she'd leave the house and drive into the city and have dinner with Frank.

Frank loved to wind down from his workday by listening to whatever musician was singing or whatever comedian was showcasing his or her material at the famous club called The Bitter End. He was also always considering new bands to sign. They spent many evenings hanging out with Bob Dylan, who lived just across the street in an awesome brownstone. Although Dylan always motioned for them to join him at his table, he never invited them to residence.

Air could hear Frank's voice in her head, "Air, when I'm at work, I want you to get out of the house and explore the town we live in rather than always heading into the city. Pearl River and the surrounding towns have a lot of history. Don't be afraid to drive around and see what you can find. Find out if there's a local art store or gourmet market you like. See if you can find a market that has those hearts of palm you love so much. If you get lost, all you have to do is call me and I will call a cab in the area to pick you up and take you home. You just need to lock the car and write down the cross streets of where you've parked. We'll pick the car up when I get home."

His words reassured her, and she felt relieved of her fear of getting lost and not knowing how to get home. The idea of being lost was terrifying to her, so she rarely ventured into town.

Air sometimes felt she was a "talked about woman" in a way that didn't feel good. She was well aware that people noticed her. She wanted to be noticed. Sometimes, she could see the look of resentment on some of the women's faces. *They don't understand my intentions*, she thought. She thought of herself as a "performance artist." She simply wanted to change people's moods for a brief moment—to pull them from a sort of numbness into a sense of joy—with the way she looked. Being in New York City, she could easily wear matching hats, gloves, shoes, and purses, along with a fur coat and feel at home. She couldn't do that in California. It really never got that cold in the Bay Area, and hats were not something that women wore.

Air felt scrutinized by other women. She had fantasies of what other women said about her behind her back. Sometimes she was haunted by the imagined conversations and had to fight off the snippets of criticism that danced in her head so she didn't feel awkward about how she looked. She didn't want anyone to think she was an elitist and unapproachable. She often wondered why she felt this way, since 99 percent of the time she was perfectly comfortable with her "overdressed look."

But sometimes the conversations played out in her head: *Oh, I know the woman you're talking about. I wonder what her story is. I'm sure she's new to the area. I've never seen her with a man. I love when I run into her in the grocery store. She obviously has a lot of money. I've never seen her in the same outfit. She wears the most gorgeous wool dresses. A lot of her clothes look like they are vintage. They look like Italian designs. She has the most beautiful coats. I think she's German, given that she has that long, strawberry golden hair and those brown eyes. I'm sure she's a man magnet. I've never seen her without a hat on. In fact, I don't think I've ever seen her in the same outfit twice. She's one of those women who fits the saying perfectly—the woman wears the hat, rather than the hat wears the woman.*

For over a year now, Air had been living the life she knew she was meant to live. She felt safe and naturally radiated a sense of magic. When Air walked into a room, every man's head turned. As much as she loved entertaining others with her appearance, she was still oblivious to just how alluring and sexy she was. She knew heads turned but wasn't completely clear as to the effect she had on men. In her world, she simply believed, *I bring joy to people. Nobody else is doing it, so I might as well do it. Besides, I love getting dressed up. It's who I am.* Air continually had to be reminded of what she looked like by going to the mirror and looking at herself.

She became recognizable in the city. There were people in Central Park, especially older men, who looked forward to seeing her. People were drawn to her beauty. When she talked with someone, she was alluring and quite candid. There weren't too many subjects that Air held sacred. She developed a knack for putting people at ease quickly. She was sincere and authentic. She had no problem telling funny stories to someone in a department store line just because he or she looked like in need of a friend.

No one, not even in his or her wildest dreams, would have believed this lovely creature who they all longed to be or to be with had endured a tortured childhood or, God forbid, had once been homeless and lived on the streets as a teen.

Air woke up early and wandered into the large, open kitchen. She looked around at all the beautiful dinnerware and wine goblets. She wondered if they would ever entertain anyone. Frank had once talked about having an afternoon catered party, but that hadn't happened yet. He wanted to have all his colleagues out to enjoy the grounds and swimming pool. The weather was warm, and Air thought about reminding Frank of the party. The kitchen was her favorite room in the house because of the massive windows on each wall. The sun was very bright that morning, and Air felt creative.

She found a note Frank had left on the table. He said he would be working late entertaining a new group the company had signed. She decided to work in her studio all day. After some coffee and a croissant, she headed down the long the hallway toward her room filled with ornate tables and paintings by Chagall and Monet. She painted for a couple of hours and then went into her sewing studio and pinned pieces of fabric onto her dress model. She then grabbed her journal and laid on one of the lounge chairs in the sun before going for a quick swim. She was just starting to write when the phone rang.

"Hi, Air. What are you up to?" Frank asked.

"I've been in my studio all day and was just taking a break. I just went for a swim and was going to write in my journal."

"I'm glad you're enjoying yourself. Sorry, I've got to entertain a new band tonight—you know, take them to dinner and show them around town."

"Oh sure, I understand. I'm just going to hang out in my studio all day."

Air was asleep when Frank finally got home. At this point, he and Air had been living together for almost two years. He felt he could tell Air anything, but tonight was going to be difficult. He was drunk and nervous. He had not called Air to tell her that, instead of going out to entertain a newly signed group as planned, he'd ended up going out with friends and getting quite drunk while they discussed the terrible events of the day.

He walked into the living room and sat down on a large, white leather chair. All of the furniture in the living room was white leather and had a boxy look. A large ebony coffee table with elegantly designed, redwood burl legs offset the white, and the room had an elaborate music system with speakers that functioned throughout the house. One of the long walls was packed solid with record albums. The music ranged from folk to jazz to classical. Frank walked over and randomly picked out an album by Mozart and put it on the turntable. He turned the music volume dial down so as not to disturb Air. He knew he would have to wake her and talk about the day he had experienced, but for now, he just needed to relax. He sat back down and stared at all the art they had collected. They went to auctions regularly hoping to purchase the work of Ben Shahn's. Frank loved his drawings. They really wanted to collect Cocteau's work, but it was out of their price range. The house was already full of priceless art.

Air would plead with Frank to not fill up the house with more art. She was afraid of being influenced either by style or color combinations.

Frank poured himself some brandy and immediately drank it in one gulp.

He poured more into his glass and sat back down. He was shaking. He had had a day from hell and had no idea how to tell Air what had happened. After about an hour of listening to music and drinking almost half the bottle of expensive cognac, he felt like he could face her.

He got up and walked upstairs to their bedroom. The bedroom was expansive. Floor-to-ceiling curtains covered the windows on the south-facing wall, allowing them to black out the morning sun and sleep in when they wanted to. A fireplace and two antique French armoires along with a matching chaise lounge dominated one corner of the room. The bed was enormous. It was big enough to easily sleep six. Otherwise, the room was stark.

"Air? Are you awake? Air, could you wake up? I have to talk with you. Air darling, please wake up. This is important."

Air turned over and slowly opened her eyes. She looked at Frank's face. "Hi, honey, how are you? Oh my God. Let me see your face! It's all swollen, Frank. Are you okay?"

"No, Air, shit hit the fan at work today. I got into a fistfight with the president of the company!"

"What? Are you kidding me?" Air asked in disbelief.

"No, man, we were in a staff meeting, and he looked right at me in front of everyone and said I'd made a huge mistake by signing Just Getting Started."

"I told him he was wrong, and he suddenly jumped out of his chair and came at me! What was I supposed to do—wait until he hit me? I could see he was raising his fist, so I hit him first!"

"Oh my God, Frank! What happened then?"

"He asked me if I liked my fingers."

"What the fuck did he mean by that?" Air asked with fear in her voice.

"Air, I don't tell you everything that goes on in the music business or the city. There are people who will cut your finger off for five bucks! And this guy has those kinds of connections!" Frank told her.

"So what happened after you hit him?"

"He told me to pack up my office, and I was fired," Frank replied and lowered his head.

"Holy shit! You're shitting me, right, Frank?" Air asked in a pleading tone.

"No, Air, I'm telling you exactly what happened. This guys had it in for me since I started working there. He knows I'm a threat to his job. I'm so far ahead of him. I could completely turn that company around for the better, and he knows it!" Frank's voice grew louder, and he looked off in the distance as if he could see the future that had just crumbled.

"What's going to happen to us now?"

"I think we have to get the hell out of here as fast as possible."

"What does that mean? You're scaring me, Frank!"

"We need to be scared. Air, you don't fuck with these people. They have no problem with taking you out!" Frank yelled.

"What do you mean, *taking you out?*" Air squealed in fear. "Frank, you're scaring me!" Air said again as she got out of bed.

"Air, these people have no problem killing people for the right amount of money," Frank said in a fearful tone.

"Oh my God. I can't breathe, Frank!" Air said. She sensed a panic attack coming.

"Air, I thought I was going to have a heart attack earlier. Jesus Christ! I have no idea what we should do."

"I have to get out this room, Frank. I'm so scared. Are we safe here?"

Frank dropped his head and said, "I have no idea."

"Should we go check into a hotel?"

"Air, if they're after me, they're going to find me no matter where we go," he said. He looked into her eyes, his expression utterly serious.

"I can't breathe, Frank. I think I'm going to die!" Air cried out.

"You're fine, Air! Now is not the time to freak out on me. Just find a brown paper bag and breathe into it. We have to keep it together," he warned.

"What! Are you joking?"

"Air, you're fine!" he yelled. "You're just hyperventilating. If you go get a small brown bag and breathe into it, you'll be fine. Get me one too."

"Frank, what are we going to do?" She looked at the clock. "Where the hell have you been? It's three in the morning!" she shouted.

"I went out with a couple of guys I work with. We just hung out at The Bitter End," he answered.

"Why the hell didn't you call me and tell me all this?" she questioned.

"I didn't want to freak you out, Air," he replied. "I wanted to try and figure out a plan."

"Good God, Frank. Do you think we should move back to California?" Air asked before she headed down the stairs, her antique silk gown flowing behind her.

"That's exactly what I'm thinking. But it's not going to be easy. All this shit has to be packed, and I think we should change the way we look!"

She stopped halfway down the stairs and looked back up at him in amazement. "What the fuck does that mean?"

"Well, first off, I think you should cut my hair and maybe even dye it another color."

"Frank, I think you're going off the deep end! What I am supposed to do?" Air gave him a look of inquiry and slowly walked back up to their room.

"For one thing, stop getting so dressed up like you usually do. Try to look normal."

"Look normal; you've got to be kidding! I don't know how to look normal," Air said as she put on her plush, pink, cashmere robe.

"Start dressing in clothes that look like something from Goodwill. For God sakes, don't get all matched up either! Wear tennis shoes. And *no hats*!" he replied, yelling now.

"Frank, tennis shoes are for tennis courts," she snapped. "I don't play tennis! I don't even own a pair of tennis shoes."

"Air, you don't understand what is happening here. I have no idea what's going to happen, but what I do know is that the company pays for this house, so we have to get out," he said as he opened another bottle of cognac.

"Fuck, Frank. This is insane! I certainly can't sleep now. We don't even have any boxes."

"Air, relax. I'll call a moving company later this morning. They'll come out and pack everything for us. They'll drive our stuff wherever we want them to," he said as he sipped his drink.

"Where the hell will that be?" she asked.

"I have a pretty good idea, but I don't want to talk about it now," he answered her. "I need to make a few calls."

"Shit this all reminds me of my childhood. I came home once to a moving truck, and the next thing I knew we were moving from Texas to California, leaving all that was familiar behind—including my grandparents," she lamented.

"Air, please try to keep it together. The last thing we need is you to have an emotional breakdown," Frank pleaded.

"How long will it take for someone to pack all our stuff?"

"Air, that's simply a matter of money. We can be out of here by the end of the week," he reassured her.

"Holy shit, you're not kidding are you, Frank? We're really moving back to California?"

"You bet your ass we are! We're not safe here anymore. You really don't understand how much I fucked up by telling the president of the company he's wrong in front of the entire staff," Frank said with a quiver in his voice.

"I can't breathe, Frank! I think I'm dying," Air said, fighting the feeling that the room was closing in around her.

"This is not a time for joking around!"

"Frank! I'm not joking!" Airstream screamed.

Later that morning, Air started arranging her studio materials for packing. She walked out into the kitchen to look for Frank. She started to panic. He was nowhere to be found. She ran down the hall toward the front room. All of a sudden, the front door opened, and Frank walked in.

"Frank, where have you been?" Air demanded.

Frank walked into the kitchen and poured himself a cup of coffee. He sat down and took a sip and turned and looked out at the gardens. The flowers were in full bloom, and he could see the gardener cleaning the pool. "Making calls," he finally responded.

"Making calls? What do you mean making calls? To whom?" she asked as she opened the refrigerator to pour herself a glass of grapefruit juice.

"I called some old friends in California. We need to have a place to go when we get there," he answered.

"Why didn't you just make the calls from the house?" Air asked, not understanding what was going on.

"Air, you don't understand, and it's better this way. I need you to get dressed and go buy some hair dye for me. I have to get rid of my blond hair. Make it a dark color. I'm going to call a moving company and have them come tomorrow and start packing. I'll shave my mustache and beard off today. I want you to dye my hair today also," Frank stated.

"Oh good grief, Frank! Aren't you the one who's losing it now? Don't you think you're being just a little too paranoid?" Air asked a bit delicately.

"No, I'm not. I'm doing the right thing. Trust me. Air, this is what I love about you so much. You are like a baby doe, super innocent and childlike. You have no clue about the big bad world out there," he said calmly.

"Frank, everyone knows your middle name is Paranoid!"

"Well, I'll take my chances," he replied, knowing he needed a disguise.

"God, Frank, I've never seen you without hair all over your face and head," Air laughed.

"Air, remember what I said," he added, looking at her sternly. "Do not get dressed up to go out."

"Okay, I'll put on something I wear when I paint."

"Okay, I'm going out again to call a moving company. Let's meet back here in about thirty minutes."

Frank pulled into the local gas station and went to the phone booth. He picked up the phone book and found the number of Bekin's Moving Company. He arranged for them to come out and begin packing early the next morning. He took a deep breath and called his longtime friend, Fred, once again.

"Fred? It's Frank. How are things going with Melinda? Did you two talk about things?" he asked, hoping for a positive answer.

"Frank! The question is, how are you?" Fred asked loudly.

"I'll feel a whole lot better when you tell me what Melinda said," he replied. He peered out of the phone booth, glancing around to reassure himself he wasn't being followed.

"Ah, Frank. You know Melinda would do anything for you. Of course, you and Air can live here with us! Melinda wanted me to tell you this is exactly why she insisted we buy the farm. She's wanted to create a communal living situation for years. We've both had it with living in the Bay Area, so now we have ten acres; a great, old barn; horse stables; and a beautiful, old, two-story Victorian home with a carriage house where you and Airstream can live. This is Mel's dream come true," Fred said excitedly. "She wanted me to tell you she can't think of living with anyone else but you."

"Is she still a nurse?" Frank asked.

"Yes, she's still a nurse. She got a job at Kaiser up north a bit. I commute to the East Bay every day. I'm still making jewelry. I have to tell you, Mel's gotten back into painting, and she's really good. In fact, she's starting to get me into sculpting again. It'll be great to sit around with some wine and talk about the days at California College of Arts and Crafts, Frank. You couldn't be coming at a better time."

"Oh, Fred, that's great news! Give Melinda a huge kiss and a hug for me. You two are literally our lifeline right now. When did you two move in there?"

"Oh, it'll be about four months soon. You know, we're both here for you. Let us know when you're on the road," Fred said.

"Fred, thank you so much. I'll be in touch in about a week. You're sure you have the room?" Frank asked, still keeping an eye on everything that so much as moved around him.

"Oh yeah. Wait until you see this place, Frank! It's a little piece of heaven. We just need to get some farm animals."

Frank drove back to the house. He met Air just as she was driving up.

"Did you get everything we'll need?" he asked.

"Yeah. Did you make your calls?" she asked anxiously.

"Yep. Everything's all set. We have a place to live, and the movers will be here early in the morning."

"I can't believe you really want me to cut your hair and dye it dark."

"Well, what kind of 'dark' did you get?"

"I bought a dark brown since you have blond hair. You don't want black. I don't think it would ever come out," she told him.

"Well, will the dark brown eventually come out?"

"Frank, your hair will have to grow out. Or you can go to a beauty salon and have a hairdresser who knows her colors dye your hair back to your natural color.

"You go cut off your beard and mustache," she said after she'd searched his face for a moment and determined he was as serious as he could be. "I'll get this hair dye ready. I guess we have to do this before the movers show up."

Frank shaved his face and walked back into the kitchen.

"Oh my God, Frank. You look so different."

"I hardly have an upper lip. That's why I have a moustache," he said, as if revealing a great secret.

"Well, there's that, but your face is half tan and half white."

"I don't give a shit, Air. Please, just dye my hair."

Air wrapped a towel around Frank's neck and squeezed the bottle of hair dye onto his head. "We need to wait twenty minutes now for the dye to work," she said after thoroughly rubbing in all the dye.

Frank sat in silence at the kitchen table the entire time. He rarely smoked cigarettes, but by the end of the twenty minutes, he had smoked four of them. Air was coughing, and her eyes were burning.

"Frank, please stop smoking. I haven't had a cigarette in over a year, and I don't want to start again. The tobacco smells good, but I can't breathe. I need to wash out the dye from your hair so please come over to the sink," she said, motioning him to the sink.

About an hour later, Frank looked in the mirror at his dark brown hair. He smiled. "It's perfect."

"Frank, how long had you have that beard?"

"All my life. Geez, I look so weird."

"Weird? You look ridiculous! The two different tones of color on your face make you easy to pick out in a crowd," she remarked.

"Good God, don't say that, Air. I'm supposed to be in disguise!"

The next day, Air heard the big moving truck coming up the long driveway. The movers arrived at precisely 8:00 a.m. as promised. Frank opened the garage door and motioned for them to come into the house.

"Most of the furniture stays with the house, but we do have quite a bit of personal items that need packing. You can start upstairs with the bedrooms. You'll need to pack everything that's in the closets and bathrooms. There's a linen closet off the kitchen that will need packing. The bed in the master bedroom will go, but the rest of the furniture stays. There's a couple of rooms with art materials that need packing, and then I'll show you the stuff in the living room, like all the record albums, books, and which pieces of artwork go. Let's start with all that and then take a look at what's left."

127

Frank turned to Airstream. "Air, would you pack a couple of suitcases with enough clothes to get us through the next week? Just leave them in the bedroom and I'll take them down to your car later," he said.

Frank had bought Air a 220 S Mercedes when they had settled in New York. He drove a Jaguar, but the company owned it. He planned on just leaving it at the house. He followed the mover's upstairs, and everyone seemed to move swiftly. There really wasn't that much to pack since the house was pretty much fully furnished when they'd moved in.

At the end of the next three days, the house looked just as it had when they had moved in. The movers had taken off to California the day before. Air and Frank were exhausted but determined to leave that day. It was going to be a very long drive.

They drove about eight to ten hours a day and then checked into a Motel 6 to get a few hours of sleep. It was a mind-numbing drive. They didn't talk much. Air was extremely frightened most of the ride, since Frank was convinced that they were being followed.

When they arrived in the Bay Area, Frank called Fred and Melinda.

"Fred, it's Frank. We're here in Napa, and we're about to cross over the Sonoma Valley and head up your way."

"It's great to hear from you! We thought we might hear from you today," Fred replied cheerily. "The movers just left. They got here yesterday afternoon and finished unloading all of your boxes. They unloaded the furniture today and put it all in the barn for now."

"Great!" Frank said. "I knew we wouldn't be too far behind them." He added, "Fred, I don't want to freak you out when you see me, and I'll tell you the whole story about why we had to get out of New York when we get there, but I want to warn you now, I had Air cut my hair short and dye it dark brown. I shaved off my mustache and beard too. I look very different, so don't freak out when you see me."

"Whatever you say, man," Fred replied, adding, "I've got great news for you guys. Melinda told me at breakfast that she thought it would be perfect for you two to live in the carriage house. I told her that I'd already told you about it. You two will have your own space. You're going to love it." Fred's voice conveyed a great deal of excitement.

"Ah man, that's incredible! I'll work my ass off around that farm of yours, Fred. You can count on me," Frank assured him.

"It's okay, Frank. We don't expect anything from you," Fred replied. "We can't wait to see you and Air. It's been so long. Melinda and I are really looking forward to meeting Airstream. Sounds like you'll probably be here in just a couple of hours. I hope my directions will work for you. If not, just call and we'll meet you."

Frank got back into the car and turned to Air, "Okay, Air, we'll be there in a little over an hour. I can't tell you how relieved I will be to get a good night's sleep! Good God, it seems like we've been in this car forever. It's so fucking great to be back in California."

"I second that, Frank," Air said. "Remember how you asked me not to call any of my friends and tell them I'm back in California?" she added.

"Yes, and you still can't call anyone for at least a month, Air. It's really important we fall off the radar screen," he warned her.

"What about my family?"

"Air, why would you want to call them anyway? They don't give a damn about you."

"Oh, I just don't want them to worry. I usually call them once a week."

"Well for now, the less they know, the better. You should consider stopping all contact with them. It's not healthy for you, Air. You always end up crying after you've talked with your mother. I'm not trying to hurt you, my love, but your mother doesn't have all her marbles," Frank said.

Air fell asleep for the rest of the trip. She had no grasp of the situation Frank was in. She had matured tremendously after two years in New York City, but she was still very naive in many ways.

After some time, Air felt Frank nudge her gently awake. "Okay," he said with a smile. "This is the street."

Air stretched and looked out the window, "Wow, we're really out in the country!"

They slowly pulled into the driveway. Fred and Melinda came running out of the house to greet them.

"Oh God, it's so good to see you, Frank!" Fred hugged Frank and turned to Air. "Hi there. You must be Airstream. Welcome to our little abode," he said enthusiastically.

"We're great, just exhausted and probably dehydrated," Frank replied for them both, as Air was a little at a loss for words. "Melinda, come here and let me hug you. It's been so long! Mel, this is Airstream. We've been together for a couple of years now."

"Hi, Airstream. It's a pleasure to meet you. And welcome to your new home!" Melinda said, smiling warmly at the younger woman.

"Come on inside and let us get you something to eat and drink," Fred said.

"Oh boy, that sounds good," Frank said eagerly. "Feels great to just walk around," he added, taking in the vastness of the property. "Fuck! This place is out of this world!"

"Wait until morning when you can really see the place. It's just what you both need," Melinda said.

Air looked at the large, white, two-story Victorian house and then turned around and glanced at the property. She looked back at the house and stared while Fred, Mel, and Frank had already started in with talking about old times. It was the house of her childhood dreams. Air counted fifteen steps that led up to the porch. The hand-carved, wooden fence that wound around the entire porch was beautiful. It was so rare to see a house on the West Coast with a porch like this. There was an old fashioned swing for two next to the front door. Air had dreamed of living in an old Victorian house with a porch all around the house and a swing for two since she was a little girl. She had seen a movie with a family who lived in a house like that, and the family was so happy there. Air had convinced herself that was all it took to be happy. A big, white Victorian house with a porch and a swing was your ticket to happiness. As she stood there staring at the house, she started crying.

130

Frank, Melinda, and Fred stopped laughing and looked over at Air.

"Air!" Frank yelled as he grabbed her. "What's wrong? What's wrong?"

"She's exhausted from whatever's going on. She's so young, Frank," Melinda whispered. "Let's get her into the front room where she can sit down and rest. She needs some water."

"Air, why don't you sit there on the red velvet Victorian chair? You love these types of chairs," Frank said, steadying her as she walked.

"You sit down too, Frank. You're both exhausted. Let Melinda take care of Air," Fred said. "How about a joint, Frank?"

"Oh my God, does a bear shit in the woods? I'm ready to get completely fucked-up!"

"Would you like a glass of wine, too?" asked Fred.

"Hell yes! You don't even have to ask."

"Great! I've found this really great wine Melinda and I drink all the time! How about you, Air? Want some wine?" Fred asked, clearly wanting to please the two of them.

"Yes, that would be great," answered Air.

"This place is unreal, Fred. It's in mint condition. Did you buy it in this condition?"

"Yes, the previous owners lived here all their lives, and the old man did nothing but work on the place daily," Fred explained. "We really lucked out. We're so blessed to have found this place. We put in a bid, and they accepted it straightaway. I think in another ten years everyone will be moving up here. Melinda's spent the last few months decorating it with as much original furnishing as we can afford."

Frank looked around. The furniture was elegant and in almost perfect condition considering how old it was. The velvet chair Air sat on had a matching chair and couch. The bookshelves were full of art books and Roseville vases. Art from the early sixties hung on the walls. One of Frank's sculptures was sitting on one of the end tables. Expensive, colorful hand woven rugs that Melinda had inherited from her aunt covered the floor. Melinda had made the curtains that hung from the ceiling to the floor out of antique lace she'd special ordered. Frank looked over at the French doors that separated the living room from the dining room. He noticed everything was dust-free.

"Wow, man, so what the hell happened in New York City?" asked Fred.

"Shit, all I want to tell you right now is that I had a fistfight with the president of the record company right in the middle of a meeting with the entire board. He looked straight at me and made a remark about how signing Just Getting Started was a wrong decision, and I told him he was wrong."

"Fuck," commented Fred.

"Yeah, the guy jumped out of his chair and came at me with his fists knotted up real tight. I was ready for him. I hit him first, and we wrestled until some of the staff pulled us apart. As he was lying on the floor, he looked up at me and told me to get the fuck of his office and pack up my office," Frank said in an intense tone.

"Frank, that's unreal!"

"What's unreal is the guy's involved with big-time mobsters. Air and I had to get out of there as soon as possible."

"Well, you're safe here, I'm sure," Melinda said reassuringly.

"Let's hope so. If I get any clue something's up, Air and I will leave immediately."

"Frank, don't blow this out of proportion. I doubt anything's going to happen now. The guy's got you out of the company. That's probably all he really wanted. You're no longer a threat to him."

"I hope you're right."

"I see you're as paranoid as ever, Frank!" Melinda laughed.

"Some things never change. Too much dope."

"Well, I say we drink to that!" Frank proposed.

"Long live, Mary Jane," Fred harped. "Frank, you're going to need a job. What have you come up with?"

"Nothing, man. I don't know what I'm going to do. I can't get back into the music business."

"Well, think about working with me if you want. I've always loved your roach clip designs. I think now is the time to get into designing anything to do with smoking dope, peace pins, and earrings. It's all up for grabs."

Frank decided to work with Fred designing hippie jewelry. Air lost interest in designing clothes but continued to pursue painting. After a few months, life became normal again. Friends came to party on weekends. Air and Frank began to spend a lot of time in the Bay Area and in Santa Cruz. Frank was always checking out possibilities of going back to work in advertising.

"Fred? Did you and Melinda throw a party to celebrate when you bought this place?" Frank asked one day.

"Funny you should mention that, Frank, because the other day Melinda said we should throw a party, not only for the farm, but for you and Air being back."

"I think that's a hell of a great idea!" Frank laughed.

"Mel thought we should throw the party over Labor Day weekend. What do you think? One of those good ole U. S. of A's favorite national pastimes—a giant barbecue! It's going to be one hell of a weekend. I'm going to tell folks if they want to camp out back on the property, they're welcome to stay the weekend," Fred remarked.

"A potluck barbecue—that's perfect! And the camping is a great idea, Fred. My God, your land will be covered with tents and cooking grills."

9

The two couples invited everyone they knew, plus some.

"You know, the house will be packed with dope-smoking crazies," Fred said. "We have to plan out the food and find a place where we can rent about ten tables and at least forty folding chairs."

Air stood there imagining what ten acres of "dope-smoking crazies" would look like. She didn't drink liquor, but she had started occasionally smoking dope. Actually, she still didn't really like smoking dope. What she liked was looking "angelic." She remembered overhearing a conversation Fred and Melinda were having about her when she was stoned.

"I love talking to her when she's stoned," Fred had said. "She's so sweet and naive, so nubile and fawnlike. When she's stoned she's even sweeter if that's possible."

"Fred, don't talk like that about Air!" Melinda had yelled. "She actually doesn't like smoking dope. It makes her paranoid, but she feels left out of the gang if she doesn't."

"Speaking of planning the food," Melinda was saying now, "Frank, you're such a great cook! What are you going to make?"

"I was thinking of putting together my favorite Galloping Gourmet dish called Forty Cloves Garlic Chicken," he replied with a grin. "I'll order twenty roaster chickens a couple of days prior to the party and then marinate them overnight in olive oil with forty cloves of garlic in each chicken."

"Forty cloves of garlic in each chicken? You're kidding, right?" Melinda asked.

"No, the guy actually stuffs forty cloves of garlic in one chicken and bakes it. It's one of his most popular dishes. He leaves the skin on the cloves, but it's still a lot of work."

"Well, it must be incredible. I've never heard of that many cloves of garlic put into anything. Are you sure about that, Frank?" asked Melinda.

"Oh yeah, you'll love it. I sort of put my twist on it by marinating the birds with a bit of teriyaki sauce. Barbecuing the chickens will be much better than baking them, too."

"Okay, I guess I'll take your word for it," Melinda replied. "And we do live in a town famous for raising most of California's chickens, so at least they'll be really fresh."

The Labor Day party finally arrived. People were spread out as far as Air could see. She looked out into the crowd and saw many of her friends she hadn't seen in a long time. She suddenly noticed one of her favorite people—RB. She'd met RB the night she'd met Frank and hadn't seen him since they'd moved back to New York. He was also in the music business but worked in San Francisco. He was a concert producer and had worked with Frank in the past. She could see he was talking to Frank.

She walked—or perhaps one should say "electro-glided"—over since she was so stoned. Standing there, imagining how angelic she looked, she listened to their conversation.

"I am becoming painfully aware of the fact I have no idea what I'm doing with my life," RB said.

"Well, I have an overabundance of energy in the plans department myself," Frank said. "In fact, at any given moment, I have at least three or four hundred plans."

"I like the simple life myself," RB said.

"What, like working in the fields picking tomatoes or lettuce?"

"Oh hell no. I'd have to join a union for that!" RB laughed.

"Well, I got problems. All of my ideas are so good, I just can't decide which one of them to do," Frank said.

"You're right, Frank," said Air. "It has to do with your head, and I don't mean inside. I mean outside. I think those goddamned beanie hats you wear have sent a taproot right down into your brain!"

"Where do you get those hats anyway, Frank?"

"Frank makes me crochet them for him," Air remarked.

"What's with the chin strap, Frank?"

"That's another problem I have. Well, it's not really a problem. It's more like an unusual situation. I've always liked hats—on my head, on hooks, on nails, or just about anywhere—but I'm particular to ones on my head, which leads me to this problem or situation or whatever it is. You see, every time Air makes me a new beanie, the damned thing keeps climbing up to the top of my head—not real fast but real slow, kind of sneaky-like, like it's too small. It gets all bunched up on the top of my head like a small soup bowl. I try to pull it down, tuck it under my glasses and over my ears, you know, just generally pull it down real tight. The son of a bitch shoots right back up every damned time!"

"So that's what's up with the chinstrap?"

"At first, it was difficult to get used to. It felt like some orthopedic device. Nearly strangled me. That's when I discovered the situation I was mentioning. My head is growing to a point—not a real sharp one but like a bullet with a blunt point, sort of like a '56 caddie bumper tit. I have all this hair, and so it's real slippery.

"Now, my pilot hat is another story! It pulled some real shit on me the other day. In fact, it almost got me killed! The damned thing spun its earflap right in front of my eyes while I was passing a ready-mix truck down by the dump."

Everyone just stared at Frank. Christ, the fact was, he looked deranged in the hat he was wearing. The cap looked like something Snoopy would wear, but it was crocheted, and he always had the chinstrap fastened no matter what the weather was like. Thank God he didn't have any goggles.

"Hey you guys have to excuse me. I have to go check on my special dish."

RB turned to Air with a look that asked, *Should I or shouldn't I?*

"You know, Air," he said. "Frank told me something the other night that was pretty strange."

"Like what?"

"Like his beanies were blabbermouths."

"He said what?"

"He said his beanies were taking turns fucking him around. I didn't have a clue as to what he meant. He looked pretty stoned on weed, so I just figured he was tripping. I didn't want to say anything to you about it. I thought it'd just pass."

Tony, a longtime friend of Fred and Melinda's, walked up and joined in on the conversation, saying Frank had mentioned something about his beanies to him too.

"What'd he say to you?"

"Well, he said he was in the middle of the Piedmont Market the other day, and suddenly his beanie decided to spin around a few times—not too much, just enough so that people noticed him."

"Oh my God!" Air said. "That's it. I'm not going to make him another beanie no matter how much he begs."

"I think he's smoking too much weed," RB said.

"Excuse me, I have to go talk to Frank," Air said and walked over to Frank.

He was talking with a big-time marketing director for Capitol Records who'd come to the party with RB. Everyone referred to the guy as either "Screaming Red Derrick" or the devil himself. She could hear them talking.

"The decision to quit the music business must have been a hard one for you, Frank. How could you just walk away from the big time? You were at the top of your game," said "the devil."

Frank looked around. He looked beyond the people, beyond the party, up toward the hills, and finally fixated his eyes on the sky. "You know, I like the fog a lot, but I don't think it gets a fair shake from most people these days. Everybody keeps raving on and on about the beautiful sunrises and the gorgeous sunsets, but nobody says a thing about the fucking fog."

"Frank, dear, could I talk with you about the teriyaki sauce?"

Air led Frank over to one of the tables with some lemons and soy sauce.

"Frank! Why the hell are you telling people your beanies are alive? Honest to God, you're going to get one of us locked up if you keep up with this crazy talk. People are going to misunderstand your humor and take you seriously. Frank, people go home dead drunk and get up the next day convinced of their memories of the party. They then go to work on Monday and drop names and polluted stories. Frank, honestly, since we've moved back to California, you've changed. I think you smoke too much dope. You've become more paranoid than ever. You don't seem to have any motivation anymore. I know you're designing jewelry with Fred, but you're so much more talented than that. I wish you'd at least get back into making sculptures if you're really never going back into the music business. We're running out of money, Frank. I'm really worried about our future."

"Viva la dead drunks!" Frank laughed.

"To hell with you, Frank!"

Air watched him as he drifted back out into the crowd. Thank God she'd talked him out of wearing his plastic, orange ring with a giant, dead black ant embedded in it, along with the matching orange beanie with the chin strap tied ever so tightly.

Folks had been encouraged to bring camping gear and spend the entire weekend. There was no special set time for anything, so at any given moment, people were sleeping in their tents or wandering about the property. There were nonstop bands playing, and people seemed to be swaying in the wind. The smell of pot must have drifted for miles. Everyone had a grin on his or her face.

By midnight on Friday, everyone had settled in for the weekend. Frank and Air said good night to Fred and Melinda and walked toward the carriage house around 2:00 a.m.

Frank opened the door and immediately staggered to the bed and passed out. He didn't even say good night. Air put her nightgown on and sat in the bed staring into the darkness. She couldn't stand the dead silence and had never been able to sleep without at least the bathroom light on. In the stillness and utter blackness, suddenly she heard and felt her heart beating. She was sure it was beating at least a thousand beats per minute

Shit! I'm having a heart attack! My God! I'm too young and definitely too crazy to die now. What would the world do without me?

Air was petrified and had no idea what to do. Frank surely couldn't help her. He was snoring so loudly she could hardly hear the band that was still playing. Air thought she'd just go to the main house and ask Melinda how she could try and sleep through her heart attack. She was a bit hesitant since she had gotten some strange vibes from Melinda that day. Air felt that Melinda was a bit jealous that Fred paid her a lot of attention. She didn't have any attraction to Fred but really enjoyed talking with him. She tiptoed out of the carriage house and into the main house. Quietly, she walked into Melinda's room. She gently nudged her as to not startle her.

"Melinda, I'm sorry to wake you, but I'm having a heart attack. I was wondering, is there any special way I should lie down so I don't disturb my heart any more than I have to? Should I lie in my bed on my back or on my stomach? Or should I lie on my left side or my right side?" Air whispered.

Melinda slowly turned over and stared blankly at Air for at least a minute before speaking. Air could see in her expression of nothingness what she'd had always suspected. Melinda thought Air was crazy. "You've got to be kidding me! Why don't you try sleeping sitting up?"

"Okay, thanks, Melinda. I'm sorry I woke you up."

Airstream went back out to the carriage house. She sat down in a big, overstuffed chair Frank called his chair. She'd never thought about her heart before. She'd been preoccupied with brain tumors since the age of thirteen. Hell, heart attacks were big-time. She'd always just been third class, second-rate with brain tumors up until then. Air didn't leave the carriage house for the rest of the weekend or even enough "brain real estate" to anticipate another ailment.

On Sunday night, the party ended, and folks left. Many people asked Frank about Airstream and why she hadn't partied much. Frank just shook his head and said, "She took to the bed with a washrag on her forehead." He added something about migraines.

For one solid week, Air went silent. She stayed in the carriage house and sat in Frank's chair as still as possible. This pissed Frank off. She kept one hand on her chest and the other hand on the phone. She would not sleep, eat, or take any drugs, which everyone, including Melinda, kept offering her.

"Jesus Christ, Air! Take this pill! You have to get some sleep!" Frank yelled.

Air took the pill and hid it under her tongue because she couldn't handle any more pressure, not from her chest or any of the people in the house. Her fear was intensifying, and she became more and more convinced she was dying. She decided she needed to get to a hospital. Unfortunately, Frank didn't have a car, which made that plan difficult, as her car was yet to be registered with the state. God forbid she should ask Nurse Ratchet Melinda for a ride to the ER. Air knew she'd tell Frank.

Finally, Air got up enough courage, or perhaps it was a decision based in great fear, to ask Fred if he would mind if she rode into the city with them and run a few errands with his car while they were at work. She said she'd be back at the end of the day to pick them up. Melinda gave Fred a nasty look, but Fred liked Air.

"Sure," he said.

After dropping Fred and Frank off, Air drove straight to Redwood High General's emergency room. The woman at the reception desk asked Air how she could help.

"I've been having a heart attack for about a week, and I just need someone to listen to my heart for a couple of minutes," Air replied.

The woman looked up at Air for a few seconds and then handed her some papers to fill out. "Someone will be out soon to take your blood pressure."

Of course, it was Air's luck that the head nurse on duty that day just happened to be Melinda. Melinda's job had her at a different hospital each week. Air had no idea she was working in the Bay Area that day. She came through the ER doors, took one look at Air, and turned around and went back through the double doors.

She came back out with the blood pressure kit and looked at Air with total disgust. Air could never figure out what Fred saw in her. She was so damned straight and looked old enough to be his mother, but she had a lot of money. Air was sure her money was the reason Fred had married her. It was Melinda's money that had bought the farm.

Air had thought Melinda was very nice when she'd first met her, but she could feel Melinda was jealous of Airstream's talent as an artist. When she found out Air had had no formal training, she'd been in total disbelief. The whole idea of a commune had just fallen under the table, and no one ever mentioned anything about the concept anymore. Air had tried to tell Frank Melinda didn't like her, but he wouldn't listen.

After she'd taken Air's blood pressure, Melinda turned and said something to one of the other nurses. Air got this feeling that she was in more trouble than ever. She'd find no sympathy or understanding here, not with Nurse Melinda Ratchet on duty.

I'm sure she has told the other nurses that I'm as nutty as a fruitcake.

Suddenly, a reassuring nurse came out. She took Air to the outpatient psychiatric unit and said someone would be right out to talk with her. Air felt safe for the moment. At least, Melinda wasn't there to give her those God, wait-until-Frank-hears-about-this-one looks.

Air waited for what seemed an eternity. Finally, a woman dressed in a gray suit with her hair pulled back so tightly her face should have been purple and tearing at her hairline came out and called Air's name.

"Hello, Airstream. My name is Mrs. Lee. Won't you step into my office?"

"Sure."

"Now, please tell me, what seems to be the problem?"

"Well, for a week now, I haven't been able to eat or sleep. My heart is all I am aware of. It just keeps beating really fast and very hard. When I close my eyes, I can hear it beating in my ears so loudly it feels like it's going to pop right out of my chest. I've never been aware of my heart before. I used to think I was going to die from a brain tumor, but now I'm not so sure. I have this pain right here."

Air pointed to the place where most people get gas pains, just below the ribcage. "I've had this pain right here for a week. I'm having a heart attack. I'm pretty sure I'm dying."

"Everyone is going to die, Airstream," Mrs. Lee said. "Do you have any shortness of breath or pain in your jaw or arm?" She was writing something on what appeared to Air to be a chart.

Great, she finally had her very own chart! Maybe now someone would finally take her seriously.

"No, I can breathe just fine. I don't have any pain anywhere except right here in the middle of my chest."

"Are you having any hallucinations?"

"Well, not that I can remember," Air answered.

Shit I'm not going to tell her about the hallucinations I had when I was younger and took some LSD. This woman was obviously not taking her as seriously as she had hoped she would. *What the hell do hallucinations have to do with my heart attack anyway?* Air wondered.

"Air, look over at the curtains. Are they moving at this moment?"

"No."

"What about the tiles on the floor. Do they seem to be moving?"

Air looked down at the black and white square tiles. After she'd stared at them for a few minutes, they did start to play tricks on her. The longer she stared, the more she realized the tiles were moving up and down like rolling hills.

I'm probably hungry, she told herself, *low blood sugar. Hell, I haven't eaten in a week, and I'm really weak.* "Yes, the floor does seem to be moving, and the curtains are swaying."

"The curtains seem to be moving to you?"

"Yeah, sorta."

"Excuse me, Airstream. By the way, that is a lovely name, Airstream. There is someone I'd like you to meet."

She left the room and returned with a huge, overweight older man.

Oh my God, what do I need a huge, old man for?

"Airstream, I'd like you to meet the head of this department, Dr. Cappy Buttz.

"Dr. Buttz, this is Airstream. Isn't that a lovely name?"

Air wasn't sure if Mrs. Lee was referring to Dr. Buttz's name or hers. *Good God, who'd name their kid Cappy Buttz? Why not just go all the way and call him Harry—Harry Buttz?*

"Hello, Airstream," Dr. Buttz said a little too softly. "How about you and I having a little chat in my office? I think we'll both be more comfortable there."

"Fine, whatever I have to do to get some medical attention. I am running out of time," Air said under her breath.

"Excuse me, Airstream. I didn't hear what you said."

"Oh, it was nothing."

Dr. Buttz led Air down the hall and into a small, sterile, bathroom size office with a white-tiled floor and a desk. He opened the closet and took out a metal folding chair. He offered Air a seat. She noticed mirrors on both sides of the room and wondered if they were being watched. He sat there for a couple of minutes staring at her. She knew the routine; she'd been in and out of therapy too many times to fall for the uncomfortable silent-stare act.

"Now, Airstream, why don't you tell me about yourself? How about the relationship with the man you live with? It says here his name is Frank, also known as Knarf. Does Frank have a last name?"

"No."

"Okay, you wrote his age but not his last name. So, Frank is a lot older than you, and it says here you are almost twenty-one years old. Is that correct?"

"Yes."

"Let's talk about your relationship with your father. Do you love your father?"

Air knew straightaway this guy was a jerk. *How could he be the head dude? He's as much of an asshole as Frank is.*

"Excuse me Dr. Buttz, but what does Frank or my father have to do with my heart attack? I don't have time for this crap!"

It's my damned freckles, she thought. *They give me away every damned time. I need those brown age spots old people get, not sun freckles. Maybe people might listen to me then.*

"Your goddamned nurses are all just standing around waiting for the 'big thrill' to arrive, and they are ignoring me. I'm the one who's dying, and your people are waiting for the meat wagon. I'm no challenge!"

"Are you on any drugs, Airstream?"

"No! And I've been asked that already!" Air yelled, her voice getting louder and her pitch higher as she went. "Jesus Christ, I'm dying. You should be giving me some kind of heart drugs! I don't want to die!"

She stared at the floor waiting to die. *Will my life flash before me?* Air wondered. *If it does, I hope I see the part when I was on my way back to New York City after a visit with my friends in California.* Suddenly, the plane had banked to the left severely, and Air had screamed at the top of her lungs, "Oh fuck! We're all going to die!" That was one of the best times she'd ever had.

Air was petrified of flying. She'd flown back and forth between the West Coast and the East Coast when she lived in New York and had experienced severe air turbulence many times. She'd always wanted to scream out something like that. In fact, she was so terrified of flying that the airline stewardesses could spot her coming a mile away. They'd put her in the back of the plane and hand her a brandy before the plane even began to taxi. Little did they know, she'd already guzzled two blenders full of gin fizzes and taken two ten-milligram Valiums.

Wide-eyed with fear, she'd board a plane hoping to sit next to someone she could tell her plane stories to—someone who would understand. She couldn't wait to tell people she'd been in the cockpit at least five times. "Yeah, the stewardesses just don't know what the hell to do with me," she'd say. "All I do is wail away the entire flight and piss everybody off. The stewardesses always end up asking me if I'd like to go up to the cockpit and talk with the pilots. They'd try to convince me that the pilots could reassure me everything was fine.

"God, if you ever have the chance, don't go up there," she'd warn her seatmate. "The cockpit is an awful place! It's so tiny, and it's jammed with sweaty men, and they can't see shit. There's only a couple of tiny windows, and that's it. It is amazing planes stay in the air!"

That memory took Air's mind off of her heart attack for a moment.

"Airstream, have you recently had your heart broken?"

"Yes, as a matter of fact, I have! By one hundred cloves of garlic, Dr. Buttz!"

"I beg your pardon?"

"I ate too much fucking garlic chicken! Listen, you jerk, never mind the patient therapy bullshit. I don't have time to play around. I'm having a heart attack! I need to speak to a real heart doctor. I need a treadmill test and a shot of some drug that will let me sleep. And you must tell them that, when they do give me that treadmill test, I *do not* want to hear my heart beating out loud! I've seen those things on TV, and you can hear the heart beating louder and louder, and I can't handle that right now. So they have to turn the volume all the way down. Understand?"

"Oh yes, I think I understand very well. We're going to need you to sign some papers, Airstream. Do you think you could do that for us?"

"What kind of papers?"

"Oh, just the usual, routine papers."

"Fine."

"Okay, Airstream, I'll have Mrs. Lee introduce you to the head nurse. I think you'll be very comfortable here. You can rest today, and we'll talk tomorrow."

All Air could figure was that she wasn't going to die tonight. Maybe tomorrow. She met the head nurse and headed out to what seemed like the north forty.

Thank God it wasn't the north forty as in the north forty garlic clove fields.

Air and the head nurse walked for what seemed forever, through many corridors and down different wings. This place was no Hilton. Air was beginning to sense she'd made a big mistake. They finally came to two huge double doors with a sign on it reading, "J-Ward."

"Right this way, Miss."

Ah, such personal pride she has about this department, Air thought and began to get really scared.

They went into a special wing of the hospital where the doors were kept locked. Air casually looked around out of the corners of her eyes and tried to check out the joint, while acting as though she didn't have any concerns. She knew she was in deep trouble. Locked doors and two men standing guard equaled a really bad sign.

They passed an elderly woman who was obviously a patient. Her hair looked as though it hadn't been washed or combed in years. She was laying out a blue pillowcase on the floor perfectly, no creases, no wrinkles, just perfectly flat. The task took her ten minutes. She kept muttering something to herself as she pressed the pillowcase flat with her hands. The instant she'd achieved her goal, she pulled up her old, worn-out, flowered smock with gigantic pockets, squatted over the perfectly straight pillowcase, and pissed for at least two minutes.

"Jesus Christ! I'm definitely having a heart attack," Air said, startling everyone. I can't breathe! Somebody help me! Could I please see a doctor for a couple of minutes, and then I'll be on my way."

Just as the old woman was finishing pissing, Air's attention was dragged away, and she turned to see a loud woman at the end of the hall. The woman ran toward her, screaming loudly. "Repent! Repent! You're a sinner! I know a sinner when I see a sinner!"

"Oh don't mind any of them, Airstream; they're all harmless," the nurse said. "The biggest event that's ever happened around here was when they used to get their dentures mixed up. They'd find a pair in the bathroom and decide that it was theirs. When they didn't fit, they'd try to flush them down the toilet. We'd have to fish them out and sanitize them. We keep them locked up in the cabinet now so there's no confusion."

Air then noticed a man in a wheelchair being pushed by an old woman who was cradling a plastic doll. The nurse saw Air watching them and again reassured her everything was fine.

"That's just Mr. Wayne and Missie Carla. Mr. Wayne has a touch of dementia, and Missie Carla has a touch of schizophrenia. She thinks the doll in her lap is her little girl. Her little girl burned to death at the age of four."

The nurse acted as though all was status quo. Air immediately forgot about having a heart attack and started trying to figure out how to act and laugh naturally. *Normal people aren't serious. They laugh a lot*, she thought.

"What the hell kind of papers did I sign?" Air asked the nurse. The nurse did not respond.

Air had the ability to change her behavior and act like someone else whenever she found herself in an uncomfortable situation. She remembered being able to do this since she was a child. She thought it had something to do with the feelin'. It was as if she'd shove herself aside and become someone totally different. Air knew she now had to begin acting extremely intelligent, articulate, and proper. One got the sense she was trustable and knowledgeable. This type of behavior was faintly familiar to Air, and sometimes she actually felt like a completely different person. This act would require someone with the name of Claire. Unbeknown to Air, she had quite a few other "personalities" within her. She did not have time to ponder this at the moment, but she would later. Now, she had just enough time to quickly go into action.

Air knew Frank would be beginning to ask, "Where the hell is Air?" He'd have heard that she wasn't parked out front of Fred's business. She knew, no doubt, Melinda had already called Frank, and he would be there any moment. Melinda probably went and picked Fred and Frank up herself. Air knew if she could get Frank to come and visit her, she could convince the guards Frank was the one who was crazy, not her.

Frank came. He brought Air a little transistor radio. The guards immediately took it apart and inspected it for any sharp objects that might be hidden in it. Nothing sharp or pointed was allowed on the "guests." In fact, Air had to light her cigarettes on this little hot spot on the wall because they weren't allowed matches. It didn't make any sense to her because one could certainly do damage to his or herself or others with a lit cigarette; hell, you could start a fire if you wanted or just stick somebody with it.

When Frank saw Air, she smiled at him. He looked perfect. He had on one of his chin-strapped beanies. He'd had Air put the initials WC (for Wacko Crazy) on the beanie, but he told everybody it had formerly belonged to W. C. Fields. His usual long, dirty blond, Einstein-looking hair was all frazzled and sticking out everywhere. His eyes were blood red from smoking too much dope. Best of all, he was wearing his L. L. Bean overalls with a red lumber jacket shirt and his favorite "old man shoes," as Air referred to them. They were funky old, backless slippers made of brown leather—the type that old men wore as they scooted along the floor, never lifting their feet. It was too good to be true. Frank looked exactly like he belonged in here. Better yet, he looked like he'd been here for years.

"Air, how the hell did you get yourself in here? I thought you said you were just going shopping."

"Frank, I'm still trying to have a heart attack, and they fucked up and put me in this goddamned J-Ward. It's really a loony bin. I have no clue what the *J* stands for, but this is a psych unit, Frank! You should see my room. Honest to God, the walls are padded. They think I'm nuts, Frank. This is all your goddamned fault!"

"What the hell are you talking about? I'm not the one who convinced these people I was loony. You've got to stop with this heart shit. You're fine; if you were having a heart attack, you'd be dead by now. Do you know how long you've been having a heart attack? For over a week now! I should know what a heart attack is. I had one when I was only eighteen!"

"Oh, Frank, bless you. You're now telling me it's possible for someone who's really young to have a heart attack. Why the hell aren't you dead if you had a heart attack?"

"Air, you did such a great job convincing these people you're crazy, they now have some legal state law hold on you—some kind of law that says if the doctor thinks you're a possible threat to yourself or someone else, they can keep you for seventy-two hours. Not even a family member can get you out. It's automatic."

It was then Air realized it was Dr. Buttz who had put her in here. He was such a butt! Everyone had neglected to tell her, "Oh, by the way, what you're signing says you agree to stay here with our lovely family for three whole days." Air had never bothered reading fine print. She was too busy on the "front lines" watching out for the land mines and being ambushed by her heart to read the fine print.

Air put her escape plan into action. She quickly pulled her hair back into a tight bun and straightened her clothes. She borrowed some lipstick from one of the women who'd been given some of her cosmetics back for good behavior. She felt a bit guilty for what she was about to do, but she had to protect herself. Frank was her ticket to ride. Frank actually looked like a permanent fixture there, like a longstanding member of the fantasy club he had created in his imagination called, "The Ruth Swartz Why Bother Club." He said that the club had only a president and one member, and he was both the president and only member. There should have been large portrait of him hanging in the arts and crafts hobby room, where everyone went to make liquid plastic, multicolored flowers. There would have been a plaque that read, "Our Hero."

Suddenly, over the speaker, someone announced, "Visiting hours are just about over, folks. If you'll kindly move toward the doors, we will let each of you out one by one."

"Who me, officer?" Frank suddenly said really loudly.

"Frank, what the hell are you doing? Be quiet. They're not talking to you!"

"I have to take a piss, Air. Where's the bathroom?"

"Over there, Frank," Air answered.

She strolled up to the guards at the door and began chatting with them. She acted very calm and made a couple of jokes about what it must be like to have a job like theirs.

"You must see all kinds in here." She laughed. "Do you have much contact with the outside world? It's quite a jungle in here! I can't imagine how you guys do this day after day. Well, I guess I'll see you guys tomorrow. They have a seventy-two-hour hold on my friend—one of those three-day legal holds. Had some sort of reaction to some drugs someone gave him. I don't really know the whole story, but I'm sure he'll be better tomorrow. Good night, guys."

They opened the door, and Air made her escape.

"Sorry, Frank, but au revoir, my buddy!"

The minute she heard the keys turn behind her, she started running down the hall. She could hear Frank yelling, "Hey, man, you don't understand! She's the one who's the fucking nutcase. Not me. You guys are blowing it!"

"Right, pal, why don't you just go back and lie down?"

"Well, at least give me back my goddamned fucking radio!"

Poor Frank. He wasn't quite sure if he would survive the night. It was his worst nightmare—being found out." Sometimes, Air realized

Frank was more fragile than she was. Or maybe it was just that he'd been around on the planet, exposed just a little longer than she had.

Frank was released the next day. When Frank would tell someone about what Air had done to him, they'd start hysterically laughing.

"Yeah sure, Frank. She was the one who checked herself in there, not you."

10

The phone rang, and Air answered.

"Hi Air, would you like to join me for lunch at the sushi bar today?" Starr asked.

"I've love to. What time do you want to meet?" Air asked.

"How about 11:30 a.m.?" Starr replied.

"Perfect, see you there."

Air and Starr had met at the Labor Day weekend party. She owned a local jewelry store in town and ordered Fred's peace symbol necklaces and earrings. As it turned out, Air and Starr had been raised just a few miles from one another in Texas. They were close in age, and each was just as wild and crazy as the other—well, maybe Starr just a little more so than Air. She was into religion and black men. Crazy with religion and wild about black men was more like it. Starr's favorite conversation was about what she knew to be true about men and their sexual desires.

"First off, Air, don't bore men with your past mistakes. The best way to deal with a man is to never tell him anything he doesn't need to know. Darling, a true lady takes off her dignity with her clothes and does her whorish best. At other times, you're as modest and dignified as your persona requires. Sweetie, everybody lies about sex," Starr would say. "The shamans are forever yacking about their snake oil miracles. If the universe has any purpose more important than a man topping a woman he loves and making a baby with her, hearty help, I've never heard of it."

They both arrived at the restaurant at the same time.

"Hey there, Starr. How are you?" Air said in a nonchalant tone, preoccupied with the thoughts about her heart.

"Hello, Air. It's good to see you."

"Starr, I'm not going to be good company today. My God, it's already halfway through the day. How dare the night start to sneak up on me so soon! I didn't get one minute's sleep last night. The darkness reminds me of what a coffin must be like and what it must be like to be in one six feet down. Nighttime, it's so damned quiet. I can't stand hearing my heart pounding."

"Too fast, huh?"

Air hated even saying the words *darkness, death,* and *heart attack.* She wouldn't let anyone around her say those words either. No one was allowed to tell her the real signs of a heart attack either. She had her own ideas about what the signs were. As long as her doctor would say, "No, Air, that's not a heart attack sign," she could calm herself down.

One time, someone told her about "referred pain"—something about a heart attack never showing up as simply chest pains. "Oh no," the person had said. "They first come disguised as pain somewhere else in your body."

Air started to have a terrible pain in her knee. She convinced herself she was having one of those, "referred pain attacks," and she looked over at Starr.

Should I say something about this to Starr? Shit, this artificial heart stuff is stealing my thunder. Maybe I should find a new anxiety like cancer or something, but I've invested too much time into this heart crap, and I just can't give up on it now!

"It chills me to the bone even on the warmest of nights, Starr. There's no way I can find the words to express how paralyzing it is. I don't even paint anymore."

"Darling, I've no idea why you let something like the nighttime get the best of you. Why, it's nothing more than the sky without the sun," Starr said, trying to console her.

"Starr, I'm trying to confide in you. I thought you'd appreciate my trust in you. I have a lot of friends I could tell this crap to, but I choose you to share my secrets with. I don't want to share this with anybody else. I thought you would understand. We seem to understand each other so well. I think it's the Texas connection. I just can't seem to stop my fear of dying."

"Sorry, sweetie. Okay, what exactly is it that's bothering you again?"

"The darkness, Starr, goddammit! The goddamn darkness! It scares the shit out of me! It has ever since I was a little girl, in fact. But now, I can't find anywhere to hide or anything to distract myself from it. Even amid the most romantic music of Keith Jarrett, even after half a liter of Bombay, and sometimes even after a couple of ten-milligram Valiums, the anxiety still has its way with me. The darkness means one thing and one thing only, and that is, I am going to die at any moment. Starr, I'm terrified."

"My God, Air. Doing this crap to your body is harmful!" Starr snapped.

"I'm such a sucker! It can poke at me with the slightest of touches, and I'll respond with the greatest of pressure on my chest. I immediately get the urge to go to the nearest ER. I panic just calculating how long the darkness is going to last. Starr, you don't have to remind me that I'm ruining my life!" Air said as she lowered her head. "I know all too well."

"Sweetie, are you sure about all this?" Starr asked, as if this was a phase Air was going through.

"What do you mean, am I sure about all this?" Air answered sarcastically. "Do you think I just want attention? That I have nothing better to do with my life than remain in a state of constant fear? To practically live in the ER, knowing that they all hate me? Shit, they just think I'm a drug addict!" she snapped.

"Okay, calm down. Well, tell me this. What is a Bombay and what the hell is a Jarrett?" Starr asked naively.

"Oh good God! Bombay is a special kind of alcohol. Gin. Jarrett is Keith Jarrett; the musician everyone is listening to these days. Where have you been?" Air said in a nasty tone.

Air leaned back in the restaurant chair and looked blankly out the window with her hand under her chin. She remembered watching her cat the night before trying to catch one of those damned dirty pigeons that were everywhere on the farm. She hated those pigeons. Even more, she hated the person who told her squabs were those dirty pigeons with a fancy name.

Isadora Duncan was the cat's name. Isa reminded Air of herself. *She's so much like me. No matter how close she comes to happiness or fortune, she misses it, just like me; neither of us can get our paws on it. That poor cat's never even experienced coughing up grass. The wind always blows in another direction just as she turns her head sideways to take a bite. Yet, just like me, she never gives up trying. You and I are real troopers, Isa. We also know how to beat dead horses.*

She looked back over across the table at Starr, who was just finishing up her sashimi. "Starr, tonight when it starts to get dark, I'll be sitting with everyone at home, smiling and acting as though everything is peachy dory creamy, while inside my head, all I'm thinking about is, any minute, I'm going drop dead. The darkness reminds me of all the promises I made to myself at the age of six and didn't fulfill."

"What? What kind of promises is a six-year-old capable of making, besides promising not to talk to strangers?" Starr asked her.

"I wanted to be a foreign exchange student and live in Paris."

"How could you have thoughts like that at that age, Air? You have to back off yourself. Besides, you still have plenty of time to go to Paris. I don't want to sound cruel, but those don't sound like real big plans or certainly big enough plans to have to die over. As I said, you're way too hard on yourself," Starr said, trying to get Air's to realize she was beating herself up needlessly.

"Time? Starr, you're out of your mind! I know one thing for sure—nobody has plenty of time!" Air leaned the chair back farther, balancing it on its two back legs. She and the chair fell over. She remained there on the floor with her eyes closed and thought, *Kill me now.*

"Airstream, are you okay? Get up. Talk to me! I can see that there are things going on in your mind that you need to get off your chest. Just not on the floor!" Starr quietly whispered. "Everyone's looking at us!"

Air got up and straightened out her clothes, "Starr, the only thing I need to get off my chest is this feeling that there's a thousand pounds of bricks on it. I can't begin to explain the feelings I have of being self-imprisoned and terrified for months now. I know everyone has demons haunting him or her. Some of us learn from our fears, and others are taken from us by drugs or suicide."

"Sweetie, you're not going to believe this, but sometimes I feel insecure too."

"You're right. I don't believe you. Your insecurities have nothing to do with forgotten promises." Air sat in the hard wood chair trembling.

I'm going to try to be strong and challenge the darkness tonight just to see what happens, Air thought.

"I always lose, Starr—always."

"Oh, Air, you just have to stand firm and say to yourself, now is the time for sleep. You need to learn how to program your mind to shut up. Sometimes, I just imagine I'm a TV and turn myself off. I actually watch myself going up to the TV and turning the power off."

"You're right, Starr, I'll try that. I knew you'd understand," Air said snidely.

"It's not so hard, sweetie. Just promise yourself you're going to wake up in the morning and talk to yourself in the mirror."

"Talk to myself in the mirror. Oh boy, that sounds like a real challenge. You know, Starr, I know you're trying to be a supportive friend, but I don't think anyone can understand what's happening to me," Air said sadly. "I'm in this alone."

Starr could never pass up an opportunity that made her come out smelling like a rose. Air chuckled out loud. *Perhaps I should really spill my guts.* Maybe it was time Starr got a reality sandwich right between her two front teeth.

"I feel as though the darkness is laughing at me 24-7. It cackles about how little time there is left to consider remembering. But it's wrong. I do remember. I can't forget how little time there is left. When the darkness comes, it whispers to me about all the hopeless situations I've found myself in. The darkness is very powerful. It knows it has the entire night to jerk me around.

"Starr, imagine not being able to sleep. It's now midnight, and you're exhausted from battling your demons, but you're too scared to close your eyes. You get out of bed and find a little electric heater. You position yourself on the floor in front of the mirrored closet and look directly at the girl you see. The heater next to you begins to get hot, and you start to relax a little. You sit there and stare at the girl in the mirror all night long. You try to imagine yourself being that girl in the mirror. She looks like she's super healthy. At about 6:00 a.m., you surrender from exhaustion and climb back into bed.

"You say to yourself, *Okay, I give up. Come and kill me! I can't take this anymore. I give up!* You're dead tired and you get a couple hours of sleep. This is how my life has been every night for months now, Starr," Air said with a pathetic tone.

"Airstream! Are you trying to tell me you're planning to die?"

"Jesus Christ, no! I'm not planning on dying! Dying's planning on dying on me!"

"Airstream, I've never told you this, but I really envy you. You seem to be one of the strongest and most courageous women I've ever met. I'm a sissy! Didn't you tell me once that your mother told you, if you ever met up with the devil, you were just to look him straight in the eyes and tell him you didn't any time to give him? Well, why don't you just imagine the darkness is the devil?"

Air just lowered her head and sensed she looked like a scared little girl. Tears fell onto her chest, and she wiped them away with a sense of hysteria. She hated to have anyone see her cry.

Air looked at Starr and tightened her lips, "There's a lot of discontentment in my life energy, Starr. Or is it that there's a lot of energy in my discontentment? Hell, all I'm sure of is that the darkness sucks up my energy and my life force. I definitely thought I'd be a famous painter by now."

"I feel so bad for you. The moment I lay my head on the pillow, out I go like a light," said Starr.

"I made my bed of thorns long ago," Air said in resignation.

"Does Frank ever help you with these attacks?"

"Hell no! In fact, he threatens me all the time," Air told her. "He tells me if I don't shut up, I'm going to be the death of him. Sometimes, I blame him for getting me into these heart attacks in the first place. Besides the forty cloves garlic chicken dish, he's always reminding me anything in life is possible. He absolutely freaks out if I wake him up in the middle of the night with an anxiety attack.

Actually, his careless attitude really pisses me off, so much that I wake him up anyway just to interrupt his sleep.

"Sometimes, when we're in bed I'll whimper for hours on purpose. That really pisses him off! Oh yes, Frank's turned out to be a real sweetie, all right. He's changed so much since we left New York. He used to be loving and completely devoted to me. Now, he's turned into a dope-smoking crazy." Air wadded up her napkin and placed it on the table.

"Well, if you had big tits and you knew Hugh Hefner, he'd stay up all night with you. Oh boy, sweetie, would you ever learn a thing or two about orgasms. I wonder if this whole heart attack stuff is related to the fact that you don't like sex. Sex is usually about love, and love usually has sex along with it."

The waiter came over and asked if she could get them anything else to eat or drink. She slammed the receipt on the table and gave them both a look of impatience. There were people waiting for a table.

"Starr, I think we're both at a point where we're mind traveling and leaving our familiar realities behind and going into the unfamiliar. It can be a lonely experience. We can lose contact with who we think we are; if we're lucky, we see a world we do not know and choose whether or not to return to who we were or become someone we don't know ourselves to be."

"Air, here's the truth as I know it. You're okay and I'm okay, no matter what. If we don't ever change one thing about ourselves for the rest of our lives, we're still going to be okay. We're still going to be able to eat, sleep, shit, screw, and do anything else we want to do. It won't matter if we grow in a certain way or don't grow in another way. We'll always be okay!" Starr said firmly.

"Sure. You got it, kiddo."

"Just one thing though, Air."

"What's that?"

"If all this story crap about heart attacks is a way to be fully self-expressed, why do you keep holding on to the same story? What is that all about?"

"I'll get back to you on that one. We need to leave. People want our table."

"Oh come on! If all this 'giving up one's bullshit' story is about living a fuller, more authentic life, why then is it that you can't see there's some huge payoff in keeping this drama of heart attacks going on? Maybe it's because suffering deeply satisfies you," Starr said meekly.

"I don't know, Starr. Some stories just have deeper taproot systems than others. For some reason, I haven't gotten the lessons or understanding of what my heart is trying to tell me. It hurts a lot. Some lessons take a few moments, others a few years, and still others require a few lifetimes," Air said, believing this was the truth about life.

"The other day, I heard someone saying the gold lies in the darkness and you have to go in there and do battle like Luke did in *Star Wars*. Remember when he fell in that dark hole and had to fight his own demons to become a Jedi warrior?"

"That might be true. If you think about having to go into a dark hole and fight your demons to be rewarded with the freedom of being able to look the devil in the eyes and not be afraid, then yes, the gold lies in the darkness," Air remarked, deep in thought about that possibility.

"Could be, Air. Think about it."

"Starr, I forgot to mention, Frank and I are thinking about moving down to Santa Cruz."

"You're kidding!" she said as she got up and grabbed her purse.

"No, I'm serious. We both have a lot of friends in Santa Cruz, and we're both tired of the country lifestyle. I can't stand being around Melinda. She hates me," Air added as the two headed out of the restaurant.

They stood in the parking lot and continued to talk for a few more minutes. The sun was very bright. Air put her hand on her forehead to keep the sun out of her eyes.

"When did this conversation about moving start?"

"Actually, we drove down to Santa Cruz last weekend."

"Wow, that's great!"

"Frank has this one friend he's known since he was a kid. This guy owns rental property just outside of Santa Cruz in a town called

Felton. We went and looked at the house, and we really liked it. It's going to be available in a month. That's perfect for us since we have so much stuff to pack."

"Oh my God," cried Starr, looking at her wristwatch. "I'm missing my dentist appointment! I've got to leave. Sorry, darling. I'm going to have to talk with you later."

"Perfect timing, Starr. Frank will be home soon. Yes, let's talk later."

Air drove home slowly. She made the turn into the driveway and saw Fred's car already there. She walked into the carriage house and found Frank in the kitchen making a sandwich.

"Hi, Frank, how was your day? I spent the afternoon with Starr at the sushi restaurant. I told her we were thinking of moving to Santa Cruz. The more I think about moving, I really do want to take another look at that house your friend has. I think it would be perfect for us. I need to get away from Melinda."

"That's a hoot you should say that since I called Tim today. I asked whether the house was still available. I told him we wanted to move and that I planned on talking with you about it tonight."

"Good grief, Frank. It's a no-brainer. Let's just do it! I really want out of here. I have always loved Santa Cruz."

"Okay, I'll tell Fred tomorrow on the drive to work. I have no clue what I will do for work down there."

"We'll figure something out. Don't worry. Good things will come from this move," Air said reassuringly.

"Well, the other thing I was thinking about is that my parents have a summer home along the coast in Santa Cruz. None of the family stays there anymore. I know we could live rent-free there for a couple of years."

"That's great! Oh my God, that's perfect! Does it have a fireplace?"

❧ 11 ❧

The conversation about the move to Santa Cruz happened the next morning during Fred and Frank's ride to work. Frank was looking at the view of the pastures and the cows as they drove down to the East Bay. He thought about how much he loved country living, but living close to the ocean was just as appealing.

"Fred, Air and I have been thinking about moving to Santa Cruz. We can live at my parents' summer home for at least two years without paying rent. That would help me out a lot."

"Hey, man, that sounds great. I'm happy for you two. Does that mean you won't be working with me anymore?"

"Yeah, I don't want to drive over that coastal range of mountains every day to get back up to the Bay Area. It's just too much stress on me."

"Okay, so when are you guys planning to move?"

"We're going to start next weekend."

"Wow, that's soon," said Fred as he turned his head and looked vacantly out at the rolling hills and pastureland. "What a difference of scenery, huh? Farmland to the ocean."

It was an awkward moment for both of them. Frank turned and looked out the passenger window at the grazing cows on the hills for about five miles.

"Yes, it will be. We've sure enjoyed the isolation we've had living with you and Melinda, though. I can't thank you enough. You know—I think everything's going to work out fine. I think I'm safe now. You and Mel have really been a godsend, Fred," Frank said, the obligation he felt clear in his voice.

"Frank, we love you, man. You're family. We'll miss you and Air," Fred said with a hint of both gratefulness and sadness in his voice.

That night when Frank came home, he told Air, "On the way into work today, I told Fred we're moving down to Santa Cruz and that we're going to live in my parents' summer home rent-free. He seemed a bit taken off guard. I told him that we would probably rent a truck this coming weekend and move over the next two weekends."

"Oh, Frank, I am so glad you told him. I will start packing up the house tomorrow. There are still a lot of boxes out in the barn I haven't even unpacked yet from New York." She looked around the carriage house. "All we really have to pack is our clothing and personal stuff. I can have everything packed in a couple of days. I'll go buy some boxes from U-Haul tomorrow. We should reserve a truck for this weekend. I think we can do the move in one weekend," Air remarked.

"Fred told me he knows a young kid a couple of farms over that could use some extra money. We can hire him to help load and then drive the truck. He can follow us down and drive the truck back up here."

"Very cool," Air said as she smiled at him. "Very cool."

Frank called and reserved a truck for the weekend. By the end of the Saturday, with the help of Fred and the young fellow, Sam, the truck was loaded and ready to go. They said their good-byes and headed down to the coast of Santa Cruz. The drive was only about three hours. They left at nine in the morning and arrived at Frank's family home at one in the afternoon. Traffic was a bit heavy since it was a beautiful, sunny day, and lots of people from the East Bay drove down to Santa Cruz to go to the boardwalk on the weekends. Frank had forgotten about this. Besides, the truck couldn't go faster than about sixty miles per hour.

Sam helped unload and drove the truck back up to Petaluma at the end of the day. Over the next two days, Air unpacked all the boxes. She set up her studio in one of the back bedrooms that had lots of light. The house was secluded among a grove of redwood trees and had a huge front deck that overlooked the ocean. The house was just seven years old and fully furnished. The kitchen was large with lots of cabinets and had a large butcher block table in the middle of the room. The butcher block had been in the family for a generation. Apparently, it had belonged to Frank's grandmother and had been used for cleaning freshly killed ducks, peasants, and wild boars.

Frank's grandparents were farmers from Nova Scotia and had moved to Colorado when his mother was a baby. The living room was very cozy with ranch-style furniture. Almost all the furniture was leather with wooden arms and backs. Handmade quilts were thrown over all the couches and chairs. The best part of the room was the fireplace. Air loved fireplaces since they were a source of heat that would calm her down during her anxiety attacks. She'd already noticed there was a least one cord of oak stacked outside the house.

Trains and train paraphernalia could be found everywhere in the house. Frank's grandmother had loved trains, and his mother had inherited her entire collection. The walls were covered with paintings and photos of trains. The hallway between the kitchen and bathroom had a bookcase full of books about trains. The curtains in both the kitchen and the front room had trains printed on the fabric.

Air and Frank made themselves at home immediately. It was one of those homes that felt just like being at Grandma's house, and you just instantly felt relaxed and safe in it. The view of the ocean was spectacular. They didn't have to open the windows to hear the crash of the waves. It was a dream for Air. She loved the sunny days and cool evenings. The house was set back far enough from the road that the traffic didn't bother them.

They had just enough money saved that Frank didn't need to look for work right away. They were on a tight budget, though. They spent their time visiting friends or having friends over for dinner parties. During the days, they both lost themselves in their own art projects. Frank had started drawing again, and Air spent most of her time knitting sweaters. She rode her bike along the coast daily, and each evening they would take a walk along to the beach to watch the sunset.

One morning, Frank looked around the front room for his favorite drawing pen. He noticed there were cats everywhere. They were either cleaning themselves or playing with one another. He looked up toward the bookshelf where the leader of the pack, Dandelion, was perched. He also noticed a book he'd never seen before.

"*Fairy Tales from an Animal Farm!*" Frank laughed and said, "I should have written that book."

Airstream was constantly trying to save Balthazar, one of Dandelion's offspring, from being made into kitty soup or kitty jerky—whichever was quicker, as far as Frank was concerned. He'd had it with the little kitty parties.

"They're just being cats Frank!"

"All seventeen of them?" he said sarcastically. "That's easy for you to say since it's *my National Geographic's* from 1904 through 1945 they've shit all over, *my* drawings they piss on, *my* favorite hats they sleep in and get cat hair all over, *my* closet they bat dead mice around in, and *my* shoes they leave just the rat's asses they don't eat in. It's *my* desk they leave gopher puke and hairballs on, and best of all, it's *my* side of the bed that all fucking female cats decide to have had their litters on!"

"Oh, Frank, come on; take it as a sign of endearment. They love you more than me."

"Shit! I should have been Conrad Lorenz's grandfather, blind as a bat with a fucked-up nose, and accepted the fact when I invited one cat into my home for brunch while preparing dessert, she suddenly gave birth to seven fucking kittens and I just didn't have it in me to kick her out! The next thing you know; I'm living with seventeen cats. Now tell me, Air, how does one cat lead to seventeen cats? This is exactly why we don't have kids! Jesus Christ, I'd have probably been better off with kids. At least they don't have any goddamned fleas!"

"Look at my legs, Air! I'm out of here. They outnumber me. Seventeen cats; three coy fish; one part-time cricket; two hundred houseplants; a crazy, ole lady who packs her bags at least twice a week, telling me she's leaving again, who checks herself into the local ER more often than the bills come; not to mention a constant collections of creatures from the unknown being brought in for viewing by Dandelion just before our dinner.

"And gee, then there's Dandy's daughter, Oona Blakely O'hara. What's it been now, seven tarantulas, five dragonflies, three five-foot gopher snakes, endless birds trying hopelessly to loosen themselves from the clutches of those razor-sharp teeth of hers."

"Dandy taught her well, Frank," Air said.

"Now, there's a case. She's the only cat I've ever seen who can walk across the room, fall over on all fours, and then turn to see if anyone was looking. She won't eat caviar unless it's served on toast with chopped egg white and, of course, the Bermuda onion!

"And, by the way, I know you ordered Dandelion an Easter bonnet the other day. I saw you go into Paralisa's, and I know that's a specialty store just for pets. So don't try and lie your way out of this one, Air."

"Frank, Dandelion was pissed you didn't come through with your promise to buy her a cigarette holder and a pair of rhinestone sunglasses. In fact, she said you tried to pass some twice frozen shrimp off on her instead. So, I figure we're getting a deal. The bonnet is a Barbie design, Dandy's favorite, and was only forty-nine cents."

Air stared at Frank. *I wonder if the good times with Frank outweigh the bad times. When will I stop messing around with words—trying to write worthy poems, secretly hanging out in bars behind Frank's back, smoking cigarettes and drinking more than my fair share of house wine? When will I put an end to the incessant daydreaming of being a famous artist, engaging in cosmic dramas, reading free newspapers that take up way too much of my earth life time? When will I stop staring out the window and wondering, isn't there more to life than this?*

Maybe, just maybe, I'll experience something worth living for and something worth dying for during my lifetime. I wonder if anyone would recognize me if I keep on forgetting my name and imagining I am disappearing among my clothes, since most of Frank's friends think I'm so shy?

She knew the answer to all these thoughts was love and truth. The truth was, she was simply not in love with Frank. She never was, and she never would be.

I am so fucking bored with Frank and his never-ending conversations about his grandfather, Agmond, his white beard, and how he loved sardines. I mean, who gives a damn? Air thought. *Oh and let me not forget Frank's parents. They visit too many weekends, and I'm sick of listening to the same stories about his grandmother, Agmonda, and her incredible train collection.*

"Trains just aren't what they used to be, darling," Frank's mother would say. "Oh, I remember the day when I took my first train ride with Frank's grandmother. Everyone was so dressed up, and the dining car was beautiful. The linen was so white and crisp. The sterling silver was as shiny as the sun and utterly gorgeous. I am so thankful I inherited her collection of all the old train books, train clocks, train aprons, special train buttons, train towels, train belt buckles, and train dishes, but I am sure you've seen almost everything here. Oh don't let me forget the old, gold train watches she collected. They are absolutely priceless!"

God, kill me now, Air thought. *Who in their right mind will ever believe I rode around in limos almost every day when I lived in New York City, had dinner with Frank Sinatra, and rode the elevator up and down with the Beatles. Who's going to believe I hung out at the Chelsea Hotel with Leonard Cohen and George Harrison, eating shrimp in green sauce and drinking sangria? And let's not forget I used to hang out with Bob Dylan.* She sighed. *From riches to rags, twice in my life—first when I left Texas and then when I left New York.*

I wonder what really happened in New York between Frank and the president of that record company, Gary Schinn, she mused. *I never questioned Frank's explanation of why we had to leave so suddenly.* She'd never understand why Frank was willing to give up such a rewarding career to just hide out, smoke dope, roll his own tobacco, listen to jazz, and drink cheap red wine.

Air sat there in a state of disbelief still staring at him. *I'm sick of being ignoring,* she realized. She was sick of him spending hours at his drafting table building another model Norton motorcycle, only to start a 1915 Hicks engine that would eventually take him another year to build. She was tired of living on fifteen cents a day and eating chicken gizzards and hearts. *And fuck, rolling our own cigarettes with cheap Top tobacco. It's so lame,* she lamented. *He used to pay me so much attention. Now, I feel like I'm invisible.*

She was completely over the edge with Frank's continuous farting, his endless complaining about running out of pot, and the never-ending stories of "them" and how "they" were out to get him.

"Hey, Air, just look at my legs!"

Air looked down at Frank's legs. They were covered with solid scabs and bloody scratches. She'd decided to buy him flea collars, one for each ankle. He put them on, saying he'd try anything once.

God, he's such a sight! Those long, skinny, white legs and black ankle bracelets.

"Black was the only color choice I had, Frank," she apologized.

A couple of days later, Air read in the local paper about some poor soul who had attached a flea collar around his neck because of the so-called "flea epidemic." He'd had a severe allergic reaction to it and suffocated to death! Apparently, he had hives down his throat, and they'd cut off his ability to breathe. He lived alone except for the forty-five cats he owned. The police reported that the minute they'd entered the guy's house their legs were solid black with fleas.

Thank God Frank didn't have any reactions.

In fact, he'd gone out and gotten a couple more, one for each wrist. If anyone would remark about the "new jewelry," he'd just mumble something about the "fucking fleas" and keep on going.

Frank was a pain in the ass, no pun intended, since he was now spending a lot of his time in the bathroom.

"I have to take it slow because of my hemmies," he'd shout.

Air didn't know what "hemmies" were and somehow sensed she didn't want to know. She tried to convince herself he hid out in the bathroom because it was the only place in the house where the "rest of them" couldn't bug him. Sometimes, she'd find smut magazines hidden in the cabinet, so she never really knew what Frank was up to. His moans could have been from his "grapes," as he referred to his hemmies, or they could have been from him having orgasms.

Frank was in the bathroom now.

Unfortunately, the cat box was in the bathroom. Air tried the door, but it was locked.

"My God, Frank, could you hurry it up in there?" Air called out, setting down newspapers just in case one of the cats decided it couldn't wait any longer. "There's a waiting line out here! Onna is circling close to the door, which always means she has to use the kitty box, and Dandelion is actually pawing at the door. Can't you hear her? How much longer are you going to be, Frank? I think she's going to piss or shit any moment. It's just a matter of time before she pukes up that Geisha tuna you gave her this morning. I told you not to give her the tuna with oil. She can only eat the tuna with spring water."

Both Dandelion and Oona were absolutely beautiful cats. They each had long, thick, pure white fur with sparkling blue eyes. They were best friends, always by each other's side.

Air dropped to the floor and tried to soothe Dandy. Oona began rubbing her body against Air over and over. Again, Air felt the pain of living a life of hell with no direction. She was beginning to feel like she couldn't breathe and started quickly praying. *Please, God, I haven't had an anxiety attack in over a month. I just cannot live in fear again.*

"My God, Frank, I cannot believe our lives have turned out like this! I'm going to start having anxiety attacks again! We used to have so much fun going out and eating at restaurants and then going to listen to music. You know, there's a great restaurant down at the wharf that has a live band on the weekends. We could go to the movies or even start going on some weekend getaways. What do you think? It would be fun, Frank. How about this weekend? We could drive up the coast to Jenner. We could stay the night and drive back on Sunday. That sounds like so much fun. I'm tired of doing nothing but hanging out here day after day. We don't even have dinner parties anymore. It makes me sad."

Listening to Frank take a dump was as painful for Air as it was for him. The moaning was torturous. Every once in a while, she'd swear she could hear him crying. She hated the thought of cooking and feeding him. She felt like she was "putting another log on the fire." She knew that, right after dinner, he'd head to the bathroom, and the moaning and anguished sighs of, "Oh Jesus," would start all over again.

She wondered if Frank's mom would still say she wished she'd fed him more as a child if she lived with him now. She approached the subject of him going to a doctor and getting his "grapes" checked out. Oh God, just saying that made him moan even louder.

"Airstream, promise me you'll never do anything like that to me!"

Sick and tired of his icky underwear, the moaning, and the incessant pacing back and forth because "things weren't ready to move yet," the day came when Air couldn't bear it any more. So instead of picking up another one of his "soiled" undies, she picked up the phone book instead.

She wondered if there were any local doctors who looked at buttholes. Hell, she didn't even know what to look under. She considered "bloody underwear," with subtitles of "colors," "grapes," "moaning," "hemmies," or "deep sighs."

She continued to turn the pages of the phone book.

For some reason, she thought back to the trip they'd made to Los Angeles right after they'd returned to California. Frank had wanted to visit some of his friends in LA and show off his rare, old VW van that he had put in storage while in New York. After about an hour of driving, he'd started in with the deep sighs. Having no idea how much pain came from sitting on his "hemmies", Air had kept quiet and offered him another hit of pot. He'd nodded yes. Once again, they had both been completely stoned.

Frank had suddenly taken an exit off the freeway.

"What's up, Frank? Are you hungry or do we need gas?" she'd asked

"No, we need to find a drug store fast," he'd said, a sense of urgency in his voice.

"There's a Long's Drugs over there," Air had said, pointing to the store.

They'd parked. Apparently too stoned and in pain from sitting, Frank had turned to Air and said, "Air would you mind going in since my legs are sore from all the driving? I don't feel like walking."

"Frank, it would do you good to walk around."

When he hadn't responded, Air had realized he didn't want to let on how much his "grapes" were killing him from sitting. She figured that, besides barely being able to drive from being so stoned, he couldn't walk with this pain.

"No, I don't mind," she'd said with a sigh. "But I'm super stoned. What do you want me to get?"

"Here's a ten. Buy me some Preparation H and get us some condoms."

"Okay," Air said innocently and walked toward the pharmacy.

Again, Airstream's naivety had come into play. She had no clue what a condom was, much less what Preparation H was. If Frank had said, "Buy us a couple of rubbers," she'd have understood, but he didn't and she'd never heard of a rubber being called a condom. If she'd known what Preparation H was, she'd would have said, "Hell no, I'm not going in there. You go!"

Air had opened the door to the drugstore and looked around. It was completely empty other than the one clerk on duty, a sweet, older lady. Air walked up and down all the aisles looking for something called condoms. By now, she couldn't even remember the name of the other thing she was supposed to buy.

The woman approached her. "Can I be of help, my dear?"

"Yes, thank you very much," Air replied. "I'm looking for something called con, con, condominiums or something close to that I think and then something else called, Operation H I think?" she said in an embarrassed tone.

The clerk looked into Air's eyes and smiled. She asked if Air meant "condoms" and "Preparation H?"

"Yes, that's it! Oh, thank you. I'd totally forgotten what I was in here for. They're for my friend who's out in the car. We've been driving all day."

"Well, come with me. You have many choices of condoms."

When the little old lady took Air to the section of what Air knew to be "rubbers," her face turned red. Then when she discovered that Preparation H was some kind of ointment used for inflammation of the asshole, it was all too much for her. She fainted.

When Air became conscious, Frank was helping her to stand up. Air and Frank had been smoking dope for hours. She was overwhelmed with a sense of panic and dizziness. She remembered the sound of her head hitting the floor and the little old lady reassured her everything was fine and helping her to steady herself. The clerk asked Frank if he wanted her to call an ambulance.

"Oh, God, no," he replied loudly.

Frank handed the clerk the ten and asked if she could package up their purchase as quickly as possible.

"Of course," the woman replied. "Then let me at least get her a glass of water."

I left that store with tears rolling down my face, she recalled. *I was so embarrassed. Damned Frank.* She shook her head and continued to look through the phone book at all the different categories of physicians and finally found "Anal Specialists."

"Oh my God!" she said out loud. *Anal Specialists? Is there really such a thing or person? Why not just call themselves butthole specialists? Good God! Who'd want to be a butthole doctor?"* she wondered.

Only one of the listings was local—the offices of Drs. Munch, Dick, and Snook. *Now this can't possibly be for real*, she thought. *Butthole Specialists with names like Munch, Dick, and Snook? How in the hell am I going to tell Frank I've made an appointment for him to see "anal specialists" with names like these? I'm way too stoned for this,"* she thought.

She decided to go do the dishes and think about this later.

12

The next day when Frank got home, he ran straight to the bathroom and slammed the door.

"Frank, I need to talk to you. I need to tell you something straightaway."

"Not now, Air. My hemmies are killing me!"

"They're killing me too, Frank! I can't take it anymore!"

"What the hell are you talking about? I'm the one with the asshole that feels like someone's got a pair of pliers and with every move I make, they're twisting my asshole just a little bit tighter and pinching the fuck out of me!" he yelled.

"I hate to steal your thunder, Frank, but I feel the same way. Today, I made you an appointment with some doctors called anal specialists. You have to get checked out, Frank. This has been going on far too long. Either that or you get me a house with two bathrooms and a washer and dryer. I refuse to do your underwear in public anymore!"

She heard him take one deep sigh and ask, "When is the appointment?"

"It's Friday, in that big medical building in town, at ten in the morning," Air answered.

She stood outside the bathroom door waiting for him to yell about how she'd broken her promise to never do this to him. She could hear heavy breathing for about five minutes.

"Thanks, Frank. I know you're going to be fine. Honestly, I'm sure you don't have anything seriously wrong with your health. You just need some medicine."

Frank was convinced he had butthole cancer. He was sure that meant surgery and that the doctors would say, "Your hemmies are fine, Frank, but we're sorry to inform you that you have butthole cancer."

Frank was so paranoid.

Friday came, and Frank was a nervous wreck. His grapes were killing him, and he could barely walk. When he did, he cried and moaned at the same time.

Air hadn't told him the doctors' names yet. She couldn't keep a straight face, and anytime she laughed about his hemmies, he'd get really pissed off and wouldn't talk to her for hours. She didn't want to do anything that might jeopardize getting Frank to those doctors. She thought she'd wait until the last minute to tell him.

They drove downtown and parked in the lot. Frank looked around and saw the lot was full. "What the hell are so many cars parked here for?"

"It doesn't matter, Frank. Let's just go in and find out where your doctor's office is located. They entered a brick building with a large lobby. Air looked at the case hanging on the wall with the doctors' names. "Down the hall, Frank."

They arrived at the door of the doctors' offices. She watched his face as he read the names on the door.

"You've got be shitting me! This is a joke, isn't it? Munch, Dick, and Snook?"

"Oh, Frank, forget about the names. What the hell does it matter what their names are? Remember the time you wanted to change your name to Mr. Pig because you were convinced no one would have the balls to simply say Mr. Pig? You said they'd all try to pronounce it like it was a European name. Like, Mr. Peeg. This isn't much different."

"Hey, wait a minute; it's not your asshole that's going to be inspected. I won't have anyone with names like Munch, Dick, and Snook probing around in mine!"

Air quickly opened the door and walked in. The waiting room was huge. It was at least four times the size of any waiting room she'd ever seen. Besides that, at least twenty people were waiting. Each of them was standing up, swaying back and forth. Air looked at all of them and then at the empty chairs. There must have been at least fifteen empty chairs.

Frank limped over and took his standing place next to a man who had to have been at least eighty years old and started humming.

"Frank, my God! What the hell are you doing?" whispered Air.

"Humming."

"I realize that! But—oh sorry, Frank, I'll try not to use that word anymore today. *But* if you don't stop, you're going to have everyone in this joint farting. They'll probably moan with each passing fart, and I can't take it, Frank! Do you hear me? I can't take it! I can't take twenty people pacing, farting, and moaning! It is way too much for me. I have no clue in heaven why your humming makes people fart, but I know for some reason it does, so please stop humming!"

"Give it up, Airstream! Don't try and take responsibility for my asshole!"

"I mean it, Frank! *Stop* the humming!" whispered Air a little more loudly and with a tone that was more demanding.

"Air, people love to fart in public, especially old people."

"Frank, I'm warning you. I'd just like to sit down and relax, but I can't as long as you keep this up."

Farting was his way of diverting folks from their ailments. He had told Air long ago that humming was a way to break the tension (or, rather, the wind). When people smelled Frank's farts, they forgot the pain of their assholes and focused on the awful smell for a few moments. The room would go quiet, and everyone would scan the room to find the culprit. Air noticed Frank was starting to get a lot of attention from the group of suffers. She overheard a couple saying they didn't believe Frank was sick at all, just another garden variety of crazy wanting drugs. The real sufferers wanted to see him removed as quickly as possible. Some of the patients acted as though the office was sacred terrain, hallowed ground on which only real hemmie sufferers could stand. It was as though they recognized one another from previous appointments and, thus, had already accepted each other into the group. Frank was a newbie. Air surveyed the group.

It seemed to her that Frank was a hemmie himself; he irritated the group almost instantly. Having hemorrhoid problems was like belonging to some secretive group of people. It reminded Air of AA, where everyone was in agreement regarding anonymity. No one knew Frank, and Air was keenly aware of the tension in the room.

Frank kept up with the group, moaning in between his humming. Farting in public was one of his greatest pleasures in life. The eighty-year-old man looked knowingly Frank's way with a smile.

That guy's an old fart himself, Air thought.

Air realized she was the only person among the twenty people in the room who was able sit down without being in great pain. She decided there was no use in trying to get Frank to stop with the farting, the humming, and the satisfying glances at the old man. The instant her butt made contact with the seat of the chair, everyone in the entire room moaned and sighed in unison.

"Oh Jesus, I'm trapped in a den of group suffers! And I thought Frank was bad. God, give me the strength to make it through this," Air said out loud, knowing no one could hear her above their own moaning.

The group continued with the rocking back and forth, shifting his or her weight from one leg to the other. She smiled at them but received only grimaces and glares in return. A sense of guilt came over her for not having a bad case of the hemmies herself. Oddly, she felt left out and lonely sitting all by herself. She tried to sit extremely still because she had noticed that, with her every move came a moan, groan, or sigh from the crowd.

There were more men than women. Most of the women were pregnant. Air couldn't figure out why that was the case. What was with all these people? Didn't they eat right or wipe theirs butts properly?

Out of the blue, Air remembered being in the car with D. J. They were on one of the exploratory jaunts to the Goodwill. She recalled that the prized dog, Kingie, had been with them. Suddenly, D. J. slammed on the brakes; almost rear-ending the car ahead of them and abruptly, causing Kingies anal glands to release a god-awful, foul smell.

"That smell is perfectly na-chur-elle. It happens whenever an animal gets re-elle scared. Some people just fart when they get scared. Airstream, honey, people who wear suits have all the time in the world to take a shit. They're in no hurry, so they never have to strain. They never get butthole problems," D. J. stated as a matter of fact; and continued driving.

Air became conscious that, if she had seen any of these people in a grocery store, she'd never have guessed their assholes were killing them. She was sure none of them would ever cop to straining or having a bad case of nerves either. "Oh, I'm eating my bran religiously," they'd say.

Frank, on the other hand, looked bizarre and was definitely a candidate for hemmies. He looked like a stress mess. He had on one of his infamous beanies, and his hair was sticking out all over the place as usual. She wanted to leave, except she knew Frank would follow. And he'd miss his calling—either by doing a solo farting act or solo humming or solo moaning, whichever would be most appreciated by the group. It seemed people were now competing with each other, in terms of who was complaining the loudest, each trying to steal the other's thunder.

Frank believed his humming had special effects on doctors too, especially when it was coupled with his standard I-can't-take-any-drugs routine. "I just usually hum through the pain," he would tell them. This usually got him an immediate shot of some kind of painkiller, plus a prescription that reduced him to a drone state, which he loved.

Frank slowly left his place in line and walked over to Air. In a tone of total seriousness, he whispered to her, "I just thought of something, Air. When it's my time for the eternal cruise, I'd like all my friends to hum at my funeral. They can fart, hum, and moan at will. Of course, no farting, humming, or moaning will be allowed during the reading of my will!"

"Frank, stop it!" Air snapped loudly. "You're not dying, and you don't have butt cancer! There's nothing wrong with you except a bad case of hemmies. Jesus Christ, Frank, we'd all be so lucky," she said with disdain.

The group became anxious as Air and Frank quarreled. One of the pregnant women asked, "Could you lower your voices, please?"

Frank's name was called next, and the group seemed elated with joy with the removal of the irritant, Frank.

They followed the nurse down a hall and into Dr. Snook's office. "Wait here," the nurse said as she closed the door.

Air looked up and noticed a shelf about a foot from the ceiling that ran around the entire room. Displayed on all the shelves was a macabre collection of antique bleeding bowls that were used in the eighteenth and nineteenth century for bloodletting practices. There was a framed notation regarding the bowls, basically informing Dr. Snook's patients that his collection consisted of a variety of bowls from antiquity through the nineteenth century. There were bowls made from stone, pottery, tin, china, and pewter, though there were a few pieces that Air could see were silver. She could see that some of the bowls had inner concentric rings that she guessed must have been used to measure the amount of blood. Some of the bowls were displayed on their sides so she could see that they each had an arc taken out of the side, which again she guessed must have been for pouring out the blood after the letting ordeal. It was the tackiest thing Air could imagine. Here was poor Frank with his asshole bleeding, and they both had to sit and look at these bowls.

"Air," he complained, "I'm bleeding as it is. I don't need to see his fucking blood bowl collection. And who the hell collects blood bowls anyway? You don't think he's going to try and drain me into one of those bowls do you, Air?"

"God no! They don't drain hemorrhoids, Frank. And what would you expect an anal specialist to collect anyway, Frank? GI Joe action figures?"

The door opened, and Dr. Snook walked into the room. He was a tall, large, older man with white hair and a long, white beard. He wore round glasses and was dressed in a floor-length linen gown that was tied just a little to tightly. Air noticed he had very thick soles on his shoes and wondered if he had feet problems. He introduced himself.

"Hello there, Sonny," he said to Frank. "I'm Dr. Snook. Why don't you drop your drawers and lie on your side over on the table. The pretty little lady can sit down here with me and observe," he added. "She just might learn a thing or two."

He might as well have said, "Sit downwind," since Frank hadn't farted in about ten minutes, Air mused. *Poor Frank. He looks so ridiculous lying on that table with his ass stuck way up in the air.*

Dr. Snook positioned two chairs at the end of the examination table; one for him and one for Air. She looked closely at the table and realized it was handmade. It seemed to be a combination of a dentist chair and an adjustable hospital bed. She looked closer at the straps Dr. Snook had put on Frank to keep him in an awkward position for his exam. She gasped as she realized they were car seat belts!

Somehow, she felt responsible for this humiliating situation. Of course, Air was used to taking the blame. She was always the one who was upsetting Frank, causing his hemmies to act up, according to him and all his friends. But this was a bizarre scene, and it didn't feel right.

Hell, we might as well hang Frank up as if he's a dartboard and just take our best shot, Doc, thought Air.

Dr. Snook was beginning to seem like a crotchety old fart. He mumbled to himself about how he wasn't having a very good day. "I've had to see too many patients today. The front desk always overbooks me," he said under his breath, but Air could hear him perfectly.

Frank started humming again, and Air gave him the evil eye whenever he lifted his head and looked her way. Actually, that was quite a feat, since his head was so low and his ass was so high. Frank's face was beet red from being hung upside down. Air thought his head was beginning to look like a blood bowl. *Jesus.*

Dr. Snook pulled up a chair for Air to join him in his exam. Before she knew it, there they were, the two of them, both staring straight into Frank's asshole, or Frank's very own blood bowl.

Frank continued to hum and moan.

Dr. Snook looked over at Air as though she was his assistant and said, "Young lady, you see this here finger?" He held up the first finger of his right hand.

Air quickly realized this whole scene was way too bizarre and wondered if it was even legal. She wished she could go out to the car and smoke a joint. She questioned how Frank could have created such a drama she now found herself in. It was a scene right out of a Lizzy Borden horror film.

"See this here finger, little lady? It's been in and out of a lot of anal canals. I don't trust them fancy new gadgets. This here finger tells me everything I need to know. Never let me down yet! This was the way medicine was done a hundred years ago, and it worked."

Air couldn't believe someone who'd seen so many assholes in his career didn't just call Frank's asshole an asshole. What was the point of being so proper and referring to his asshole as an "anal canal" after fifty years on the job? Hell, after all that time, you'd think he'd be comfortable with calling it like it was. Air was in total shock. She wanted to smoke a joint so badly. This was just too surreal.

"Hey there, little lady. Don't miss this!"

Dr. Snook didn't bother putting on gloves. In fact, he made a point of not putting gloves on. Slowly, he stuck his index finger up into Frank's asshole, or "anal canal," as the case may be, and moved it around a bit.

Frank cried out in pain.

"Hang in there, little buddy."

He pulled his finger out and put it to his nose.

"Jesus Gods! I'm out of here!" Air screamed.

In Air's mind, the tape started to play, *"Mademoiselle, would you like to smell this lovely bouquet? It's a 1966 Chateau La Tour de la Frank. It was a great year!"*

"Calm down!" Dr. Snook said. "Everything's just fine. See here, little lady? I just learned everything I need to know about your boyfriend. He's as healthy as a horse; just needs to relax. I'm just real glad I didn't find any foreign obstacles."

"I beg your pardon?" Air sheepishly said. "What do you mean foreign obstacles?

"Obstacles! I never know what I might find up an anal canal nowadays. Nothing surprises me anymore."

Air had no idea what he was referring to and didn't want to.

Suddenly, Dr. Snook noticed Frank's "friend."

"Friend" was what Air always called this cylindrical mole Frank had growing on his hip. When Air first noticed Frank's mole, she was reminded of discovering James' mole on his ear. *What's with me and moles?* The mole was about half an inch long. Frank named it "Jimmie." Jimmie and Frank had been friends since elementary school. As a child, Frank would talk to Jimmie when he was in bed at night. Sometimes he'd make references to Jimmie and what *his* feelings were on certain matters.

"Listen here, Sonny. You have to get rid of this mole!" Dr. Snook said. "The little lady here can do it for you. It's easy and painless and in your own best interest."

Dr. Snook turned to Air. "When you get home, take some silk thread and tie a knot around the base of the mole real tight."

Air stood there processing the information she'd just received.

"That will cut off the circulation of blood to the critter. And before you know it, it'll dry up and just fall right off."

Please, God, kill me now, Air thought as she slowly turned back toward Frank.

Dr. Snook walked over to the sink and washed his finger with great care. Frank stayed on the table as though he'd received very bad news, like when someone you really care about dies suddenly.

"You can get down now, Sonny. We're all through here. You're as healthy as a horse. I'm going to prescribe some medicine. Take it for about three months, and you'll be fine."

Air loved it when really old men called men who were in their late thirties, young man or sonny. She was preparing herself for the scene she imagined Frank was going to put her through when they got out to the car. She knew Frank was completely a basket case by now and would probably take it out on her. After all, she had promised to never do this to him.

"Come over here, little lady. Now, I want you to just take a look at some of these things. They're just a few of the obstacles I was referring to earlier—things I have found up inside different anal canals."

He brought out a shoebox that was full of oddities. Air looked into the box. She was stunned. The box held two 100-watt light bulbs; one twenty-inch, white beeswax candle; and about fifteen golf balls. She sensed these "found obstacles" had something to do with a very different lifestyle than anything she'd ever known.

"You see what I mean, little lady? You just never know."

"No sir, I don't see what you mean," Air gasped. "Are you into golf? And, are you preparing for a blackout?"

Her mind screamed, *Are you simply out of your fucking mind or just a fucking weirdo?* She realized the less she said, the quicker they could get out of there.

"Well, sonny, I'll call you when the results come in. But from the smell, I'd bet my last bottom's dollar you're just fine. No pun intended, young man. I mean with the last bottom's dollar bit."

Frank could barely walk. He was speechless and exhausted.

Air grabbed her purse and Frank's coat, and together walked out the door and down the hall. No words were spoken between either of them. They drove home in silence.

Frank pulled into their driveway and turned the car off. He turned to Air and asked, "Air, do you have any silk thread?"

They went inside, and Air headed straight to her studio. She found her silk thread, and she knotted off Jimmy.

That night, Frank had a nightmare. He dreamed he was in bed sleeping with Air. Instead of Jimmie drying up and falling off, it was Frank's circulation that got cut off. Frank saw himself dry up and fall to the floor, leaving Jimmie in bed with Air.

The next morning, Frank took the thread off, saying he'd thought it over and he'd really miss Jimmie. "Jimmie and I go way back. Fuck that doctor! Jimmie and I are going to be together for a long time!"

"That's fine, Frank. I like Jimmie, too. I've gotten used to having him around. You're right; things wouldn't be the same without Jimmie."

About a week later, Frank received his test results. Dr. Snook wrote a note saying, "Told you so, sonny! There's nothing wrong with you except a bad case of nerves. Try to relax and take your medication."

Enclosed was a prescription for 100 ten-milligram Valiums.

"Oh, this is great, Frank!"

Frank looked at Air and, with a smirk on his face, said, "It was the humming. It always works."

13

Frank was up drinking coffee when Air walked into the kitchen the next morning.

"Air, are you hungry for anything? A croissant maybe?"

"Yeah. That sounds really good. I think I'd like a couple of eggs, too—sunny-side up."

Frank set his coffee down immediately and stared at her. "When was your last period?"

"Why?"

"Because you hate eggs, remember?"

"Oh yeah, that's right. But they sound so good, especially with a croissant and some fig jam."

"Oh God, Air, I bet you're pregnant!" Frank exhaled loudly.

Air thought about it for a moment. He was right. She couldn't stand eggs or cottage cheese, and suddenly she felt like she couldn't get enough of either.

The phone rang. Air got "the feeling" it was her mother, since her Southern spider senses were going haywire.

"That's for me. It's my mother. She's going to tell me I'm pregnant."

Air picked up the phone. "Good morning, Mother."

"Airstream, honey, how did ya know it was me?"

"You taught me well, Mom. What's up?"

"Wh-elle, I've been just sittin' hear a readin' this here book called *Fa-Rude*."

"You've been reading what, Mother?'

"*Fa-Rude!*"

"Oh, you mean, *Freud*."

"Wh-elle, that's what I said, honey!"

"Oh, uh-huh, so what's up?" Air groaned.

"Wh-elle, I've read this here first chapter three times, and I've come to the conclusion that readin's fer the winna-time."

"Okay, reading is for the wintertime. Is that what you called to tell me, Mom?"

"No, not really. I had a couple of things on my mind. One is, you know you're pregnant, don'tcha?"

"Yes, Mom, I just found out. Frank told me, and now you're telling me. Okay, I'm pregnant. Anything else?"

"You know, honey, I was sittin' here in the kitchen just a readin' away when I heard sumthin' a callin' to me. At first, it was like a real faint voice. It kept saying, 'Little Janie, Little Janie, come over here. We need ya.'

"Wh-elle, Airstream, honey, I looked around, and I didn't see nobody. I looked outside and there wasn't nobody, so I went back into the kitchen and listened real close. The voices were a comin' from over near the sink. I went over to the sink and looked around. Air, honey, I ain't a kiddin' ya, it was kinda spookie-like. There was this here pa-lant in the windasill and it was a talkin' to me!"

"Sure, Mom."

"Ya outta come up here and see it for yourself."

"Okay. I'll be drive up and spend the afternoon with you."

Air hung up the phone and turned to Frank. "I have to drive up to visit with my mother for the afternoon. I'll be back late this afternoon."

"What about your breakfast?"

"I'll have my mother fix me something."

When Air arrived at her mother's house, D. J. immediately took her into the kitchen to see the "talkin' pa-lants."

"Lookie here, honey."

"My God, Mother! What have you done? Why do all the flowers have some kind of white padding around the rims of their pots?" Airstream was in total disbelief. She stood in her mother's kitchen staring at the shelf above the kitchen sink. The wall had four large windows, each about four feet wide, and each had its own shelf. There must have been about twenty small, potted plants placed right next to each other. D. J. had taken clippings of Wandering Jews from the neighbor's backyard and had started her own plants.

"What in the world is going on here, Mom?"

Air looked at the plants. She gently but deliberately turned her head and closed her eyes. At a snail's pace, she shook her head back and forth in a way D. J. didn't notice. She raised her hand to her chest and rubbed up toward her neck because she could feel her throat beginning to choke up. She wanted to cry—cry because here was a woman she knew who didn't have enough "Earth time" left to work through her shit, to cry because here also was a wizened, old bird destined to sit on a nest of bitter eggs for the rest of her life. Mostly, she wanted to cry because this woman was her mother—a mother who was proof there was alien life form on planet Earth. A mother who didn't deserve to be called Mother, but Air still desperately wanted to be told she was loved by this woman.

"You know plants talk to ya, don'tcha, Air?"

"Come on, Mom. How many times did you make me practice listening to plants talk to each other when I was little?"

"Wh-elle, like I said, I was just sitting here trying to read when they started calling out to me."

"They said, 'Little Janie, our arms are a hurtin' us. Help us, please'. All I could think of was to make these little pillas so they could rest their arms on them as they made their journey over to the other side of the pot."

Shit! Air thought. *You've always talked about the other side—the other side of the fence, the other side of town, the other side of the ocean, the other side of the universe—and now, it's the other side of the clay pots.*

Air looked closely at the "pillas." She realized D. J. had taken one square piece of toilet paper and carefully folded it until it was about an inch square and placed the padding under each and every stem of every plant that was "heading for the other side." The shelves were lined with pots that had rims of white toilet paper. Each of the pots must have had at least ten pads.

"The journey to the other side, huh?" asked Air.

"Yes, darlin'. Plants are religious, too. They have a long journey ahead of them, my little sweet Wanderin' Jews. You know, they told me at the beginning of the spring they were preparin' for sumthin' big. I just hoped they wouldn't all leave me at once. It gets kinda lonely around here."

"That's great, Mom, just great!" Air said with remorse.

Air thanked her lucky stars she hadn't brought Frank along. He thought D. J. should be reported for anything and everything. He just didn't know to whom. Air thought how two of them were peas in a pod. She wished that imaginary place Frank called "the Demmie Home for the Bewildered," which he often referred to whenever he no longer had the desire to live, was real so that she could make one telephone call and check both of them in together.

"Are you working on any new projects, Mom?"

"Yeah! I'm going to carve this here elephant out of wax." She showed Air a picture of an elephant she'd cut out of a *National Geographic* magazine.

Air's brain pushed the memory rewind button. She was back in high school on the day she'd come home from school and saw "them." Since she was a child, she'd never known what she was going to come home to. This time, she'd been greeted by life-size, cement alligators D. J. had made and placed in the front yard. D. J. had Air's dad go out into the front yard once a week and move those three hundred-pound gators to a new spot to make people think they were really alive and moving around the yard, foraging.

"Are you going to carve it true to size, Mom?" Air asked in sincerity.

"Oh goodness, no! It'll only be about eight inches high, honey."

Thank God, Air thought. She imagined a life-sized elephant made out of wax standing in the front yard as though it were grazing in the trees.

Air had actually lived enough now to love hearing, "Wh-elle, would ya lookie here," or "Would ya jus' look at that, honey."

Whatever her mother was referring to, it was something that made her as happy as a "pig in shit show." D. J.'s art varied from hillbilly art projects to really wild and far ahead of her time creations.

185

Air recognized her mother definitely had her own unique style. D. J.'s projects provided her with a sense of freedom she would never have had without them. There were people who admired her work and asked if she'd been in any art exhibitions.

"Wh-elle, I'm jus' waiting to be discovered," she'd answer.

Air remembered the project her mother called, "In Glass." According to D. J., it was a kind of mosaic, or as she preferred to call it a Chinesey dragon wall-hangin'.

For months, D. J. had saved green, red, and black bottles. Air would watch her mother carefully wash out the bottles and hide them in the garage. She and her brothers had no idea what she was up to, and they didn't want to know. But they knew they would soon find out. The day of inspiration came as it always did. She took all the bags of bottles she'd been saving, grabbed a hammer, and headed for the backyard. The kids looked at D. J.'s face and saw that all-too-familiar Lizzy Bordenish expression, almost like the devil himself. She started breaking the bottles as fast as she could with no regard as to where the glass was flying. One would think she'd have done this "murderin'" out in the garage or in a paper bag so cleaning up the mess would have been easy. But D. J. had a thing about being "freestyle."

Glass went flying everywhere. Everyone had to wear shoes for months. Air remembered D. J. taking the vacuum cleaner out into the backyard. She tried to vacuum up all the slivers before Daddy got home. Air had watched as the machine started smoking and the electrical cord started sparking and then caught fire.

"Oh shit!" D. J. yelled. "Oh, wh-elle, it's sure gonna look purdy when I'm done."

As usual, Air had looked around to see if any of the neighbors were watching as her mother vacuumed the backyard.

D. J. was good at hammering out whatever shapes she needed, like claws, horns, snake scales, and fangs. The dragon ended up being an enormous, five-foot-by-five-foot wall piece. She bought a sheet of plywood for the backing. She also bought white crushed rocks that are used in front yards for those who don't want to be bothered with anything green, much less a dragon. The white rocks were the background. She gave the dragon red glass teeth and huge, black glass claws. She was determined to finish the dragon before her first big Amway meeting. She worked on it day and night for over two months. She was convinced it would bring her good money luck.

"You see, honey, I've spent my whole life working through my unfinished shit with my past. I have to finish this here dragon; it's part of my learnin' this time around."

Each time she glued a piece of glass on, she'd stand back and look at her creation and murmur something like, "Ya know, everythin' I de-zign is somehow connected to one of my past lives. I just know it! And this here dragon is gonna bring me lots of sales."

"Past lives, Mom?" Air had asked reluctantly.

"Sure, honey, we all got 'em. You know that. Close your eyes and listen to your heart. Look at what you see in front of you. You've had at least six lives that I know about."

Suddenly, Air remembered back to when she was in seventh grade and D. J. had called her into the kitchen one afternoon. "Airstream, honey," she'd instructed, "I wantcha to go to the library for me and check out some books about fossils, minerals, Egyptian art, and history."

D. J. would send her back to the library two or three times a day, checking out more books on the subjects. She'd read the books all afternoon.

One night at the dinner table, the family was quietly eating, and suddenly D. J. blurted out, "I was Queen Nephritides in a past life! This here link with my past helps me with my art projects. It also helps me to finish up my old business with my past, so I can stop returning to this reoccurring life and finally journey on."

Mitchell pushed his plate forward and threw his fork down. "God dammit, Debbie Jane, would you stop with all this lunacy. You're making the kids have nightmares, and I've simply heard enough of your shit!" he yelled.

D. J. got up from the table and ran to her bedroom.

"Daddy, Mom scares me," Air said timidly.

"Listen, Airstream, at least your mother has given up her spider hunts," he said.

"You mean she's not getting into any trouble these days."

Trouble was D. J.'s middle name. She'd never walk away from a fight. Nor did she hesitate to start one.

As Air stood at the kitchen sink still staring at the Wandering Jews, she remembered old Rowena—yeah, that was the bitch's name. Air could still hear her mother yelling. "Honey, ya gotta take up for yourself. If somebody calls ya a bad name, ya call her one right back. Don't ya ever let me see ya gettin' bullied!"

Rowena, who was five years older than Air and quite fat, had walked by Air and called out, "Hey, skinny, don't turn sideways or we'll lose sight of you!"

Air, who'd been eleven at the time, had simply ignored the older girl.

"Hey you! Carrot top! I'm taking to you!" Rowena had shouted.

Air had continued to ignore the taunting. But D. J. had come running out of the house. "Tell her, Airstream!" she'd yelled. "Tell her! Tell 'er she's fat and ugly, honey!"

"My Airstream says you're fat, honey, fat! As in F-A-T! You got that, fat girl?" D. J. screamed at the top of her lungs.

Fat Rowena came up to Air and asked if what her mother had just said was true. The rest was history. Air remembered her mother telling her what to say and do.

"Hit 'er, honey! Hit 'er ree-yal hard! Kick 'er! Protect your face, honey!"

By then there was a crowd. Air thought for sure someone would stop them, but D. J. wouldn't let them. Air got her ass kicked. D. J. put her on restriction for having lost. She hated that there were always smoke signals coming from their house.

She remembered when the dragon was finally finished and hung in the family room. D. J. had Mitchell make a frame for it. Jesus, the thing was dangerous as all hell. Three-inch-long, jagged shards of glass stuck out everywhere from the thing. If anyone were to get dizzy looking from the dragon down to the three-tiered waterfall with water flowing from bowl to bowl and back, he or she would surely lose balance and fall against the dragon. Instant death. Or, if the person happened to be really unlucky, he or she would only lose an arm. What a way to go. Punctured to death on D. J.'s dragon.

Come to think of it, that damned dragon wasn't as bad as the sweater she'd bought from a thrift store. The sweater was plain black, too simple for D. J.'s taste, so she'd glued aquarium rocks all over it. Air remembered telling her she might as well go ahead and glue some guppies on it as well.

"Airstream, honey, these are not aquarium rocks. These are tumbled gemstones! Not ree-al great quality, but there's a lot of garnets, amethysts, and bloodstones here and there. The red stones are garnets, and I really think they set the sweater off. Don't ya think, sweetie? When I get finished with it, I'm a gonna wear it to my monthly gem and mineral meetin'. You just watch; those old ladies are just gonna love it! Of course, your daddy thinks I'm nuts, but I don't give a damned. He don't know nothin' 'bout style."

Air remembered her mother wearing that sweater everywhere. It was like she slept in it. She'd wear it to the supermarket every week and insist Air accompany her. Air hated going with her. D. J. looked like a walking rock garden.

"Mother, that sweater looks ridiculous," Air would insist, "especially with those pink tennis shoes. Where are the laces to those things, Mom?"

"They got all tangled up while they were in the spinnin' cycle of the washing machine."

"Well, don't wear them then. You look terrible!"

"Airstream, honey, you've got no ee-mag-gin-nation I'm an artist, and I know my colors. They may not be in style right now, but believe you me, sweetie, I'm just ahead of my time," D. J. would announce proudly.

Now D. J. stood by the sink still talking to the plants. She turned and looked at Air. "Airstream honey, you okay?" she asked. "You seem miles away. Whatcha thinkin' 'bout?"

"Oh, I'm sorry, Mom. I was just thinking back to when I was a little girl."

"Wh-elle, honey, you ain't no little girl no more. You're gonna have a baby! It'll be the only time ya ever go into a hospital and come out with somethin' instead of leaving somethin' behind."

"Yeah, I know, Mom."

"Wh-elle, whatcha gonna do about being pregnant?"

"I'm going to have an abortion, Mom. Kids just aren't in my deck of cards."

Air left thinking kids shouldn't have been in D. J.'s deck of cards either. Anybody who's A didn't make it to Z shouldn't have kids.

"I think I should go home, Mom. I need to miss the traffic going over the mountain. It's over a two-hour drive. You do know that, don't you? I drove all this way because you asked me to. I actually do worry about you more and more the older I get. You have fun with your plants. We'll talk soon."

"Wh-elle, I'm just gonna spend the day helpin' 'em pack for their journey. I wish I knew where they were headed. I guess I'll jus' have ta get me some more."

Air drove home feeling sick. She didn't know if it was morning sickness or the experience she'd just had with her mother.

The ride was long, and Air had too much time to think about how her life might have turned out differently if she'd had an "idyllic childhood," as she often heard other women refer to theirs. Or sometimes she heard her new friends remark how they had had a "blessed childhood, full of love and laughter." It was too painful to imagine what either of those childhoods might have been like.

Yet, somehow, as excruciating as her childhood had been, she couldn't help but examine intently the lives of her friends and the quality of lives they had had so far. *Perhaps my purpose in life is to be able to have the insight and compassion for others that could only come from my agonizing experiences growing up. I would not be as creative as I am; that's for sure. The beatings are still a mystery as to their lessons.*

Still, she thought, *I do know people who are living wonderful lives, making a difference in other people's lives, without having suffered as children. If only I could ask mother why I've had to go through this pain "this time around." I wonder if she knows something I don't. Or is she just too caught up in her own world to think about other people's life paths?*

It was getting dark as she finished the climb up and over the mountain and began the descent toward the ocean and home. She was exhausted but grateful that she'd gone to see her mother. *Funny how I feel good when I go visit D. J., even though I still don't feel a sense of love for her. Why do I even have her in my life? Is it that I keep hoping she's going to tell me she's proud of me? That she'll remind me I'm a natural born leader as she did when I was a child?*

I think I am far too forgiving, she concluded.

She pulled into the driveway, half expecting Frank to come out and welcome her home. No such luck. He was as absent as her mother. "Hey, Frank," she yelled out. "I'm home."

Frank was sitting at his drawing desk and looked up at her and asked, "So, what was the big deal with your mom? Or dare I ask?"

"Do yourself a favor and don't ask." Air laughed.

Just as Air was hanging up her coat, the phone rang.

"I'll get it, Frank. It's probably my mother again."

"Hello?'

"Hey, Air, how are you?" asked James.

"James! Oh God, it's so great to hear from you!" Air took the phone and went out onto the deck. It was a beautiful, sunny evening, and the sun was beginning to set. Air could see the tide was low. People were playing in the waves, and dogs were running after balls. She sat down in her favorite flowery art deco chair. She put her legs up. There was a slight breeze. "I wish I had the energy to tell you where I've been and what a scene it was," she added with a giggle, "but I'll spare us both. Let me just say, I just got back from visiting D. J."

"Oh jeez, I don't want to know. Besides, I'm in no mood. Air, people love to talk about themselves, and most people don't like to listen. I just listen and endure all their boring stories, and I have a new friend for life."

"James, do you ever pray?" Air asked.

"Only to the Valium God. I pray that someday he will make twenty-milligram valiums and they will come in the color purple."

"You and Frank! I made an appointment for Frank to see a doctor about his butt, and I think the only reason he went was to get drugs. It was a horrible experience, but I just couldn't take it anymore. And he needed to know that he doesn't have butt cancer. He's just a stress mess. I don't know how much longer I can handle living with him. I'm starting to have my anxiety attacks again."

"Ah, Air, I'm sorry to hear that. You were doing so well. Maybe it's time for you to leave him. You're not in love with him, right?"

"'Tis true. It's just that the change scares me. Unfortunately, I don't have a lot of extra money right now," Air said sadly.

"Air, I have something to tell you, but you can't tell a soul. Promise?" James asked sounding like he really needed reassurance.

"Of course, you know me better than that. Who the hell would I tell anyway? It's not like we have the same friends anymore or live near each other. You're in Emeryville, and I'm all the way down in Santa Cruz. Shit, when was it that we even saw each other last? Too long, that's for sure. So what's going on?"

"Air, I just found out that I have hepatitis," he said despondently.

"What? What's that? That's something to do with your liver, isn't it?" Air glanced up at the sky. A large number of pelicans were flying overhead. *What does that mean?* she wondered. *Pelicans? Are they trying to tell me something about James?* She ignored the thought for now, but she knew it would come back. She felt her body tensing, knowing James had the scummiest doctor one could imagine. His name, oddly enough, was Dr. Sincere.

"Lately, I haven't been feeling good. No energy. And I swear, Air, my face started looking gray and then turned yellow. My whole body has a yellowish tone. So, I decided to call Dr. Sincere and have some blood work done. It came back positive for hep," James sighed. "I wish you could have been with me when I saw him. You know how strange he is. I swear he's gay and he's married! But he's forever putting his hand on my knee.

"This time when I got to his office, there were other people who were already waiting to see him, and yet I got to go right in. He asked me how he could help. He followed that with, 'You know I'll do anything I can for you, right?' He then immediately asked if

I needed a new prescription for my tension. I told him I thought I might have something wrong with my liver since my skin was a little yellow," James said.

"He told me it was no problem, that he'd just take a blood sample and run some tests, and we'd know in a few days. Sure enough, the lab work came back and I tested positive for hepatitis!" he told her.

Air got up and started walking around the deck. She looked over the railing and watched the squirrels down below seemingly hiding nuts. She was worried. She didn't trust Dr. Sincere and felt his license should be taken away.

In her opinion, James's doctor had already prescribed him too many highly additive drugs over the years to James. The wind started to pick up. It became a bit chilly so she decided to go back inside. She went into the kitchen where Frank couldn't hear her conversation.

"James, I sure hope to God you've stopped drinking brown liquor since you got this information!" she said, not knowing what else to say.

"Hell no!"

"Good grief, James. When you have hepatitis, you don't drink. Your liver is already fucked up enough." Air started to cough.

"Well Air, if you cough up a liver, I'll take it." He snickered.

"So, what did the doctor tell you to do about the hep?" Air asked.

"Well, Dr. Sincere said the best cure for hep was to drink like the kitchen sink."

"Oh my God! You've got to be kidding! You must have misunderstood him, James. What kind of doctor would tell a hepatitis patient to drink like a fish?"

"Beats me, but that's what he said. I'm sure of it. In fact, he took out his flask and handed it to me."

"Oh my God!"

↭ 14 ↭

Air sat in the kitchen all alone. She didn't want to share any of her conversation with James with Frank. After all, Frank didn't care too much for James anyway. *He doesn't like James because he's jealous of how close we are. He wants me all to himself.* She made some peppermint tea, put on a coat, and went back out onto the deck. She stared out at the vast Pacific Ocean and thought about James.

I can't believe he still works at Ford's. He'd worked there since he'd graduated from high school. He was such a natural at interior design. He'd been promoted to manager within his first few months of working there.

Air remembered when James had moved into his trailer in the lower flats of Emeryville right after graduating from high school. Rent was cheap, and it was close to work. He had a black cat named Etta, and she was his life. Etta was fed before he ate. Most the trailers in the park were fairly new and had well-kept yards. Not James's trailer. His was the most outdated, disgusting, rusty-looking trailer in the park. Paint was chipping off everywhere, and rust crept in between the chips. The old style TV antenna looked like the Leaning Tower of Pisa. The left side of the trailer had dents on top of dents from his many attempts at parking his car at three in the morning after a night on the town.

Air remembered teasing him. "Too bad there's nobody in the park who needs a three a.m. wake-up call."

After returning from New York, she'd drive down from Petaluma and spend the weekend with him. Some of her fondest memories were of the times in "trail," as she'd refer to his home. They'd spent many weekend nights laughing and listening to his ultra-scratchy records of Judy Garland over and over. He loved Judy.

"Doesn't everyone just love Judy, Air?"

"No, not me." She would chuckle.

"Whenever I listen to her, I drink and smoke more."

"Jesus, James, you use any excuse to drink and smoke more."

"Well, I say whatever makes the party happen is right up my alley, girl."

He'd seen every movie Judy had starred in and sang along with her verbatim. Air remembered that, whenever a Judy movie was on, James would turn down the sound. He could lip-read her songs and would sing loudly just to torture Air. His secret dream in life was to be a singer. The problem was, his voice was terrible, especially when he was drunk. Air didn't have the heart to tell him. He was so happy when he was singing for people. Old people in bars actually loved to hear him sing. Of course, they were shit-faced themselves, and anybody who sang the "oldies but goodies" was simply a fabulous singer in their minds.

There was a liquor store just two blocks from the trailer. He was a weird bird about keeping liquor in the trailer. He would buy just what he planned on drinking at the moment. Of course, he'd make at least three trips back to the store in one night because he could never gage just how wasted he was.

Air could never figure out how the hell the guy could stay up all night drinking and be at work by seven in the morning—reeking of alcohol, but never late. Of course, there was the fact he was also head of his department. No one wanted to mess with him because they were all his "best friends."

James was a fun drunk. He was not the kind of person who turned into Dracula and sucked the fun out of the party. "Gullible" and "skittish" were his middle names. Air loved to play practical jokes on him.

While still living in Petaluma and really bored, the prankster part of her would decide it was about time to pull a hoax on James. *What could I do to really freak him out?* she would think. One time, she'd come up with a brilliant plan. She would cut out letters from the newspaper and create an anonymous death threat note. Then she'd drive down and tape it on his front door. He'd find it when he got off work and never suspect her since she lived over an hour away.

Air had spent an entire morning cutting letters out of the newspaper. She'd glued them onto a purple poster board. Purple was his favorite color. When she had finished the note, she'd taped it to the wall and imagined what it would look like on his door.

Dear Mr. James Fundelle,

You are nothing more than a queer, weirdo wimp.
    Don't ever come back to Ford's if you know what's good for you.

Air read the note and decided it wasn't scary enough.
I know, she'd thought. *I'll cut out the obituaries and tape them to the bottom of the note. Shit, he's going to know straightaway I did this.*
Air had looked at the clock. It was just past noon. *Oh good, I have plenty of time!*
When Air had arrived at the trailer park, no one seemed to be around. It was very quiet, and only a few cars were parked by their homes. Air had quickly grabbed the note and some tape and jumped out of her car. She'd looked around, and she'd suddenly remembered that feeling of looking around to see if any of the neighbors were watching as her mother was up to something totally embarrassing. No one seemed to be aware of her, so she'd taped the poster board to the door with duct tape. When she'd gotten back in her car, she'd noticed a role of toilet paper she kept in the car because of her never-ending runny nose.
Oh my god, I have to throw some toilet paper around his trailer just for the hell of it.
She'd stood in front of the middle of the trailer and tossed the roll as high and hard as she could, hoping it wouldn't hit the neighbor's trailer. She'd promptly walked around to the other side and picked up the roll and tossed it under the trailer. She'd continued to throw the roll up and over about three more times. She'd wanted to totally wrap it, but she only had one roll of toilet paper. She couldn't help but laugh out loud when she was done. She'd made so much noise she couldn't believe no one had come out and asked what in the hell she was doing.

She'd driven home and waited for James to call when he got off work. She knew he would call her the moment he got home. Air waited for over an hour, and when he still hadn't called, she'd decided to call him.

"Hi, James, what's new? I haven't heard from you for a couple of days."

"Airstream," he whispered, "you won't believe this. Somebody's trying to kill me!"

"James, I can't hear you. What did you say? Why are you whispering?"

"I said, someone's after me. Somebody's trying to kill me!"

Air had to pinch herself to keep from laughing. "You have to be kidding me. Who'd want to kill you?"

"Air, when I got home there was a death threat letter on my door! You should have seen my trailer. Someone had thrown toilet paper up and over the middle part. It was completely white. It was like what we used to do in high school to the front yards of kids we didn't like."

"Oh my God. What did the note say?" Air asked, as though she was scared as well.

"It said, never come back to Ford's if you know what's good for you. Air, they even called me a queer fagot! Plus, they taped the obituaries to the bottom of the note. I am freaked out. My best friend, Dave, from next door is here, and so is Denise. Plus, I have my mother's gun. I think I'm going to go stay with Aunt Laura for the next couple of days because I'm too freaked out to stay here alone."

Hell, James had never talked to a soul in the trailer park the entire time he'd lived there. Now he was "best friends" with someone named Dave, and good God, having Denise there was like having a ticking time bomb around. She was ready to go off anytime. She was more into drugs and a bigger drunk than James.

Air smiled at the memory of that day and glanced down at the beach. Lots of kids were still running around, screaming with joy. Some families were still busy building sand castles, taking advantage of the last of the fading light.

Oh my God, Air thought. *I remember how serious he was; he wasn't playing around with me at all. He was genuinely freaked out, and he had a gun! Jeez, this was a guy who jumped ten feet when the lights flickered.*

She remembered growing worried. She could just see the headlines: "Young Man Accidently Shoots Himself and New Best friend to Death During Electrical Failure."

Out of the blue, the sky grew cloudy and the wind was a bit colder, as it often did along the coast in the evening hours. She pulled her coat more tightly around her.

"James, are you sure you're not drunk?" she'd asked.

"Nah, I'm just fine, Air," he'd said. "Don't worry about me. I'm going to call the police after we're through smoking this joint. Anyway, listen, Dave and Denise are here, and I feel like I'm ignoring them, so I better go. I'll call you when the police leave."

"Sure. Maybe I should drive down."

"Oh God, would you, Air?" he'd pleaded. "I know it's a long drive, but try to come, if you can."

Air hung the up phone and thought about what he'd said. Anytime he told her he wasn't drunk and in the same breath said he was going to call the police, she knew he was messed up on something. She grabbed her purse and headed out the door. If he called the police, and they found her prints all over the death threat note, she imagined she would be arrested. She hurriedly wrote a note to Frank. She simply told him she was out shopping to clear her mind. As she drove, she reassured herself that the police would determine the scene was not a hate crime.

She'd made it to James's in less than an hour. From a block away, she remembered seeing two police cars already parked out in front of the trailer with their lights still flashing. *Oh shit,* she had thought. *Maybe because he's so antsy and paranoid, he's already shot Dave or Denise or one of his other new "friends" from the trailer park as they were coming out of the bathroom. It could have been a case of "out of sight out of mind," and then when his new friend came out of the bathroom, he thought they were the would-be killer.*

She had run up to his kitchen window and listened. All she could hear was James talking.

"Here is the death threat, officer. It was taped to my front door, and my entire trailer had toilet paper wrapped around it."

"Is this your home, Mr. Fundelle?"

"Yes."

"This looks like a prank to me," the officer had said.

"Yes! Yes!" Air remembered saying to herself.

"No, begging your pardon, officer, I'm sure this is for real. You see, I sold some marijuana to this guy at work because I needed the money. The guy I sold the dope to got fired, and I'm sure he thinks I had something to do with it."

Oh my God! He's in there spilling his guts to the cops, Air had thought, gasping inwardly. *Shit, he's definitely drunk, and this has gotten way out of hand. They're going to end up arresting him, especially if they find out he has a gun that's not registered to him. I have to go in there and shut him up.*

Air remembered walking in the door just as Denise, who was as deranged and as doped up as James was, stumbled and fell flat on her face on James's glass coffee table. The table had shattered, and everything had gone flying across the room, including a giant bottle of scotch.

Air remembered looking at James and could tell from the look on his face he was one twisted son of a bitch. His eyes were extremely blood shot. In fact, all three of them were one giant bust. The cops asked if they could keep the note in case they needed it as evidence.

"We're pretty convinced no one is seriously out to kill you Mr. Fundelle," one of the officers had said. "If this were really a crime scene, no one would have taken the time to toilet paper your trailer. That's a high school prank and takes quite a lot of time. It was very risky for the person or persons who did this. It's highly unlikely he or she wasn't seen by one of your neighbors. Don't you agree? I think they would have called us if they thought there was a real crime being committed."

"I don't know, officer. I know some pretty crazy people," James had replied.

"Well, let us know if anything else unusual happens." They'd left without even asking about the marijuana.

199

Air thought back to how she'd tried to convince James she was the one who had created the death threat and put the toilet paper all over his trailer.

"James, I confess, I drove down and did this whole thing," she'd said. "I spent the morning cutting out those letters and pasting them onto the poster board. I just wanted to play a trick on you. I didn't realize you wouldn't immediately think of me. You have to give that gun back to your mother!"

James had loved all the attention he was getting. Hell, everyone in the trailer park was now his best buddy! He'd refused to believe her, but he had insisted she call his mother and cop a plea to her, "just to relieve her anxiety."

"She's been so freaked out, and if you say you did it, you know she'll believe you. Sorry, Air, but you know how crazy she thinks you are. So will you do this just for me?"

"James, I did all of this!" Air had insisted.

"Here's the phone. Just relieve her anxiety," James had said as he'd handed her the phone.

She never understood why he wouldn't believe she was the one who had created the whole horrible scene in the first place. He knew she had a key to his place, and he knew she had pulled pranks on him almost every other month for at least a year prior to this one. Once, she'd stuffed a pair of men's pants and a shirt with newspaper. She took a pair of her black nylons and stuffed them into the shape of a head. To finish him off, she put a black sweater cap on the head and sewed it to the body; the "intruder" even had shoes on. The dummy had catsup poured all over his chest and had three steak knives stabbed into his chest. She'd pulled that prank more than once; positioning the "dead man" in various discrete places in the trailer. James would come home from work so tired that the dummy would catch him off guard and make him scream every time.

Now, Air remembered how she'd called James's mother and confessed to pulling the death threat prank.

"How can you do this to my son? Are you ever going to grow up, Airstream?" his mother had screamed before slamming down the phone.

"Okay, James, are you happy now?" Air had said. "And would you please give her the gun back?"

"I think I'll keep it for just a couple more days," James had replied. "But, I think I should go back to work tomorrow. I'm way behind in my orders. I talked with work today, and they told me I had some pretty pissed-off customers. I missed showing up for appointments I'd made for the last week. I was supposed to measure their homes for new drapes."

Air had been glad to hear that. "I think it would be a really good idea for you to go back to work," she'd told him. "It'll take your mind off of all this. Call me when you get home tomorrow night, okay?"

"Okay, Air, thanks for trying to calm me down by telling me you did it. You're really the one who's my best friend you know. I just need to drink a little more and calm down. Denise will stay here with me tonight. I won't go to my aunt's house until tomorrow after work."

James and Denise had poured themselves another drink and announced they were going to finish off the rest of the gallon of brown liquor before the night ended.

Air remembered walking back to her car and driving home in total disbelief.

Air stretched out in the chair and watched the sunset. She pulled her coat tighter to her body and, before she knew it, she'd fallen asleep.

"Airstream, wake up," Frank said. "It's dinnertime. I've made us something to eat. Come inside the house. It's really cold out here. I've made a fire. We can eat dinner in front of the fireplace."

The next day, Air set up her easel on the front deck and painted all day, stopping only to eat. Frank came out and told her that she had a phone call. She put her brush into a can of water and covered her paints with plastic wrap.

"Oh my God, Airstream! You're not going to believe what happened to me this morning! I had an appointment in Newark to show this couple some drape samples. I left my trailer early. The appointment wasn't until eight a.m., so I decided to buy a six-pack since I was so hung-over. Denise came over last night, and we drank until we both passed out on the couch."

"Holy shit, James. You're going to kill yourself. I'm telling you, you're drinking and smoking yourself into an early grave!" Air yelled. "You're still taking antibiotics for your hepatitis."

"Fuck that. Listen to this!" James said to her. "This morning, I felt like death warmed over, so I bought some beer and drove to the street where I had my appointment. I parked and just sat in my car chugging down the whole six-pack, one after another. I had the passenger window open, so I just tossed the empty cans out into the gutter.

"Suddenly, I looked over at the house I'd parked in front of and noticed there was this old man mowing his lawn. He was just staring at me. Air, I'm sure he watched me drink every one of those evil beers, but what the hell did I care, right? I thought I'd never see the guy again. Well, I sat there for about half an hour until it was time to go. I got out of my car and opened my truck. I took out my suitcases full of drapery samples. I picked up my appointment book and started walking down the street. Guess what happened then?"

Air had already been feeling a little anxious that day. She knew this was not going to be a good story and wondered if she should make up a story about cooking dinner and needing to hang up. "I can't imagine, James, but the story is going to get worse, isn't it? Maybe you'd better not tell me. I've had anxiety all day."

"I totally messed up on the house address. I thought I had parked up the street from the house where my appointment was. Air, I had parked exactly in front of the house where I had my appointment!"

"You're kidding! Oh my God, you've got to be kidding. James, tell me you're kidding. Don't make me laugh while I'm in the middle of an anxiety attack."

"I'm not kidding, Air!"

"Oh my God! What the hell happened?"

"Well, I ended up walking back down the street to my car to check the address. I looked around, and the man who'd been working in his yard asked me if he could help me in some way. Air, I could have died of embarrassment. He'd watched me drink every one of those beers! Can you imagine? A complete stranger suddenly pulls up in front of your house at eight in the morning and proceeds to chug down a sixer and then tosses the cans out the car window into your gutter! And if that's not bad enough, the stranger turns out to the man from Ford's who's there to show you some drape samples."

"I'm in total disbelief, and at the same, I think it's the funniest damned thing you've ever done in your life!" Air smiled, imagining the scene. "What did you do then? Your ears must have been red with embarrassment."

"I tried to act like everything was fine and that I wasn't drunk. And get this, straightaway he says to me, 'Well, you came to the right place, little buddy. The missus is inside waiting for you.' So I just followed him into the house."

Air burst into laughter. "Fuck, that's the most hysterical thing I can imagine. I can hardly catch my breath, and I don't like feeling like I can't breathe and being elated at the same time. This is way over the moon, James. Oh my God!"

"Their names were Mr. and Mrs. Emanuel Tell. And get this, Mr. Tell offered me a drink as soon as I sat down—brown liquor even! I almost accepted, but I was so full of anxiety I acted like, who me? Drink at eight in the morning? Are you crazy?"

"Were they already drinking? And did they order any drapes from you?"

"Yes, Mrs. Tell was having a glass of brandy when I walked into the kitchen! They ordered drapes for both the living room and the den. They both drank like fish the entire time I was there."

"Well, it sounds to me like everything turned out okay. Besides, you said they offered you a drink, right? So I wouldn't worry."

"Yeah, as a matter of fact, Mr. Tell asked me if I'd ever been to a bar called the End Zone. I think he might be gay, Air. In fact, I think I recognized him. When he offered me a drink he said, 'How about a little cocktail, Kitzie-Dat?'"

"Kitzie-Dat?" Air asked between bouts of laughter.

They both started howling.

"Yeah, I think he'd already 'kitzied his dat' years ago. You should've seen his nose. I swear he looked just like Rudolph!"

"James, I don't get the Kitzie-Dat thing. Is that something gay people say?"

"God no! He had a lisp, and that's why I think he's gay. Plus, I think he was already drunk when I got there. Jesus, Air, my Aunt Laura says that to me all the time, but she waits until at least four in the afternoon. And, it's always, 'How about a little cocktail, Kitzie-Cat?'"

"Isn't she the one who does tons of crank and Valium?"

"Yeah, God did I ever get wasted at her house the other night? Talk about a little slobber and piss in the pants."

15

The fog rolled in thick along the coast that night. It seemed colder than usual. Air and Frank kept a fire going steadily almost daily. It was difficult to see the waves sometimes, but tonight the waves crashing onto the beach were loud. It had been raining the week before, and it had been almost impossible to leave the house for any reason other than to go grocery shopping. Air didn't mind because Christmas had finally arrived, and she insisted Frank cut a tree from the property of one of his friends as soon as possible. Frank was not interested, but he did it for Air. He didn't help her decorate the six-foot tall noble fir, so she hung the ornaments herself. Frank's only request was that Air hang all his grandmother's vintage, handmade train ornaments.

On one of her shopping trips in New York City, Air had found a year-round Christmas store that specialized in one-of-a-kind vintage, handmade ornaments from all over the world. She'd bought dozens of boxes of unique German and French glass ornaments, ranging from traditional Christmas ornaments to delicate mermaids and pigs. She also loved to buy miniature glass deer with red noses and tiny green ribbons wrapped around their necks whenever she found them. The two Christmases she and Frank had spent in New York had been some the most exciting times in Air's life. She'd loved decorating the house with garlands and wreaths. She'd spread a red tablecloth over the dining room table, set out green linen napkins, and placed a wreath-decorated runner down the middle. She'd bought a full set of Christmas dinnerware—twelve place settings in all. The design was a holly ribbon design, and each piece had a rim of 14-karat gold. She'd had fantasies about a future with children and grandchildren and how special Christmases would be for them. She'd imagined she would entertain the family at Thanksgiving time too. Frank would have the tree already cut before each Thanksgiving. It would be standing over in the corner waiting until after everyone had finished the meal. Air would have all the ornaments and lights ready so everyone could decorate the tree together. Even then, she'd known she was trying to replace her childhood memories of the family without a tree and no presents after they left Texas. She'd taken special wrapping classes and learned how to wrap presents the way the Japanese wrapped boxes. She'd delighted in choosing unique wrapping paper and would over-trim each present. She'd bought presents for her family in California and shipped them back. She'd felt a sense of personal accomplishment and wanted her parents to know she was living a lifestyle they would never have imagined for her. She would usually start buying gifts in August and hide them in the George Washington wing, and by the time Christmas arrived, the presents would fill the room.

This year would be different though. Frank had cut down the tree, like usual, but now they didn't have the money to buy presents. The thought of Christmas gave Frank extreme anxiety. "Extreme anxiety" translated into overly long hours in the bathroom coupled with overemphasized moans.

"Airstream, this is serious!" he'd grumble. "People have heart attacks from straining."

He'd been without work for months. Frank's biggest concern was not work; nor was it Christmas presents. Instead, he worried about where he'd get his next joint. Weed was high priority, and a jug of Red Mountain was next. He was still terrified of going back into the music business, and his art was not selling.

Air had a basketful of yarn she'd been saving for years, so knitting something for everyone was a no-brainer. Frank decided to do a drawing of his old model Norton motorcycle for everyone on his list. Between the two of them, they'd come up with presents for everyone but D. J.

D. J. was a tough one. Not much impressed her, except for things like Egyptian art and history, poisonous snakes, black widows, Louis Comfort Tiffany, dogs, curlers, juicy fruit chewing gum, makeup, fossils, crystals, rocks, and especially petrified wood.

If you gave her something she didn't like, she had no problem telling you her true feelings. Air remembered her saying once after she'd worked really hard to find something she thought would fit her mother's unique taste, "Oh now, honey, I don't like that at all. You can just keep it for yourself."

Air had become an excellent cook. That night, she prepared salmon filet, topped with ginger and garlic, sun chokes, and a spring salad with red pear and walnuts in a poppy seed vignette. After dinner, she walked over to the fireplace and stared at the flames. She looked over at Frank, who was sitting at the dining table preparing to roll a joint. It was dark outside, and she wondered if all the cats were inside the house. She didn't like going out in the dark since the raccoons that would come were as big as dogs. She walked through the front room and turned on all the lamps, gathered her yarn, and pulled her favorite overstuffed, velvet art deco chair in front of the fireplace.

Air set down her knitting and reached over to take the joint Frank was holding out in her direction. She knew better than to get into discussions with Frank when he was stoned, but when wasn't he? So now was as good of a time as any. Air took another hit off the joint and turned to Frank. "Frank, what the hell are we going to give my mom for Christmas?" she asked.

"I vote for a going out in the woods and finding her a redwood burl."

"Frank, I'm serious!" she retorted.

"So am I," he replied without looking up from the sketch he'd taken out and begun working on. "Your fucking mother is so weird. You figure it out."

"I know one thing she's wanted all her life."

"I know, don't tell me, a dried rattlesnake coat!"

"Goddamn it, Frank! I'm really serious. The one thing I know she's wanted all her life is a monkey. She has always wanted a monkey."

Frank started laughing so hard and loud Air started to worry he might not be able to catch his breath. "Oh my God, Air! That's so out there! I'm getting a cramp from laughing so hard."

"I'm not kidding. She's always wanted a monkey. I swear, since I was a little girl that's all she said used to dreamed about—a monkey so she could dress herself and the monkey up in one of her own designs. You know, so they'd look like twins."

"Yep, that sounds just like your mother!"

"I saw an ad in this morning's paper, and it said you could buy a squirrel monkey for only $12.95. It says they make great Christmas presents. The monkeys come from this place called Your Friendly Pet Store."

"Right, a squirrel monkey?"

"Oh, come on, Frank. Please?"

"With exactly what money are we supposed buy this monkey?"

"I got our AFDC check in the mail today. I forgot to tell you."

Airstream was pregnant again. She planned on getting another abortion. Until then, her and Frank qualified for the Aid for Dependent Children Program, and they received eighty dollars a month from the county. They'd been living on practically nothing for months. For food, they would invite their city friends down for the weekend. Frank would strongly suggest they bring plenty of weed, food, and wine with them. With the little money they had, Air would buy chicken wings and backs during the week for twenty-nine cents a pound, and they'd live on soup until the weekend.

Air had had it with the poverty life. Thank God, Frank's parents had four cords of wood stacked out back since the fire was their only source of heat and entertainment during the winter.

Of course, that was not always as entertaining as it may sound. The fire came with a price. Air always had to endure the incessant endless stories about Frank's grandparents and what a hard life they'd led. Stories of Agmond and Agmonda always ended the same. The two of them both choked to death kissing each other good night while each was sucking on a Victor Brother's cough drop.

Air sat there each time and listened. She would imagine her and Frank dying swallowing their tongues while kissing because they'd be so stoned on weed they'd forget what the hell they were doing.

There were only two days left before Christmas. They didn't have a checking account, so it was going to be hard to cash the eighty-dollar check. Usually, they'd sign it over to one of their friends when they came to visit. But no one was coming before Christmas.

"Let's just go look at the monkeys tomorrow, Frank. Please? It would be good for us to get out of the house."

"All right."

The following morning the sun was out, and it was a windless day. Air went out onto the deck and looked at the waves. They were about six feet high, and it seemed to be high tide.

This must be a good sign, Air thought.

It would turn out to be a sign of the "second coming."

The house was six miles from the downtown area, but it took them an hour to get to the pet store. They decided to take the coastal road into town. Since they were so stoned Frank didn't drive any faster than about five miles an hour, and he had made two wrong turns. They smoked dope the entire drive because both were trying to give up smoking cigarettes. They were trying to just stay calm from the withdrawal effects by smoking weed.

"There it is," Air shouted. "Just past that gas station on your left."

Frank pulled into the parking lot. They got out, and Air turned around to make sure they'd locked the car.

"My God, Frank, you parked right in the middle of two parking spots."

"That's so I'll remember where I parked the car."

Air sighed and said, "That's just not cool, Frank. The parking lot is full, and you've taken up two spots."

"Tough shit! I don't want to spend an hour looking for the car."

They entered the pet store and immediately realized they were both definitely too stoned. The store was too huge and had way too much to look at. Finally, they spotted a gigantic cage full of monkeys in the middle of the store. It had to be twenty feet by twenty feet and twenty feet tall. Air estimated there were at least ten different species of monkeys. They stood in the doorway of the store staring at the cage of monkeys beckoning to them for what Air was sure was at least twenty minutes. They couldn't move. They were "tripping," and through her fog, Air was vaguely aware that that had become obvious to the salespeople.

A man came over and asked if they needed some assistance.

"Yes, could you call us a taxi?" Air replied. "We're entirely too stoned to be here and quite incapable of driving ourselves home at this point."

"I beg your pardon, miss?"

"I said we're interested in a squirrel monkey."

The salesperson pretended he hadn't heard what Air had first said. "Sure, it's the smallest one you can see," he said, gesturing to the cage in the center of the store. "They make great pets. Let me know if I can be of assistance."

Frank and Air made their way over to the cage and scrutinized the monkeys again, this time from even closer. They both found the smallest monkey at the same time, and both were quite taken with her. She was beautiful. She looked like a small, delicate child about three or four years old. Her face was absolutely gorgeous. She had large, dark eyes and a chiseled face. She stared back at them with a look Air and Frank decided was one of compassion and understanding. Stoned and unable to move, they both went into a trancelike state and didn't take their eyes off her for about twenty minutes. In fact, neither of them even said a word to each other.

"Frank, she's so beautiful," Air finally said in a dreamy state. "We have to buy her."

"Excuse me, sir, how much is the squirrel monkey again?"

"She's $12.95 in total," the clerk replied.

"We'll take her," Air said.

The salesman opened the door to the cage and went in. Air and Frank watched as he approached what Air recognized as a Woolly monkey from a *National Geographic* issue. He lifted the Woolly's tail and revealed the tiniest monkey they'd ever seen. They couldn't believe their eyes. There, huddled as close to the Woolly monkey's asshole as it could get, was a coke bottle-sized monkey.

As the man reached for the squirrel monkey, it seemed to have disappeared up inside the Woolly's asshole. Air looked up at Frank. There was a look of pain in Frank's eyes that even made Air's asshole hurt. Assholes were always a source of pain, whether they were people's or, as in this case, a monkey's.

"Excuse me, sir. We want the squirrel monkey."

"Yes miss," the salesman replied, "I realize that. This is the squirrel monkey."

Frank immediately started freaking out. "I'm not buying a fucking monkey that's been some other fucking monkey's toy!"

"Frank, cool out!" Air whispered. "Sir, how much is the monkey up on the branch in the middle of the cage?"

"Oh, that's a spider monkey, and she's eighty dollars."

"Sir, the spider monkey is the smallest monkey in the cage. We had no idea there was another monkey hiding up some other monkey's ass. Now we have our hearts set on the spider monkey, and we both thought she was the smallest in the cage and only $12.95," Air said pleadingly.

The salesman stood there, looking completely bewildered.

"Good grief, Frank. Come on! I can't take a little monkey that smells like shit to my mom! Besides, she's called a spider monkey, and you know how much my mother is into black widow spiders."

"You're right. Let's just get the hell out of here since that's all the money we have to our names. How will we buy dope, wine, gas and chicken gizzards? We're both too stoned for this."

They stood there for a moment, silently saying their good-byes to the monkey they'd fallen in love with. She sat there curled up on a branch, motionless, looking back at them.

So pitiful, Air thought. "God, she's beautiful, isn't she, Frank? I almost feel like we're leaving our child at an orphanage. She looks so sweet and gentle. I sure wish we could buy her."

"Hell, yes! Let's buy her. Your mom's probably never gotten a present she's really wanted in her entire life, right?"

"She's eighty dollars, Frank, and that's all we have."

"It's okay," Frank said.

"Excuse me, sir. Would you kindly take a county check for exactly eighty dollars for the spider monkey? After all, it's Christmas, the time for giving."

The salesman looked around at the other customers. Air saw him notice a young couple heading toward the door. He turned back to them, muttering something about monkeys not being big sellers anyway. It was clear he wanted Air and Frank to leave because they were causing such a scene.

"Sure. Why not?" he said. "You're right. It is almost Christmas. Tis better to give than receive. I'll even throw in a carrier box, a collar, and the chain for nothing."

Oh my god, Air thought gleefully, *my mother is finally going to have her very own monkey. I can't wait to see the look on her face when we give it to her.*

The salesman put the collar on the monkey and gently dropped her into a tall box. He connected a chain to the collar and snapped it to the hook on the inside of the box.

"She's all yours. Merry Christmas!" he said and escorted them to the front door of the store.

"Well, Air, let's get her in the car and go home," said Frank. "I'm really exhausted. And," he added with a silly grin, "I can't wait to get home and cuddle with our new little girl."

I can't believe we bought a monkey. Air was elated until the next thought hit her. *And now we have no money until the beginning of the January.*

As they drove home, they both felt like new parents. They wondered how they would ever be able to give her up.

"Oh my God!" Frank said.

"What wrong?"

"I passed our exit miles ago!"

"It's okay, Frank. Just turn around. We're not that far past our exit."

Frank turned around, took the coastal road exit, and headed toward the house. As soon as they were in the driveway, Frank turned to Air and said, "Take her out of the box and let's just sit here with her for a while."

"Let's wait until we get her in the house," Air said. "It's freezing out here. Besides, maybe she needs something to eat or maybe she needs to shit."

"What does a monkey eat besides bananas?" Frank asked.

Frank and Air realized they didn't know what the spider monkey ate. Nor did they have any idea where she went to the bathroom. Was she like a cat? Should they get her a box of sand? For that matter, did they need to walk her?

As Air stared at Frank looking back with a happy grin on his face, a thought occurred to her. *This is strange. Frank's afraid of animals other than cats, and now he wants to sit here with the monkey so close to him?*

"Go ahead, Air. Let her out of the box," he coaxed.

"Well, her collar is chained to something inside the box to keep her in there. I have to find it first. Let's go inside, Frank. I'll let her out inside the house."

They carefully took the box with the monkey into the house and set it down in the middle of the front room. Air put her hand down into the box to pet the monkey. Without warning, the monkey grabbed Air's hand with her teeth and began shaking it back and forth with such force Air felt as though she was being attacked by a great white shark. The monkey would not let her hand go.

"Frank! Quick! Close the lid to the box! She's biting my hand really hard, and I can't get her to let go," Air yelled.

At the same time the monkey was biting Air, the clasp that held her inside the box was accidently released. Air looked at Frank's face and saw sheer terror in his eyes—just before he turned and ran down the hall toward the bathroom.

"Frank! Where the hell are you going? We've got trouble! This goddamned monkey's got my hand in her mouth, and she won't let go! Besides that, she's now loose and almost out of the box," she shrieked. "I need you Frank! Come back here!

"Frank! You can't leave me alone out here with this goddamned, freaking ass monkey! She's going to kill me! Frank! Where are you? This goddamned monkey is still biting me!"

The tiny, tender, beautiful child suddenly let go of Air's hand. Air looked at her hand, and there were deep teeth marks like those of a child. She hadn't broken the skin but Air was in a lot of pain. The monkey climbed out of the box and stood up. Air could not believe her eyes. This monkey suddenly had an arm span of about six feet and had gone from Little Princess to Queen Kong!

Frank was still in the bathroom, and Air knew he could hear her yelling. Before long, she heard moans coming from behind the closed door, and she imagined him sitting on the toilet, moaning ever louder in an attempt to drown out her screams.

"Hey, you motherfucker! Get out here and help me, Frank!"

Suddenly, the monkey decided to jump onto the couch and recoil back into her small size—the size she was at the pet store. She just stared at Air.

Frank finally cracked the back door and yelled, "Is she back in the box yet?"

"Fuck you, Frank! I need help. This bitch is hysterical, and she's about to rip the couch apart."

"Well, just get her back in the box," he coached. "Don't be afraid!"

Air was terrified. She felt like she was in a cage with a wild animal. Suddenly, the monkey jumped off the couch and onto the table with the display of Grandma Agmonda's antique train sets. She started throwing the trains all over the room. She ran into the kitchen, jumped up onto the sink, and pulled on the kitchen curtains with all her might. Down came all the curtains within moments. She let out the most incredible screams Air and Frank had heard in their lives.

Frank slowly opened the bathroom door and yelled, "When you've captured her, just kill her!" He'd slammed the door as hard as he could.

Air checked her hand again. The monkey had bitten her right between her thumb and first finger.

Thank God, she didn't break my skin. I'd probably have had to go and have a tetanus shot.

She looked over at the monkey, who was now ripping apart Frank's mother's wool blanket that she'd just crocheted a month earlier.

"Frank, we've got real trouble out here! You know that beautiful wool blanket your mom just made and let you borrow for sitting in front of the fireplace?"

Frank opened the bathroom door about an inch and whispered, "Yeah."

"Well, the monkey just ripped it apart! I have no fucking idea what to do, and I'm afraid she's going to attack me. Frank, she doesn't seem friendly at all, and I am way too stoned for all this. I'm just going to open the front door, and maybe she'll run out. I'll close the door right after she walks out onto the porch."

Frank slowly cracked the bathroom door, a little wider this time. "Wait a minute! I have an idea," he said. "Roll up a ball of some of those dope brownies you made that are in the refrigerator and give her one. Make sure it's a big one."

"Frank! That might kill her."

"Who the fuck cares? What the fuck else are we going to do? We can't take her back the store. It's closed now. Just do it!"

"I'm too scared to move," Air cried. "She's just sitting here staring at me. Frank, this is insane! When she stands up, she's got an arm span of six feet. This fucking monkey is out here terrorizing me. I'm stoned out of my mind, and you run and hide in the bathroom, claiming your hemorrhoids are acting up. Get out here and help me!'

"I can't, Air. My grapes are killing me."

"Well, in a couple of minutes, this fucking eighty-dollar monkey is going to kill me. I can't believe this! I'm going to die either from this fucking monkey or your fucking hemmies!"

Air inched over to the refrigerator. She slowly opened the door and reached for one of the brownies squares. Reshaping it into a ball, she rolled it over to the monkey.

The monkey snatched it off the floor so swiftly Air barely saw her pick it up. The monkey's eyes never left Air's as she ate the brownie.

Jesus, that damned monkey is so smart. She seems so cunning and guile. I can feel it. She knows I'm scared of her. This was how she'd felt when she was a little girl and Paige was after her.

"Air," Frank yelled, "did you roll up the brownie and give it to her?"

"Yes," Air snapped. "If you were out here, you could watch her eating it. She's actually eating it like a human. Her little hands are holding it ever so daintily. She's taking small little bites at a time. You can come out here now, Frank. She seems to have calmed down."

"No, I'm not through in here."

"You're such an ass, Frank. I always knew you wouldn't protect me when I really needed you. All you care about is yourself!"

Air slid down to the floor about ten feet from the little queen and wondered what the hell she should do next. Within ten minutes, the monkey simply fell flat on her face. Air was sure she was dead. The fall was so abrupt. Air was sure the monkey had just suffered a heart attack or a stroke. Shit, leave it to a monkey to steal Air's thunder. Air slowly tiptoed over to the monkey and put her hand on her chest for any signs of a beating heart.

"It's okay. You can come out now, Frank! She's passed out on the floor," Air called out.

She heard the toilet flush. *That goddamned jerk! I hope his asshole is really messed up, and he won't be able to sit down for hours.*

Frank walked into the kitchen and looked directly into Air's eyes. "Air call your parents right now and tell them we're bringing their Christmas presents tonight," he said sternly.

"Frank, that's over a two-hour drive, and it's already late!" Air protested.

"I don't care. Call 'em! I'm not sleeping in this house tonight with that goddamned, wild-ass monkey. You're as nutty as your crazy-ass mother! I don't know how I let you talk me into going to that pet store in the first place!"

"Frank, I'm afraid by the time we get to my parent's house the monkey will be a dead monkey. My parents still think I'm off drugs. I promised them there'd be no more drugs in my life. Now how's this going to look when my mother opens her present and finds a drugged, dead monkey? And the coroner's report will say she died from an overdose of brownies laced with marijuana."

"Tell them you got some tranquilizers from the vet for the ride."

"Frank, they won't believe that, and you know it."

"Look, I don't give a fuck! That monkey's going, and she's going tonight! So call them. Besides, Air, by the time we get there, the dope will have worn off."

As they were backing out of the driveway, it started to rain again. Air was all too aware they were at the beginning of a two-hour drive in an old VW van, with a stoned, crazy-ass monkey. Air kept looking in the box to see if the monkey was moving at all. She was sure the monkey was dying.

Air sat quietly and a bit rigidly as they rode by exit after exit, town after town in silence. Air stared at the windshield. It was raining so hard they couldn't see more than three feet in front of the car.

I know I overdosed her. Shit, if my parents don't figure out she's stoned, they're at least going to wonder why she died. Imagine giving your mother a dead monkey for Christmas.

"You know, Frank, I feel like we're Joseph and Mary with the little baby Jesus, except this little baby Jesus is female and a monkey, and instead of three stars pointing the way, there are freeway signs telling us which way to go."

Frank just stared straight ahead.

"I want to stop and buy some wrapping paper for the box, Frank," Air insisted.

They found a drug store near Air's parent house. Air went in and bought some bright red foil wrapping and a giant green bow. As she wrapped the paper around the cage, she couldn't help but feel like she was sealing off a coffin.

As they pulled into her parents' driveway, she heard movement in the box. *Thank God!* she thought.

They got out of the car and knocked on the door. No one answered, so they just opened the front door themselves.

The family was still eating dinner when they walked in with the gigantic box and the other presents.

"Merry Christmas to everyone!" yelled Air and Frank.

"Wh-elle, Merry Christmas to you!" exclaimed D. J. "This is surely a sir-purr-rize!"

"We have presents for everyone," Air said. "We hope you all like them, especially you, Mama."

"Oh! Ground shakes alive! Y'all didn't have ta go and buy me anythang. We didn't buy y'all anythang. We just put up that old aluminum tree we bought twenty years ago and didn't bother with any ornaments. I hope ya don't mind. Seems like y'all got ever'thin' ya need, especially you, Airstream. If ya don't have it, ya jus' make it yourselves. There ain't nothin' y'all can't do."

Frank walked over and sat the big red package in D. J.'s lap, "Be careful, Mama, you never know what might be in here."

D. J. pushed her chair back from the table. As she did, she felt the box begin to rock from side to side on its own. The monkey was beginning to want out, and the longer the box was in D. J.'s lap the harder it was to kept it stable.

"My goodness, feels like there's somethin' alive in my present! It's like it's movin' all round in there. Oh my, y'all think I outta open it up? It ain't gonna hurt me, is it?" she asked with a sincere look of fear.

"Go ahead, Mom! Open it up!" yelled Air's brothers.

Air watched as D. J.'s eyes widened with anticipation. "Yep! I kin hear sumthin' a rattalin' around in here. Oh my, it's gettin' kinda heavy. Airstream, honey, are you sure this is safe?"

"Go on, Mama, open it up!" Frank motioned with his hand toward the box.

D. J. sat the box on the floor. She slowly opened the lid a little and peeked in. "Wh-elle, would ya lookie there. What is it? A raccoon?"

All of a sudden, the monkey leaped out of the box and ran straight into the living room, shrieking as though as she was being shot at by arrows.

Oh my God, she's acting just like she did earlier at the house. This is going turn into a nightmare. She looked around for Frank and heard the bathroom door slam shut.

Air's brothers started laughing while Mitchell stood up and demanded, "Airstream, contain whatever the hell that animal is."

"Everyone stood in utter disbelief, terror, and horror. Helplessly, they watched as the monkey scaled the curtains as though they were trees. Within moments, the curtains D. J. had taken weeks to make lay shredded on the floor. The monkey was in her own world and squealed with delight. She obviously had an addiction to curtains.

"Is it legal to have a monkey?" Jimmy asked. "I saw some gorillas on TV last night, and they can kill you. Is this monkey going to kill us?"

Frank came out of the bath and grabbed Air's arm. "Come on!" he shouted. "Let's get the fuck out of here!"

"Airstream, honey! Do somethin' quick," D. J. pleaded as she stood peering out from behind Mitchell. Mitchell had grabbed a baseball bat and was holding it like it was a gun.

"You boys should go to your rooms and let us take care of this."

"But what about our presents?" Ron asked.

"I think we have enough presents on our hands at the moment.

Just then, the monkey jumped up onto the dining room table, grabbed a cube of soft butter off the butter plate, and chucked it against the wall. She then reached around to her butt, shit in her hand, and threw it right at Mitchell's face. She stopped for a moment and looked around.

The monkey jumped down and followed the boys down the hallway. The boys started running into their bedroom and closed the door behind them as fast as they could. The monkey continued down the hall and into the bathroom. She stepped into the bathtub and grabbed the bar of ivory soap. She came out screaming and threw it straight at D. J.

Then the worst possible thing happened. The monkey looked around the kitchen, and for some reason, she decided to jump up on the kitchen stove. This was the worse decision she could have made. She landed right in the middle of the griddle. Unfortunately for the monkey, "griddle" was D. J.'s middle name. D. J. "griddled" everything. The griddle was still extremely hot from dinner, and the monkey severely burned all four of her paws.

Oh my God, this is worse than getting a beating from my dad, Air thought. *We're going to have to take the monkey to an emergency pet hospital.*

Everyone gasped and even D. J. turned her head away. It was too painful to watch. The monkey looked as if she was doing a little jig on the griddle while shrieking horribly.

Fuck, now D. J. can add "Griddled Monkey Paws" to her How to Live on Griddled Foods *scrapbook*, Air thought.

"Airstream, honey, you'd better take that critter back! I don't think this is gonna work out," D. J. said.

It needs to go to a hospital, Mom. It's burned its paws mighty bad, Air thought. "Mom, you've always wanted a monkey," she protested. "Ever since I was a little girl, that's all you talked about. You would tell us how badly you wanted a monkey. You wanted a monkey even more than you wanted us kids. I'm just trying to make you happy."

"Wh-elle, that ain't completely true."

"Look, Mama," Frank said. "We just spent all our fucking money on that goddamned fucking monkey. We don't have the money to take it to a hospital since we just spent all the money we had for the rest of the month. And that's not to mention we drove for over two fucking hours to get it here! Your daughter was trying to make you happy. She wanted to give you something she thought would bring you great joy. And for your information, it's rude to try and give back a Christmas present to the person who gave it to you. If you ask me, Airstream is right! You are a selfish, wizened, old blackbird still sitting on a nest of bitter eggs! So Merry Christmas to all, and to all a goodnight. Come on, Airstream. We're leaving! And I will not ever visit you people again! Take that goddamned monkey to a pet hospital."

Air looked at her father. "I'm so sorry. I guess I just can't do anything right. This is my fault entirely. I hope to God you get that monkey to a hospital."

As Air and Frank backed down the driveway, they could still hear the monkey making horrible squeals of pain. This time, Air didn't look around to see if the neighbors were curious as to what was going on. She looked up at the house. D. J. was standing on the porch.

"Y'all can't just leave without taking this damned critter with you," she yelled. "What am I supposed to do with it? Airstream, don't y'all leave without this monkey. I ain't kiddin'! I just can't imagine what on earth made you buy me a monkey!"

The rain had stopped. They drove the entire way home in silence. Air wanted to talk to Frank, but she knew it was not the time. When they arrived home, Frank went straight to the bathroom. Air got into her pajamas and went straight to bed. Frank finally came to bed, and not a word was spoken between the two of them, not that night nor the next. The subject of the monkey was never mentioned again between them.

The next morning, Frank went for a long walk. The phone rang, and Air knew it was her brother, Ron. She usually had the feelin' about who was calling when the phone rang.

"Hi, Air, I can't talk long. I just wanted you to know that Mom kept the monkey in the guest room all night. It was awful. The poor thing was like a child crying with pain. She told all of us to stay away from the room. Dad tried to talk her into calling an emergency pet hospital and having them come and pick up the monkey so they could take care of its paws, but she said that it would be fine. Something about animals had their own natural way of licking their wounds so they could heal themselves."

"Apparently, this morning, D. J. went into the room to try and catch her and put her back in that box you packed her in. Well, you'll never believe what she found."

"Oh, Ron, I can't imagine. I'm sure she'd pulled the curtains down at least. She had a thing about curtains. What else did she do?" Air asked sheepishly.

"She found the monkey with her favorite black sweater," Ron said.

"Oh god, not the one she'd personally enhanced with the 'real gemstones.' Oh, Ron, tell me she didn't ruin that sweater," Air said with a tone of disbelief.

"Yeap, the monkey pulled off all the stones on the sweater and then hid them from her. Mom went crazy. She was yelling about how no one fucked with that sweater. She threw a blanket over the monkey and immediately put it in the box and drove it to the local pet shop.

"Oh wow, that's really too bad. That really pisses me off. The only good thing about it is, hopefully, the pet store will get the monkey some medical help. I'm so sorry you have to put up with Mom in the state she must be in. I'd leave the house if you can."

"Mom's coming back in the house. I have to go. Thanks for the sweater you made me. I love it. Bye," he said and hung up the phone.

A week after talking with Ron, Air received a letter from D. J. She briefly mentioned the monkey—something about how she'd taken it to a pet store. "It just kinda didn't work out, honey."

221

⌁

After the holidays, Frank and Air said very little to one another. They simply ignored each other and did their own thing. Needless to say, Frank was going off the deep end. He finally announced he was leaving her and "them." Once again, he threatened he was headed for the "Demmie Home for the Bewildered." Air had heard of the place many times but still had no idea where it was located or if it was even a real place. The conversation ended there, until about a week later.

On morning, Air and Frank were sitting out on the deck having breakfast. It was another beautiful, sunny, warm Santa Cruz spring morning. Both of them ate and stared out at the ocean. Out of the blue, Frank turned to Airstream and said, "I am leaving now. You all outnumber me! It's you; seventeen cats; three goldfish; a part-time cricket who comes and goes; at least one hundred houseplants that require constant watering; and a continuous collection of tarantulas, dragonflies, gopher snakes, and squealing wild birds brought in for viewing just as we sit down to dinner each night thanks to Dandelion.

"Fuck it! I'm getting the hell out of here! Don't tell anyone, but I'm going to the "Demmie Home for the Bewildered" once and for all."

"Frank! How can I tell anyone? I don't have a clue where the place is or even if it's real. What about Dandelion? How can you just leave her? What's going to happen to me, Frank? Do you have any idea how the hell I am going to make it without you?"

Frank got up and kissed Air on the forehead. "Airstream, I've adored you from the first moment I saw you. I've loved you beyond my wildest dreams. You are the most fanciful woman I've ever known or had a chance to live with. You are naturally talented and someday you will be famous. Trust me. I watch you paint, and I ask myself why I wasted time going to college. You're gifted and your paintings will be in museums, it's just a matter of time. I hope you will still be alive to see how much you have contributed to people's lives with your art. I'm still blown away you've never taken an art class and don't even know what the primary and secondary colors are. Your

222

paintings are stunning and emotional. I've never gotten tired of looking at them, and I see something different in them every time I spend time with them. You must promise me to keep throwing paint around and explore all the mediums you can. There's nothing you can't do. I gave you my eyes long ago. Don't let me down, Air."

Before getting into the music business, Frank had been a famous sculptor. None of his friends understood how he could just walk away from the art world and never look back just as he had with the music business. He had been an established artist and was commissioned by wealthy and famous people to create unique dollhouses. He'd had long conversations about art with Airstream and had taught her how to see beyond what was right in front of her.

"You're fun, spontaneous, gorgeous, and so sexy. But you know, Air, Libras and Cancers aren't compatible. I've been a lucky man to have you in my life for as long as I have. I've taken you as far as I can. You need to take the next step up the ladder, and I don't have the skills to show you the way. You'll do just fine on your own. I'm just a stone around your neck now."

Frank picked up his packed bags and left. Air was reminded of her father leaving her mother when she was young. Maybe he would be back. Maybe he wouldn't. She suspected he wouldn't. He didn't leave a forwarding address. He was so paranoid. He would never put his real name in the phone book, and none of his bills ever came addressed in his real name.

When the mail came, Air never really knew if was for Frank or simply a wrong address. He'd decided long ago the safest name, in terms of remembering who he was at the moment, was to just to spell his name backward. Oddly enough, nothing ever came addressed to "Knarf."

❧ 16 ❧

After Frank left, Air couldn't move. She felt empty and sad. *I don't know why I should feel so sad. This is what I wanted. I wanted Frank to leave me.* She repositioned herself in the chair so the sun did not burn her skin. She looked at the table and remembered when they had found the set at the local flea market. It was an exquisite, ornate antique Parisian rod iron breakfast set. Air loved having breakfast out on the deck. She sat motionless for hours. She just watched the waves and felt waves of memories flowing over her. She thought of all the years she'd spent with Frank. He had been her savior. He had taken her under his wing and had saved her from a life of danger and despair. He was a decent man. *I owe him my life*, she mused. *I'd be dead if he hadn't asked me to stay with him.*

She waited for James to get off work and went into the house and called him.

"James, Frank left today," she said.

"What do you mean, Air?"

"I mean that Frank packed his stuff and left me."

Air started crying. Dandelion jumped up in her lap and started purring.

"Well, isn't that what you wanted?" James asked.

"Yes, it is. I just have no clue what to do now. He told me I could stay here for a couple more months, but after that, I have no clue what to do. I think after I move out, he'll move back in again. His folks rarely come down anymore. I know Frank leaving me was the best decision, but I'm starting to have a really bad panic attack being all alone," Airstream said. "I feel like I'm headed to the ER again soon."

"Air, when was the last time you saw Dr. Shepard?"

"Oh about three weeks ago."

"Does he know Frank left you?"

"No, how could he?"

"I think you should make an appointment with him. He's always helped you in the past."

"I'll call him tomorrow," Air said.

Airstream had endeared herself to a doctor who couldn't resist treating her. He found her charming and adorable. He was determined to reassure her she was healthy physically except for her phobias. He would see her whenever she was in the depths of her panic attacks about her heart.

Air would always wear clothing she'd designed herself just to impress him. He loved how she seemed to have no inhibitions. He could sense how creative she was just by listening to the stories she would share about the different projects she'd been involved with. One day, she asked him if he would consider bartering with her. He didn't hesitate to answer yes. She offered embroidering designs on the cuffs and collars of his shirts instead of paying him money. He wanted to help her and agreed to her offer.

Dr. Shepard would schedule her at the end of his day, partly because he knew there was nothing wrong with her and partly because she was such a treat to wind down the day with. The nurses knew he didn't charge her and would always give her a nasty look when she came for her appointments.

The next day, Air called Dr. Shepard and told him about Frank leaving her.

"Dr. Shepard, I can hardly breathe, and I'm terrified. I'm starting to have severe panic attacks again. Could you order lab work for me and I could come and see you next week?"

"Of course, Air," he said. "I'll call over to the county hospital, and you can go in tomorrow. Make sure you fast for eight hours. I'll see you next week with the results. I'll transfer you back to my front desk, and you can schedule a time to come in."

"Thank you. You're the best."

⟶❦⟵

The following week, Air was sitting in his office waiting for test results. Dr. Shepard's office was very different than any other doctor's office Air had ever seen. It was almost like an artist studio. The building was on top of the Santa Cruz Mountains secluded in the redwood trees. His walls were covered with shelves full of handmade baskets and small sculptures of naked women. Air thought they had something to do with the body and medicine. There was a large collection of medical books as well as art books. A long, antique leather couch from the forties for clients was positioned right across from his looming, gigantic oak desk. He had hand-woven rugs on both the walls and the floors, which he had brought back from a trip to Jerusalem. The room was brightly lit by the sun streaming in through the windows on three sides of his office. He had incredible views of the ocean and the hills leading down to the cliffs. Air loved his office. She felt safe there.

The door opened, and Air jumped up to hug him.

He smiled and said, "It's good to see you."

"I'm so happy to be here. I could sleep the night away on your couch, you know."

"Air, I have the results of your blood work here. As usual, unfortunately, I can't find a thing wrong with you. I hate to tell you this, but I think you're going to live to be a ninety-nine-year-old woman. I want to talk to you about something serious, and I want you to hear me out before you react to what I have to say. Have you ever considered hypnosis to deal with your panic attacks?"

"Hypnosis?"

"Yes. It has been proven to be very effective for some people who suffer from multiple personality disorder. Air, I've been treating you for months. Every time you come to visit me, you seem to be a slightly different person. Sometimes, you're very proper, and at other times you try your best to seduce me. You know what I am talking about."

"Multiple personality disorder? What the hell is that? Hypnosis?"

"Air, I believe you're someone who has more than one personality. Each personality has his or her particular beliefs system, style, and interests. Instead of being someone who most people would describe as a person with a certain type of personality, you're someone who has many personalities. Most people have a difficult time understanding you and probably think you're a little loony. For instance, one day you tell me something you deeply believe in, and the very next time I see you, you contradict yourself with a new concept and belief. Have you ever noticed you have at least five different 'looks'?"

"Looks, what do you mean *looks*?"

"What I mean is, you seem to have at least five different sets of wardrobes. Each one depicts a particular personality. I have seen you come here dressed as though you worked in the corporate world. The next week you dress like Audrey Hepburn without a care in the world. The following week you'll come in looking like you just got back from the horse races. I've seen the side of you that is incredibly sensual and sexy. This is what I mean. Does any of this ring true to you?"

"Well, to tell you the truth, I've often wondered why, out of the blue, I have this desire to go home and change my clothes. It's like I don't feel like myself suddenly, and the clothes I am wearing feel awkward. Sometimes, I'll change clothes four or five times in the same day. Each outfit makes me feel like a different person. I have a hell of time packing for a trip because I never know what kind of mood I'm going to be in. That's all I ever thought it was—moods."

"Well, Air, I'm thinking it might be more than just moods. I've come to know you pretty well. I would like you to see a very good friend of mine. Her name is Dr. Susan Hill, and she's the best in her field. Here's her number."

"Does this mean you're not going to see me anymore?"

"Air, you can come and see me anytime you want. I really want you to give Dr. Hill a chance. You're influenced by your personalities more than most people. I think Dr. Hill can assist you in bringing all of these personalities together, which will give you a sense of oneness."

"Please don't misunderstand me, Air," Dr. Shepard added. "You need all of these personalities. They are all parts of you. As it stands now, it's as if they all live in different houses in different cities and hold different jobs, and all have varied interests and routines. What we need to do is to get you and all your parts into one communal house, where everyone is working together.

"I hope someday you will come to appreciate all of your parts for exactly who they are and their importance. Your dark side is every bit as important as your light side. You are a rare and unusual human being in this world. I must confess, Airstream, I'm struck by your independence and self-sufficiency. You are truly a free spirit. You have a type of magic that beckons you to go dancing no matter what is occurring in your life, even while amid your anxiety attacks.

"It seems to me you want to share yourself with others, not as a way of losing yourself in them or sacrificing your independence or somehow forgetting your spiritual center, but somehow from the intimacy you create with another person. You continually grow stronger in your individuality, more connected to the world, and more open. You come across so intense most people feel as though you are about to devour them. I believe you are completely unaware of how your presence affects others, Air.

"Someday you will be someone people are drawn to for healing purposes. I am sure of this. You are already wise beyond your years. You have had a very difficult life, and you have survived, Air. You are strong, and yet you don't believe you are. You continue to move forward because you have a little crystal of hope in your hand. Life gives us magic and life brings us tragedy. But after you have seemingly devoured your prey, you allow them to pass through your body, so they too have a chance to be reborn into a fuller, stronger, and a wiser self," Dr. Shepard said in a strong tone of voice.

"I deeply believe there are very few people who really know who you are. You are a marvelously passionate human being, Air. I think you have difficulty in deciphering your realities sometimes. It would seem to me that this persistent irritating thing called 'reality' confuses and, frankly, frightens you. You end up in here, convinced you're dying. It amazes me how you are the last to know what a gift you are, Air. Please go and see my friend Dr. Hill."

"Okay, I'll call her but only because you want me to, Doc."

Air called Dr. Hill as soon as she returned home. The receptionist told Air there had been a cancellation the next day and Air could meet with Dr. Hill around noon. Air was a bit hesitant, but she took the appointment.

After hearing about all the different personalities she had and recognizing her need to change clothes all the time, Air was befuddled as to how to dress. *What personality is going to see this new doctor?* she asked herself. *I have no clue how to dress. I guess I'll just wear a vintage dress and a straw hat. No, that'll just make me look like a little girl. I'll wear some jeans and a T-shirt. I'll look normal.*

It turned out that Dr. Hill's office was only a mile from where Air lived. Her office was in one of those expensive complexes with other psychiatrists. Air recognized the complex. Air entered the building and walked down the long hallway until she found Dr. Hill's name.

She took a deep breath and opened the door. A young girl who looked as though she was still in high school greeted her with a beaming smile.

"Hello," Air said quietly, "my name is Airstream, and I'm here to see Dr. Hill at noon."

"Yes, hello Airstream," the girl said cheerily. "I have a little bit of paperwork for you to fill out if you don't mind. Here's a clipboard and pen and just answer anything that is appropriate to you. The doctor will see you as soon as you have finished." The girl seemed to be too happy.

I guess that's a job requirement, Air thought. *I'm sure most of the people who come here are basket cases and she needs to be cheery.*

Air filled out about five pages of medical questions and handed the clipboard back to the girl.

"Great," she said, smiling from ear to ear. "I'll let the doctor know you're ready. Just one moment."

Air could hear a door open, and Dr. Hill came out into the waiting room to greet her. The first thing Air noticed was how tall Dr. Hill was. She was dressed in clothes that told Air she was definitely from the sixties. She immediately felt at ease and knew she was going to like this woman, whether she helped her or not.

"Hello, Airstream," Dr. Hill said. "Would you please follow me back to my office?"

Air stood up and sheepishly followed her. *Why do I feel like I'm being led to slaughter? I'm so fucking gullible and naive. I believe anything and everything anybody tells me. I have no idea why I agreed to this. I hope to God I'm not making another one of my stupid decisions. I just have to trust Dr. Shepard. I know he cares about me and would never advise me to do something that would hurt me.*

"Please sit wherever you'd like," Dr. Hill said, pointing to various seating arrangements.

Air looked around. Dr. Hill's office was very informal. It looked like a comfortable living room in a hippie's house. A couple of large beanbags sat on the floor, and large pillows with paisley prints were stacked in the corner. The windows were small, and plants drooped over the sides of their ledges. Air briefly remembered her mother's Wandering Jews and their journey "to the other side." There were paper shades for curtains. Air looked at the black-and-white landscape photographs that were jammed against each other. She couldn't stand it when a piece of good art wasn't given the space it needed to be acknowledged as fine art. She noticed all the photographs were signed by someone with the same last name as Dr. Hill. The floors were decorated with handmade braided rugs.

I bet this woman smokes dope, Air thought to herself as she chose a reclining leather chair facing Dr. Hill's chair.

"Airstream, I want to acknowledge your courage in agreeing to see me," Dr. Hill said. "I know Dr. Shepard very well. We are very good friends and have been colleagues for a very long time. Would you like me to call you Airstream? Or is there another name you'd prefer me to call you?"

Oh God, is she thinking I might be somebody other than myself at the moment? Hell only knows what Dr. Shepard has said told this doctor about me. "You can call me Air, if you'd like. Most of my friends call me Air."

"Fine, I will call you Air. If you feel comfortable with calling me by my first name, Susan, that's fine with me."

"Great, I'll call you Susan. Susan, what are we going to do today? Do we really have to waste fifty minutes with you taking notes on my history?"

"No, we don't. Actually, we're going to have our first hypnosis session today. Have you ever been hypnotized before?"

"God no!" Air said as though being hypnotized was something ridiculous.

"You will experience being in a very deeply relaxed state. You will allow your body to let go of any tension or tautness. I will begin to count back from ten to one out loud. With each number, I will ask you to relax and feel yourself sinking deeper and deeper into the chair. I will ask you to try to go back in time. Air, I am going to allow whatever you experience to just let it take its own course. I know you are here with the goal of bringing all your different personalities together as one, but let's see what comes up for you and just flow with it like a stream. Is that okay with you?"

"What do you mean *back in time*? How far back in time? Will I remember what happens?"

"If you want to remember, you will. When I decide to bring you back to the present, I will ask you whether or not you want to remember what we've discussed during the session. It will always be your decision."

"Oh, pretty cool."

"Are you ready to begin?" Dr. Hill asked reassuringly.

"I guess so."

"Okay. I'd like for you to fully recline in the chair with your feet up, and we will begin."

Air pushed the recliner back as Susan had asked, and almost immediately she heard the doctor beginning to count back from ten very slowly.

"Ten, nine, eight ... you're beginning to feel more and more relaxed. You're starting to go deeper and deeper back in time. You can feel yourself sinking deeper and deeper into the chair, and your body feels very heavy. Your body feels so heavy you cannot lift your arm or legs. Now, Air, when I decide to bring you out of this state of deep relaxation, I will simply count slowly from one to three, and you will be present in the room again. Do you understand?"

Air could feel herself nodding her head up and down. At first, Air didn't believe she was "under." She felt as though she could open her eyes and lift her arms anytime she wanted. *This is just a game*, she thought. Abruptly, thoughts she'd either suppressed since childhood or had never known about began to emerge.

Susan noticed Air's breath had suddenly become labored. "What's happening Airstream? Where are you? How old are you?"

"I'm four years old," Air answered in a little girl's voice. *What the fuck is going on? I'm talking like a little kid.*

"Where are you? And do you know your name?" Susan asked quickly and decisively.

Air looked around. "I'm in an old kitchen. It seems like a log cabin, and there's just one big room. There's a huge black, woman and I think she's getting ready to give me a bath. I'm sitting in a huge, round metal tub full of water in the middle of the floor. There are a lot of tiny windows above the sink and cabinets everywhere full of jars and canisters. The floor has wide, wooden planks that seem to be really long. The door is open, and it's a sunny day. I think it's morning. I hear birds outside. There are about ten stools around this large, wooden table. I don't see a refrigerator, but I do see a large stove with wood stacked up along side of it. The place seems run-down. I feel the presence of other children, but I don't see them," Air responded, this time in her own voice.

"What's happening now, Air?"

"The big black woman is getting something out of the cabinet. She's wearing a dirty long dress and an apron. Her hair is covered with a dirty white cloth, and it has a knot on the side. She's kneeling down beside me now and starting to bathe me with a washrag. The water is cold."

Air started to shiver as she sat in the chair. Susan began to think something was wrong. Air became aware a part of her was sitting on the other side of Susan's office watching the whole scene. She couldn't tell if there was an actual body there or just a presence she sensed. "The feelin'" came over Air that this part who was watching was beginning to feel anxious. Something was wrong.

"What's going on now?"

"I think there is something wrong with me."

"What do you mean by wrong?"

"I think there is something wrong with my body, like I'm severely retarded or something."

"What is the date? Do you know the date, Air?"

"It's 1849. I mean 1949! I mean 1849! Wait a minute; I was born in 1949. It can't be 1849. This can't be happening! I'm scared," said a frightened little girl with a voice that quivered as she spoke.

"What is your name? Who am I talking to?"

"Suzie. I mean Airstream. But my name is Suzie. This can't be!"

"Just stay with me, Air. Just stay with this. I'm here with you. What's happening now? You're four years old, and the year is 1849. Your name is Suzie, and a black woman is giving you a bath."

"She's starting to push me down into the water. I can't breathe. I can't breathe! I can't get up! She's holding me down! I feel pressure on my chest," yelled Air.

"Airstream, I'm going to count to three, and when I'm through, you'll open your eyes and be back in this room safe and relaxed. If you want to remember this, you can. Do you want to remember this, Airstream?"

"Yes!"

"One, two, three."

Air opened her eyes. She took a very deep breath. She was stunned and sat there staring at Susan. She couldn't move. She felt like she couldn't open her mouth to talk. She remembered everything and, oddly, felt a sense of embarrassment.

"Do you remember what happened?"

"Yes, I remember everything," Air said with a petrified look on her face.

"Do you want to talk about it? We still have a little time left."

"I don't understand. What just happened?"

"I'm as surprised as you are, Air. I was expecting to talk with one of your personalities and instead you had what we refer to as a "trans life regression" experience. If I had thought this might happen I would have prepared you, and I am very sorry I didn't. Do you believe in past lives?"

"Yes, I do," responded Air firmly.

"Only you can make sense of what happened and how it fits in your present life or your life before becoming who you know yourself to be now," Susan said in a slow soothing tone. "It certainly appears to be obvious that your anxiety attacks about heart attacks have significant meaning for you. I don't believe it is a coincidence that you felt pressure on your chest and the sensation of not being able to breathe; after all, all of these feelings are all present in your life now. It is my belief that these current heart-related experiences, which you fear so greatly, actually come bringing 'gifts' for you from the past. You are fortunate enough to be a multisensory person among your many other qualities." Susan paused for a moment, a perplexed look crossing her face.

"Now, I'm not saying you don't have multiple personalities, and I believe each one was created from a traumatic experience during this lifetime. You are a highly sensitive and a quite intuitive person. These attacks you feel, which are so paralyzing, might be worth their weight in gold. But, Air, you must be willing to put on your hard hat and take out a flashlight. You must be willing to embrace parts of yourself you don't like. Some of these parts you are experiencing now have come with you into this life because much of your traumatic childhood was very much like your past lives. The kind of trauma you've experienced most people don't survive. They live out their lives as victims. You appear to be someone who is unstoppable. Even though you have these anxiety attacks that have you landing in the ER, they don't stop you. You have found a way to live with them, or perhaps I should say tolerate them. Just because we have learned about one personality from the past does not mean that personalities from the present will come out. I am surprised you experienced past life regression so quickly."

Susan held Air's gaze for a moment. "What I want to work with you on is having your personalities become more infused with one another. I am certain there are more personalities along with Suzie.

Even though Suzie appears to be in a past life, I am quite sure she is here with you now. We need to work together to reassure each of your parts that they need each other. They are actually the flip side of one another. For instance, how could one know love without knowing hate?"

"What do you mean?" asked Air, puzzled.

"Did you know that a hundred years ago, children who were born with any type of disability were put to death almost immediately? In some families, a disabled child or even an adult who became a burden to the family was put to death. Deformed newborns were usually drowned immediately after birth. I'm surprised you were allowed to live until you were four. Back in 1849, everyone in the family had to carry his or her own weight. Perhaps you suddenly became very sick and were living somewhere that a doctor could not be called," Susan said, her tone informative.

"You're kidding!" Air said leaning forward to hear more of this mysterious and baffling concept. "I've never heard of such a thing before."

"All of this is historical truth, Air. It's been going on for centuries."

"I can't believe this! In 1949, I mean 1849, I was drowned because I was retarded?"

"I don't know. What I know is that you said you couldn't breathe over and over. It appeared to me indeed you were having difficulty with your breathing, but I don't know. What do you imagine drowning to be like?"

"I don't know. I can't even swim."

Susan looked up at the clock hanging on the wall and said, "I'm sorry, Airstream, our time is up. Would you like to come next week?"

"I guess," she said, a bit dazed.

Air didn't tell anyone about her sessions with Susan. All she could think of for the rest of the week was the reality that she might be being haunted by events of her "past life."

I hope to God my next session isn't as bizarre as this last one was, she found herself thinking. *I can't handle any more evidence that my belief systems related to "life after death" are real. I like telling people I believe that crap, but I don't want to know that it really happens. That would mean I could actually have a dead person visit me or that it's possible I really do create my own reality.*

"Good afternoon, Airstream. How are you?" asked Susan.

"You're really asking how are *we*, aren't you?" Air retorted.

"Not at all, Airstream. I see you as a total person. I'm glad you chose to see me again. Shall we get started?"

"Let's go for it."

Air sat down in the recliner and took three deep breaths. Susan began counting down from ten to one. With each number, she told her she would be going into a deeper and deeper relaxed state. Air relaxed immediately.

"Air, where are you?"

"Oh my God! I seem to be lying on the ground, and the sky is gray. I can see old stone castles and peasant-looking people everywhere. There is a huge crowd around me. I have no idea what the commotion is about. The crowd is very loud and people are shouting something. I don't understand why I am on the ground. It looks like the 1600s."

"What is happening to you?" asked Susan.

"There are men trying to hold me down. I think I am a man. I can hear someone yelling for me to be executed for having committed adultery. I can feel I am lying on cobbled stones, and now strangers are coming toward me and placing stones one by one on my chest. The stones are mounting, and I am starting to not be able to breathe! I can hear someone saying that my chest is about to cave in. I'm dying! Oh my God, I'm dying! This is so frightening! I have this horrible sensation of an incredible amount of weight on my chest!"

"Air, I am counting to three, and then I want you to open your eyes. One, two, three."

"What the hell was that all about?" Air asked as she gasped for air.

"Air, haven't you ever heard of people being stoned to death centuries ago?"

"No, I've never heard of such a thing. And what about me being a man! I know I was a man—a man who had committed adultery! And I was being stoned to death. Oh my God, I've never heard of such a thing. That was awful. I could not breathe. They just kept coming and placing stones on my chest hoping for my chest to cave in," Air said in exasperation.

Air could hear the part of her who sat across the room laughing hysterically. She or he thought that Air was talking about being "stoned on drugs" back in the 1600s. Air had still not told Susan there was a part of her in the room making sure Air was safe.

Air looked at Susan and said, "Susan, I'm really starting to freak out. Up until now, I really believed we were sort of playing a game. For the most part, I didn't really believe in all this past life shit. But now, experiencing this … this being stoned to death back in the 1600s and you telling me that this used to really happen makes me feel like I'm always going to have panic attacks because I've done really bad stuff in my past lives. And by the way, I've always told people that I believe in shit like that, but I honestly was just saying that to look good. I swear to you, I have never heard of people being executed in that way, so how could I have just had that happen to me? I wouldn't even know to make it up. Nothing like that has ever crossed my mind. I don't want to admit there's some validity to all of this. How could I have experienced such an event if I've never heard of anything like this? Shit, I want out of here."

"Air, I want to reassure you that you are safe here. I will not let anything happen to you. Remember, it is your decision to remember these sessions. It is my professional obligation to emphasize that you seem to be reliving past life occurrences that correlate with your present-life dilemmas. I am referring to you feeling like you cannot breathe and thinking you are having a heart attack," Susan said. Her tone was stern, yet there was a slight pleading in her voice, as if she was trying to convince Air to stick it out.

Fuck, there's no way I can look the other way anymore about this past life crap. Air wished she could tell someone about what was happening to her. The experience of being stoned to death had felt weirder than being drowned had felt. She was beginning to feel more worthless than ever, but now all of her anxiety attacks seemed to make sense. *How the hell am I going to make amends with the damage I've done to so many people in my past lives? Am I doomed this time around? Is this why I've come back, just to suffer for all the pain I've caused others?*

"Shit, Susan, even back in the 1600s I was messed up." She let out a long sigh. "Being a man is a little farfetched, don't you think? I must have gotten the vision wrong. I must have been a woman who had messed around with some other woman's man.

"I've got to get out of here and go get drunk with some of my friends," she added before Susan could respond. "I have to be very careful about what I say. None of my friends know I am seeing you, much less that I'm going through hypnosis. I can just see myself getting plastered and starting in with this past life crap. God forbid I should lose it and say something like, 'Yeah, today I was at my shrink's office, and she hypnotized me. I remembered when I was a man back in the 1600s, and I committed adultery. I was stoned to death.' She heard herself laughing, but she didn't really feel like it was funny.

Air looked at Susan, feeling like she was stranded and up the creek without a paddle. *If you only knew how shitty I feel right now*, she thought. *I've been a loser all my life, and it doesn't look like things are getting any better.*

Weekly sessions with Susan had been going on for months now. Air was finally beginning to find out about her different personalities. She didn't time travel much anymore. She discovered she had about seven strong personalities in her present life. It took about two months before anyone wanted to come forward and reveal his or her identity. Eventually, each personality made an appearance and talked about him or herself. Initially, they all wanted to talk about how difficult it was to get their due time during the day with Airstream.

Air's personalities had very little in common. They had different names, manners, styles, and dress and varied interests. She even had a set of twin girls, both with the same name, Little Suzie. They were four years old. Susan informed Air that personalities didn't age. They were born during a time of specific trauma and would always stay the age they were when they emerged. This meant Air had twins within her with the emotional mentality of a four-year-old. Susan explained to Air that she had created these characters instead of staying in her body during times that were too painful. One of the twins cried incessantly, while the other was always up to something and a delightful little prankster. It was interesting to Air that they were four years old. She found it more than a coincidence their names and ages were the same as the little girl in her past life who had been drowned. Air now understood why she'd had so many countless nights feeling like a little girl who was crying and incapable of stopping. These memories brought Air a lot of sadness and grief.

At the beginning of one particular session, Air sat down and promptly said to Susan, "When we start our session, I would like you to ask the Little Suzie who constantly cries if she knows about the other Suzie who lived in 1849."

Air was afraid of the emotions that might be released if Little Suzie did know that little girl, but she felt strongly that she needed to know more about the deep sadness and somehow, if possible, reduce the pain. Air and Susan never knew when crying Little Suzie was going to show up. At this point, she'd appeared only once briefly. Susan had questioned her about her sadness, but Little Suzie hadn't uttered a word. Air became Little Suzie and knew she was sitting in front of Susan sobbing. When she left, Air's facial muscles were very sore. Air knew she'd cried the entire time Little Suzie had timidly emerged. Despite Susan's many questions, Little Suzie hadn't replied. Air could feel the nonstop tears running down her face and realized she must look ridiculous with mascara all over her face.

"Air, I couldn't tell that you were crying at all," Susan had said. "There were no visible signs that you were crying. When Little Suzie came out, you just sat there in the chair motionless. I didn't see you crying; nor do you make any crying sounds. To me, you looked the same as before she visited me. Air was in total disbelief and immediately got up and went to the mirror Susan had hanging on the wall. Air wore water-based mascara, so she expected her cheeks to be streaked with black lines. She'd vividly experienced the deep sobbing. Yet as she looked at herself in the mirror, there were no visible signs that she'd shed tears.

"This is impossible! I felt the tears running down my face! There's not a bit of black smudging under my eyes—not even any white lines through the blush I had packed on my cheeks today!"

"I have no explanation, Air. There's not a lot of information about hypnosis."

During the following sessions with Susan, Air had met her most predominant personality—Claire. Claire constantly reminded Air to be "perfect." She was charming, gracious, and very intelligent. Air could sense Susan enjoyed talking with Claire. Claire sat quite stiffly and crossed her legs properly. She would talk slowly, unlike Airstream. In fact, she used words Airstream never used and, on occasion, words Air had never heard of.

Veronica was Air's sexy, teasing, languid, sensual part. She was great. Air loved watching her. Air was amazed at how self-assured Veronica was with her body and sense of beauty. She would slink down in the chair, slightly raise one hip, and pucker her lips. Veronica always put one arm on her hip and the other under her chin and ever so slyly tilted her head to the left so she was always looking at you from the corners of her eyes. It was as if she had one eye on Susan and the other on everything that moved in the room.

Faye was Air's favorite personality. She was her wild and crazy part. She was spontaneous and creative. Her middle name was "Dare." Air could not resist a dare no matter what, unless it wasn't safe. Faye was Air's part that allowed her to dress uniquely and unabashedly. She held very little sacred. She loved to talk about subjects that made most people very uncomfortable. Faye had no problem with second thoughts. They simply didn't exist; nor did regrets or failures. Everything was a learning opportunity, and Faye made the best of every possibility that came her way. She loved dancing and partying all night long and would urge Air to drink wine, play music, and draw all night long. Air felt liberated when

Faye was around. She rarely thought of heart attacks or had panic attacks when Faye wanted to play.

Oh God, then there was Joe-Bob. When Joe-Bob first made his appearance both Air and Susan were stunned. Susan and Air had been dealing with her fears about having a heart attack whenever Air made love with someone.

"Let yourself go. Way back," Susan had said. "I'm counting back from ten, and by the time I get to one, you'll be very deeply relaxed. You're going deeper and deeper and deeper."

Susan waited to see who would make an appearance. She waited for about ten minutes.

"Is anyone here with me now? Who is here with me? Do you have a name?"

The leather recliner suddenly moved into an upright position. Air took on a very rigid posture and spread her legs wide open. She leaned over toward Susan as if to tell her a secret. The part of Air who always sat across the room and watched everything about died because she knew Susan could see her underwear. She was horribly embarrassed.

"Listen here, Doc. I don't like screwin' no man. It just ain't right! I ain't no goddamn queer," Air said in a very deep male voice.

Susan's facial expression changed from one of listening to extreme alertness. She raised her eyebrows and asked, "Who am I talking with? Do you have a name?"

"Yes, ma'am, sure I gotta a name. Name's Joe-Bob."

"It's a pleasure to meet you, Joe-Bob."

"Pleasure's all mine, Doc."

"Joe-Bob, what makes you feel it's not okay for Airstream to have sexual relations if she feels she wants to. She's quite capable of making her own decisions."

"You don't understand, Doc. You just don't understand. I feel like I'm some sort of queer when she's screwin' some guy."

"Ah, is this why Airstream has been having feelings of wanting to have an affair with a woman? Are you suggesting this to her so you yourself can have some sex?"

"Well, all I know is I ain't no goddamned fagot!"

"Joe-Bob, do you think we could work out some sort of agreement so everyone concerned will be happy?"

"Like what are ya proposin', Doc?"

"Could I talk to the part of Airstream that feels like she's going to have a heart attack whenever she makes love?"

"I'm here, Doctor."

"Can you tell me who am I talking to?"

"Veronica."

"Hello, Veronica, we have a problem. Joe-Bob feels as though he is a queer when you are making love to a man. He feels so uncomfortable about it that he is giving Airstream suggestions of having a heart attack or pursuing a lesbian affair.

"My suggestion is, when you are planning to make love, you let him know so he'll have time to make other arrangements, such as going to a football game or a baseball game. Perhaps he could take the crying Little Suzie to the park with him while Air is making love. How does that sound?"

"That sounds reasonable to me."

"Okay. Thanks. Great! May I please speak with Joe-Bob again? Thank you, Veronica."

"Are you here, Joe-Bob?"

"I don't like that crying Little Suzie. Nobody likes crying Little Suzie. Shit, all she does is cry all the damned time!"

"Okay, I understand that. Otherwise the football game sounds good?"

"The baseball game does," says Joe-Bob.

"Fine. Let's try this out for the next week and see how it works. Thank you, Joe-Bob. I am going to talk with Airstream now. Air, I'm going to count to three. When I'm through, you'll be awake, refreshed, and full of energy. One, two, three."

Air opened her eyes. She was shocked and could hardly look at Susan. She wished Susan had asked, "Do you want to remember this?" She'd have said no, so she could just smile and say, "See you next week," and slither out the door. But oh no, she had to deal with this one. She sensed Susan's eagerness to talk about the session. She almost seemed excited, which was not in the script for a therapist.

"Do you remember what happened?" Susan asked.

"Yes, unfortunately."

"Do you want to talk about it?"

"No," Air remarked quickly.

"Okay, I will see you next week, Air."

After her session with Susan, Air stopped by her favorite bar to have a glass of wine and reflect about this multiple personality crap. She took out her little black journal that she always had with her wherever she went. She opened it and was about to write when she heard an internal voice saying, *What the hell have you learned, dear? Do you really think you're changing?* It was Joe-Bob.

Not much if she still sees that little ballerina that was dancing on the ceiling in our bedroom back in Texas. I used to stare at that dancing lady when I'd get caught doing something bad and get sent to my bedroom! said someone deep within her. It sounded like the prankster Little Suzie.

Still trying to find your own sense of personal freedom? said someone Air was familiar with, Veronica perhaps.

Hey, give her a break tonight. She's had a rough year, and it's almost her birthday, remarked a sympathetic inner friend that sounded like Claire.

Parts, parts, parts. I am so sick of them and their constant internal chatter to me. As time went by, Air had found herself more imprisoned by all her parts—or at least more accountable to them. Her mature and responsible parts were becoming even more responsible and mature, despite her desperate attempts at keeping her wild abandonment and her sense of free-spiritedness, and this was driving her nuts.

She thought about how Susan had told her parts remained the same age as when they'd first appeared. And all of these parts wanted "Air time" at the same time. It was difficult playing out a four-year-old named Little Suzie and then suddenly switching the conversation to one about community development just to give Claire the same amount of time—tormenting to say the least.

I'm waking up almost every night in an altered state of consciousness, and I ask you, whatever happened to that wonderful young girl "we" all used to know and have fun with? Veronica would ask.

Sometimes I wish I'd grown up to be a race car driver and made contact with the outside wall rather than making contact with my inner personality friends, Air thought, hoping "they" were all listening.

Damn, she thought. *None of you will ever experience freckles or moles. Some of you won't grow up to find out your tits are never going to be big enough. None of you will ever have the opportunity of going through a crisis and finding out you can count on yourself.*

Airstream, I think you should lighten up on yourself. Besides, you have luck these days remember? Faye said.

I'm scared, Air thought back. *All of you know I have nothing left in my bag of tricks. I mean, I've done everything I know how to do, and none of it has gotten me anywhere. I have nothing left to do. I have no marketable skills or talents to ensure financial freedom, and that's always been my goal—to be able to make decisions that weren't fear based. It's all about money!*

You know it hurts us all to feel you suffer so much emotionally. You simply never trust yourself. Plus, you're so damned impatient, said Claire.

I do know, added Faye, *where there's a will there's a way, and we're going to be just fine. Air, trust me.*

No! That's not true, yelled Joe-Bob. *Or you wouldn't be wasting your short and tricky time on the planet with this heart attack shit.*

Air closed her journal and lit a cigarette. She looked over and motioned for the bartender to bring her another glass of wine. She was definitely going to get drunk and shut all her parts up.

17

Air was working in the garden when she heard the doorbell ring. She kicked her gardening shoes off and walked into the house. She could see her friend Patty peeking in the window.

Before Patty and Air had become good friends, Patty and her husband, Gerry, would often stop by and visit Frank. Patty was always stoned and disheveled-looking. Nothing she wore quite matched, and most of the time she was missing something, like her purse or an earring. She wore extremely short cutoff jeans with the pockets hanging down below the cutoff line and see-through T-shirts. Her long hair always looked as if she'd just gotten out of a convertible after a long drive along the coast. She hadn't been very friendly toward Air in the beginning.

One evening, during dinner, Air had asked Patty about her past.

"Well, I graduated from Cal Berkeley and used to live for being a high school teacher. I went to school with Gerry, but I didn't realize he cared for me. I started receiving love letters from him. We dated and fell in love. I quit teaching and we moved to Santa Cruz," Patty had said giving a matter-of-fact summary.

Air suddenly realized that Patty had been her math teacher in high school. Many students had thought she was too young to be a teacher. She'd dressed extremely conservatively—two-piece gray suits with gray pumps—and had styled her hair in a French roll back then. But sure enough, she was the same woman.

"Oh my God!" Air had exclaimed. "I know you! Were you a math teacher?"

"Yes, I taught math at De Anza High for about five years until I got pregnant."

"I cannot believe this. You were my math teacher in tenth grade. You were always so straight looking, and now you're such a stoner!

You always wore your hair all pulled back, and you were really strict! I can't believe this. I've been trying to figure out how I knew you. Oh my God, what a trip!"

"Well, I've changed," Patty had replied quickly, adding "I'm not much older than you are. I think we're only four years apart. I would love to hang out together. Let's go shopping on Pacific Avenue next week."

They'd become very close from then on. There were no secrets between Patty and Air.

Air waved to Patty and yelled, "I'm coming. Hold on. I need to wash my hands."

"Hi, Air," Patty said as soon as she'd stepped through the door. "I stopped by to share some absolutely incredible news. I know you've been looking for a place to live since Frank left, and I wanted you to know that there is going to be a room available at the West Cliff house."

"Really? When?"

"The beginning of next month!"

"Oh my God, I'll take it!" Air screamed. "Patty, this is a dream come true. I can't believe this. This is a dream. Will I have to go through that interviewing process I've heard you talk about?"

"Yes, but you'll have Gerry and me totally vouching for you, so you won't have any problems getting in. Don't worry," Patty said reassuringly.

The West Cliff House was a large Victorian house built in the late 1800s. Poised right on the ocean cliffs of Santa Cruz just a mile up the road from Frank's parents' house, the house was absolutely unique and ornate. It had three floors and sat on an acre of land. It had been restored ten years ago by the owner and was rented out as a communal living space. The West Cliff household consisted of twelve people, who had given the property its name. The house was one of Santa Cruz's oldest homes, and the bottom floor had once been used as the town's local grocery store. There were three guesthouses along the side of the main house that were for couples. A newly married couple had renovated the old barn and turned it into an incredible live/workspace. The main house had four bedrooms and these were for single people.

The room that was available was located on the bottom floor of the house. Two large windows faced out to the ocean, and the room had its own front door. Air couldn't believe her luck.

All week, she put up yard sale signs for the following weekend. She sold almost everything, keeping only her bed, her art, her drawing table, and her art supplies. The West Cliff House had a communal kitchen that was fully stocked with everything anyone needed, so Air sold all her kitchen stuff as well. The ground floor of the house had only two bedrooms and a large, communal recreation room with chairs, books, and a pool table.

The following weekend, Air was completely moved in to West Cliff House. She had the entire bottom floor to herself. The person who rented the other bedroom on that floor was out of the country, and no one in the house used the large rec room.

Air felt a sense of freedom she'd never known. She'd never before felt like she didn't have to answer to someone. She stayed up late at night drawing, writing, drinking wine, and listening to music that made her sad.

Air continued to see Susan. She couldn't wait to tell her how happy she was living at the West Cliff House.

If it hadn't been for the fact she'd fallen in love with a guy named Paul, who didn't feel the same about her, she would have said it was the happiest time of her life. Air had met Paul soon after Frank left. She'd been dating him for about four months. She had convinced herself he was "the one."

Air's friends could see that Paul was not the one. Paul's mother had recently visited and met Air. She'd realized Air was not, by any stretch of the imagination, the one for her Paul, so she'd quickly offered him a job back East—an offer that was too good to resist. Within two weeks, he had moved to Vermont to make his fortune in real estate. Air loved scenes like that though. They presented themselves as a challenge, an opportunity, as she would tell everyone.

When Air arrived for her appointment one day shortly after the move to West Cliff, Susan was waiting for Air out front.

"How are you doing, Air?" Susan asked as the pair walked back to her office. Air seemed a little over excited.

"I'm terrific!" Air beamed. "I am incredibly happy with my new place, and I spoke with Paul a couple of days ago, and he misses me terribly. I know he wants me to fly back there and be with him. I know I am the bigger one, so I'm going. He just can't stand up to his mother, and he knows that I will come to him. I'll surprise him and just show up. I can rent a car and drive to West Virginia from Washington. I looked at a map, and it seems like only a two-hour drive."

"Don't push the river, Air. Just don't push the river," Susan said.

"You know, I don't know how not to push the river, Susan. I'm driven to push, push, and then push some more! What's the big damn deal? If I don't push, then who will? Somebody has to push. Otherwise, things won't change. There's not enough time to just flow with the river. Who the hell wants to just flow with the river? Not me! I have no clue where the river will take me! In fact, I am suddenly remembering the song I used to listen to as a kid by Nat King Cole called 'Time and the River.' The words were something like, 'Time and the river, how quickly they go by.'"

"That's called imprinting, Air. You let those words in so deeply as a child that you're run by them now. You need to see that belief system doesn't serve you any longer. You're supposed to just flow and see where it takes you. Air, I have to admit, I get tired of reminding you of your talent. Most artists spend their lives working on developing their artistic talents. Not you; you're a natural. But, Air, you have to stop drinking so much and smoking so many cigarettes, and you have to let go of your self-pity. I think you're stuck and you like it. What are you doing with your time on the planet today? I appreciate that you are here today and that you are trying very hard to change your life, and I acknowledge that you are suffering deeply. But I have to get through to you somehow that you have everything you need to have a wonderful life. Your only problem is that you can't stand being in your body," Susan said, hoping Air would think about her remark.

"Susan, I think I'm doing really well," Air replied. "My parts all seem to be getting along and I haven't had a panic attack for over a week."

"Don't misunderstand me, Air, but I think your new move has sent you into a manic state. You spent years with Frank, and I don't think you've processed his leaving you. The move into a new environment takes your attention off the sadness you have about him leaving. We have to deal with your feelings regarding this issue. Do you want to talk about that today?" Susan asked, a hint of pleading in her voice.

"No, Susan, I don't. I'm happy. I'm going to go visit Paul, and that's where I want to put my attention," Air said with a smile.

"Air, I want to bring something up that we haven't talked about in a long time. Is that okay with you?"

"Oh God, it depends on what it is."

Air leaned back in the chair and stared at Susan. Susan stared back at Air. The tenseness suddenly became too overwhelming for Air and she looked over at the sun streaming through the window. *What in the fuck could she be talking about? What could she possibly want to talk about that we haven't talked about for a long time?* Air wondered, bracing herself.

"Air, I want to talk about Keith."

"Keith! Why?"

"I spent the last evening reviewing my notes on all our sessions. During one session, you spoke of having found your soul mate. You expressed your feelings about Keith to me and I must be honest, Air, I have never seen your face light up the way it did as you spoke about Keith. I saw and heard an Airstream that literally lit up the room with an almost delirious happiness and ease. You were solid and centered as you spoke to me about him, and I've never, at any time since I met you, seen you that clear. I know you told me he is the lover of your best friend, James, but you said that didn't matter to you. I remember you saying that you could not convince your heart that he was unavailable in more than one way. You told me that he was the one person in your entire life that you would love until the 'twelfth of never.' Airstream, what did you do with those feelings?"

"Susan, what can I do with those feelings? Nothing. I don't want to talk about this."

"It's important Air," Susan said in a demanding tone.

"I have nothing to say about Keith. I know I can never love anyone the way I love Keith. I know that I will hold any other man at bay, allowing him to get only so close, so long as he maintains a certain distance from the door of my heart that's marked 'Keith.' I just accept the way things are, and I know there is nothing—*nothing*—I can do about it. Keith is James's lover. He has no idea how I feel about him. And what if he did? I know that James has seen the way I look at Keith when they are together, but he doesn't say anything to me. Let's just leave this conversation on the shelf."

"I believe the only time in your life when you've come close to authentic intimacy is when you spoke of Keith. I want that kind of love and emotional intimacy for you, Air. You did not have it with Frank. Nor do you have it with Paul. I'm convinced you keep your love for Keith sacred, and you do this by choosing men who are emotionally unavailable to you. They never get close to the door of your heart. You have reserved that indefinitely for Keith."

"Susan! Stop. My time is up. I will see you next week, and I never want to talk about Keith again." Air stood up and glared at Susan.

"Next week, Air. Take care. I am happy you are enjoying your new home."

Air had just gotten back to her room when a knock sounded on her door. She yelled, "Come in."

"Air, you're home!"

"Patty! Come on in and make yourself comfortable. How was your trip to Tahoe this past weekend?"

"It was wonderful. Gerry and I had so much fun hiking and cooking outside. I love camping."

"I was just about to go up to the kitchen and cook some dinner. Are you hungry?" Air asked.

"I thought you drank your dinner!" Patty laughed.

"Usually, but tonight some tofu and veggies sound really appealing."

"You're not pregnant are you?"

"Oh good grief! I wish every time I said I felt like eating something people wouldn't ask me if I was pregnant."

"It's just I never see you eat anything, Air. You are always drinking a glass of wine."

Air thought about ending the conversation then and there. She knew Patty wanted to start in about her plans to go back East. Susan had been trying to dissuade her from following that course for weeks. *Why won't people just see that this is what I want and leave me alone?* Still, she couldn't just avoid Patty. "Would you like to have dinner with me?" she asked.

"Thanks, but we just ate," Patty replied. "I came to tell you my dear friend, Brett, has finally returned from Europe. He's been in Los Angles the last couple of days visiting his parents, but he left early this morning and will be here in about an hour."

Brett rented the other room on the ground level close to Air's room. Air had heard a lot about him from everyone in the house. He apparently had been one of the original people to start the cooperative household. All of the members of the house spoke of his exquisite woodworking abilities, but more importantly, everyone knew he was going back to college to study to become a doctor. Everyone in the house said he would someday be a famous psychiatrist just like his father.

When Air heard this kind of chatter, it meant one thing to her. Brett was on "a path." He did sound interesting especially since she knew the woman he'd left behind. She lived in the house too, and she thought Air was a bitch. No one in the house liked her except hungry men. She was a venomous creature, sort of like one of D. J.'s "wida's." She was always ready to take whatever was an easy kill. *I wonder*, she laughed to herself, *what would happen if I took some Aqua Net hair spray to the bitch. Would her legs cramp up and would she slowly go to sleep? I could pin her into a position that reflected her true nature, legs spread apart.*

Air found it curious that Brett was coming home just a couple of days before she was to leave for the East Coast. It was almost as if Patty had sent for him, thinking if there was anyone who could stop her, it would be Brett. *Patty thinks if she creates a circumstance such as this "oddity," I will say, "There is no such thing as a coincidence." Maybe, just maybe, Patty will think, this will be enough to me tease into putting off my trip for a few days. She's hoping Brett will have enough time to change my mind.* She looked at Patty with a smile.

"He left his parents' house this morning and should be here around 5:00 p.m. I want the two of you to meet before you leave."

"Sure."

"I care deeply about him, Air. We go way back. He needs to get in touch with his craziness. He's so damned rational. I care a lot about you too, and you're so damned crazy, you need him to help you land back on the planet. I'm worried about you. Therapy doesn't seem to be doing you any good. I feel as though Susan has failed you. It's an odd feeling."

"Patty, you know I landed on the moon years ago. Great view from up here."

"Well, Brett's very down to earth. His parents are both psychiatrists, so your frame of reference will be very different from his. At the same time, you need a place to just be calm. He'll offer you a place to stop shaking for a while. He won't ask many questions. He's more the listening type. You'll have the whole stage to yourself."

"Of course he's the listening type; he comes from a family of psychiatrists. You know, I appreciate what you're trying to do. I really do, but it won't work. I'm leaving for the East Coast in a couple of days. I love Paul, and I know Paul loves me."

"So you're all packed and ready to go?" Patty asked as she looked around Air's room.

"I am."

"Okay, if I see your light still on later, I'll bring Brett over to meet you."

"Great! Sounds fun, Patty."

Air forgot about dinner and went back to journaling at her desk. She looked up at one of her drawings on the wall. One of her poems was written on it:

I'm going, since I don't have time to ask the wind more questions …
I can scarcely walk properly since I am in such a hurry …
I guess you know that wild, wild things can turn on you by now …

Half the time I write; I get too drunk because my goddamned personalities keep trying to make me change the words to my poems. Sometimes I get up the next day and I don't remember anything about the night before, Air thought to herself as she opened another bottle of her favorite Zinfandel and began to lose track of time.

The phone rang. It was Patty.

"Air, I was just heading to bed, and I noticed your light is still on? Did I wake you up?"

"Oh no, I'm just finishing a drawing, listening to music, drinking more wine, and wondering if I should prepare another canvas for a new painting when I return."

"It didn't occur to me you might still be up until I saw your light. It's really late, and Brett left about an hour ago. He told me all about his travels, and I told him all about you."

"Do you think he's still up?"

"Oh I doubt it. He was exhausted from the drive up."

"Well, I guess that means I'll just have to light a candle and go knock on his door. Is he in his old room now?"

"Yes, he's probably in bed. Are you really going to go see him?"

"Sure, why not?"

"Well, it'll blow his mind. It's just what he needs. Now, remember he's never met anyone like you before. Go easy on him. He's first class in 'the world according to Airstream.' I love it! I can't wait until morning. Oh my God, don't you dare leave the house tomorrow without coming by and telling me everything!"

Patty hung up the phone and thought about how she simply loved Air's zaniness.

Air went over to her armoire and opened the beveled, mirrored doors. She looked inside at her collection of beautiful, antique, silk lace nightgowns. She wondered which one had the appearance of a slightly overdressed swan. She wanted to look delicate, fragile, sort of helpless, but then again, she wanted her webbed feet to be able to turn into cat paws if need be. And if that were the case, he'd barely come out alive. Or maybe she'd use her beautiful long, sleek, pearl white neck to suddenly turn python on him and suck the very breath out of him.

She thought for a moment. It would be her beauty that would suck the very life out of him, a beauty that radiated from inside her, the way she presented the left side of her face to him that would make him uncomfortable. But, in the end, it would be her lips. She had a killer pucker. She pulled her long, golden strawberry blonde hair to one side and looked in the full-length mirror. She had chosen a see-through silk and satin gown with T-straps and lots of antique lace.

Besides having a great pair of lips, her shoulders were to die for. They were as broad as her hips. Her long neck accentuated them even more. She was looking for someone else when she looked in the mirror—someone she'd long forgotten. There was no connection between the young woman Air saw in the mirror and how she felt inside.

Air looked around for a candle. The drama was about to begin—the night Airstream walked into Brett's room. She grabbed a couple of glasses, put a bottle of wine under her arm, and set out for unchartered territory, Air's middle name.

Slowly and quietly, she opened the door to Brett's room. She listened for a moment. It was dark.

"Jesus, we're going to have trouble," Air whispered. "I can't sleep with the lights out. I hope to God he has a window open; if not I'm leaving straightaway. That will tell me everything I need to know about this guy."

As she walked by his windows, she held the candle close to see if they were open. No! *Too bad*, she thought.

Brett was asleep in his large antique brass bed. Air sat down carefully at the foot of the bed. She looked around. She'd never been in his room. It was too tidy for her. His clothes were folded too perfectly. His three pairs of shoes were all lined up too perfectly. His room was immaculate. He had a place for everything, and everything was in place.

Air knew if she came back in twenty years, the room would look exactly the same. She sipped her wine and watched him sleep. She couldn't really see his face because of the shadows in the room. It didn't matter to her anyway. She was only doing this to please Patty. Air smiled to herself and imagined what must be going through Patty's mind at that moment. She looked over at the window, half expecting to see her standing there.

Brett slowly rolled over and raised his head calmly, "Hello, Airstream, I've been expecting you. I've heard so much about you from Patty and some of the other members of the house. You're quite a celebrity around here. Everyone seems to be delighted you live here. Apparently you're quite entertaining. And judging by your clothes, I'm sure I'm not going to be disappointed either."

"I'm just doing Patty a favor."

"Oh, that's too bad. How much did she pay you?"

"What!"

"I just assumed with your nightgown and all. It's been over a year and a half for me, you know."

"Oh really? It's been four months for me."

They both started laughing.

"Would you like some wine?" Air offered.

"Sure. We'll drink to your trip back East."

"She told you, huh? She thinks I'm wasting my time and money because I'm in love with a man who left me a few months back. I'm flying back there to be with him."

"Well, here's luck to you and sadness to us that we didn't have more time to get to know each other. Patty is playing cupid, you know."

Air looked at him awhile before she spoke again. He stayed right with her face, and she liked that; that—a person's willingness to just "be" with her face—said a lot about him to her. She could sense his "path," and she was sure he'd always have a path. She felt she'd missed the boat because she'd never had a path. That was her path, to not have a path.

Wouldn't it be wonderful if I could just live happily ever after with a man who had a path? Air could hear all the voices in her head. *Run with his sense of being rational and show him the way to his wild, abandoned zaniness! It's what the gods have ordered. Why the hell do you think he's showing up only a couple of days before you leave? How many times have we said there is no such thing as a coincidence? Air, trust your spider senses and us.*

"You have the greatest lips I've ever seen," he said.

"Such a pucker, huh?"

"Such a pucker! Airstream, you're quite flashy. I can just imagine you flashing around town turning heads wherever you walk. I like you. I think I'm going to nickname you, Flash."

"Well, as a matter of fact, I'm going to nickname you Pokey. I imagine you poke around life, expecting your 'path' to last forever."

"I'm not sure I like that, but I do like the combination of Pokey and Flash. Sounds good."

This was definitely the last thing Air would have expected to happen between her and Brett. She was leaving in a couple of days for her dearly beloved Paul! She leaned forward and kissed Brett.

"Are you sure this is what you want?" Brett asked.

"No."

Are we going to sleep in Brett's bed tonight? Veronica asked.

Air had a very strong feeling about Brett's presence; he would be tender to her, and she would feel safe. She crawled under his quilt. Brett's bed had an antique Hudson Bay blanket. It was old and reassuring like at Grandma's house. Her hands were shaking.

She could hear Faye whispering softly, *Air, you need a place where you can stop shaking for a while. We all do.*

Air was scared. Her eyes couldn't focus on anything, if indeed they saw anything at all. There seemed to be stars and pinched lines floating together and blurring. Perhaps it was because there was no reason to focus anymore. She put her head into the part of Brett's neck she knew could hold an ocean of her tears.

"He's gone. He just left me!" She started to sob.

"Who's gone? The asshole that let his mother buy him off?"

Her hands still trembled. Her fingers teased as if they were resting on some vague trigger that could, on close inspection, blow apart the void. The birds of love had suddenly stopped singing their song of love for her and Paul.

She tried to manage an occasional smile whenever her eyes met Brett's. She could feel Little Crying Suzie surfacing. He stared at her. She felt as though she was under glass, like some dehydrated bug from the Far East being rehydrated for exhibition in some museum. She imagined her wings being stretched out, ready for flight again, not prepped for clear, glistening fingernail polish.

He sensed she was like a great white shark that someone had thought he or she could keep in a backyard pool. He wanted to be with her as much as she would let him. He held her tightly. He thought of how many times he had dreamed of holding a woman like this. *This is a woman worth dying for*, he found himself thinking. But how could this be? He'd just met her.

Here was a man who was returning the laughter she'd had taken from here years ago, eating her full to the last drop, playing her like she was a violin, and giving her back feelings she'd felt had been stolen long ago. She imagined him screaming, *I recognize you, Airstream! I am here for you with stretched out arms of enthusiasm. Stay the night with me.*

She must have been dreaming. Unfortunately, she wasn't. She knew she was going to spend the night. She knew too that, in a couple of days, way past the time her plane had departed, she would still be in Brett's bed and his arms.

"Oh, Paul. I'm sorry."

"What did you say, Airstream?"

"I said, thank you, Brett."

"Just rest your heart now, Airstream. You need rest and someone to love you. Let me love you, Air. I will be good to you."

He is almost saying the exact same words that Frank said to me long ago.

"I should go."

"Yes, I can hear that; it's very loud. I know that what you resist persists. So, for now rest. It's simple. Just close your eyes. Give yourself permission to have sweet dreams. And if you can't, then I give you permission. Everything is all right. Everything will be all right," he said as he stroked her hair, which looked golden in the moonlight that poured through his windows.

Reluctantly, Air closed her eyes. She felt as though someone else had taken responsibility for something she had refused to do for herself. Half-drunk, half-saved, and half-willing to let go of Paul, she started to relax.

Tears ran down her face as she thought, *I will tightly seal Paul away in an evaporated jar—a vacuum-sealed jar that will slip by somehow, by mistake. I'll file it under "mistake."*

"Good night, Airstream."

"Good night, Brett."

Air fell into a deep sleep. She dreamed she wrote a letter to Paul. It read:

Dear Paul,

I now live in a room with a man who seems vaguely familiar to me. His name is Brett. I wanted to be the one to tell you. I sense it's taken almost a third of my lifetime getting here. Twenty-seven smooth years? Why of course! Just a few miles of worry in between a pair of beaches, West and East, plenty of men, and loads of heart attacks. A red-haired, freckled girl with big, brown eyes and lots of teeth, trying to word everybody to death, complete in *How to Live on Fifteen Cents a Day.*

Oh yes, Paul, it's been a breeze. Six months ago, I'd have said it's been rough. I'd have begged for a place to just rest my yesterdays and promise not to ask about the future. Maybe I'd offer you another glass of Zinfandel and a game of "oh hell" and ask for an explanation of what you meant when you said you can't handle living with me.

I never thought I'd say this to you, Paul, but there's not the stunning loneliness without you any longer. I have golden wings now, Paul. So I raise my glass to us. Good Queen Shadow, hello! Good King Skeleton, good-bye!

The next morning, Brett woke up, and Air was deep in sleep. Brett was surprised to find her still in his bed. He longed for her lips. He let her sleep.

❧ 18 ❧

Airstream woke up just as Brett closed the door so she could sleep more.

"Airstream, I'm glad you're awake. I need to talk to you," whispered Claire's voice. Everyone thought it would be best if I came and talked with you. We need to talk to you about the book you're writing about our life."

"Book? I'm not writing any book! What are you talking about?" Air answered.

"Let's start with that you just accept you're writing a book and you're unaware of it. Can you accept that there's a possibility you're writing a book and just don't pay it much mind?" enquired Claire.

"No. But I do want to hear what you have to say. I'm fine now and don't need of my personalities to start in on me! So, tell me what you have to say and go away!"

"Air, I've guided you out of dangerous situations many times, as well as being a stand for you to support yourself on your own, allowing you to be free of the suffering and misery whenever you would consider suicide. I am the one who has been at your side during each and every visit to the ER. I am your *will*. You've always listened to me, and if you search your heart you will know how intricately woven the two of us are."

"Shit! I need you to leave. Brett could come in at any moment! Plus, you sound much older than I am."

"I am all of you, Air—your past, present, and future. I cannot leave until we have talked."

"What do we need to talk about? I've worked very hard on pulling all my personalities together with Susan, and as torturous as it was, I did it! We've all been living together just fine as far as I know.

No one has acted out and caused me any trouble. Are you saying you are here to tell me that my parts are fracturing again?"

"In a way. You could look at it that way. You just need to listen."

"Well, I don't have much time."

"Yes, I know, and this shouldn't take long," Claire responded. "Air, I showed up in your life when you were five years old. This was a time in your life where you experienced severe sexual abuse at the hand of your grandfather. You have hidden it so deeply you can't remember what happened between the two of you or if anything happened at all. I know you remember that your grandfather spent Sundays with you, but all you can remember is that he came and picked you up during the summer and took you for car rides. You don't remember anything at all once you drove away from your house. You don't remember where you went, how long you were gone, or how you got home. You continue to suffer deeply from this, and I am not sure if you will ever remember anything of what happened. You just have to trust me on this, and I know you do know what I am talking about.

"You're saying you've been with me since I was five years old, and yet Susan told me none of my personalities age," Air replied, sounding surprised.

"Never mind that now. We both have the same parents and have lived the same life. I am a part of you. You are writing this story right now as we speak, but you're not aware of it. I want to talk about why you keep writing stories about parts of our life that were as devastating to us as they were to you but telling them as though they were a joke. Excuse my language, but it pisses us off when you make fun of our life."

"Listen, let's get one thing straight here," Air broke in. "No one tells me what I can and can't do! You are just a part of me, and frankly, I would like you to leave now."

"I can't until you promise to stop telling the story of our life in ways that didn't happen. We've had the same life as you have experienced, and I don't like that you are telling the reader about horrible events that happened during our life and making them sound like they were funnier than hell!" Claire retorted.

"Well, I disagree," snapped Air. "D. J. was crazy as hell and a borderline schizophrenic. We were just little kids left with someone who loved the dogs more than us."

"Oh, are you referring to how she never cooked for us but would make hamburgers for the dogs?" Claire countered.

"Yes, just to mention a few of the ways she displayed her preference for them. So what do you want from me, Claire?" Air inquired.

"What I, what we, want is for you to tell the truth, as painful, exceptionally lonely, and isolating as it has been for us," Claire said. "I'm sorry you still have issues with her, but most of us have reached a point where we now see her as a total hoot. We've accepted we didn't have a mother. That's it, end of story. I've tried to tell all the other parts we have a weird, absentee, temporarily displaced mother. Everybody has weird mothers. Our lives haven't been that tragic compared to others. It's been absurd and bizarre, by all means, and I don't deny the embarrassment through the years. I understand your bitterness, but you have too much pity-party crap going on. I just want to live life through a cat's eyes."

"Oh to hell with you!" Air responded loudly.

"Wait, wait, wait! I know at times we see the world quite differently. I'm sorry you're writing a book that is upsetting us. We all love you, Air. None of us want to see you in pain. That puts us all in pain, and I am tired of the pain! You take life too seriously, and you're always beating yourself up. Sometimes it seems nothing's sacred to you. We hear all sorts of words and images fall out of your mouth inappropriately. And then there's Keith. Why aren't you telling the reader about the one true love of your life? You have a brief conversation about him with Susan, but your readers have no clue how much he means to you. Why in the world would you write a book and not reveal such depth of love you have for another human being? Don't you want the reader to know you're capable of loving someone you'd die for?"

"Go fuck yourself, Claire. My feelings for Keith don't belong out in the world. He's too precious, and my love for him lives on a gossamer thread of hope. It's too private. It's like having someone going through my underwear drawer.

"You are just excreting nonsense!" shouted Claire. "If you're going to spill your guts about our life, then let the world know you're in love with your best friends' lover!" Claire cried out in total bewilderment.

"I can't. Not yet." Air lowered her head. "It's too painful. I love him more than life itself."

"Air, we've been blessed with the ability to live in both a non-reality and reality-based world. The problem you've always had is making decisions—at times about which of the two worlds you should be coming from when dialoguing with another human being. This is certainly your problem with Keith. If you had just communicated with him rationally, you would have had the relationship you longed for. But you've always chosen to speak to him in very illogical language. By the way, he left James. You need to call James and find out what happened."

"What difference would it make anyway? He prefers men," Air sighed. "But that doesn't matter to me one bit. I fell in love with him the moment James introduced us. His incredibly sparkling blue eyes pinned me against the wall immediately. I've never recovered from that moment. It actually startled me. I felt breathless and weak. I remember not knowing what to say, which was really embarrassing. In that moment, I realized why God created love. It's the most extraordinary feeling on earth. One who finds someone who burrows into his or her heart and puts down a taproot is absolutely helpless. There's nothing, I mean nothing, you can do to ever stop loving that person. Other relationships can come and go and not effect that true love one bit." Air sighed. "Sad thing is, you can find yourself with someone who loves you the way you love someone else, and that person will never really have your heart they way he or she deserves. But it's lonely out there in world, and like someone said, 'If you can't be with the one you want, love the one you're with.'"

"Good grief! This is exactly what I'm talking about. The way you experience the world is beyond his understanding of the beauty of acceptance you can offer him. You and Keith were meant to be together, and I tried to guide you in that direction. At any rate, we are all curious to see how you are going to bring him into the book.

You don't even share much about James's personal life and that he has a lover who's bisexual. God, I've suddenly forgotten why I am here. I got off track with this Keith shit."

"Oh yes, I remember now, it's true we all need each other, and we're the same person. I acknowledge we hold each other as sacred creatures among the many who are still journeying along with us, but Airstream, I'm the one who should be writing this book, not you. You're not capable of speaking the truth because it's too painful for you. I insist you let me tell our life story as I saw and lived it. You must allow me to develop as a character, or a 'personality,' if you will; otherwise, we're both wasting our time! We all know you are the character with whom the readers will relate—the one they'll find endearing, as long as you don't drift into us. When you become one of us, you make things sound disjointed, and we lose your whimsicalness and start to overwhelm our readers."

"Claire, you're the one who showed me how to lose my faith in everything that was solid in the world, everything stable and sure, in order to get a glimpse of something more powerful than the mind. You showed me how to look beyond what my normal eyes told me was the truth. What you didn't show me was how to live with the isolation, knowing everybody else thought I was everything from insane to flighty." Air pulled the sheet over her head. At times, she was so childlike. Tears rolled down her cheeks and onto her chest, and as unusual she grabbed at them with a sense of hysteria.

"This is a part of your spiritual journey, Air. I'm proud of you. You have been a monument to being unstoppable. You're a true stand for the existence of awesome love against all odds and have been willing to be thought totally crazy for believing this type of love exists. We are truly making the most of this earth-life experience. I urge you to acknowledge yourself!" Claire said, her tone full of encouragement and acknowledgment.

"I also have to bring up another question," Claire continued. "Why is it that you don't talk more about all our successes as an artist? Why aren't you telling the reader about our outrageously successful community public art projects? Seems to me there's some major withholding here! Could it be you won't go there because it's far safer to stay with the story you're writing than the one of truth, which is that we have intimacy problems? You know, you're not bragging when you share that you're becoming a well-known artist. It's just another side of you and something that brings you both joy and money! You need to talk about the exhibits you've been a part of, not to mention the work you do with the university."

"Fuck you, Claire! You all are too impatient. I haven't even written half the book yet. Give me a break. I plan to tell them about my success as an artist, and I intend to write about Keith. It's just not been the right time. I had to let the readers know about my childhood."

"Airstream, trust me. The reader's not stupid. And please, I'm telling you this from a loving place. Intimacy is your problem, and you're not alone in that; people love to hear about others who suffer from the same thing. Some of the stories you write about are really irrelevant. Successful books need love, sex, romance, and drama. All you have in your book is talk of love and romance but very little drama and no sex. What is up with that? We all know you're having sex. Why not write about it?" Claire asked inquisitively.

"Okay, you have to leave now. I've heard enough," said Air in a tone that was a bit threatening.

"Look, we've invested too many years in keeping ourselves distracted from our sacred path with this Keith stuff. The truth is, you hold onto telling yourself Keith loves you because you know you'll never be required to go to that place of intimacy with him. Airstream, you're a fraud, and you're deceiving our audience! We need to share the possibility one can move toward the light and embrace our inner love without the need to partner with someone. It's your growth path. We have it in us to open our heart to ourselves! Isn't Keith just your 'ghostly lover'? He's simply a soul who does not judge people by sex. When he loves, he loves deeply. He loves when he finds the person who holds the world like a child. We all, including Keith, feel the electricity between the two of you—a non-corporeal knowing of a love that was meant to be, a love that would be worth the journey. Yes, Airstream, it is about the journey."

"Claire, I asked you to leave. I'm going to get out of bed, and you'll have to leave then. I'm getting out of bed now Claire, so leave."

"I'll leave if you promise me that you'll let the readers immerse themselves in the inescapable truth that the two of you, Keith and us, have a love only known to gods, one that's sacred and written on the walls of a long-lost world where the great lovers of the world once loved many past lifetimes ago—a love so uninhibited that all we could do was cry with joy all the time."

"Oh good grief, Claire!"

"Air, listen up, we have major intimacy issues, among abandonment issues and betrayal fears. Is the reason we are so in love with Keith that we know he will never want to make love to us? God knows he's had plenty of chances. Remember, we've already spent a week with him in Mexico when him and James were separated for a few months. Remember? We slept in the same bed with him every night. If he had wanted to show us he loved us, he would have turned over and looked us straight in the eyes and said, 'Air, I love you.' A man is not going to lie next to an incredibly sensual woman for whom he cares in a loving way and not make love to her!"

"Listen, I am in no mood to do this. The book needs to be finished, and there's no way I can deal with our intimacy problem right now—period."

"Yes, we can."

"How do you propose *we* do that?" Air asked with snappy tone.

"Keith's mother, Elizabeth. She's our portal," Claire answered decisively. "She will tell us, 'Save the last dance for him.'"

"What in the hell are you talking about?" Air asked as she looked at Claire with disdain. "You have to leave. Brett will be back to check on me any minute, and I have to look like I've been sleeping."

"You see, what you don't know is, Keith has been journeying toward us, and we have been journeying toward him. He too has intimacy problems. He doesn't know how to love. He just wants to be loved. He didn't want anyone like us to come into his life, just as we didn't want anyone like him in ours. The mere thought of him brings all of us turmoil. He adores us and then feels anger toward us. The same is true for us. For him, we are a constant reminder of his inability to be emotionally available."

"You are wrong. I can feel he has ability to love and show intimacy. He loves and desires us very much. His struggles are our struggles. Time has nothing to do with this," Air stated.

"Listen to the words you've written about Elizabeth's whispers to you in our dreams. It's just a matter of time now, Air. The question is, did you ever think you would end this book with Keith and us finally getting together and fully committing our souls to one another for the rest of our lives?"

"Why the hell do you keep talking about Keith? I thought you came to yell at me about how I'm not writing the truth about my life, or 'our lives,' I should say."

"I did. And I will end this conversation very soon, as I see I am getting nowhere with you!" Claire said coldly.

"So, if I understand you right, you're saying Keith is asking me to save the last dance for him and I'm not hearing it? I think I ought to call the book, *Prairie Doggin' it with Airstream*." Air laughed.

"This is not a joke, Air. I'm saying he is on his journey toward us as we speak, and it's simply an *is*. Timing has nothing to do with it as far as we're all concerned. And you? You're still pushing the goddamned river! Air, I think you should tell the readers about the night Elizabeth visited us in your bedroom in Mexico while you were involved with your project out at the dumps with the homeless families. Which by the way, you still have not let the readers know about that adventure either. You were so freaked out you got out of bed and wrote it all down in your journal because you knew that you'd fall back asleep and that, when you woke up, you'd think it had all been a dream. It was not a dream, as frightening as it was. Do you remember calling her in the States the next day and asking her if she believed in out-of-body experiences?"

Air sighed. "Yes, I do. I remember she said she'd had many out-of-body experiences in her lifetime," Air said, reaffirming Claire's memory. "She told me her first out-of-body experience was at a party. Everyone was dancing. For some reason, no one could see her, so she decided to lie down on the dance floor and raise her body about a foot up, parallel from the floor, and float in between the legs of people as they were dancing."

"Remember she was really sick when you left for Mexico and was bedridden in Berkeley at the time of her visit to you in Mexico, and yet she woke you. Do you recall the conversation the two of you had about Keith?"

"Yes, I do. And when I asked her about it, she said it sounded very familiar."

"Then why not share this with the readers?"

"I'm still scared about that night. I still question the reality of what really happened."

"Airstream! This is what Susan was trying to get us to talk about. Again, you're pushing the river! How about trusting what you wrote in your journal about Elizabeth's visit. Why are you afraid of where the path will end? Why not trust that this is the beginning of a life for all of us and that we will live with an abundance of joy?"

There was a long silence in the room.

"Hello, Claire? Are you still here?"

Silence.

Air lay in Brett's bed and thought back to the night Elizabeth had visited her in the middle of the night. It had been around three in the morning. Claire was right; it was a significant event and one that had challenged Air's entire belief systems. *It altered my life path forever*, she realized.

This was what was so magical about Air. This was what was so wondrous about her. This was what drew people to her. She had never lost her childlike approach to life. She actually processed life's experiences like a child. People sensed this about her and were intrigued, watching her every moment. At gallery openings, people would line up just to say hello. She had a way of putting people at ease, even if they knew nothing about art. Air was never pretentious. Nothing was off limits to talk about, and strangers loved this. She could bring up subjects most people didn't even dream of talking to their friends about, and no one would be offended because Air would joke about whatever she was talking about. Many handsome and successful men were attracted to her, but she was always able to remove herself from conversations she knew were headed toward seeing one another again.

"We are an angel, Airstream," Claire whispered in her head. "Just stop trying to fly in the rain. Angels can't fly in the rain."

19

Pokey, Aka Brett, wanted Flash Aka Airstream. He didn't care if she was on the half shell, in a fresh spinach salad, a la carte, drunk, or amid an anxiety attack and bolting for the local ER. He wanted her free-spiritedness deep within his soul. He wanted to be taken to a place without expected behavior, without rules, without "interesting" supermarket conversations. Flash could take him to that place, but he was afraid to journey along her path, which he felt was the path of a warrior. He knew she didn't care about the consequences of her behavior, or maybe in the end, even him.

Pokey sensed he could be easily butchered, and yet he knew his utter existence was being beckoned by the possibility of being transformed by Air's deep, life-learning experiences, her discoveries of "the unknown." He knew he had to trust Flash, but did anyone dare trust Flash? *Hell no!*

Oh yes, Pokey wanted Flash, and she was going to be the most real experience Flash had ever had. He would make sure of this, since he was risking so much.

Flash didn't know how to want anything other than freedom from heart attacks, rent, cats, memories of Frank, her love for Paul, a broken down Opel Kadett, her love for cigarettes and alcohol, and her deeply hidden feelings for Keith. Probably no one would get out alive.

Airstream decided to let Pokey call her Flash. She thought it did represent her personality. Everyone in the house was talking about the new relationship between the two. Actually, no one could believe Pokey had it so bad for Air. They were so very different. Everyone whispered all hell would eventually break loose. It was like one person needing to get crazy and the other person needing to get sane.

In the beginning, Flash ran as fast as she could, but Pokey chased. Flash loved this drama. He wanted her in his dreams, in his work, in his force. He knew it would be up to him. Flash was incapable of making decisions about anything other than art and liquor. He knew anything was too much to ask of Flash. Trying to get her to light on anything besides the moon longer than two minutes was too much to ask of her. The only thing she'd wait for more than two minutes was Pokey's cock.

Tolerance. Pokey had tolerance. Incredible tolerance. Sometimes his tolerance drove Flash right out of her mind. He had a hell of a time tolerating her smoking, but Pokey was one for accepting truths. He knew Flash was an intense person who had to be an intense smoker. He would come home, and there would be three different cigarettes burning in three different ashtrays in three different parts of the house.

"It's hard to imagine he lets her smoke in his room," Patty remarked to one of the other house members. He hates the smell of cigarettes."

Flash knew she was pushing him beyond his limits at times. She loved having that power and, at the same time, appreciated his constant reaffirmation of his love for her. Not once had he given her hell about her smoking, drinking, foul mouth, or exceedingly loud orgasms that everyone in the house could hear and complained about.

One morning, Pokey woke up around seven o'clock and rolled over. Flash wasn't in the bed. He looked around the room. She was curled up in his old Victorian wicker chair next to the window. The sun was shining beams directly onto her face. Her hair looked electric, as though it was on fire. Her enormous, brown, doe-like eyes and her faint freckles reflecting in the sun reminded him of a picture he'd seen of her as a child. She was the most sensuous woman he'd ever been with. She looked over at him and slowly smiled. He continued to gaze and had to refocus on her since it was such a bright morning.

She was wearing another one of her vintage silk nightgowns, and her hair rested upon her shoulders in golden locks.

"So ivory, rhino ivory," he said quietly, yet Air heard him.

"What did you say? Did you say something about a rhino?" she asked.

"Your skin. It's as white as rhino ivory. "I didn't know you could hear me."

"Would you like some wine?" she asked coyly.

"No thanks. I'm going to have some granola and yogurt if there's any in the kitchen."

"Oh sure there is. I made some myself just yesterday."

"The granola or the yogurt?" Pokey asked almost sounding surprised.

"Both of course, you silly."

"I didn't know you liked to cook. Would you like to have some with me?"

"No thanks. I never eat breakfast. I'm drinking mine."

"Why did you make the granola and yogurt then?"

"Because I love making the people in the house happy," Flash said. She returned to reading her journal, smoking a cigarette, and drinking her glass of Zinfandel.

Air knew Pokey was having a very difficult time with her morning routine. He clearly had no clue how to react to finding her sitting here drinking wine at seven in the morning. She figured that the cigarettes were probably not such a big deal to him, but the wine was. *I'm just too avant-garde for him*, she thought with a sigh. *Somewhere deep within his soul he knows I'm crazy, as clearly as he knows his own breathing. Nevertheless, I can see in his eyes he thinks I'm too goddamned exciting, too fascinating, too appealing, and too convincingly convinced of my "path. He's not even sure who's doing the driving, if anyone at all. Perhaps he'll realize we're both on autopilot.*

Flash had never realized she too had a path until now. She'd always felt stuck along some roadside rest. She made a point of being sure everyone knew she was eccentric and delightful in spite of her unaccountability.

"What are you writing, Flash?"

"I'm not writing about anything, Pokey. I'm reading what I wrote last night. I'm never sure if I wrote what I'm reading or not. Half the time, I don't remember writing what I read the following morning, and I often question whether I wrote it or not."

"What do you mean whether you wrote it? Who else writes in your journal?"

"You're misunderstanding me. For instance, right now I'm reading this page on which I drew a picture of a nude woman sitting in a chair looking over her shoulder. Her long hair covers her tits, but her butt is showing. And it is gigantic. The only thing she's wear is a pair of high heels. Over the image, I wrote a couple of lines and I don't remember writing the lines. Listen, to this. 'That spring night I spent pillowed in your arms never really happened except in a dream. Unfortunately, I'm talked about anyway.' What I mean is that I could have read those lines in some poetry book of mine. Or maybe I really wrote the lines myself. I don't remember if those are my words since I do write really great lines like that," Air said, shaking her head despondently. "It really sucks since it seems to be happening a lot lately. Sometimes I wonder if I drink too much."

"Flash, do you ever consider getting help with your drinking? These constant questionings you have of yourself, both of your writings and your drawings might simply be what's called blackouts," Pokey replied, clearly hoping Flash would ask more about his remark.

"Blackouts?" Air snapped. "What the hell are blackouts? Does the sun go somewhere?" She looked out the window. "It looks like we're in a blackout right now. The sun has disappeared, and it looks like it's going to rain any moment."

Pokey looked out his window and saw dark, looming clouds rolling in. The bright sunlight had been replaced with thick, low fog. It wasn't unusual for the weather to change drastically and quickly along the coast. "A blackout usually means forgetting what happened the night before when you drank too much," he explained. "During blackouts, people forget the details of where they were, who they were with, or how they got home. You've never heard of a blackout?"

"Nope. Oh well, love is so short and the forgetting so long," Air spouted.

Pokey stared at Flash and said, "You know, Flash, I'm drawn to you on many levels. Your ability to yell and scream and take great pleasure in arguing is very appealing. My parents never raised their voices as I was growing up. I'm not personally familiar with any of the tales you tell about your childhood, especially when I think of my own. It's as though we came from different planets. I thoroughly enjoy your silly ways. I can't believe your talent! I love to watch you paint and wonder why you aren't more driven to exhibit your work. It's not like you. You care about people so much, and your art would bring many such pleasure. Your work is so different than any art I've ever seen. What about you, how do you feel about me?"

"Well, I'll confess, I'm not familiar with any of your silly ways either. I'm so damned indecisive. For me, it seems that, at any given moment, there are so many paths one could chose. I just break down. For you, there seems to be only one or two choices to be considered. Life seems easy for you. I hope you realize how lucky you are you weren't born a Libra. It makes decision-making almost impossible, not to mention aggravating as hell. I've always seen all sides to everything, and it seems all are legitimate in some way or other. I could never serve on a jury because I would clearly see both sides and why the person did what he or she did," Air said as she took her last sip of wine.

"Don't take this wrong," she added, "but sometimes I think you deny what's exciting in favor of what you think is best and acceptable. I'm out of sorts compared to you. I'm a constant stranger to both you and to myself—you know, Miss Non-direction herself. And you are Mr. Path himself."

"Flash, I think it's just your unwillingness to totally commit yourself to anything that borders on normal. For some reason, I think you think that, by committing to something 'everyday normal,' you are giving yourself a death sentence."

"Oh cut the therapy shit, Poke! Jesus, it's raining now! It was just sunny a few minutes ago. Listen, I've been in goddamned therapy for years. It's become a sport, and I'm as good at it as you and your parents. You know, you should have a glass of wine with me and lighten up. This is good therapy and a lot cheaper. And you know what else? Sometimes, I hate your guts. Why don't you just go upstairs and eat the healthy granola and yogurt I made."

"Flash, I've come to know you well enough to know that, at this very moment, what you would really like is for me to force you onto the floor and make passionate love to you. Admit it! You just can't ask for what you want."

Pokey grabbed Flash by the arm and forced her to the floor. She loved it! Paul would never have done this. Paul never forced Airstream to do anything. She loved playing the game of resistance.

"Stop it, would you!" she cried.

"No, I won't. This is what you want, and you know it. Let go, Flash!"

"It's not! Now, get off me right now," she said with in a tone that wasn't so convincing.

Flash had always wanted a man she loved to force her to the floor and make love to her, but she was caught between the feeling of being dominated and submitting.

"I'm going for a bike ride!" she announced.

"Flash, it's pouring rain outside. Plus, it's cold out there; it's only seven in the morning."

"So what?"

"Flash, you are welcome to use my bike. Just be sure to wipe it off when you get back; otherwise, it might rust."

Pokey stood in front of his window watching as Air rode off into the morning rain. *Who would go for a bike ride in the early morning rain, especially in an antique silk nightgown?* Besides that, everyone in town used the coastal road to get through town and to the freeway. *Crazy! Fucking crazy*, he thought. *I wonder if I have the slightest chance of making her happy. She's insatiable, and I'm obsessed with her.*

The rain was coming down so hard Air could barely see the road.

Why didn't I just let go and enjoy the moment? Air asked herself. *Why didn't I just give in—give in to the freedom of self-expression and the security that someone really wanted me? I'm afraid of being found out, being discovered as a fraud. I act like I know so much about being sexual, and I don't have a clue how to act like I know what I'm doing. I'm sure I'd disappoint Pokey after he had the nerve to risk pushing me to the floor like we were in the movies. I'm already beginning to give up quite a bit of my freedom with him. I feel like I spend too much of my time with him as it is. I should be painting and writing more like I used to. I feel like the nails are being driven into my coffin.*

At the same time, she knew deep within her spirit that the security of being with Pokey was just an easy way out of being responsible for herself. She'd just started to relish her newly found personal freedom when Pokey had come into her life. Loving Paul had been on her terms. She knew there was no real love with Poke, just the sense of reassuring solidness.

It began to rain harder, and the cars were starting to spray her with water as they drove by. She decided to turn around and head home. She could barely see, and her silk nightgown was clinging to her naked body. Her skin was glistening with a mixture of body lotion and water, and her long hair was a mantle of dripping ringlets. Air could see the glares from women as the cars passed her by. The glares felt like daggers. Suddenly, she decided to stop and pick some roses from a yard that was full of all sorts of different flowers. She put some in her hair and the rest in the basket on the front of the bike. She continued to ride home.

I'm nothing more than one of Pokey's woodworking tools, she mused. *I'm a special tool that has been perfectly designed to complete and fulfill a magnificent task. He plays me as though I was his prized tool during sex, and that's why I resisted him this time. I won't allow him to do that to me again.*

Pokey went upstairs into the kitchen. He opened the refrigerator and found the yogurt Flash had made. He looked around for the granola.

Patty came into the kitchen to make herself a cup of coffee. Brett finally found the granola in a giant jar in the cabinet.

"Good morning, Patty."

"Good morning, Brett. How are things? Where's Air?"

"She went for a bike ride."

"A bike ride? In this rain?"

"Yeah. You know, Patty, just as I start to believe her absurd act of pure and enjoyable craziness, she flips out and goes nuts on me."

"I don't understand. What do you mean?"

"Well, take last week. You know that we drove down to Los Angeles to check out a couple of med schools, since I'm working toward getting my master's degree in early childhood education. I asked Flash to come along so we could look at apartments down there. She came to all my interviews, but she kept saying she couldn't breathe from all the smog. She started having anxiety attacks from this sense of breathlessness. She asked me to buy her some wine, so I did. She said she just had a small amount of pot with her and wanted to save it for the ride home. She drank the whole time we were down there. She was getting ripped every day—I mean so ripped that, one night, she ran out of cigarettes, and she couldn't find my damned car keys. I mean this was after midnight, right? So what does she do? She takes my father's keys to his Mercedes, and we don't see her for over three hours," Brett said with a look of total disbelief.

"When she got back to the house, she pulled in the driveway and idled the car for about ten minutes. The radio was blasting at volume ten, and instead of using the house keys to get back in, she pounded on the front door yelling, 'Pokey! Hey, Poke! Let me in!'

"Patty, my parents put me through the Spanish Inquisition. My stepmother kept asking me over and over if Air was on drugs. The worse part was the ride back up here though. When we got to San Luis Obispo, I realized she hadn't said a word to me for over an hour. She wasn't even looking at me. I tried to start conversations, but I couldn't get a response out of her. I decided to drive really close to the car in front of me because that drives Flash right out of her mind, and she'll usually start yelling at me.

"Nothing, not a word for over two hours. She continued to ignore me and just stared out the window. Then when we enter the Salinas Valley, about twelve miles outside of the town of Salinas, she suddenly turns her head really quick toward me and yells something real loud and fast. I couldn't understand a word of what she was saying. She turned back and continued to sit there quietly just staring out the window.

"I calmly asked her what she'd said, and she turned again, looked straight into my eyes, and yelled, 'Take me to the hospital the minute we hit Salinas!' I started laughing; she started crying."

"You're kidding, Brett." Patty said sadly as she filled the teapot with water and added coffee grounds into the French press.

Brett laughed. "I wish I was," he said. "Apparently, she'd gotten herself too stoned on weed and convinced herself her tongue was going to fall down her throat if she didn't hold onto it with her front teeth. I had no clue she'd been holding her tongue all the way from Santa Barbara to Salinas. That's why she wasn't talking to me! She was too freaked out to talk since she'd have to let go of her tongue. She was sure she'd swallow it and die if she talked. Can you believe that?" Brett shook his head and stirred his granola.

"Shit! I think that's hysterically funny. I can just see her sitting there gripping her tongue. Poor thing. Did you take her to the hospital?"

"Hell no! I finally convinced her she was just too stoned and only dead people swallowed their tongues, which, by the way, was a big mistake. I should never have mentioned the word *dead*. I ended up taking her to Rosaria's in Watsonville and putting some food in her. Her blood sugar was all screwed up from drinking alcohol for four days straight. After we finished eating, she had a bad case of heartburn and started farting the rest of the way home. I don't know which was worse, the tongue swallowing bit or her gas. Actually, her farts were."

"Oh my God, Brett. That's funnier than hell. Never a dull moment with the Flash! Hey, did you find a school or an apartment?" Patty asked as she sat down at the kitchen table with her coffee.

"Actually, I did. There's one school I really like, but it has a two-year waiting list. I'm sure my dad can pull some strings. I'm grateful Flash insisted I needed to go back to school now while I'm still young. You know, I really love her despite everything," Brett remarked as he glanced over at the windows to check the weather.

"What do you mean despite everything?" Patty asked.

"We fight all the time. I hate it, and she loves it. I never know when I'm going to be ambushed. I think she still has so much bitterness about Paul. I don't think she's gotten over him. She'll hold his deserting her against every man she meets for the rest of her life. I just wish she'd admit to herself he never loved her and that he's an asshole for not seeing how wonderful she is. He's the loser, but she's convinced herself there's something wrong with her.

She's convinced he's going to wake up one morning and realize he has to have her—that his mother came between them, that he sold out, and that his love for her is more important than any career gain. She is a hopeless romantic," he added as he pushed the empty bowl toward the middle of the table.

"No, Pokey, unfortunately it runs deeper than that. Air doesn't feel she deserves to be loved. As a young child, her father told her daily she was a worthless piece of shit and that no man was ever going to love her. When you're a little girl, you believe your father. She's played out this scenario by continually choosing men who are emotionally unavailable. This ensures she's never required to be intimate or make a commitment. She can then hide out behind her story of how she knows he really loves her, and it's up to her to get him to see it. It's a very safe place for her to be.

"Fortunately, she's one of the strongest-willed women I've ever met. She has a spirit that takes a constant stand to keep her from sabotaging herself this way. It shows up as her anxiety attacks, which are all related to her heart. The 'heart attacks' are simply symbolic of her mission in life, which is to open her heart and trust she's a wonderful and compassionate human being who most certainly deserves to be loved.

"Everyone she meets absolutely adores her, but she chooses to put her attention on the men she can't have. I talked with her therapist, Dr. Hill, and she said she's spent months with Air and feels she's really let her down. She feels she's made no progress with her at all. I don't know if you are aware of why Air sees a therapist?" Patty asked as she walked over to the sink to wash her cup.

"No, it's never come up," Brett said as he joined her at the sink.

They washed their dishes and walked into the front room near the one large main window. They were both looking for Air. It was pouring rain now, and both shook their heads at the same time.

"A year ago, Air's primary doctor diagnosed her with multiple personality disorder. He referred her to Dr. Hill, who uses hypnosis to treat her patients. She doesn't talk about the sessions much with me. Apparently, when she first started seeing Dr. Hill, she had some past-life regression experiences before her personalities began to emerge. It was all pretty overwhelming for Air. She doesn't like to talk about what she's found out about herself. Brett, you're the only man she's ever met who is emotionally healthy and available for her. She's scared of you. Unconsciously, she'll do anything to disrupt the relationship the two of you have."

Pokey sighed and sat down in one of the wooden chairs Tom, the woodworker who lived in the renovated barn, had made for the house. Tom's designs were simple but beautiful since he used expensive hard woods like black walnut. The main living room in the West Cliff House was dark. The walls were made of dark paneling. Almost all of the furniture was made of wood without upholstery. A very large hand woven rug, that at one time had been colorful but now was faded and quite worn, covered most of the floor. End tables from the fifties sat beside a couple of the chairs and a long, plain, dark brown couch. The group had decided not to have a TV in the room, so there were bookshelves that offered a constant supply of traded books from the household members. Brett and Patty sat quietly staring out the windows at the ocean and then glancing at the front door, half-expecting to see Air coming through.

Brett lowered his head and said, "Sometimes she cries so hard and so deep at night that it scares me. I don't think I've ever heard anyone make the kind of sounds she does. It's almost like a wounded animal. She's strong though; you're right. She's almost inhumanly strong. She's a steam train, and nothing can stop her. My hunch is, as she gets older, she'll calm down. You know, she's not going through anything most people don't go through at some point in their lives. It's just that Flash has this peculiar way of making everything so intense, experiencing life to the maximum, especially with her emotions. She lives more life in one month than most people do in their entire lives!"

"I hope you're right. I hope moving to LA is what she really wants. She said something last night in reference to not wanting to lose her job."

"What job?" Pokey asked.

"There are times when she works up at UCSC in their extension department. They call whenever they need her. She's very intelligent, Pokey, although she doesn't always seem to be. She took two semesters in community development, group dynamics, and communication skills. She met quite a few people who work at the university through Frank. They invited her to sit in on some of their seminars dealing with community development," Patty explained in an upbeat tone. "They wanted her to give the seminar leaders feedback after their lectures and workshops. She was a natural at being able to see what was really going on in the groups and the thoughts behind what people were really saying. They were so impressed with her ability to notice people's behavior and attitudes they asked her to lead one of her own group dynamics class for some nurses from Africa about a year ago. She received raving feedback from the group members. They loved her so much they hired her. She makes good money when she works."

"You have to be kidding me!" Brett said, surprise in his voice and expression. "How could I not know this about her?"

"She doesn't talk about her accomplishments much," Patty stated. "I've always wondered why she's so secretive about parts of her life. Flash is so incredibly talented—and not just in the arts. She loves to lecture in front of a large crowd and present thoughts and methodologies most people have never considered. After Frank left her, she became very involved with the folks up at UC. She's facilitated workshops with different city council members, county supervisors, Clorox corporate executives, the police department, teachers, school principals, and different community leaders. I've hired her to work with me a couple of times when I'm called to do a DUI class for the county. She's completely a different person when she's at work. She even dresses differently. You wouldn't recognize her. She's really good, Brett. People line up to talk to her when the workshops are over. In fact, we have a workshop together tomorrow. She's giving a lecture on time management. I need to talk to her before tomorrow."

"Time management? Now, that's funny! Someone who has a belief system that 'time is short and life is tricky' giving a time management lecture? What does she say, get out your credit cards and live for today?"

"Actually, I'm wrong about that. She's leading a seminar around group dynamics and communication skills. You should sit in on one of her lectures. She always has the group mesmerized, and she's highly respected in the university's extension department. She has the ability to be incredibly clear and rarely gets derailed. People will wait for up to a half an hour to speak with her after the sessions."

The next day, right after her lecture, Airstream decided to get the hell out of Dodge for a few days. She found a phone booth and called James.

"Hey, James, can I come up and visit for a couple of weeks?"

"Hell yes, girl!"

"Great, I'm on my way home to pack and work a quick project, and then I'll head to the Greyhound bus station. I'll call you just before I get on the bus and let you know what time I'll be arriving."

Airstream stopped by the bus station, bought a one-way ticket up to the Bay Area, and headed home.

Air went upstairs to the kitchen and rummaged through the garbage can. She was looking for an empty milk carton so she could glue a note on the side of it for Pokey. She finished the project and put the carton in the middle of Pokey's bed. She packed some clothes and left.

"Patty, did Flash do the seminar with you today?" Brett asked.

"Yes, why?"

"Take a look at this."

"What is this?"

"Another drama scene. She's missing."

"What do you mean, she's missing?"

"I found this in my room in the middle of my bed. You know how they're putting missing kids' pictures on the side of milk cartons now? Well, this is her adaptation."

"Let me see that." Patty grabbed the carton out of Brett's hands.

She stared at the milk carton in horror. On one side it read, "Missing. SWF, 5'4", pretty, has always gotten everything she's ever wanted and it was still never enough although she'll tell you she's had more than her fair share. She's probably a genius, but sadly, she's the last to know. She's the most amazing person we know. She's fearless, so be careful. She'll take on anything and can make whatever she wants happen. Men look at her all the time, but she's oblivious to it; she's completely self-absorbed. She's bird-boned in stature, feminine, and clueless about her sexiness. She's insecure but won't admit it, listens to Maria Callas's *The Voice within the Heart* over and over, and burns easily in the sun. Her shoulders are as wide as her hips, and her tummy is quite flat. She has a great pucker and killer lips. She has big, dark brown eyes, and she looks sad. At times, her eyes gleam like no other, especially when she's telling one of her stories. She lives in 'Airstream World,' and we think that's where she's gone. It's just that nobody knows where that is."

"Good grief, Pokey! Where is she?"

"Your guess is as good as mine. Her clothes are gone."

20

"Hi, Patty, I'm up in the Bay Area visiting James for a couple of weeks." Air took a drag of her cigarette and raised herself up on her knees to flick the ashes out the tiny window in the kitchen of James's trailer. "This way, I'll create an opportunity for Pokey to leave me."

"What do you mean you're creating an opportunity for him to leave you?" Patty asked. "I hate to tell you, Air, but it seems to me that you just left him!"

"No, I'm sure everyone thinks I've just left for a couple of days. Pokey's moving to LA and wants me to go with him. The fact is, it was me who convinced him to go back to school in the first place. I just had no idea he'd chose a school down south. Patty, you know how hard I've worked to get my position at the university, and I also need to get back to my art. If I leave with Pokey, I'll be giving all that up. Instead of just telling him I don't want to be in a relationship with him anymore, I've set up a scene that will lead to us arguing so intensely it will be natural for him to leave me," Air announced loudly.

"What I know is Brett is completely broken. What the hell was that joke with the milk carton?" Patty snapped angrily.

"I wanted to let Pokey know I wasn't coming home," Air said. "Pokey will understand the situation. I just need more time to talk to him. It's just easier to create a terrible scene first, hurt him, and let him take the responsibility of telling me to fuck off!"

"I wish you'd keep things simple for a change," Patty replied with a sigh. "You can't hurt people who love you the way you do, Air. I'm pissed you've really hurt my dearest friend."

"What? Me? Keep things simple? You have to be out of your mind! You know me better than that."

"Air, someday you have to learn how to enjoy life and stop with all the drama. I wish you'd get how important it is to just tell the truth. How dare you stand up in front of a group of people and lecture like you have tons of integrity and immediately after act so childish?"

"I don't know." Air bit her lip. "I just don't know. I'm sorry, Patty. I think my parts are fragmenting on me again. I just needed to get out of town. I plan on looking around for a live-in work studio in Emeryville while I'm visiting James. It might do me good to get out of Santa Cruz and start taking my art more seriously. I'll see you in about a week or two. Patty, I am sorry I hurt Pokey. Bye." Air hung up the phone, looked at James, and let out a long sigh.

"James, I think it's time I moved back up here to the Bay Area," Air said. "I'm sitting on a stack of artwork that needs to be shown out in the world, and I can't do that in Santa Cruz. There are very few galleries in town and most of them are too conservative for my work. I was thinking maybe we could drive around Emeryville and look for studio space—one that I could live in and paint."

"Air, I've been telling you that for over a year. Your work is completely unique, and you need to have a solo show," James said in a supportive tone. "You know that Emeryville is full of artists. I'm sure we can find you a place. You could live with me if I had the space, Air."

"Oh my God, James. That goes without saying. Don't give it another thought. I'm just so grateful that you're letting me stay with you. I know your feelings about guests. You've always said, 'Guests are like fish; they go bad in three days.'"

"Well, I have said that, but it doesn't apply to you, sweetie. You're always welcome in my lil ole trail." James laughed reassuringly and with love.

"Since you have the weekend off, do you think that we could drive around Emeryville tomorrow and check things out?"

"Is the Pope Catholic?" James grinned. "Hell yeah, girl!"

James and Airstream got up early the next day.

"Air, I'm going to make some breakfast. I think I'll cook oatmeal and add some fresh fruit. The oatmeal is organic. Would you like some?"

"Yeah sure. I need to take a quick shower. I'll be out in a minute."

"Do you want a beer with your oatmeal?" James yelled.

"No, I'm going to have a glass of wine. You're welcome to have some if you want."

"No thanks. I'm going to have a beer or two."

Air showered quickly and walked into the kitchen just as James was setting their plates down. She slid into the built-in, yellow leather-cushioned seats. The table was just big enough for two. James set out the oatmeal and wine.

"This looks great. I usually never eat breakfast," Air said. "As I was showering, I kept waiting for the smell of bacon. I know how much you love bacon. Did you stop eating bacon?"

"I'm out. We need to stop by the grocery store. My refrigerator is empty. We'll figure out a dinner plan while we're out and about."

"James, remember how we couldn't wait to go to your house after school and slice up a bunch of potatoes. Then we'd cook them in that bacon grease your mom had in a can sitting on the back of the stove? Fuck, that stuff had to be rancid as all hell, but we loved them! Do you remember us doing that?"

"Yeah, I remember your mom had bacon grease in a dog food can on your stove! I think everyone's mother kept pouring bacon grease into the same can and just left it sitting there forever. They cooked everything in it. It's amazing we're still alive. I'm sure a whole generation of folks were raised on rancid bacon grease."

Air and James laughed long and hard. They knew everything about each other, and almost any memory they shared and revived was hysterically funny. Nothing could or would ever come between them. They had lived a life of, "Wanna Hear Another Funny Story?"

At first, they drove up and down streets looking for "for rent" signs. Air became frustrated and suggested they go downtown, where there were a lot coffee shops where artists hung out.

"Air, let's park at the end of the block and just walk in and out of all the cafés. We'll look for bulletin boards with listings for rentals."

"Great idea. Let's start right here," Air said, pointing out the window. "This one is full of artists."

They walked to the back of the café. Air took out her journal and a pen and started reading.

"Air, here's a listing for a studio that say it's two thousand square feet with skylights!"

Air didn't look up but continued scanning her half of the corkboard wall, which was so full of advertisements she wondered if the shop owners ever cleared it off.

"Air, did you hear me?"

"Is it live/work space?" she asked.

"Yeah," he said. "It's very close, and it's in a good neighborhood."

Air looked toward the ad he was reading, "Does it say how much it rents for?"

"No, just lists a number. Let's call and see if we can see it."

"Okay, I'll call."

Airstream went over to the phone that was hanging on the front wall. She called the number, and a soft-spoken woman answered the phone.

"Hi, I just read your posting for a live/work art studio. Is it still available?"

"Yes, it is," the woman replied. "I just put the posting up this morning."

"I'm very interested in seeing it. Do you think we could make an appointment to meet?"

"Sure, I will be there in a couple of hours, so let's say at four o'clock?"

"Thank you very much. By the way, my name is Airstream."

Air and James decided to get something to drink and wait until it was time to go see the studio.

"Oh man, Air, if you like this studio and the rent's not too much, you should take it."

"You're reading my mind, James. I could still commute down to Santa Cruz for seminars and just live and paint here. Oh, I'd love to be close to you again!"

"Air, let's just drive over to the place now. We can look in the windows before the landlady gets there. Besides, you'll know if you like it the minute we see it from the street."

They walked fast to the car, drove over to the street, and searched for the addresses. They both saw it at the same time and started screaming.

"Oh my God. It's awesome," Air squealed.

The building looked like it had been built in the forties. Just for the hell of it, James turned the doorknob, and the door opened.

He looked over at Air and said, "Oh shit, do you think we should go in? She'd not due here for another forty-five minutes."

"Fuck yes, let's go in!"

They opened the door and walked into what seemed to be the last of the wild, wild West.

"Oh my God, you don't see buildings like this anymore! Look at the skylights," James said, grinning.

"This is perfect, James! I hope the rent isn't too much. I'd move in here tomorrow. I love that there are no walls except for what seems to have been a small office. Let's go check out the back," Air said happily.

"Look," she exclaimed, "there's a kitchen in the back part of the building under that huge loft. I've never seen such a large ladder to get up to a loft. Hell, I could sleep up there! This is too good to be true. I love it, James!"

"Air, it's time you had luck on your side. I know you're going to get this place!"

"My spider senses are on red alert. I absolutely know I'm going to get this place," she said as she turned to James.

"Well, howdy, neighbor!" James said with a sigh that encompassed both relief and anticipation of the future.

21

Patty hung up the phone with Air and walked over to the main house. She went downstairs to Brett's room. Slowly she opened his door and peeked in. Brett was just sitting in his chair with his guitar. Somewhere between dying and not dying, he remembered the song Flash had written for him just a couple of weeks ago. It was about how much she loved him and how good he was for her. It only had two chords, but it was the way she sang it to him, especially when she sang the words, "Oh, baby, you're such a good thing."

He thought about writing a song. He searched the margins of his memories for a name for her besides Air or Flash. There were moments when he found her "unearthly" and couldn't remember her name at all, but he didn't apologize for forgetting. Flash was someone who did and did not exist. After all, someone said she'd come to Earth with Jupiter dust in her hair.

"I guess this had to happen," Patty said. "But you have to admit she's made you into a warrior now. You now know about the dark side, and it is there that the gold lies. You now know how to fight your demons and survive. She teaches people that, you know—survival. Her life has been about surviving, and it has brought her gifts most of us will never know. Most of us are too afraid to venture into the darkness, but not Air. She loves it. She swears that's the only way to live."

Brett kept discreetly searching for her name among his belongings. It was strange, since Flash had left only two days ago. She must have left behind something, a slant of a smile, a picture of herself when she was eight, or maybe her fake eyelashes or fingernails.

Brett dropped his head into his hands and began crying. "She deceived me," he said through his tears. "You know, she disappeared long ago. She'd reappear, convincingly disguised in my clothes. The crazy part is I don't think I have a clue as to who she really is. I haven't the slightest idea what really makes her happy."

"I think that's part of the game," Patty said. "But, I do know the happiest I've ever seen her is when she's doing her art. I really believe someday she'll be a famous artist."

Brett continued to slump down into his chair.

"She's left me no peace," he said, shaking his head in disbelief. "How can one so tender and full of wild abandon leave me so disjointed? How will I ever forget her? She was so full of excitement. She was so willing to put herself out there on the planet—so ready for whatever there was to absorb. I don't know myself anymore," he said to Patty as if he was looking straight through her. "It's like I forgot how to drive."

"That's certainly clear, Brett. But it doesn't matter anymore, except she'll probably publish your story, and that will be another gift she will give to you."

The tears now fell from Brett's eyes uncontrollably. He continued to hold his head in his hands. "I wanted it to work! I love her so much! I've never felt so much emotion and allowed it to pour through me!"

"Another gift Flash gave you. Be grateful," Patty said to him in an almost pleading tone.

The tears seemed to have nothing to do with anything. It was just that, somehow, Brett felt like a loser. And being in his heart instead of his head was something new for him. Allowing another human being to see him in such pain was something new for him, even if it was his very best friend, Patty. It was true Flash had done this for him. She had gotten him in touch with his heart and out of his head.

"I thought the heart never lied," cried Brett.

"Oh yes, it does," Patty sighed.

He wondered how he could have ever mistaken her for his "chosen one." "How could I not have seen this coming? I've been living in a trance. She came into my life telling me she'd already chosen her 'chosen one.' I thought I could change her mind and her heart at the same time. How crazy is that? Me, changing Air, what a joke! She has a lot of endearing traits, but mercy is not in the portfolio of Flash's life. In the beginning, I thought I could resist her. I thought she would resist me. She was just as you said she was. You warned me, Patty. I'd just never experienced anything so close to being real since the death of my grandfather. How could I walk away from an opportunity to say and be all the things my grandfather had tried to tell me? Air is so much like him. He was a true free spirit among a bunch of 'numbies' for a family. My grandfather knew there was more to life than what was right in front of him, just like Air does. That's probably why I was instantly attracted to her."

He started hysterically laughing and finally blurted out, "Do you remember when Flash and I flew down to LA for my grandfather's funeral?"

"Yeah," she said, patting his shoulder reassuringly. "That was pretty soon after the two of you met. I remember being surprised you took her with you."

"I remember waking up the morning of the flight. She was looking through her clothes for something to wear since she'd already spilled a glass of wine on herself. For Christ's sake, she drank all that morning, and I think she even took a couple of Valiums. I swear, she didn't seem fucked up at all but she cried the entire drive to the airport. She kept telling me she was terrified of flying. Just before we went into the boarding section, Flash turned to me and looked straight into my eyes and said, 'Pokey make sure you get your grandfather's Mercedes.' She meant it; she was not joking."

For about five minutes, the room was silent. Both Brett and Patty sat close to each other holding hands. Brett continued to look around for something she'd left behind, and Patty kept glancing at the door as if Air would walk in at any moment.

"I have to find a way to say good-bye to her," Brett said quietly. "She's too damned nuts for me! But, I haven't the slightest idea how to let go."

The room fell silent again. Patty wanted to hold Brett and cry with him, but knew she had to keep it together for her friend. She started thinking about Air's cruel side and reconsidered. It wasn't that Air was cruel person it was just that Air never thought about the fact that her behavior had consequences for both her and others. Patty had always known Air's beliefs about fate and self-realization. Whatever happened in life was meant to be, Air would say. And if anyone were to have a true epiphany about him or herself, it would always show up as real bad news. Apologies had no possible reality to live in. She believed the same when it came to regrets and failures. Air reminded Patty of this belief of hers often.

Brett gripped Patty's hand more tightly. There were no words to be spoken. Just memories. Brett moved closer to Patty. He thought about the past summer when the love between him and Air was still fresh. He remembered having a fantasy of being fourteen and riding in the back of a hay truck with her. She was lying on top of a bale of hay naked, sunning her perfect body. She was stretched out freely, and yet one knew you needed permission to touch her. He fantasied about kissing her breasts. He knew this was what she wanted, so he bent over and began to kiss her breasts teasingly. He remembered how his fantasy had turned into a nightmare.

"Oh my God!" she'd screamed.

She had a way of twisting her mouth into the most disgusting look. She gave him that look. Pokey got up immediately and looked at her breasts. There was blood all over her chest. He'd had a nosebleed and hadn't even known it! In his daydream, her passion for blood sprang forth from hiding, and it fell upon her. After her initial reaction, she'd smeared his blood all over her body. She'd left him trembling—left him naked, remembering the taste of his own blood in his mouth.

"Shit! Farewell to all this craziness. I can't take it anymore. I'm drained, and spending a day with Air is exhausting. At least that's what I'm going to tell myself. She's making me contradict every belief system I've ever had," he declared to Patty.

Patty looked around Brett's room. She felt helpless. A part of her felt guilty for introducing the two. "I don't think she'll ever forget your name either, Brett. I think, no doubt, the two of you will always try to fly, and your passion for one another will live forever. I'm sure she's feeling quite butchered herself, if not by this affair, certainly by the one with Paul. He tore her apart as much as he could get his hands on her. You know, she's afraid of apologizing for being so crazy. I think she convinced herself long ago you could never spend your life with someone like her. She once told me she felt you were someone who could be president someday, and then they'd find out about her past, and she'd ruin everything for you."

Patty just sat there not really knowing how to comfort her dear friend of many years. She heard a voice whispering in her head to tell Brett about Keith. She wanted to simply say, "You don't know this, but there is another." Just like in *Star Wars*. But she couldn't inflict any more pain on her friend. Yet, she wondered if she was being a friend by withholding this sacred secret.

"I don't think she knows how to accept kindness from anyone. She gives so easily and then freaks out if someone wants to do something for her. I am beginning to think I too am deeply satisfied with suffering," he said, though there was a question in his tone.

"I don't think it matters, Brett. What's important is that you allowed yourself to fully open your heart. You allowed yourself to express your feelings openly and freely for the first time that I've ever known you. I've never seen you laugh so much and display such affection as you did with Air. Say what you will, but she was good for you. I suggest you get off your pissed-offness and embrace her gifts. Not too many people are going to be lucky enough to cross her path like you did."

"I can't say I don't love her anymore," he replied after a moment. "But I am beginning to lock our love successively into smaller and smaller boxes, one at a time, deeper and deeper, one less accessible to the other. She told me the reason she left was because we had come to the end of our 'Earth school lessons' with one another. She said she had nothing more to give to me, and she had nothing more to take from me. What kind of crap is that? She said we were meant to spend time together so that we could learn from each other. Our relationship and the knowledge we gained from its experiences would prepare us for our next relationship."

"Brett, that is her belief system. She believes partnering with someone for a while is like taking a class in college, so you can graduate and be ready for the path you were meant to travel."

"Patty, I realize that she meant to set up impenetrable barriers. I knew there would be no middle ground with her. I knew I was experimenting with a new way of being—a way that took me to a place where I didn't know myself. I tried not putting down rules and regulations. I let her be as free as she needed to be. But as amazed as I was by all of it, I was also just as horrified by our connection. At times, I was repulsed by my own behavior. I argued with her more than I've ever argued with anyone in my whole life."

"She'll be back."

"Oh yeah, I know she'll be back, except I won't be here. I'm going to go ahead with my plans to move back down to LA and finish my medical training. I'll be down there for a couple of years. That should be enough time to get her out of my heart and for my skin to grow back over my exposed nerves, don't you think?"

"I've known her for a long time, and I've never seen her in a healthy relationship. She thinks she has to experience more of the world, like her art, before she settles down."

"No, Patty. I'm 'Flashed' out. She's hurt me too much. I am not so sure she changed my life for the better. I do know I needed someone to push me in the direction I'm headed now. But we're through! You know, she's the one who forced me into looking at the possibilities of going back to school. I'd probably have been just as happy hanging out in the garden or helping Tom build furniture for the rest of my life. But Flash sees things in people, and she takes it on like it's her mission to get them on their path. She takes on the responsibility as if she alone can get people to see their path, their true contribution in life—the one that will live way past their own lifetimes."

Patty heard some voices in the community room. They weren't familiar voices. She got up to take a peek. It was Tom and some of his friends playing a game of pool.

"I'm so happy that you have this space down here. It's very unusual for people to be in the community room. Otherwise, you'll have this bottom floor all to yourself now that Air has left."

Brett was in his own world. "She'd have been a great ER nurse," he remarked. "She can go into an emergency situation, suture everyone up, get them on life-support belief systems, and tell them what they need to do to in order to move their lives forward. Then off she goes—just like that—never to be seen again. Shit! People don't ask her to fix them. All we want is for her to love us the way we are. I'd still have my old beat-up Studebaker if I hadn't let her talk me into selling it. I loved that car, but Flash said it embarrassed her."

"Well, Brett, I hate to remind you, but you gave her the nickname Flash the night you met her. She was brilliant enough to name you Pokey. Someday she will come into her own sense of knowing. She has a lot to offer the world, and her art will be the portal. I am certain she'll be a well-known artist, someone who's really going to make a difference in the world. She'll be famous, you mark my words."

"Well, what I know is, no matter how much money I make, I still want a Volvo, and that just pisses Flash off. I am a 'Volvo sort of guy,' and Flash will always be a 'Gull-wing gal.'"

"I don't know about that, Brett. My hunch is you're going to be about as famous a psychiatrist as she will be as an artist, and I'll bet she'll be a different person by then. And so will you. And I bet you both will have luxury cars."

"How much do you want to bet?"

"Well, we could exchange a great massage for some therapy sessions for a few months."

"Deal."

℘ 22 ℘

It would be many more years and many more national and international exhibitions later when Air would receive a large, white envelope made of exquisite paper that had on it a series of sparking, colorful stamps. It would be handwritten to her and postmarked from Italy.

She would open it with care, to read that she had been nominated and juried into exhibiting her work in the famous and prestigious Venice Biennale in Italy. At this point, she would already have received much notoriety regarding her art, including a National Endowment for the Arts Fellowship. She'd been a three-year recipient of the California for the Arts Fellowship and the founder and creator of an extremely successful, internationally known environmental public project. She'd received many private foundations grants; had two mini-documentaries for TV made on her projects; and had many letters of recognition from presidents, senators, and congressmen and congresswomen. She'd accepted many commissions from countries around the world to share her projects with their communities, been featured in countless newspaper and magazine articles, and had lectured around the world about environmental art.

All this would culminate in Airstream's dream come true. She was to have a solo show at the New York Museum of Modern Art.

And thus, Pokey, the now famous Dr. Brett Rhodes, head of Cedars-Sinai Hospital, author of over ten books and countless magazine articles, and lecturer on childhood education, would receive the following beautifully embossed announcement:

The New York Museum of Modern Art is proud to announce

The Solo Exhibition of the Internationally Known Artist "Airstream."

You and your guest are cordially invited to a private reception to meet the artist and view her latest series of collagraphs and etchings:

"Somewhere Outside My Window"

The exhibit will run from July 1 through August 31.

The reception will be held Thursday July 5, from 5–7 p.m.

Please RSVP with the enclosed card and envelope.

Dr. Rhodes would close the invitation slowly and slide it back into its ochre-colored envelope. Sitting in his overstuffed chair, in his fancy office, with all his accolades on the walls, he would stare out the twenty-second-floor window taking in his private view of Los Angeles. Actually, it would be more accurate to say that the doctor would collapse into the chair, clutching the envelope.

"Oh God," he would say out loud. "I haven't thought of Flash in years. Shit! Why do I still feel a slight sense of regret and missed opportunity?"

He would wonder about Patty. It had been so long since he had spoken with her. He was sure Flash had sent an invitation to her as well. Leave it to Flash to have the invitations printed in some strange color like ochre, too.

He would chuckle out loud, "A mustard-colored invitation and a private reception."

"Why?" he would ask his empty office. "Why would Flash send me an invitation after almost twenty years?"

He would know there was no reason. Air was simply still pushing the river. He would wonder why, all of a sudden, his stomach hurt. He had been nothing more than a drop in her bucket of life.

Why the hell is she sending me an invitation after all these years?

A sense of numbness would come over him. It'd been so long since he'd felt her body next to his, seen her face smiling and her gorgeous golden hair blowing in the ocean breeze. Shit. She'd been so much fun, until the end. There had not been anyone in his life since her who'd played in such a "high-drama arena."

"I've almost forgot your name so many times," Dr. Rhodes would whisper, staring at the envelope now lying on his leather-covered desk.

The memories would run over him like a slow freight train. He didn't want to remember, but he couldn't help himself. A short breath went in, and a long one came out. So much of him still ached for her.

"Why?" he would shake his head and laugh out loud at himself. "I'm not in my body at this moment. My sign reads, 'Dr. Rhodes is Out of the Office. May or may not return'."

The phone would ring, bringing him back to the present. He would quiver at the possibility of it being Flash.

"I'm just going to let it ring," he would say out loud. He wouldn't resist. "Hello?"

"Brett?"

"Flash?"

"Flash?" The woman on the other end would giggle.

"Is this Flash?" he would ask again.

"Good grief, Brett! Are you all right?" Patty would ask.

"Who is this?"

"It's Patty, Brett. How are you? It's been too long."

Brett would start laughing. "You got one too, huh?"

"I'm so happy for her! She's always wanted to have a show there. It's a dream come true. During so many of our times together, she'd tell me nothing mattered more to her than having a solo show at the Museum of Modern Art in New York. I've followed her career all these years. She's famous, Brett. Were you aware of her success?"

"The last I heard was that she living somewhere in the Bay Area and that she'd been interviewed on a lot of TV shows regarding different projects she was involved with. I didn't think much more about it. I heard she founded two highly acclaimed nonprofits that had stemmed from her public art projects. Did she ever get married?" Brett would add inquisitively.

"I don't know anything about her personal life," Patty would tell him. "I haven't talked to her in years. Someone along the line told me she was writing a book. I have no clue what it's about or if she finished it. Remember I told you that she'd write a book. I've read articles that have been published in the various Bay Area newspapers. I read an article of about her in the magazine called *Art in America*. There were lots of photos of art and her studio. She looks great! She hasn't changed a bit. It's like she been dipped in wax."

"I remember when we were together she'd say she was going to be an awesome old lady. I always knew she'd dress very avant-garde even when she was in her nineties," Brett would reply.

"Yes, I agree," he'd hear Patty say in the background of his visions of what Airstream must look like now. "She was always perfectly at ease with dressing very couture. She designed clothes in New York, remember?"

"So, did she write anything special or personal on your announcement?" Patty asked.

"If you consider mustard personal, then yes."

"Run that one by me again."

"Oh, I was just being snide. I'm not sure where that came from. Anyway, no, there's nothing written on the card. You know the now-famous, mysterious Flash. I know the message is in the color ochre, but I'll be damned if I can make any meaning of the color," he would reply with dismay.

"Well, I say we hit New York City and go to the private reception," he would hear Patty say.

"It's an interesting thought," he would reply after a moment's hesitation before deciding to share a dream he'd had about Air a few nights before the invitation had come. "I dreamed we were making love in some field of dried weeds. As a matter of fact, that damned field was all ochre colored! Hmm, that's very interesting. Anyway, somehow the field caught fire, and before we realized it, we were surrounded. I kept yelling, 'Let's get out of here!' All Flash did was lie there screaming, 'No! To hell with the fire; make love to me!' She just kept screaming that over and over. Weird dream. Patty, to this day, I'm still uneasy around her."

"Do you mean maybe you'd have let the field burn up around you while you were making love to Flash? Or do you mean you'd ruin a perfectly wonderful dream by telling her you wanted to save your life?"

"All I know is, I'm self-destructive when I'm around her."

"Listen, you're successful now. Come up to San Francisco. You can stay with me. We haven't seen each other in years, and we'll fly to New York together. You'll have the opportunity to thank her for pushing you in your direction of medicine and early childhood education. Just think of all the people you've assisted along their journeys this time around. Air had a lot to do with that. Besides you've both changed and we're all older now."

"I can't go," he would say sadly.

"Oh yes you can. You must! If you don't, the two of you will have way too much unfinished business. This is why she has sent us invitations."

"Patty, I know there's a hidden agenda here. What's up?"

"You're starting to sound like Flash. You're the one who will probably end up publishing our stories, but it won't have the ending you want."

"I am not going to her opening," Brett would say bitterly. "I won't be missed either. The lady's made it. She's doing exactly what she always wanted. I bet there are no men in her life either."

Patty would remain silent.

"You're right, this is exactly what she's always wanted to do," he would add, "live life on her terms. And she's survived. She survived big-time!"

"Survived? I'm not sure that *survived* is the word for her. Perhaps *exposed* is more accurate. She's always exposed herself to the dark side of life because, remember, she always said, the gold lies in the darkness," Patty would say firmly. "By the way, should I remind you of our bet just before you left for LA? You owe me a therapy session, and I owe you a series of massages."

23

But long before Airstream would plan her exhibit at MOMA, she was finding reasons to celebrate, learning more about herself, and enjoying her new home. "I can't believe it's been over five years since I moved into this studio," Air said, cradling the phone and gazing into the belly of her home/studio from her loft view. "It seems like yesterday we found this place and I left Santa Cruz. I can still remember unpacking the endless boxes of stuff I hadn't seen in years and how excited I was to begin a new life. It was like Christmas going through those boxes that had been in storage for so long! Emeryville is really the coolest artist district on this side of the Bay. I'm actually beginning to run out of space. There are so many canvases leaned up against the back wall. I wish you'd come over. We haven't seen each other in a couple of weeks. I can't believe I've had over five exhibits already this year, and I need to crate up a couple of pieces to go to Spain by the end of the week. It's hard to imagine how my career just took off so quickly!"

"Air, I've been as busy as you. If I'm not working, I'm just hanging out with Keith."

"How is Keith?"

"He's fine. We're still going to AA meetings a couple of times a week. You know how Keith is; he doesn't say much. I'm the one who has to figure out what we're doing."

"I wish you guys would stop by and visit."

"Air, I didn't really want to get into it with you, but we're not seeing each other that much these days. Our relationship has been so on and off over the past two years that I have no clue if we'll make it as a couple. He works nonstop, and he's always drunk. Sometimes I stop by his office, and he won't even answer the door. I know he's in there, but he just doesn't want me to see he's drinking. He's so behind in his orders. I keep begging him to hire someone to help him run his office so he can focus on making his jewelry, but he's too freaked out to have anyone around. I never realized what a loner he really is. I've begged him to move in with me, but he pretends to not hear me. I don't know if we're going to keep seeing each other."

"I am so sorry to hear that. I haven't heard from him for over a week myself. I think 'our' boyfriend maybe MIA." Air laughed.

"I've about had it with him. He's so distant with me. I try to give him affection, and he acts as if doesn't faze him. He hasn't spent the night with me in weeks. When we're together, he just wants to watch movies. If I didn't know him better, I'd think he was seeing someone else. I don't know, Air. Maybe it is time to let him go. I met this guy the other day at work, and he asked me if I wanted to have a drink with him after work. I almost said yes."

"Wow, James, I'm sort of shocked. Keith is probably just in one of his manic episodes. You have to wait it out. I feel so sad for him. I really think he wants to be more intimate; he just doesn't know how sometimes. Give him some time." Air wanted to tell James that she had been having conversations with Keith via her fax machine for weeks, but Keith didn't want James to know. Air didn't want James to know either. Air knew Keith was not interested in James anymore. He'd told Air that James just wanted to live in the past, and he was bored with his immaturity. Air felt she was deceiving James, but she couldn't resist communicating with Keith. She loved Keith more than life itself. She hoped James would change the subject. She hated what she was doing but her love for Keith was stronger than her morals.

"I need to clean this trailer. It's a mess, and there's no room for anything to be put away."

"That's funny. My studio is completely packed. There are paintings everywhere! All the surfaces are full of small art objects. The bookcases are full of art books. It's a curse that I have two delivery doors. On the positive side, it allows me to paint quite large canvases and get them out the doors. The negative side is that I can now buy super large items. James, I miss you. We used to go to the movies and dinner at least once a week."

"Yes, but you've joined so many art cooperatives, and you're hanging your work in some gallery every month. Didn't you just tell me you hired a professional photographer to come in and take photos of your work? Plus, you're busy putting together packets of your work and mailing them out to as many New York City galleries as you can. You've become too well known. You're 'blood in the water' these days. It's fabulous you're selling so much art though. Are you able to save money?"

"I wish. It costs so much to ship my work. I have to commission special crates, not to mention the framing costs. I'm doing okay though. I'm able to pay the bills and travel with my work. I'm going be exhibiting in Greece this coming October. I can hardly wait to go, but that's not going to be cheap."

"Maybe you could stay with Leonard Cohen."

"I wish. You know I'm not connected with the music business at all anymore. I really miss it. I think about those days often. They were a blast. It's hard to imagine that life now. I can hardly believe I actually used to sit in the Chelsea Hotel with Leonard and George Harrison and drink sangria and eat shrimp in green sauce. God, I wonder where Frank is these days?"

The predictable day finally came when Air received a call from the prestigious Vonne Gallery in New York City. The gallery representative told Air the owner of the gallery was interested in exhibiting a couple of her smaller paintings in a group exhibit of emerging artists in the United States. She was told she would need to send her work back to New York in eight months.

Air hung up the phone and screamed out loud, "Oh my God! I can't fucking believe this!" She stood there completely paralyzed with a mixture of excitement and disbelief. She quickly called her very close friend and fellow artist, Sandy. She'd met Sandy a year prior after reading an article in the local newspaper about him. It was an announcement for his solo exhibition and reception at the most prestigious East Bay gallery, Simon Arts. The article had photos of him working in his live/work studio that turned out to be just around the corner from her. She'd decided to attend the reception and introduce herself. They had become good friends quickly.

"Sandy! Oh my God! You're not going to believe this. I just received a phone call from the Vonne Gallery in New York City! They want to include a couple of my pieces in an exhibition they're having this coming October!"

"Airstream, I'm not surprised at all," Sandy said. "Congratulations, gorgeous! You deserve it."

"I can't believe this! My God, how things can dramatically change overnight," she said.

"Hey, I just finished cleaning my brushes. I've been painting all day, but I'm through now. How about I come over and we'll celebrate?" Sandy asked.

"I'm really sorry, Sandy. I'm on an incredible deadline before I leave for Mexico."

"Mexico? Are you going to Mexico for a vacation?"

"No, I wish. It will be a working vacation. Last month, I received a letter from the Mexican government. They invited me to go down to Puerto Vallarta and set up an environmental art project aimed at the homeless families who live out at the dump. The families send their children into town each day to beg the tourists for money, and the government wants that to change in a positive way. I'll be training a group of local artists to work with the homeless families. These artists will show the families how to pull paper safely from the waste streams. They'll recycle it into pulp. They'll learn how to put the pulp into large containers of water and, using papermaking screens, which they'll make themselves, dip down into the water, pulling up newly made sheets of paper. They'll incorporate 'found objects' into the pulp. The families will be shown how to create their own greeting cards. They will be given the opportunity to sell their cards at some of the local business in town. My main job will be teaching nine local artists how to keep the project going after I leave."

"Wow, that is awesome! How'd you pull that off?"

"I've been going down to Puerto Vallarta for years and have a lot of artist friends down there. One of my friends owns a gallery, and she is a member of the Rotary Club. There is an increase of baby boomers moving to Puerto Vallarta, and the business owners want to clean up the streets—you know, stop all the begging and keep the locals from pestering the tourists for money. When the issue of how to deal with the problem came up during the meeting, my friend talked about my zero paper waste project in the schools. Puerto Vallarta has a strong environmental group, and someone from that organization contacted me to see if I had any interest in participating. The plan is that I will be there for six months with the project, but I'm considering staying longer. I have a very good friend, a muralist, who's willing to sublet my studio while I'm gone. I leave in about two months, and I still have a couple of local commissions to finish. Plus, I now need to prepare for the exhibit in New York!"

"Ah come on, Air. Let me come over for just a few minutes. I haven't seen you in a couple of weeks, and now you're going to Mexico for six months or longer! I can't believe you didn't tell me about this commission. How did that slip by? At any rate, I have a great bottle of champagne. We can have a couple of glasses and I'll leave. You can keep working on whatever you're doing. I'll just sit and watch you. I'll entertain you with a story from my childhood."

Sandy was the CEO of a high-profile tech company in Emeryville, as well as a very talented artist. He was handsome, and Air felt totally at ease with him. She loved laughing with him and teasing him, since she knew the relationship would remain friendly and nothing more. "Okay, for a little while," she acquiesced. "See you soon."

Air walked back to the canvas she'd been prepping when the call from the gallery had come in, except this time she looked at the image from a different point of view. It became obvious to her that only two colors on the canvas—black and blue—made sense. "Good God, this image reflects exactly how I feel," she said out loud. She enjoyed the sound of her voice as she worked in the large, spacious studio. "I'm in a tremendous amount of pain, and I'm burying myself in my art. Leaving for Mexico without Keith is an unbearable reality." She couldn't imagine not being able to look into Keith's eyes and hold him close to her body. Of course, he had to be drunk for her to hold him and sometimes sing into his mouth. Without her, he wouldn't have anyone to make sure he hadn't fallen and hit his head on one of the pieces of huge metal machinery in his warehouse. She found him on the floor all the time. His face would be smeared with blood. "He needs me to help him through the day," she said softly. "His life has become hopeless. He's struggling to find reasons for living." She reflected on the words he'd recently said. "Oh my God, I have an awful ache in my heart, Air. You are the only one I can share this with. I've lived in darkness for decades."

Air heard Sandy knocking on her front door.

"Hey, I forgot to mention," Sandy said as he came in. "I got your phone message the other night. You seemed pretty upset—something about a guy you went on a hike with over the weekend saying some weird things that really hurt you. You said he thought you were beautiful, in spite of all your wrinkles, small tits, sagging ass, varicose veins, and bunions? But you looked great for thirty-eight. What's that guy's problem? Is this a guy from the personals? He's just a little weenie, Airstream. You do know that, right? He's just a guy who finds traveling into the nothingness, just to peek, way too scary. He's just a guy who is weak of heart, a guy who's really not looking for a traveling companion, a guy who isn't up for dreaming about birds and muffled conversations in foreign tongue, a guy whose dreams are cold, a guy with way too many shadows who doesn't see them as being as precious as the sun." Sandy smiled his charming smile. He gently grabbled Air by the arm as she walked by him. "Don't give this ass another thought. You are perfect, my dear."

They both laughed as Sandy opened the bottle of champagne. Air handed Sandy a couple of her "special times" crystal champagne glasses. They toasted to Air's exhibit at the Vonne Gallery.

"This guy is someone who is not up for the risky side of life, Air—a guy who thinks you're too exotic, too adventurous. And I bet, above all, he thinks you were way too dangerous for him, but he's too arrogant to ever admit it!"

"He didn't find me to be one of those 'good girls.' We both know good girls go to heaven, and bad girls get to go everywhere else! Shall I go on?" Air asked as she tossed her golden locks back away from her face.

"By all means!"

"I think he caught a glimpse of my teeth. In fact, I'm sure of it because I made a point of referring to myself as being a lioness in a past life. I told him how I loved to lie in wait for a wildebeest just like him, trotting slowly across the great African ancestral plain. I told him I'd love to pounce on him and munch on his haunches and smear his blood all over my lips and face and call it makeup and then announce to him I had to go and put on my party dress. I had to go dance the dance of love and life!"

"Ha! You didn't really say that to him, did you?"

"You bet your ass I did—my 'sagging ass' that is!"

"So what other trouble have you gotten yourself into lately? I heard you put another photo of yourself on one of those dating sites. I hope you didn't post the one with the long hair? That one's a killer! You're going to have every guy in the US slobbering over you."

"Of course I did."

"Oh boy. How many responses did you get?"

"Actually, I've spent most of the morning revising a grant for my latest art project. I was taking a break for a moment from painting. So, I haven't even had a chance to check my e-mail today. To tell you the truth, it didn't even cross my mind. I need to concentrate totally on this piece. I'm almost done, but my mother called me out of the blue this morning. She wanted me to know she saw me on TV the other day. All I'll say about my mother is that she became an incredible jeweler and sold her work at Gump's for years. Her philosophy on children is, 'Wh-elle now, honey, I birthed ya; now you're on your own!'"

Air backed up and nervously looked at her canvas. She was pleased with the direction the painting was headed but sensed it was far from complete. She needed to paint every day.

"Sandy, talk to me while I paint," she said. "Talk about anything in the world, like the bonding and emotional connection that occurs between two people. That is one of the great mysteries of my life. I long for that so much. I ache for that—the unbelievable bond two people can have when they are truly connected to each other and share their feelings and values. It's what I'm looking for in life and something I am committed to achieving with a man this time around. If I am fortunate enough to find that, then I will be a fulfilled and happy woman for the remainder of my days on earth. My partner will be the beneficiary of an immeasurable amount of love, loyalty, generosity, and respect. And since I am so candid, I also want a man who desires cultural exchange, someone who admires and appreciates people and traditions that are different from what I was raised with. I want a man who wants to get to know me and all the regions of possibilities of knowing ourselves in ways we don't yet know ourselves to be."

"Well, Airstream, I'm happy we didn't meet online. I tried the online thing once, more on a dare from my friend than with the hope of really finding somebody. If you were just ten years younger and still into wanting babies, I'd ask you to marry me in a flash. I think you are the most fascinating woman I've ever met. I know you understand my desire to have kids. I've always loved big families. Maybe I'll never find the mother of my children and regret I didn't just grab you up and head to Venice, marry you, and make love to you for the rest of our lives!"

"You know I don't believe in coincidences, Sandy. I find it very interesting I met you the very day I decided to delete my profile and pictures from half of the dating sites I was on. After our first meeting, my spider senses told me I should put my profile back online but, this time, express what I'm really looking for. No more of this 'evidence of greatness' crap, just the authentic me. Honestly, I've always thought no amount of money could buy me. I decided to stop saying I can't be bought. I've decided to tell the truth. I can be bought, but it's just going to take more than health insurance and a house to buy me.

"I've learned in life that there are no such things as accidents or chance meetings. I deeply believe that things like regrets and failures don't exist either. Those are concepts that have no probable reality in which to live. I will say I have lived long enough to contradict myself though—daily in fact! I can say to you I have a certain 'blah, blah, blah' belief system, and you'll tell me your way of thinking. And I'll turn right around tomorrow and say something like, 'Chance rules everything in the universe except for the human heart.' We alone make the choice of love, although it may have been an accident that gave us the opportunity to make the choice in the first place. But you know what? I don't know shit! I don't even think I'm making sense anymore. I've had to much to drink!" Air concluded, feeling a bit tipsy.

"Well, you say you want a man who will open up and share his deep feelings with you. I was raised in a family where my father worshiped my mom. As a child I watched him hold my mother and cry once. It scared me, but at the same time, I watched as my mother continued to kiss my father's eyes as he cried. I remember him telling her he didn't feel he was good enough for my mother. He kept telling her how loving and understanding she was. I started crying and they heard me. They asked me to join them, and the three of us held each other so tightly. In that moment, I realized it was okay for a man to cry and to be intimate with his family. My mother was 100 percent Italian. She was born there, but her parents came to the United States during the turn of the century as immigrants. I love Italy and often dream of retiring there. She was the most loving woman and my father never missed a day telling her how beautiful she was and much he loved her," Sandy said.

"There's no place in all of Europe like Italy. I once took a tour of little towns outside of Florence and fell in love with this one small town in the Chianti district called Greaves. It was so beautiful. I got off the bus and decided to spend the day. The bus came back later in the day, so I knew I wouldn't get stranded. I decided to walk on a dirt road that led out of town for miles. I felt like I was walking through time. You have to get out on those little roads to really sense what life is like there. There were green rolling hills with vineyards as far as I could see. I walked by ancient two-story stone homes with gardens full of vegetables and flowers that were more romantic than anything I'd ever experienced.

"I found a very old church and sat on a wall of hand-gathered stones for at least an hour. I tried to imagine what everyday life was like. It was just too different than anything I'd ever imagined. I think it was because it was centuries old, because I was raised on a ranch and used to being out in the middle of nowhere. This was just so different. It was heaven. I'd never experience such serenity and beauty in my life. It was so seductive, and I fantasied about how I could possibly live there.

"Of course, there's Venice too. I spent three weeks in Venice discovering small neighborhoods tucked between canals. Some days, I sat on benches in secret courtyards watching grandparents playing with their grandchildren. I was astonished at the patience these people had with these screaming kids throwing fits. They would talk to them until they stopped crying and then they'd hold them in their laps for over an hour, just rocking them back and forth. It was so touching.

"I remember feeling such sadness that I had missed out on a childhood like what I was witnessing. I'd listen to the chatter of people who'd gathered at little cafés after work before heading back home. I'd watch them sip small glasses of wine in regular water glasses along with a small glass of water, or some just enjoyed a cup of espresso. I'm now finally comfortable traveling alone, but a place like Italy is best experienced with your partner who is also your traveling companion. It's just too sensuous to enjoy all by oneself," Air said with a faraway look on her face.

"I didn't realize you'd been to Italy."

"Yeah, I exhibited there late last year for about a month in Florence. I then spent seven weeks traveling throughout Spain."

"You know, Air, on the surface, it seems to me we have a lot in common. Maybe that's the reason you seemed to be intrigued with me and responded to my invitation to that gallery opening last spring in the city. I'm a pretty good writer in the sense of conveying feelings into words, but I'm much better and ultimately prefer the face-to-face variety of communication. I remember the night when we met. I thought you were such a knockout, and then after spending the evening with you, just laughing and watching your eyes and your lips, geez, I was blown away with how easy it was to be with you. I will admit, though, I was disappointed with the way you talked about kids. I definitely got the message you weren't interested in having any kids, and I still wanted a family," Sandy remarked.

Air continued painting and listening intently.

"You know me pretty well by now, Air. I'm a very passionate man about many things. I love life and all it has to offer, and I refuse to be a bystander and let events control me and sweep me along. The idea of being in love again is very strong in me. I believe passion and romance with the right person is a wonderful feeling."

Air set down her paintbrush, slowly walked over to her butterfly chair, and sat down. She loved those chairs. She looked over at Sandy. *I wish I had chemistry for him,* she found herself thinking. *He's such a decent man.* But even if there was chemistry, her heart belonged to Keith. She just played on the online dating sites when she was bored.

"I don't have to tell you how challenging it is to find the right person to trust your innermost desires, dreams, and intimacy with," Sandy said. "I know I'm responsible for my outlook on life and my heightened state of sensory perception. I love to share stories of the sights, smells, and sounds that emulated from the homes of families on both my Italian and Spanish sides as a child. My Italian family has had by far the greater influence on me. Most of all, it is the interaction between the men and women that remains with me— the way they communicated and expressed their feelings to each other. They found joy in everything—food, music, relationships, and passionate debates."

Sandy paused, and Air could see in his face that he was reminiscing.

"Air, you asked me to talk to you while you painted. Now, you're sitting down. Am I boring you?" asked Sandy.

"Not at all," she assured him. "I find what you are saying incredibly fascinating. I'm listening to every word. You're intriguing me, and that's hard to do." Her eyes became more focused and intense as she looked at her work and tried to do a quick critique.

"I'm convinced," Sandy said slowly once Air's gaze had returned to his, staring directly into her eyes, "that I could learn about the gentleness of life from you. I still believe in the ultimate triumph of the human spirit over adversity, pain, and suffering. Tragedy is so common in our world. I think of myself as pretty fearless. I'm not afraid of commitment and being an engaged, proactive, decisive man in a relationship who is, at the same time, an equal and respectful partner with the woman I am involved with. Of course, I wasn't always like this."

Air turned back to the canvas. She got up from her chair, walked over to it, picked up her paintbrush, and began painting with a different color. "Look at this painting and tell me what color is missing. What's going to make this image really pop?" Air asked Sandy.

"Oh more blue, for sure!" he said encouragingly. "I think I'll come over there and get a different perspective."

Air, too, backed up about ten feet and said, "You're right, there's still too much black. I need to mix some darker blue and push it up against the black."

Sandy walked over to the canvas and said, "I think you're almost there. It just needs a bit more depth."

"Is there any champagne left?" Air asked.

"There's just enough for both of us to have half a glass. I'll pour," he said, walking back over to the coffee table.

As he poured, he continued to share very personal thoughts. "I have learned, painfully at times, that, above all else, relationships are built on responsibility to oneself in order to love and to respect the person you are involved with. For the relationship to have meaning and to last, each person has to have a great sense of self-esteem. Love is blind, and you may not ever get back what you put into it. But relationships are all about interaction and compromise with the person you are involved with. They're about give and take."

"Sandy! Enough with the relationship chat! Can you change the subject?" Air snapped as she looked at him with a compassionate smile and dropped her chin a bit charmingly.

"No, I haven't finished my thoughts. Cut me some slack. I'll be through soon. Now as I was about to say, love may eventually be the outcome. Relationships are often better than heartfelt, but often are blind and end up as unrequited love."

"Sandy, I'm like you. I am a person of honor and integrity. I also demand the same from the people I choose to trust and love. I believe in the power of words, but actions and how one visibly lives his or her life communicates who the person is better than words. I am an intellectual to a certain extent and socially liberal, but by no means do I believe that my views and politics are necessarily the correct ones in every circumstance. I am open-minded, but I also have the courage to act on my convictions. I love to have fun and enjoy this wonderful life we have been given to the fullest! I try to laugh at myself and not take myself too seriously. I love to talk about any subject any time, including fears and expectations. Now what color do you think I need?"

Sandy surveyed the canvas, scrunched up his face in thought, and then said, "I think you should try adding some purple."

Air instantly dismissed his idea and said sweetly, "Good grief, Sandy, this is a black and blue painting. I need to stay with this 'beat-up' sort of feeling. I don't have a clue what to do. I'm thinking I need to add more shades of blue."

"Yeah, I agree," said Sandy. "It's interesting that you sense the image as being a 'beat-up' feeling."

"Well, think about it. I didn't set out to have it symbolize a beat-up feeling. Somehow, it just ended up being all black and blue. Maybe that's what I'm really feeling at this point. What do you think of when you think black and blue? Don't you think of being beat up?"

"Yeah, you could see it that way. Or you could look at it as being in a very 'cool state of being.' Leave it up to your audience," he said.

"Okay, I'm going to introduce a couple of lighter shades of blue. You can finish your relationship story and then let's chat about something different," Air pleaded.

"All I want to add is I am available because I have chosen to put myself out there again. No grandiose, breathtaking, majestic truths of awe and wonder. I'm just sick and tired of living in my old, worn-out, run-down house of belief systems. I'm starting to think they are outdated. They worked for me for a long time, but I'm thinking about throwing away my rearview mirror. I'm moving like atoms in a rock into a new house," he said firmly.

"I'm well aware of my power as a woman," Air replied, "yet when it comes to matters of the heart, there seems to be an invisible magnetic field where I lose my power to move past certain circumstances I know will never occur again during my lifetime. I haven't the slightest clue how to just walk away, to let go; currents run too deep. I know I sound cryptic, but there's something about me that very few others know. I've been in love with a man named Keith for over ten years. He has my heart and will until the twelfth of never, but he doesn't feel the same way about me. I try to go to a place of love and compassion and tell myself he is on his path to his higher self, even though the path seems overgrown and strewn with thorns. These are his lessons his soul must learn in order to heal himself.

"My corporal self wants to say to him, 'I hope to God this is the last incarnation in which you have to suffer and be so alone, but I am only that corporeal.' He tells me I am his heart. And yet, this is all I get from him. Even those words came through a fax or e-mail, not face-to-face. Do you want to hear the saddest part? I've never even kissed him, much less made love to him. Yet I'd do anything to be with him. I'd sing. I'd dance. I'd jump off a cliff on a bicycle with a parachute. I'd eat oysters, which I've said I'd never do in my lifetime. I'd even try to have a baby when I'm fifty! I'd promise to never buy another materialistic thing in my life. I'd even beg him to take me to a Kentucky Fried Chicken joint if I thought it would make a difference. And you know how I feel about the Colonel," Air added with disdain.

"Well, well, Missie Airstream, you're human after all! You're just as messed up as the rest of us rug rats. I understand and applaud you for being unstoppable and taking such a stand for love. It is the right thing for you to do. I believe you would betray yourself if you gave in to someone just to not be lonely. I know how you feel about that. You're pretty cool. You know, there sure are a lot of men out there who would give their last bottom dollar to be loved like that by you, including me. What's with this guy? You've never mentioned him to me. He actually sounds a little weird, like that the guy who made all those dumb ass remarks about your body. Guys like that should just simply take a gun and point it at their big toe. The real question is, why the hell are you wasting your time with guys like this? The guy you've loved for ten years doesn't deserve you either!"

Sandy suddenly stopped what he was saying and shouted, "I have an idea, Air! We could adopt!"

Air wanted to slam her paintbrush into a can of water, but instead she gathered her composure. She took a deep breath and, with a lot of thought, she said, "Ah Sandy, there's nothing simple about developing self-understanding, independence, and self-respect. I think we are among the lucky ones. There are so many folks who make every choice based on fear. We've chosen to have our journeys be full even at the high cost of being terrified. We have filled our lives with the energy of personal ambitions and our own sense of responsibility to our families and friends, accepting each of them with their strengths and their weaknesses. I just want to grow old with Keith and share our joys and fears intimately—an opportunity I imagine only a few people recognize or have the willingness to do."

"Well, Air, I think you're awesome, and I know there are no shortcuts to becoming a whole person. Certainly intuitive abilities aren't the answer. You can have my heart anytime you want."

"Please allow me to say this emphatically, Sandy. I want to be clear about my thoughts and how I create my own reality. You know the saying, 'You're the parents of your fate,' right? I'm beginning to consciously choose to see, feel and do things differently with my life. I accept that Keith and I are never going to be together. I have begun to entertain the idea that I am deeply satisfied with the suffering I have with him. It is as though the relationship, as it is, serves as my muse. It is a wealth of inspiration for both my art and my writings.

"If he were to be here for me, I might question whether or not I'd be willing to choose a life with him or the one I've created in my mind. The one of suffering is appealing since many of my most successful pieces have been created out of my complaining," she said.

"Wow, Air. That's some canvas you have going on in your head. It's huge! What is it, thirty feet by thirty feet?"

"Exactly," Air answered as she turned back and looked at the highly textured, abstract, black and blue painting. "I believe life occurs exactly as it should for each person. The opportunities are there for the taking, if not in this lifetime then perhaps the next incarnation. I am grateful I am wealthy and rich. I do not mean with money; I mean with integrity, health, and the insights of choice and intention. I have the possibility of choosing to live without lies, and this is a challenge I'm working very hard on. Thank God, I'm not living on the streets anymore. And honestly, I look back at those times in my life and see them as huge gifts. It was one hell of a scary gift, and I am lucky to still be alive, but my past has taught me a lot. Here I am in this incredible studio, living in an almost extinct abode. For me, it's one of the last frontiers. I don't know too many people who will ever get the chance to live in a studio that could house a bowling lane! I feel like I'm in a sacred garden that is unknown to the rest of the world. From the outside, no one would ever guess how cool it is in here.

"I don't think too many people drive by this place and realize there's a Japanese pond in the floor with live coy swimming around, playground swings hanging from the twenty-foot ceilings and real recreational park slides, thirty-seven pinball machines, two jukeboxes, two eight-foot span gliders, two 1930 Schwinn bicycles hanging from the ceilings, not to mention the pool table and Jacuzzi in the backyard! And that's just how I want it. I like that it looks like an empty warehouse from the outside. No one notices it. They just drive right by. The only drag is I can never have a garage sale because then people would wonder what other incredible treasures are inside this place. It's like a museum in here, you know. I mean, I have everything from petrified dinosaur poop to a real Chagall print on the wall!"

Sandy leaned back in his chair and looked around at Air's studio. He glanced around at all the things she'd pointed out. Her space was like no other, and that was because there was simply no one like her. Her talent extended way past painting and fashion. Everything she did or had or arranged was done with an innate sense of eclectic style.

"When we're at gallery openings, I notice people are drawn to you, whether they want to be or not. I remember you didn't deal with this attention well at all. You used to overreact or would have an immediate inappropriate reaction to certain people, especially women. Then again, there were men you felt were coming on to you, and you'd make some pretty nasty remarks. I used to think you felt threatened by other women artists who were getting as much attention as you were. I want to acknowledge how hard you've worked on yourself this last year, Air. I can see the changes in you from the work you've done with the Landmark seminars and those DBT classes you took for months. I forget what DBT stands for, but I know you've radically changed since I first met you. Your knee-jerk reaction has all but completely vanished. Your what I call 'everyday common anger' has subsided immensely. Your talk of 'intention' has been actualized. You can't stop it now.

"I think you've finally accepted you are not your stuff. You are not a National Endowment for the Arts grantee. You're not an abundance of materialistic stuff that proves your success and greatness. Nor or you just another pretty face with good stories. You've realized what's really important in life. You're making the best of your circumstances while knowing you are not a victim of your circumstances. I know how easy it is to live out one's life as a victim."

Sandy walked over to Air and took the paintbrush out of her hand. He gently lifted her face with his hand and leaned down and kissed her forehead. Tears started to roll down Air's face, and she buried her head in his chest. He held her for almost a minute before she wiped her eyes and looked up at him.

"Thank you for being such a good friend. I'm so grateful to have you in my life and that you accept me for who I am. You've been here for me when even my best friend, James, wouldn't listen to my struggles. People just assume that, because I've received so many grants and won so many awards, I don't live with devil demons. I know in this past year, I've not always been easy to be around. It's been really difficult to honestly look at myself and admit that I've done things I regret," Air said with a heavy heart.

"What? Oh my God, did I just hear you say the word *regret*? Are you telling me that you've changed your belief system to allow for such feelings as regret? Wow, that's really big, Air! How did you do that?"

"I realized in DBT, which stands for dialectic behavioral therapy, by the way, that I wish I'd handled certain events in my life differently. And yet I accept that, if I hadn't dealt with those events the way I did, my life would be quite different. I have given this issue a lot of thought, and I know in my heart I would do whatever the nasty behavior was exactly the same. I can now say, 'I love you, Airstream.' So, to be clear, I don't think I've thrown out my belief that there's no such thing as regret, but I do have room for there being exceptions to every rule."

"I can hardly believe what I'm hearing," Sandy said with a look of amazement on his face.

"I have to sit down. I feel dizzy," Air remarked. She sat down in her butterfly chair and invited Sandy to join her. "We're out of champagne, but I do have some good French wine. Would you like a glass? Or I have some Italian sodas, if you'd like. What can I get you?"

"I'd love some wine," Sandy said with a grin.

"Are you hungry? I have some great cheese and smoked Norwegian salmon. Does that sound good?"

"Yeah, sure!"

Air opened a bottle of French chardonnay and poured two glasses of the wine into hand blown crystal wineglasses. She looked around for her large art nouveau platter. She set the triangle of triple cream cheese with truffles and the smoked salmon onto a plate that had been made by a woman who exhibited her ceramics with Ansel Adams. She added a couple of the artist's smaller plates for each of them and a sterling silver pâté knife for the cheese and set the two glasses of wine onto the beautiful sterling silver platter. She was an utterly divine hostess. She collected only handmade serving platters, plates, and bowls so that she could serve up the many different ethnic foods she knew how to cook. Her favorite foods for aesthetics were those that looked great on her black plates, like Petrale sole with golden beets and prosciutto-wrapped asparagus. Her collection came in all sizes, colors, and shapes. She loved to impress her friends with her ability to cook and decorate a table. She would often invite friends over just to bring out her beautiful, rare collection of ceramic pieces by well-known artists—a collection she'd amassed over years.

She walked back to the middle of the studio where she had arranged comfortable seating with a small eating table and said, "You know, Sandy, truth is, I rarely see Keith in person. We started communicating through faxes, and now there's e-mail. I could count on one hand how many times I've looked into his eyes, which, by the way, are the most gorgeous blue eyes I've ever seen. They pin me against the wall every time I look at him. When he e-mails me, I rapidly read his note, scanning for what I ache to hear, giving little room for the 'true intention' behind the words he sends me. I rapidly trip, stumble, and tumble over my own personal power to love myself enough that, no matter what he says or doesn't say, it's okay. I am grateful for the fact that he writes, and I try very hard not to get stuck on what he doesn't say that I want to hear. In the end, it's okay to simply enjoy his correspondence and acknowledge he takes time out of his life to write to me."

Sandy stared at Air. He shook his head, knowing she had no idea how beautiful she was and the effect she had on men.

"Don't get me wrong. I do stumble over such primal joy, such simple joy, my own simple smile as well. All distilled down, Keith and I are two people who eventually will become dust and one with the cosmos. We don't even have to write to one another ever again to know the truth between us. A silk, gossamer thread binds us wherever we are on the planet. I know he is thinking of me when I am thinking of him. Writing is just one of those corporeal, measurable results with which our five senses run us and jerk us around. It is one of those sacred contracts we made with each other before entering these corporeal bodies."

"Airstream, do you *realize* we are having one of those intense conversations we both long for?" he said, with an emphasis on *realize*.

"I know our high celestial spirits have put us together for lessons far beyond our capability to comprehend," Air said to Sandy, whose gaze remained fixed on her. "They keep us physically apart for reasons unbeknown to me outside of my 'state of grace.' By this, I mean a place that is past our five senses—a multisensory place where there is 'knowing,' and it can't be put into words. I have also taken on the challenge; if these states of grace and illumination can last up to five or ten minutes at a time, there is no reason in the world why they can't last for as long as I want them to!"

She smiled and added, "For me, I've been lazy and irresponsible with the power I have. I can no longer deny this ability or act like I have nothing to do with the fact that the phone will ring right when a conversation I am having with someone starts to get intense in some way. I will make someone call me to get out of the conversation."

The phone suddenly rang. They both laughed.

"That's my friend, Brenda. She's calling to ask if we can talk what we call the 'gig's up talk.' By that we mean having a conversation much like the one we're having tonight. No bullshit. No withholding. Just pure, honest gut feelings and thoughts. She's the one who finally nailed me on my power. She has said the same thing to me as you have, about people being drawn to me for some unknown reason. Before we go to receptions, she asks me to try and notice how many people will steer themselves to be near me. She says it's not because I make things happen. It's because they can feel the opportunity of something they have no idea about occurring. They can't help themselves. She says they know deeply on some level that I have the power to heal them. I'll just let the phone ring, and she'll leave a message."

Air stood up and walked over to a beautiful piece of Japanese furniture called a tansu. It was the equivalent of an American antique pantry cabinet. It was made of cherry wood and was in excellent condition. She had been collecting Japanese tansu's for years. Japanese sewing boxes were her favorite items to buy. The pieces she had were rare and expensive. She'd had to save for a year in order to purchase many of the sewing boxes. She also had a step tansu that fit under the stairs leading up to the loft. The Japanese were geniuses at designing furniture for all space since they had so little room in their homes. Air kept all her treasured items in the drawers of this particular cabinet. It had secret hidden drawers, and they held Air's sacred possessions.

"You want to read something I wrote last night? I write letters to myself that I want Keith to write to me," Air admitted.

"Sure, I love to read what you write. In fact, I honestly think you should focus on writing rather than painting. You're a really good writer."

Air lifted the lid to the top of the cabinet. There were several bundles of small envelopes each nestled next to each other as though they were in a cradle. Each bundle was wrapped differently from the others. Some had dried flowers on them, and others had different thicknesses and widths of velvet ribbons. Air unwrapped one of the bundles and reached for a letter that was wrapped in paper she had made herself. Dried flowers were embedded into the paper. Sandy noticed that all the bundles were wrapped with her handmade paper. She turned and walked toward him with an envelope. She handed it to him.

Sandy carefully unwrapped the letter. It read:

To my dearest Airstream,

This is a gift to you from my heart. Every day for many years, I have thought about you; imagined your face; heard your wonderful, almost childlike, devious laugh; thought about how you're always up to something and how I wish I was with you, dancing the dance of love and life, holding you so close that you can barely breathe. I whisper into your ear. It's just me and you, no one else, my love.

I wish I could choose to celebrate every moment I'm alive with you, Air. I want to be mindful and be present with you and only you. I want to be present for life with you, Airstream. I know our lives and each moment we breathe are a miracle. I don't want to live one more moment without telling you how much I want and need you. I don't want to put off enjoying my life without you one more minute.

I really appreciate the long, thoughtful e-mails you send me. I wish I could send you more than 996 bit/s, but I'm afraid to open up to you. I'm afraid I won't live up to your standards and expectations, much less meet your needs. I'm afraid I can't count on myself, so how in the world could I possibly offer myself to you and expect you to be able to count on me? I deeply appreciate your continued stand for me and for "us," Air. I love that about you. You are wondrous! I ponder at your words over and over telling me to just do it!

Sometimes, because you believe in me so much, I think I can. Then for some reason, I stop, and the demons tear and rip my flesh, leaving me with a dark, brown, winter feeling and all tangled up with thorns. Then, I hate you. I wish you didn't exist! I wish I'd never met you.

And yet, in the middle of the night, in the dark darkness, I want to cry out your name, Airstream. I would love to make love to you, Air. I want to touch you in a way that makes our hearts merge and become one forever. I am overwhelmed with life. These are things I wish I could say to you Air, but I never will. I do want you to know how much I care for and adore you.

You are my heart, Keith.

Sandy put the letter down. "Wow, that's pretty intense!" he said.

"I've written so many letters like that, Sandy. It's pitiful. Then again, each one was a muse, an inspiration for whatever art I produced that day or the next," Air said, her voice almost apologetic.

She went back over to the desk, returned the letter, and held up a stack of letters she'd written, each one a different version of Keith's voice. Sandy walked over and asked her if she cared if he looked through them.

"No, not really, but they get really gushy."

As Sandy glanced through some of the letters, he began to feel her deep pain and just how much her heart was suffering. It was hard to understand. She could have any man she wanted. Why the hell was she holding out for this guy? This guy didn't deserve her. She kept her suffering hidden inside so well. Maybe that was why she overdressed and always wore hats with matching purses, shoes, and gloves. She became a different person—an invisible person. This was a different Air from the one he knew so well, and yet still, it was the real Air. She didn't know to act phony. She was authentic no matter how she looked. She couldn't hold back the words that fell out of her mouth. Some people loved this about her. Others were offended. What a gift she was for everyone. Her best quality, he thought, was her compassion for others. There wasn't anything she wouldn't do for others.

"Air, forgive me for saying this, but this guy should kiss your ass! *This* is the guy for whom you should turn yourself into that lioness that resides deep within you, full of passion, and lie in wait and spring forth and fall upon him and devour him to the very last drop. Let him be the one to catch the last glimpse of you as he gasps for air. Ha, that's funny—gasping for 'air,' no pun intended. Then leave him, alone, to die a slow and agonizing ancestral death. You should slowly walk away, occasionally turning back to look at him for one last time with your shining teeth gleaming and your wet tongue and blood dripping from your luscious, red lips.

"Let him be the last one to hear your voice echoing, 'You don't mind that I devoured you do you?' Then skip away with a wicked smile and become completely reinvigorated. Leave him behind for the thunder and lightning and the buzzards!"

Tears began to run down his face as he held the countless letters she'd written. *God, I wish I had a woman who loved me this passionately*, he thought. *She'll always be in love with this asshole because he's incapable of love and she'll live off the few grains of love he throws her way. This guy has major control issues, and Air can't see it. He actually has the best of all worlds. He knows as long as he holds out on her, he'll have her loving him and him only, for all time. What a bastard!*

He inspected the letters more closely. They were all handwritten, very artsy, and written on the most beautiful paper he'd ever seen— paper she'd made herself. The words were written with special pens; the artistic quality of the lettering made the lettering almost seem to literally dance and float on top of the page. Each word was written so distinctly that, visually, you could "hear" the intonation. He noticed one that stood out from all the others. It was doubly tied with a red ribbon.

He turned to her, "Air do you mind if I read this particular one with the two ribbons around it?"

"No. Be my guest. But again, I warn you, you're going to get very bored."

He slowly untied the ribbon. The paper was an ochre color. Air had an amazing ability to mix dyes for her pulp. The letter read:

To my dearest Airstream,

I'm lying in my bed, and I am reminded of the time we had a full moon on one side of the plane and the setting sun on the other as we were ascending into the skies toward Mexico not so long ago. I will never forget that sight. It was beautiful and magical for me. It is on nights like this that I miss you most. I have tried for years to find something as spectacular as that memory, to change my thoughts every time there is a full moon. I cannot. I lie here with the covers pulled up to my chin.

I can hear your voice as clear as the stars out my window. Air, I know how I hurt you when I say you are my heart and yet I keep myself from you. I know the tears we share sear our faces like acid as they roll down. I'm so sorry, Air. I wish you were here with me. I would ask you to put your head on my heart, and together we would climb the ladder to where dreams are made.

Keith.

Sandy didn't say a word to her. He knew he'd regret it later. He wanted her. He wanted her spirit, her mind, her body, and especially her soul. He thought about making love to such a sensual creature. He'd never known a woman who gave so much and received so little in return.

"Air, I'd better take off. How about lunch soon? My treat. Call me anytime. I mean anytime, okay?"

"Sure, I'll call you the next time I'm feeling playful."

Air resealed the letter Sandy had just read. It was another letter that would never see the open mouth of a mail slot waiting to devour her passion and her longings.

24

Air was relieved Sandy had left. She continued sitting in her black butterfly chair, staring at her canvas. Her head was swirling with thoughts—she knew she could be difficult to be with sometimes. She knew she could be self-centered when it came to her work. She felt she had to be. No one else was paying the bills. She didn't know anyone who was as busy as she was. She burned the candles at both ends, as they say, often up until two or three in the morning and up at dawn. She didn't have any artist friends who wrote grants to foundations asking for funding to create a community-based public art project with families, along with continuing to do their own personal work.

She had artist friends who no longer talked to her because she was able to receive grants the first time around without really being "known." "Who is this person named Airstream?" was the murmur around the artist's community. Other artists resented the fact that she hadn't gone to an art school and that she didn't spend her days *practicing* her art. She'd never sketched in her life. Her style of creating was to just prepare a canvas, choose a tube of whatever color appealed to her in that moment, choose a brush, and simply see what happened. She never had an image in her mind. Nor did she know the next color that would be chosen. Air never created a piece that was an experiment. Every painting was a successful piece and could be marketed. She had protected herself from the "rules," and this worked wonderfully. She had no clue what the "cautions" were around taking an image to the edge of the canvas. She had no problem with creating an image in the middle of a canvas or using colors that others told her to stay away from since they would not appeal to the general public. She didn't care what others said and demanded not to be told what worked and what didn't work. She allowed herself to create very unique pieces both large and small. Her work became recognized because of its uniqueness. She'd often overhear people say, "I bet that is the work of the artist named Airstream."

As she sat there, she realized how difficult it was to want to be alone and just paint, not knowing how to ask someone if he or she would please leave. Since she had a live/work space, many of her friends, including other artists, considered her available any time. There seemed to always be a knock at her door in the middle of the day. Most of her non-artist friends didn't think she had a real job. She wondered how they thought she could afford the lifestyle she lived. They didn't understand Air was also a "corporate artist," which meant she had an art representative who would stop by her studio monthly and look at her latest work. The rep would then tell her which pieces she liked and asked Air to recreate them in the latest colors, handing her a color swatch of about five different colors. These commissions went to hospitals, banks, big-time corporate offices, and the lobbies of attorneys' offices.

Her big break had come when she'd received a National Endowment for the Arts grant she'd written requesting funding to work in local schools creating zero paper waste projects. She'd received eighty thousand dollars for two years. Creating public art projects had become Air's bread and butter. Designing art projects for kids in underprivileged districts in Alameda County was a shoo-in with foundations since the districts' funding for art and music had been completely cut years ago. These projects were easy for Air to create since she loved working with children and empowering young people through the arts. Air had a deep belief that all traditional education could be learned through the arts. It was her passion for this belief that got her the grants as well.

Overnight, Air had found herself unexpectedly playing in the big leagues. Well-known artists in Northern California and the San Francisco Bay Area quickly became aware of her and her work. She hadn't realized that funders talked to each other, to prominently established nonprofit organizations, and to successful artists. Once word of Air and her successful art projects had circulated within the funding community, she had no lack of projects and money. She received invitations to participate in projects from well-known California artists she'd previously only heard or read about. Before she knew it, collaborating with other artists became routine. She was often invited by other public artists to lecture on and demonstrate her traditional Japanese papermaking skills over a weekend with the families of the artists she worked with.

Air's studio was like no other artist's studio she knew of. One prime distinction was that she had the entire building to herself. She didn't live in one of those giant buildings with thirty other artists all looking over each other's shoulders and influencing each other's work.

Her building had been a machine shop back in the forties and fifties. It was located in what was called the Golden Gate District of Emeryville since it bordered both Berkeley and Oakland, and the fog came directly through the Golden Gate Bridge to her studio. The building was rectangular in shape and made of bricks. It had an art deco facade that Air loved. Walls had always given her anxiety. This need for open space was almost an obsession with her. One of the first things Air did when she moved in was remove the bathroom door. The only door she kept was the one at the end of the building that led to another room attached to the main building. She didn't care if guests were intimidated by having no bathroom door to close. As far as she was concerned, they could just hold it or trust that she would not head back into the area where the bathroom was located when they were using it.

The ceilings were twenty feet high, and the floors were dark wood. There were delivery doors both in the front and the back of the studio. The building ran parallel with the San Francisco Bay. The side that was aligned with the bay had two-by-one-and-a-half-feet tall, rectangular, cloudy glass windows separated with metal inserts. Every ten feet, a window about the size of four by four feet could be opened, allowing for a very sweet bay breeze. The studio had six-foot-wide skylights that ran from the front door to the back door.

This intense light coupled with the almost floor-to-ceiling windows made the place extremely bright. The sunlight was so intense that, during her first summer months, she went to one of the nearby beaches along the bay that had been an old landfill dump for glass companies back in the thirties. The beach was full of old, tumbled broken glass of all colors. Each day, for two weeks, she gathered as much glass as she could carry in a backpack. Her intent was to defuse the light. With the backpack on, she would climb a ladder up onto her roof each day. She made many trips up and down that ladder, until eventually she created a stained glass effect that reflected down into the studio. She depended on the light to both paint and to wake her each day. Now, she had the perfect amount of light with a beautiful cathedral feeling.

Off the back end of the building was a separate room attached to the main building that had its own entrance. Air set this room up as her private getaway. The room had a small vintage wood stove that kept her quite warm in the winter months. Old-fashioned, wooden-paned glass windows offered views of giant yellow rose trees that secluded her from all the neighbors. She didn't bother putting up curtains. Almost daily during the early spring months, wild Yellow Canaries would flock to the roses. The canaries sitting on the branches along side the wild yellow roses was an amazing sight to see.

Air rarely invited anyone into the room. It was sacred ground to her. She had created a small, friendly space with chairs and a large coffee table to entertain in the main space up front. This room had its own door, and she kept it closed until the end of the day. She had a way with design that was uniquely her own. Just when you thought not one more painting or off-the-wall piece of art could possibly find a home in her room, Air always easily found a spot to place it. She had a collection of over a hundred beautiful, glass paperweights. She could have easily opened her own clothing store, jewelry store, vintage hat store, or designer shoes and purses boutique. She also had first editions by her favorite authors, Edward Gorey and Maurice Sendak, which were precious to her.

There was no hiding herself from the public when they entered her private space. It was as though one was looking in her underwear drawer. Everything in her studio was sacred to her, and heartfelt memories were everywhere. Hanging on one wall was the first antique silk nightgown she'd owned, the one she'd worn to the party that had changed the course of her life. On another was a framed letter of acknowledgment from President Clinton for her outstanding artistic community work.

This back room, oddly enough, had French doors that opened up onto the patio she'd created. When she'd first moved in, the small backyard—almost unheard of for an art studio—had been filled with dirt and weeds. Air loved to garden, so she'd pulled the weeds and brought in rolls of sod. She'd planted a wide variety of annuals that required minimal care, including cosmos and carnations, along with a small vegetable garden. She'd lucked out and found a Jacuzzi at a garage sale for only five hundred dollars. It was in perfect working condition, just a few years old. She'd hired help to deliver and install it for her. She was extremely possessive of the Jacuzzi, never letting anyone other than herself use it.

Each morning, rain or shine, she'd wake very early and go out onto her patio. She'd get into the Jacuzzi and wait for the sun to rise. She loved starting the day off this way. Her private space was like being inside her own body. By sitting in this room, you could get to know this woman intimately. Everything had been chosen with great regard and reflected who she was. It was as if someone had just said to her, "Now, you claim to be an installation artist. Let's see what you can do with a sixteen-by-twenty-two-foot space." If it were an exhibit, it would have been called *Inside Airstream. Come Join the Other Organs of her Body.*

Instead of heading to her private quarters, Air decided there was still an hour of light left to paint. She was starting to feel she was close to finishing the piece. When she worked, it was as though someone else had entered the room and asked her to just take a seat. She had a habit of talking out loud while she painted, and she was typically in deep thought about something completely different from the work itself. She loved this; it meant that, when the work was completed, she had no personal attachment to it at all.

"I don't feel comfortable with myself," she'd say out loud. "I don't know what to expect from myself anymore. Perhaps I'm giving up some of my 'control madness' syndrome. My mind is weary. My heart's exhausted. *My spirit says, Relax, Air. I love you.* I've always been one to follow my heart. When I listen to my head, I've always contradicted my heart. I get severe anxiety attacks and end up in the emergency room, whispering to the attendants to hurry before I die from a heart attack again."

"You must begin to recognize yourself, Air!" A voice shouted within her head. *"They don't understand you. You live in a multi-sensory dimension, a non-corporeal reality. I just can't communicate this connection to them!"* The voice, which sounded like Claire, grew louder as it went on.

Suddenly, Air would feel an overwhelming sense of sadness. She'd question her sanity and the obsessive world she lived in. She'd start to beat herself up about being a stand for love and how she'd convinced herself that someday Keith would realize how much he loved her.

Sometimes while she was painting, she'd suddenly put down her paintbrush and walk over to the wall with all the windows. Many times, she would wish she could see through the windows, but that meant curtains, and Air felt the same way about curtains as she did about walls. She'd lean against the wall and stare at her pool table and remember playing pool with Keith.

Slowly, she'd slide to the floor like a rag doll. In her mind, her life was always like a movie. The projector was always rolling, and the director was always yelling, "Quiet! Action on the set."

Oh, Keith, why can't I tell my heart the truth? Why doesn't my heart just slam its door shut when I think of you? I know your ability to be cruel and ruthless with me, how you believe it will all work out; "trust me." I know your pride in your photography shows, your ability to repair bicycles, your appreciation of the Japanese culture. I remember you leaving sorrel soup on my porch whenever I've been sick. I remember when you rented *The Night of the Iguana* and we watched it together before we flew to Puerto Vallarta the first time. I remember you playing the song "Unchained

Melodies" on my jukebox and holding me so close. You played it at least three times. Each time you whispered into my ear that I was your heart. I think of your ability to not get sidetracked with your business and you taking responsibility in the "real world" all alone because you can't handle other people around you. You're so scared. Well, I'm even more scared!

I remember you and I building a battleship together and the time you dressed up for me in your pink Don Juan DeMarco shirt with its puffy sleeves and took me out for my birthday. You jumped that four-foot hedge to catch up with me once we'd parked since I'd headed on toward the restaurant without you. You gave me my favorite flowers, Casa Blanca's. You said you were going to start laughing any moment because you knew how afraid of spiders I was and that I would be convinced somewhere hidden in all those flowers was a spider just waiting to bite me!

You spent the night with me that night. You'd planned it all along. You'd dropped your dog off at a friend's house, and I kept waiting for you to leave. You wanted to dance until the wee hours of the night. I asked you when you were going to leave and you said, "Let's go to bed. I'm tired." I was terrified. I'd never been with you that way. I was paralyzed when our bodies touched. I froze. I didn't even want to breathe for fear you'd leave. You ran your hand slowly over my body, and I didn't move. You seemed to be exploring, and I let you get to know my body. Then you stopped and put your arm around me and fell asleep. You left before I woke the next morning. We never talked about that night. I didn't want to hear that you didn't remember because you drank too much.

I remember how angry you'd get whenever I'd knock on your door unannounced. I'd keep knocking, and you'd finally answer, standing there with your hair a muss, wearing two different shoes, both untied. I think of your undying awe of your mother, your gorgeous blue eyes, and how you always picked me up and swirled me around.

I think you suffer from a dual personality—one day you're completely nonsocial with me, and the next day, you say, "You're right, goddamn it! Let's go to the party!" I love your talent for writing such touching, intimate poetry to me, Keith. I've kept everything you ever wrote to me, you know. I remember the time we decided to cut each other's hair really short. We looked dreadful! I think of your dreams of buying a sailboat and calling her *Innisfree* and how long it took you to accept the death of that pelican that got caught between the rocks at Point Lobos. I remember how you hate that I wear fake nails and how I dye my hair, how utterly free you are when you drink, and how utterly cruel to yourself you are the day after for having had so much fun with me.

"Cut!" the director would yell. "Perfect, Airstream. You can go back to your canvas now."

Air loved these private dramas she would give to herself alone in her studio. They inspired her. They excited her. She'd return to her painting, reinvigorated, with a new perspective. She thought about how much she loved writing. She wondered what it might be like to be a famous writer. But thinking of the intimacy of her writings, she knew she could never let strangers read or see them. She wrote to bring joy and perhaps a sense of sanity and release to herself.

When Air had moved into her new studio, she called D. J. and told her she'd moved from Santa Cruz and was now living in Emeryville.

"Airstream, ain't that close to where that guy, Keith, works?"

"Yes, actually my studio is very close to his business," Air replied.

"I don't think you outta see him anymore," she said. "Why, his platforms aren't even high enough. He ain't really all that purdy. He's nothing more than a twenty-five-watt light bulb tryin' ta screw himself into your hundred-watt socket. Listen here, Sweetie, what you need is a man with some muscles! There ain't nothin' like a man with muscles. Oh! When he puts those big arms of his around ya, you'll know what I mean."

"She's never experienced how magical you are, Keith," Air said out loud. "But the thing is, no one wants to rescue magic shows anymore. Everyone's leaving the big top arena of dramas, except me. I need some more wine," she murmured to herself. She went to the kitchen and poured herself another glass. It was getting late and cold. She wanted to get drunk, to forget about Keith. She missed the old days when she felt everything was possible, but she felt she knew too much now.

Life's cruel that way. It requires you to participate, giving you experience, and tries to make you mature from your knowledge.

She closed up her tubes of paints and washed her brushes in the kitchen sink. She wandered into her back room and built a small fire.

I'm halfway—halfway drunk, a half-ass artist, and a halfway dreamer.

She sat down on her 1940's art deco couch upholstered with burgundy velvet and let the heat of the stove seep into her. Her mind wandered back to her dear friend Patty. Patty used to always say, "Another year, and the dreams thin out."

Air thought about what she wished she could say to Keith. "Watch out!" she'd tell him. "I'm going from faithful to unfeeling. And my mama told me, 'There's flying saucers and there's flying cocks, and they both take you to the same place.'

"Besides, that twenty-five-watt bulb that represents you, it's painted into this hundred-watt socket, and I can't unscrew it even if I had something to stand on to reach it. The moths can't even find it. Even though I've come to know my nights without your body, I go on hungry in my dreams, searching endlessly for you, always hunting you down. I can scarcely walk properly, and I won't ask the wind any more questions. I won't be in such a hurry because I now know that wild things can turn on me. My love is a like a child crying, reluctant to leave your arms. I leave it to you forever, Keith. You are and are not my 'chosen one.' There are no clouds out tonight. Just me. There are no signs of dawn, so I find myself again recollecting. I remember, in the cool of the night breeze, all I had and all I didn't have with you. All that I am and all that I am not is here with me now. I am completely paralyzed within the defined role of being the deserted, proper stranger. All I ever get from you is, 'Things are as they've always been and always will be.'

"I realize I have little intention of letting you go," she'd tell him. "I don't even have the slightest idea of how to let go of you, but my life will continue to continue. I'll go on to be the famous artist and hope that you'll realize you love me."

Air took a sip of wine and again thought about her canvas. *Needs more black*, she thought. I hurt more than I know. She looked up at the photographs on the wall and felt an overwhelming sense of loss. The photos were of her and Keith in Puerto Vallarta the first time he took her there. *We look like we are joined at the hip and meant to live out life together. What happened? Was I too demanding? Did I want too much too soon?*

"Soon, very soon, I'll be in Mexico. You're such a fool, Keith. Unfortunately, I've done so much internal work I'm well aware it's me who's the fool. I'm the one who is drunk, broken, scared, and lonely. And you? You're happy to be alone. I can hardly wait to leave this town and go to a town where everywhere I look I will see you. Who am I fooling? I must truly be out of my mind to move to a country where both our hearts reside."

25

Air woke early as usual and started her normal routine; after her Jacuzzi, she turned on the coffee machine and then headed to the computer to check her e-mail. The morning was already warm. She needed to call all of her funders and let them know she'd been commissioned by the Mexican government to do one of her environmental projects over the next six months. This commission would reinforce her funders' past decisions to fund her projects. They'd convey the information to their contributors. Everyone would feel their previous decisions to back her were, indeed, wise. As the saying goes in the investment world, "You're only as good as your next best act." And this act would remind all of them that they had had a part of Air's continued success.

The phone rang, and Air answered. "Hello?"

"Hi, Air. It's Bren. I think this crap you got going on about 'living life at 150 percent' is causing you too much stress and anxiety. Aren't you getting sick and tired of working on yourself? All I ever see you doing is reading those goddamned self-help books. I, too, go to places most people wouldn't think of, but my places are so dull and ugly that it takes a brilliant philosophical mind like mine to see the beauty in them. But then my stunning philosophic quips are something I have in abundance—something only we Virginian gals know about. By the way, I did read the profile you wrote about yourself on that personal dating site you joined. I noticed in your profile you're looking for a guy who makes $175,000 a year?

"I can promise you this, girly; all you're going to find on those sleazy sites are guys who make $7,500 a year! I also noticed you say you like to travel and stay in five-star hotels. You'll find a guy like that all right, but only after he's won some funky lawsuit. And he'll never again be as a good as his first act! And for sure, you're going to get some guy who tries to tell you he's an artist too—specializing in the morose and self-pitying poetry. He'll try to tell you how he has mastered the art of positive thinking. About as close to positive thinking most of those guys get is finding ways to rationalize why the hell they were dumped by their New Age girlfriend!"

Air could not handle hearing anymore from Bren. "Bren, I can't talk right now. I need to call my funders and let them know what I'm up to. Sorry. I'll call later, okay?"

"Oh sure, Air. No problem. Talk later," Bren replied.

Air went to her computer and looked at her e-mail responses. She sipped on her coffee as she read the first response.

"Dear Woman Who Lives Life at 150 percent. I live life at about 75 percent, which if you balance it out with your numbers, would equal an average of 100 percent. I think that's probably an ideal situation. I say this with the utmost affection for you. You seem to be a wondrously odd creature!" It was signed, An Admirer.

Air chuckled and headed for another cup of coffee. She was amused by such replies. The never-ending, "I, too, am conceptually compulsive and will literally go to the ends of the earth to pin down a loose concept," was old. Air couldn't figure out if the personals were a desperate attempt on her part to connect with someone or whether she should she give herself a badge of courage. She was too picky and complicated and unwilling to date anyone who didn't amuse her.

She was also uniquely qualified to survive without a mate. Her mother had made sure of that; she was covered in the residue of her black widow days—must devour the mate. Air briefly remembered how her mother was mesmerized by the thought of coupling and then eating her mate. However, she found herself battling bouts of loneliness, even though she'd had many offers of marriage, health plans, and beautiful homes. She was all too familiar with long periods of voluntary abstinence from sex.

She loved a dare. If she found someone who seemed intriguing, quirky, and as curious about life as she was, she'd fall completely in love, laying all her cards on the table—which usually turned out to be a fatal mistake.

She stared at the computer screen. There were eighteen new responses. She knew they all said the same thing. She thought back to her high school days and what it had been like to be a teenager in the sixties. She thought about her mom.

"Honey, there's more to life," she'd say. "And if you don't just go for it, you'll always be left asking yourself, 'Is this all there is?' There's sumthin' out there, honey—way out there, on the other side. I'm talkin' on the other side of the fence in the backyard, in the town, way past them there Texas skies, and the deserts. And hell honey, there's even an ocean you ain't never even seen. And believe you me, there's even sumthin' underneath that and on the other side of that! Even past this here thing called the you-knee-verse.

Air remembered the time D. J. had leaned in and added, "I know for certain cuz ever' night I get a visitor I ain't ever told ya nothing 'bout. His name is Adack, and he comes from a place twelve billion light years away. I see him at the end of my bed, and his body is only waist high." D. J. had pointed to her waist. "The you-knee-verse continues to expand and fill its own void," she'd added, as if that explained everything.

Air had simply shaken her head. *God, my mother's a trip. There's something on the other side of everything!* Air thought about the voids she still had that needed filling, but she was more interested in the places inside herself where she would go and there were no rules. Then, there were the places she dared not go—the deep voids where even chaos refused to go.

Airstream knew there was a world that separated her and her mother. She knew she had her mother's wildness and her intimate relationship with being primal. She realized, too, she had now lived long enough to appreciate D. J.'s wild-ass craziness. She was beginning to see that when men said things like, "I say this with the utmost affection; you're a wondrously odd creature," they were really talking about her mother, who they could see in her.

"Eat or be eaten!" D. J. would say to her.

Always the spider talk. D. J. was definitely a hunting beast. Anyone who spent time with her couldn't help but wonder about this eat-or-be-eaten bit. Of course, D. J. had no clue about the great ancient Hindu doctrine—we are all devourers and all prey. We all feed on the universe, and the universe feeds on us.

Airstream smiled. She knew if she told D. J. this, she'd just go off on her, like she had that time in the movie theater. The two of them had gone to see *Cleopatra* on opening day in the city. It was the only time Air had ever gone to the movies with her mom. The minute Liz Taylor came on the big screen dressed as Cleo, D. J. immediately stood up in the theatre and screamed, "That bitch! I was Cleopatra before Cleopatra was even Cleopatra!" Air remembered sliding down into her seat.

Even though her family had moved to California when she was twelve, much of the core of Air was still Texas. Even back then, she'd seemed to know too much. She smiled when she remembered being a little girl, lying out in her backyard and peering up at the big Texas skies. Her knees would knock against each other, and her shoulders would shiver, all because she knew that there was too much—too much immensity, too much uncertainty, too much of everything. Anything was possible, even without D. J. putting in her two cents.

She remembered how she'd desperately tried to catch lightning bugs night after night, convinced she could make herself a ring that would show her "the way" out of there. But D. J. would always remind her, "Airstream, the only way out is will! And you got it in ya. I kin see it in your eyes. Where there is a will there is always a way."

The phone rang again. It brought Air back to the smell of another freshly brewed coffee she'd just made.

"Hi, Brenda," Air answered. "Why are you calling me again? I told you I'd call you later." Air heard the slight harshness in her voice.

"I'm sorry, Airstream, but have you seen the article in *The Tribune* this morning about your new exhibition in the city?"

"No, is it a good review?" she asked sheepishly.

Air had been invited to have a solo show at one of the most prestigious galleries in all of the Bay Area—the San Francisco New Vision Gallery.

"What's it say, Bren?" Air asked.

"Listen to this! Let me read it to you: 'Airstream's images point out an entirely more evolved vision of the human as both beast and a spirit. Her intricate images indicate her intense desire to share herself with others. She offers the viewer the possibility to go from intimacy to a place more connected to nature, leaving the viewer feeling devoured by her. The exhibit is marvelously passionate.'"

Air put her coffee cup down and starting jumping up and down and screaming. "Wow, that's pretty intense. How cool! Maybe I'll sell something. That *devoured* part is odd. The concept of devouring is a theme that keeps showing up in my life for some reason."

Again, Air wondered about the comparison of being devoured. *Did the reviewer sense that my exhibit would devour my audience? Of all the times the theme of devouring has shown up in my life, it's now being captured in writing by some* Tribune *reviewer?*

Had she maybe, just maybe, created a scenario in her life she couldn't shake no matter what—the hunts and the spiders? Was there more to those experiences than just her memories and her stories of crazy-ass D. J.? But she didn't say anything about that to Brenda; she just continued to listen.

"Wait," Bren was saying, "it goes on. It says, 'Her subconscious is very rich and textured. The premier piece of the show is entitled, "The Ocean as the Universe." Airstream seems to be luring the viewer into becoming comfortable with the contradictions of life almost suggesting the universe is too vast to have one single meaning or one single truth. When interviewed, the artist remarked, "I go to a different presence of being when I'm painting. It's as though I am painting with words, not paints. When I am around people, I've never been comfortable with being in my body. My body suddenly operates at warp speed. I feel like the part of me that is the trunk of my being simply leaves me, simply disappears among my clothes, like it got out of the car and is waiting for me at the corner or on the other side of the universe. It knows I will eventually show up after I've put the spark plugs back in the car. It's tough getting back into my skin!"'"

"Jesus gods! Air, did you really say that shit?"

"Yeah. I think when I was interviewed by the journalist I'd had too much to drink. I was just trying to be amusing."

"Well, you sound totally disconnected, alienated, and like a blabbermouth to me. But somehow you got this guy hooked into portraying you as the most gut-centered artist in the whole Bay Area! Great screening device, Air." Brenda laughed.

"I was once told, 'If you don't tell the art critics what your art is about, they make it up for you.' So, I made it up for them. Sounds like it was effective."

"Thank God you didn't go into that crap about how you've lived several full lifetimes before this one. For some reason, that irritates the living shit out of people!"

"Ah, but I hook 'em anyway, don't I, Bren?"

"Oh yes, the sweetest little social deviant I know. What do they say, a wolf in sheep's clothing? Honestly, sometimes I can't figure out if you're devilish or devious," Brenda said, almost instantly regretting her words.

"Thanks for loving me anyway, Bren. You know, they wanted to know about my art background. What I really wanted to tell them was about the time back in the seventies when I was still living with Frank and there was a bunch of us just sitting around this beautiful, old Victorian home. We were smoking this killer dope. All of a sudden, Frank announced he'd given me his eyes and wasn't going to be drawing or doing anything that was creative anymore. He said he was beginning a different path.

"We all just sat there stoned for so long, not being able to comment at all. Then Frank told everyone they were sitting with someone who was going to be a famous artist someday. Everyone was really surprised, since Frank was famous himself. Somebody suddenly suggested we change our names as a distraction to Frank's ramblings about me. Everyone wanted to keep it simple, something like spell our names backward. That's how Frank got the name Knarf. We all started laughing so hard when we realized he'd be known as Knarf and I would be Ria."

"Well, thank God, you didn't do that. Listen, sweetie, I need to get going. I just wanted to be the one to read you the article. We'll talk later."

"Hey, thanks for calling. And save the article for me?"

"You bet. Later."

Air thought back to the show's reception the week before. She'd worn a beautiful, rust, T-strapped dress with red crystals and beads.

She loved to show off her shoulders. She'd overheard someone remark about how she moved with such grace and charm. She remembered meeting a man who had left her feeling empty, only to be made full again. He told her how she'd captured his heart from the moment she'd entered the gallery, though he hadn't realized at the time she was the star of the show. She had noticed him watching her from the top of the stairs as she entered the gallery. She could sense, long before he approached her, he was watching her with great interest, watching her uniqueness unfold before him. She could see he was losing himself in her deep, dark brown eyes.

She remembered glancing around the room, looking for anyone besides him and her funders. He was dressed in black on black. He was the man she'd always fantasized about. He looked to be of Armenian descent to her. He told her with his eyes he hoped the projector would never stop, but the feeling of being captured crossed her mind. She made sure he lost contact with her. She took up residence far away from his stares. She felt he, too, had come to Earth briefly with Jupiter dust in his hair, just to remind her to never sell out.

He'd found her again. This time there'd been no escaping. The moon was full, the room was full, and there was no place for hiding anymore. For the moment, she'd lost sight of him. She'd felt a slight touch on her lower back. "I understand you are the creator of all the magnificent art," he said. "I'm enthralled by your imagination and your style. I imagine you're a woman who's made time on earth an intensely felt adventure filled with lots of possibilities," he whispered into her ear.

She remembered purposely interrupting his words with one of her devilish smiles, as if to invite him to dance with her—to dance to some ancient drumming only the two of them could hear. She wanted him to leave her alone and did not know how without causing a scene. She was prepared for such situations.

"My name is Airstream. I would enjoy a visit from you. Here's the address of my studio." She shook his hand and handed him a business card, knowing she was giving him an outdated card, one from the second set she kept separate from her current ones for

341

occasions such as this. Then she had slowly turned and walked away, smiling at him one last time and saying over her shoulder, "I will warn you; I am one to keep turning out sweet dreams in my garden of strawberries and dead onions, and I am prone to uncontrollable moments of silliness."

She loved to say strange lines out of her poems to people she knew she'd never see again. There was a part of her that never wanted her body to be touched. There was also a part of her that fully understood the "nature of being human" and was willing to allow her intellect to go off and enjoy an afternoon at a baseball game, leaving her body behind to go to heaven on Earth.

She remembered what a wild reception that had been for her. She'd felt exotic, defiant, and flamboyant. Air knew she would always look for him at each of her receptions. He'd simply disappeared in the black hole of time. Perhaps he had emerged "on the other side."

"That was really a great reception!" she said out loud, laughing to herself.

She shut off her computer and looked over at her painting. *I am going to finish you today*, she thought. But, she didn't feel inspired. She decided to take Sandy up on his offer of lunch. She looked through her Rolodex and found his number.

"Sandy?"

"Hey there, gorgeous. It's great to hear from you! What's up?"

"Are you swamped with work?"

"No, actually. I just finished up with an international, three-way conversation with one of our venture capitalists. Want to do brunch?"

"Yes. That's why I called."

"Sounds like just what the doctor ordered. Want to meet at the same little French café?"

"Yes. How about in an hour?"

"You got it. See you there. And by the way, the article in *The Tribune* today about your exhibit is awesome. The photos of your work are great, and you look beautiful as usual! I'm so sorry I didn't make it. I was working late that night."

"That's okay. I'll see you soon. Bye."

As Air put on her coat, she wished she were meeting Keith. Deep in her heart, she could hear her mother's voice. *Life is short, and time is tricky. Don't wait too long. Life ain't like riding a bicycle.*

Even though she continued with her online matchmaking games, in truth, Air had no intention whatsoever of connecting with anyone. On one level, it was a front to keep her friends from hounding her so much about being alone and pining away about Keith. Primarily, it gave her a break from her art projects. She was intrigued with her thoughts that came pouring out of her in written form. Her playful missives when she'd respond to someone didn't sound at all like the Airstream she knew. She knew where she stood on matters of the heart and her deep beliefs about life. She found the space that held these online encounters was a world she could easily break free of. All she had to do was turn off the computer.

Often, the day after responding to someone's profile and then rereading what she'd written, she would question whether or not those had really been her thoughts. She felt as though she was viewing an art piece for the first time in some museum or gallery exhibit. She realized writing was a world in which she totally lost the concept of "self" and became free of her self-imposed daily belief systems. She entered into her "state of grace and illumination," as she referred to it. The written word was an arena where she could "hide out" and become whoever and whatever she desired.

She loved what she wrote and would hold off as long as possible before meeting a potential "match," if the potential partner in any way inspired her to dig down deeper into her creative mind and spar with words. She believed it was just not possible that a face-to-face conversation could be as good as what was shared through written word correspondences. Meeting carried with it the risk of losing the magic the two had in their written relationship.

Just as Air was leaving, the phone rang. She hesitated to answer since she would be late meeting Sandy, but it could be a newspaper reporter wanting to interview her at her studio.

"Hello?"

"Air! There's another article about your exhibit in the *San Jose Mercury*, and it is unbelievable! Your show is a total success, and the art critics love your work. *The* Mr. Kenneth Ricker wrote an article about your exhibit."

"Bren, thank you so much for sharing the info with me, but I'm on my way to meet Sandy for brunch. I was really excited about getting dressed up and going out and about for a change. But now I'm feeling so sad it's not Keith I'm meeting. I feel inauthentic and like I'm wasting my time. I don't have much time before I'm supposed to leave for Mexico. This painting is done, but it still needs to dry before I can have it delivered. I was thinking about the way I fear the dullness of a real-life conversation when I go out with a man, even if it is male friend. It seems silly to try and chat over brunch as if we were meant to be together. I have to keep reminding myself I'm only meeting Sandy, but I still feel like I'm wasting my Earth-life time. He's not Keith. I don't have time to meet with anyone other than Keith, but now I've made a commitment to Sandy, so I have to go."

"Air, lighten up. All you've been doing for the last month is painting. Go have fun with Sandy," Brenda said.

"The other problem I have with meeting a man is I know how extremely powerful I am, not to mention the fact that I'm a self-sufficient woman who doesn't want or need a lover to tend to her. Honestly, I don't like to be physically touched by a man. For me, touching always turns into being dominated in some way. I hate the feeling of being dominated! I have no idea why I feel this way, and I often try and explore that about me. Bren, I wonder if Keith would ever try and dominate me, given the chance?" Air added offhandedly.

"Oh my God! Just go, would you?" Bren shouted.

"Let me just finish this thought. As independent as you know I am—I travel all over the world and give lectures on our environmental crises and how to set up recycling programs—the last thing I need is a man assuming that just because we've shared some time together and some slight physical joy, somehow he can come charging into my life and start critiquing my work and come along on my travels. It's like how I always have to say out loud the word *travel* whenever I get on a binge of wanting a dog," Air remarked.

"Air, you're off the deep end. What's been going on with you this morning? You know how you are ambiguous about any future potential relationship of any kind, outside of having one with Keith. You enjoy meeting men; you feel wonderful when they give you their attention. I've seen you with my own eyes! You just don't like the concerns you end up having about his feelings being hurt by something overly sentimental or old-fashioned you say about what love or intimacy is really supposed to be like," Brenda said sympathetically.

Air sat back down in her chair and ran her hand through her hair. She did this when she was nervous. "Bren, why do men tell me they love to receive e-mails from me? They aren't prepared for a woman who possesses the heart of a poet. I suppose it's because I hold nothing back. When I decide to respond to someone, I think he reads too much into what I write. He takes it too personally. I should tell them all that I just cut and paste all my responses to men. I want to ask them if they really think I really have the time to respond to them on an individual basis.

"Bren, doing this online stuff is like painting words on the canvas of the monitor of the receiver's imagination. I give each man the opportunity to view my words as a piece of art, as though the words were gracefully swaying and moving to the beat of some far-off drumming, just for him. I respond to men as though I was writing to Keith. I respond to each man as though I was kissing Keith. I make myself intoxicating. I always leave them gasping for breath, waiting with anticipation of the arrival of my next storm of passion. After the next downpour of my words that are like a hard rain that washes over them, they beg to be devoured by me once again. I am thunder. I am both wicked and soothing at the same time—like lightning. This is all men want. They are simple creatures."

"Air, that's cruel and hurtful. Guys are suckers for believing what women say to them. Air, all distilled down, you're too demanding and unreasonable. You throw your dolly down in the dirt way too often. You love to write some stupid, cryptic words like, 'Is this abalone or just real bad chicken?' These guys are just ordinary men with ordinary jobs, and they just want to watch TV with a woman when they get home from work. You, you're like a bottle of 1949

Chateau Margaux. You're a taste that never leaves a man's palate for the rest of his life. You leave him asking for more than his fair share."

"Bren, I have to go. I will call you when I get back to the studio. I love you."

"Love you too."

26

Sandy and Air walked out to the parking lot of the café. "That was an excellent brunch, Air. How about a ride up the coast? Feel the ocean breeze, breathe in the fresh air?" Sandy suggested. "It's such a clear day and I bet there's no fog along the coast."

"I'd love that," Air said, beaming. "We can watch the sun set!"

"Let's drive up to Point Reyes. It's early enough that we'll have at least four more hours of sun. We can go in the little shops and stop in my favorite bookstore. Sound good?" he asked.

"Absolutely! I need to get away from painting for a day. Just laugh and have fun! Sandy, you're a doll! You always seem to sense when I'm sad. I hope I've been there for you when you've needed me."

Sandy had a BMW convertible, and normally Air would not want to ride with the top down. Her skin was so sensitive that, when her hair brushed against her face from the wind, it felt like whips; besides, she sunburned so easily. Today, she told herself she was going to enjoy the top down and pretend she was riding a horse.

The coast was just across the bay, but they needed to cross over the San Rafael Bridge to get to Marin County. From there, they drove down the rolling coastal hills. The view was breathtaking. The drive took just over an hour, and with a cloudless sky and no fog, they could see all the way to the horizon.

They arrived in Point Reyes and parked just outside the Point Reyes Art Gallery. As Air got out of the car she looked over at Sandy. "I don't think you know this, but I had a solo exhibit here about four years ago. I exhibited a series of six canvases that were seven by seven feet. I'd worked on them for two years. I actually amazed myself with how the hell I was able to adhere my handmade paper to canvas and then paint on the surface. To this day I have no clue how I was able to do that. I keep in touch with one client who bought one of the canvases and it looks just like the day I created it.

"Honest to God, Sandy, I've stared at that canvas and for the life of me I have can't remember how I did it. If my life depended on it, I couldn't tell you how I was able to glue paper to canvas and have it stand the test of time.

"I'm going to tell you something I've never told anyone. I can't tell you how many times I've started a piece and want to use a color that was in my last piece and I'll have no idea what colors I mixed together to come up with that awesome color. For instance, on some of my paper pieces I can't even tell you what fibers I used or how I manipulated the fiber to get the wispy effects.

"You know the pieces I have in my studio that I say I don't want to sell because I love them so much? Well, the truth is I don't want to sell them because I think I'll never be able to create anything that great again. I am terrified that I'm like some musician who produces his or her first CD and it becomes number one on the charts. Everyone is dying for the next CD and when it finally comes out, it sucks. It's like sequels to movies. The second one is never as good as the first one," Air remarked.

"Why don't you keep a journal and write down the paints you are mixing? And have samples of paper from the different fibers you collect?" Sandy asked.

"Lazy. During the exhibit I had here I met a woman who was a member of the Mendocino County Arts Counsel. She asked me if I'd be interested in coming up to Mendocino County and working in their schools with my zero paper waste project. I told her to send me a proposal. She did, and I worked in almost all the schools in the county! I was there for a month. They arranged my housing with families in the community, and I made some really good friends. Plus, the project was a total success."

"You never cease to amaze me with all your adventures! You did that all alone?" Sandy asked her.

"Yeah, I did. There were only about twenty schools in the county. The real problem was they were so far away apart. Sometimes I'd be staying with a family for a few days, and the school would be twenty-five miles away and on winding roads. That part was tough, but I enjoyed being up in nature a lot. The forests were magical."

"I bet you're really glad you chose to move back to the Bay Area instead of staying in Santa Cruz. You're far too talented to be cut off from the art world."

"I agree, and that's kind of you to say to me."

"But it's true, darling. Just speaking the truth. Shall we just start walking up the street?"

"Yeah."

"I love to window-shop first and then go back to the stores that interest me. What about you?" he said.

"Whatever you want to do is fine with me, as long as we stop in the cheese store."

Air and Sandy wandered in and out of all the stores. Sandy bought a book with paintings of Marin County landscapes. Air bought some of her favorite Gouda cheese stuffed with truffles.

"Let's go see what the gallery is exhibiting this month," Air suggested. "This is the same month I had my exhibition."

"Sounds good."

They turned around and walked back to the end of the street and looked in the window. There were abstract paintings and metal sculptures of women standing in a row.

"I swear to God, sometimes I have no clue how this crap gets into a gallery. These paintings are terrible!" Air said.

"Well, that's because your work is so much better and no one is doing what you are doing."

"I think we should head home so we miss most of the evening traffic."

"Okay."

"I had a lot of fun, Sandy. Thank you for suggesting the drive."

Air was home by six in the evening. She loved opening the front door to her studio and walking into the secret world she'd created. Air went straight to the phone and stared at it. She wanted to call Keith. She wanted to reach out to him and plead with him for "the box."

One day, after an angry conversation with Keith on the phone, Air had stuffed all the letters she had in a shoebox and sent them to him. She thought if he realized she no longer cared for him, he would reach out to her and let her know how much he cared. But over a month had passed by, and she hadn't heard a word from him. She hoped to God, he'd held onto the sacred box. The thought of losing all those letters was devastating to her, and she cursed herself for being so flippant with her emotions. When they first started corresponding they'd fax each other almost daily. She knew that, as time passed, those faxed letters would fade. Fax paper had a short shelf life, and she wanted to write over the fading type with a pen, to save what had been written.

If he really doesn't want to be with me, then maybe he did throw the box away. What, if any, value would they have for him? Oh God, please don't let him have thrown that box away. She'd thought when she sent the letters that she'd read them so many times she'd never forget what they said. Now she could no longer recall the once familiar words, and that scared her. *I want my letters back. I sent some of my best writing ever to him, and I want them back!*

The thought prompted her to grab the phone. She gave no thought to Keith's feelings or the fear of his response to hearing from her. She was willing to risk hearing his rage about her bothering him, since this wasn't about him; it was about her desperate desire to possess her heart—the heart she'd sent in a box—and the memories of her deep love for this man.

"Hello?"

"Keith, it's Air. I need you to return the box of letters I sent to you, please. You still have them don't you?"

"Air, I've been so busy I haven't had the time to open that box. I think it's around here somewhere. When I find it, I will send it back to you."

"Keith, I understand you're busy with taking care of your sick parents and trying to run a business, but just to let you know, I'm going to Mexico in a month to do a six-month art project in Puerto Vallarta. I might not even come back after it's over. I will e-mail you my address."

"I will do my best to find the box, Air. I want you to know I will miss you," he said sincerely.

Air had already hung the phone up while Keith was still talking. She knew what he was going to say because she'd heard his excuses too many times and needed to stay based in reality when it came to him. She'd spent too many nights and too many mornings thinking about his redundant remark, "You've done so much for me. I often wonder what I've brought to you. You're such a wonder, and I do love you. You bring such joy into my miserable, dark life."

The fact he'd posed the question of what he'd given to her was, in itself, a gift. Being "the Air" they both knew her to be, she'd turn the unspoken present of his not knowing where the box was into one of his disguised emotions for her. She'd inspect and inquire into that remark every which way she could. She'd make up all manner of meanings out of it, all of them untrue. She needed to believe that someday he would keep his word, and they would be together in time.

Air looked over at the fax machine, remembering the countless rolls of paper she'd put into that machine.

What has all of these years of holding back a tremendously sacred part of my heart gotten me? Why do I go just so far with other men and then, when we start to become intimate, we run into the door that has Keith's name on it? We've now entered "Keith territory," and I run the other way.

She could hear Brenda scolding her. *Air, this so-called perfect love, by its very own nature, is imagined. I think that's what Keith means when he says all that stuff about ghostly love. Maybe because of the relationship's very essence, there's part of your heart that never has to be challenged or actualized. Maybe you're hiding out behind this so-called love for Keith because you don't know how to truly love anyone. Have you ever considered the reality that maybe you're totally freaked out about being intimate with a man, so you hold on to this drama with Keith?*

"Oh who cares if I am capable of becoming one with another man?" Air said to herself in a cold tone.

It was getting late, and Air was tired. She went back into her private room and built a small fire and sat down in the burgundy velvet chair. Thoughts rushed through her head as she looked at the canvases she'd painted the year before. They were all painted in earth colors—reds, oranges, rusts, and greens. She associated the colors with her thoughts of birds and flight. There seemed to be a theme of transformation, movement, and journey in these colors since they were autumn colors, a time of change, but it seemed all very convoluted and distant. She thought about getting old. Nothing frightened her more than getting old and wrinkled. Looking into the mirror and seeing some old woman was something she thought would never happen to her.

I've always been pretty, and lately, life hasn't been easy. I see how men look at me. I am alone, and I'm not crawling into bed with anyone. If my friends knew how much pain I suffer from being alone, they'd blow me off. I have everyone fooled. It's been so long since I have been with a man.

Tears ran like water from a broken dam down her face, and her stomach churned with torment. She ran to her bathroom and stared into the mirror. As usual, she quickly brushed away the tears.

"Soon I will be in Puerto Vallarta," she said to the woman in the mirror. "Who knows what might happen there? It will be a new beginning emerging from a deep, remote center somewhere within me. I want to toss away my deeply sad past. Hope. I'm sick of hope. I wonder if it's crazy to talk out loud when there's no one around. But I have no one else to talk to. Besides, I enjoy talking to myself."

She walked out of the bathroom and into the middle of her main space. She surveyed the paintings hanging on the walls. "When I look at my paintings, I see circles of my life," she said. "And my mind carefully walks those circles, wondering where they will lead me. I think about the circles and how my life has been like a mandala of travel. I search, and I collect ideas and objects for my inspiration and my ring of creativity. I think it'd be a powerful exercise to reflect on the writings in my journals and the images I've painted, once I'm settled in Puerto Vallarta. I need new adventure, new stories, something beyond this mundane life of mine everyone else thinks is great. I have a need for permanency or, perhaps, normalcy. I relish solitude and my ability to explore and discover new places and new horizons on my own. I've now lived long enough to know that you don't have to understand it all. I think I'm supposed to tap into something among my words, my passions, desires, fears, insecurities, pride, and knowledge."

Although the real truth, all the way down to my core, is that I am scared to death of what will become of me. I've been winging it for so long, I wonder if anyone will be there for me when I finally throw in the towel?

Air opened the refrigerator and looked inside. Not much there—pickles, garlic hummus, eggs, cheese, smoked salmon, capers, pickled ginger, mayonnaise, peanut butter, and a couple of red pears. She slammed the door shut and shivered at the thought of having to go to the market. She looked over at her shelves and, again, not much to eat. She did see a bottle of wine and thought about the smoked salmon. She wasn't really hungry, just bored. She grabbed the bottle of wine and opened it. She always treated herself to a glass of wine in a beautiful, hand blown crystal goblet. She returned to her private room and fed the stove more wood. She loved entertaining herself as though she were her best company. Again, she returned to her favorite velvet chair and stared at the small, ornate antique wood stove as it slowly heated her room.

"This constant questioning of what happened to my life and how I ended up here is driving me insane," she said loudly. "I often imagine just driving my car at a high speed into a freeway overpass with the hope I don't wake up."

Sipping her wine, Air continued her monologue. "My life is so different than it was when I was young and really scared. Who would have ever thought I'd turn out to be a successful, well-known artist who's exhibited in Europe and other countries? My God, I've been commissioned to do public art in over four countries! I dress like I have a million dollars. I have a studio that looks like a museum of very expensive, eclectic art and beautiful furniture. It's all very unique. Just like my mother said, "We're unique, honey.""

Air continued to examine the pieces of her own work she'd hung in her private space. *I think my earlier art is reflected in the outer rings, and now I am progressing toward the center, discovering as I go. The innocent and naive part of me shows up as pure and uncontaminated in its colors, revolving at the center, and high tide is being measured somewhere beyond it. The lines of previous tides are becoming the rings, concentric but not even, glowing, glistening,*

353

foreboding, brooding. They're way beyond the outer limits of the circle. My color palette is imposing, engulfing, enveloping, and frightening in many of my paintings. It's as if some part of me is hard at work trying to sabotage my next move.

But you know you love the unexpected, Air. You've never been one to let fear stop you from anything. You want to marvel at how things happen when you least expect anything to happen!

Fame is dangerous for artists. I've had my fifteen minutes of fame and more. I want to live in the shadows of the last few years that have taken my breath away. Now, I crave anonymity. I want to forget who I was. I want to discover who I'm becoming. I want to be the blank canvas I'm painting on. I want to be stretched on stretcher bars and leaned up on my easel as a "possibility of who Air could be." I'd like to make a copy of a photo of a blank canvas and just sign my name at the bottom. I'd like to glue it to the side of an empty milk carton with the caption, "Missing. Have you seen this woman with the doe-like eyes?" Like the one I made when I was younger and really crazy, the one I left for Pokey to find in his room."

Incessant thoughts poured through her mind in an unconscious stream. She wanted them to stop, but she felt captive to her ramblings.

I would stare at me every day. I would wonder, had I simply said good-bye or was I so preoccupied with being out of my body that I didn't hear the door close behind me as I left?

Would I just get up and leave with a comfortless, dreamless grin? Would I intend to leave a "keeper of a well-preserved, pickled love" that only I know so well, which lived in one of those tiny, perfect moments with Keith? Would I ever find my relentless friend, who once pleaded with me to be with him as we grew old?

Air smiled at her pursuits of half-ass craziness and considered painting those words onto the canvas. They would stay on the canvas of her imagination instead.

I've now lived long enough to have outgrown the need to desperately grasp at holding on to this imagined love. I am now holding on to myself, and sometimes it hurts like hell. Why I never gave up on us is a grand mystery the universe has given to me. You, "my ghostly lover," have given me much. So wonder no longer. Just smile when you think of me. Know in your heart my obsessions have their wondrous flip side. One cannot know heaven without knowing hell.

Air was breathless. She begged herself to stop thinking. She sipped at her wine mindlessly. She looked at the clock. It was almost midnight. Sitting in silence for almost an hour, she finished off the bottle of wine, washed the goblet, and replaced it carefully back on the shelf. She checked on the wood stove, changed into her nightgown, and headed up the stairs to the loft. She was exhausted and fell asleep the minute her head hit the pillow.

27

Goddamn it! Isn't the sun ever going to show its face? Don't tell me it's going to be another cold, gray day! She went to the back door and looked out at the grayness. The fog was rolling through the Golden Gate Bridge nonstop. Air couldn't see her garden. She closed the door and went into her private space and started a small fire. She sat down on the couch and realized just how tired she was. *I need a day of rest,* she thought. She put on another sweater and stoked the fire some more. She looked at the windows. They looked as though gray curtains were covering them. The doorbell rang. She got up and walked through the studio at a fast pace. Most of the time when the doorbell rang, by the time Air had walked from her private space through the front two thousand square feet and opened the door, no one was there. She'd thought of buying roller blades.

"Hey, girly. What's up?" James said.

"Oh my God, it's so good to see you. I'm just finishing packing up the canvas today. Come on in. Have a seat. I'm so glad you stopped by. I'm having a big-time case of the blahs. It's so good to have a friend with whom there is no withholding and no secrets come over," she said. "James, would you like something to drink or eat?"

"Sure, I'll take a beer. And if you have any nuts, that would be great," he answered.

"Yes, I have some nuts. Hold on. Let me put some in a bowl and open you a beer. I'm going to miss you so much!"

Air went into the kitchen, opened the cabinet, and brought out some nuts. She got a couple of beers and sat down next to James.

"Air, I know you so well that I'll believe you're leaving when I see you actually leaving. Until then, I've heard you say you're sick of your studio and you're moving too many times before," he said.

"I don't think you know this, James, but my middle name has become eBay now. I've been selling so much of my stuff through that site these past couple of months. Hey, look over there under my loft stairs. Do you see my step tansu? Look around. Where are all my pinball machines? When you drove up, did you notice "It's Her" is not parked out front?"

"You have to be shitting me!" he shouted. "You sold your Studebaker? No fucking way!"

"Way!"

Air had bought "It's Her" from the original owner some five years back. She was a 1950 Studebaker, in mint condition. She'd ordered the vanity plates, ITS HER, from the DMV because the moment she saw the car with a for sale sign in the window, she'd started yelling, 'It's her. I want that car!' She had sworn to everyone, she'd still be driving it around when she was a hundred years old. Everybody knew "It's Her" and Air were one. She was like riding around on a big overstuffed couch. James was in total disbelief.

"I've gotten rid of almost everything," Air told him. "Whatever I didn't sell or throw away is going into storage. I'm keeping my antique Victorian bed since it's so rare. It's from the late 1800s and has all this ornate hand carving on the headboard. It has a matching armoire with beveled mirrors and a bedside cabinet that contains a porcelain chamber pot."

"Air, how would I know about your bed, since I've never been allowed back in that room?" he said, taking a gulp of beer and looking sullen.

Air smiled sweetly and touched her friend's arm. "I'm sorry, James. I keep telling you to not take it personally. I don't let anyone back there. Well, I take that back. Keith was back there once, but I'm not going to go there right now. I'm keeping all my bedding since it's Egyptian sheets with a high thread count; a couple of expensive, white duck down comforters; and a beautiful, handmade, reversible silk quilt with matching slip covers for my pillows. I've already packed up five exquisitely embroidered silk nightgowns for my princess bed. Of course, I'm keeping my BMW and all the valuables among my knickknack collections—you know, like my handmade paperweights and rare books. I'm storing my all vintage hats and designer clothes, shoes, purses, and jewelry in plastic containers. I long for nothing more than I can carry around my waist, and that's probably just a plastic card. I've had more than my fair share, James. What's left is all going into storage for now."

James chewed a handful of nuts and surveyed her quietly. "Hey, you're serious," he finally said. "Did you rent a storage unit? Or are you going to put all of it out back in your shed?"

"Out back, except for my car, of course. I'm storing her in my friend Sandy's garage." Air snuggled into her chair, thinking how perfect it was that James had been the one to stop by. "James, back when I first moved into this studio, I was doing just corporate work to survive. I've realized I've become a very powerful businesswoman— you know, always writing grants and meeting with funders. I've taken the skills I learned from being a corporate artist and applied them to the business side of art. Unfortunately, most artists don't have this ability, much less the ability to even market themselves, but I do. Now, after all these years, I feel like I've really run with these talents and have totally done the art scene. I'm sick and tired of living here in this studio and doing art day after day. I know, you're going to laugh, but there are too many beautiful evening dresses that I've never worn that are just hanging in my armoire. There are just so many receptions and funders parties I can attend. And the reality is, I don't want to be seen at another funders party. No more grant writing for me. C'est fini!"

"Good grief, Air! Air, you're crazy?" James shook his head in disbelief. "You're really going to go and live in another country? And this crap about giving up the art world is just that, crap. For Christ's sakes, girl, what have you been drinking? You are art! You're romanticizing the life of leisure. You are so lucky that you don't have a boss. And no matter how hard you work your ass off the boss is still on you for more and wanting a little piece of it, too. My boss is always pinching my ass, and he's straight!"

Air finished her beer and looked at James. "I know what you mean about my silliness, my daringness, my incessant irritating behavior." Air turned her face from James to keep him from seeing her tears. "I want to set the memories of my childhood free. They are still harbored inside my soul. I need to move on with my life. Letting go of all the material stuff has helped me to sense a new free life. I know I must give my heart the chance to live fully without reserve."

She leaned forward. "Remember how Keith and I used to fax each other messages every day? I'd saved every one of them. I didn't tell you this, but one day, I got all pissy and boxed up all the years of correspondences between us. I sent them to him in a shoebox, thinking he'd come running to me professing his love."

"Yeah, I remember. You did tell me about doing that. I remember also thinking how you'd regret doing that," James said.

"Oh, I don't remember telling you I did that. Anyway, I thought I had reread those letters so many times I'd never ever forget one single word. But I was wrong. I did forget. For me, some of my most wonderful writings were to him. There's one in particular I long to have back. It was a letter in response to a fax he'd sent me. I think he was drunk when he wrote it because I could barely make out most of his writing. So I took to being playful with his intentions, guessing that perhaps he meant this or perhaps he meant that. It was a long, playful letter, in which there was this dialogue between two people about the meaning of words.

"Anyway, that night was one of the most memorable nights of my life. I loved writing that letter to him. It brought me great joy. I was so proud of myself. It was as though I'd had a date with myself, and I had a fabulous time. I was in my bed with a fire going in my little wood stove and tickled myself silly with words to him, actually, with words to myself. Now, I'm freaked out that he threw that box away and I really want those letters back."

James looked around the studio. He couldn't believe he hadn't noticed that the pinball machines and pool table were gone when he'd first come in. He couldn't believe she'd sold the Studebaker. He looked up at the ceiling. The gliders were gone, and now there was just empty space. The studio almost looked like it had when they'd first discovered it many years back. "Air, you have to realize an immature woman sent Keith that box—a woman who was convinced the man she loved would never, could never bring himself to throw the box away. Perhaps he never opened the box, but he certainly stared at it with disdain if he placed it in full view. And if not, he at least put them in a place where they would someday be resurrected by some explorer to discover the essence of humankind, even if we were to be labeled idiots.

"Air, I know how much you love Keith," James added softly. "I've always known there was something going on between you two when I lived with him. Why do you think that I didn't introduce the two of you for a year? I knew you two would hit it off. I was too freaked out that I would lose him. I know everyone gives you shit about still pining away for him. I know nobody besides me even wants to hear the name Keith. You'd think he'd be all over you. God, you're gorgeous and almost every man's dream woman. One thing is for sure; he'll never find anyone who loves him more than you. I didn't even love him that much!"

"Hey listen, let's not talk about him anymore," Air said, looking away. Then she turned to him with a playful smile. "I'll have another beer with you. Want one?"

"You know, I love you and will listen to you forever about your sadness. But I'm sorry, Air. He isn't worth it. He doesn't deserve you or me!"

"James, being in Mexico is my true passion in life now. You're probably the only one who knows that writing brings me more joy than painting. I was writing long before I ever started painting. Puerto Vallarta is what brings me the greatest happiness I've ever felt though. In fact, I'd never experienced a state of true happiness until I was there. Happiness is a real state of being. I would have never known happiness existed if I hadn't gone to Mexico with Keith years ago."

"You're nuts. What about all your projects here and all the grants that are about to come through? Are you telling me that you want to walk away from all the hard work you've done and just move to Puerto Vallarta?"

"No, I just want to walk away from the intensity of the professional art world," Air explained. "I've always been run by the thought that, if I didn't create something artistic every day, I would slowly die. I'm reevaluating that belief system, and I don't think it works for me anymore. I find it's become destructive for me, actually."

"Well, I know how hard you've been worked on climbing the art world ladder, and I know it hasn't been easy doing all these art projects alone, but simply walking away now and moving all the way to Puerto Vallarta? Just simply ditching everything—for what, happiness? Air! People know who you are now. You're famous. I mean you have the awards every artist only dreams of. You have the world at your fingertips if you want it."

Air stood up and stared out the window into the fog that was still pouring from the bay. "All I want to do is write," she said softly. "The rest is meaningless to me, James. I hold all those accomplishments as something I can cross off my to-do list. You know, all those awards are hanging in my bathroom. You're only as good as your next best act. I just want a dinky little studio and my laptop. I'll be happy as a pig in shit down there. Anyway, my body doesn't feel good here in the city anymore. No one seems to speak my language. I've lost my interest in making people happy, and I feel a little less compassionate than I used to. Does that make me crazy? For sure, I think you're crazy!"

They both laughed. James walked around, looking at the empty space.

Air took a deep breath and said, "The truth is the more stuff I get rid of, the more I realize that the 'reliquary' really lies inside my head." She walked back to her chair and sank into it, gesturing around the studio. "All two thousand square feet of the stuff that was here in this studio is now meaningless and gone, but the weight of my head is becoming very difficult to hold up. In all honestly, I would have never known that there was this feeling of being weighted down inside me. I wish I could have started clearing my physical world sooner to understand this truth.

"The last time I was in PV, I was introduced to a great gal who owns an art gallery. We instantly hit it off, and now she's helping me find a place to live after the project is over. The government is taking care of where I'll live while I'm there doing the project, but want to stay longer. Forever. I want something simple, with just one room plus a kitchen and near the beach. That's all I need. Oh, to be near the beach and hear the waves would be awesome! I want to sit in the darkness, alone, and not be afraid. And of course, I have fantasies of Keith coming to live with me. He's always talked about retiring and moving to Mexico."

James walked over and took the seat next to Air so he could be close to her. He held out his hand in an offering for her to move closer to him. "This all reminds me of the British movie I watched the other night while I was waiting for Gary to show up for dinner," he said. "Of course, he didn't show, but the movie was so you and Keith. Actually, I missed the beginning of it, so I don't know the title, but there was a woman who was married to this prime minister, yet there was no love between them. I think it was during World War II. She meets a man and falls deeply in love with him, and he loves her. They start seeing each other discreetly. One day, they're in a hotel room, and they'd just finished making love. He was kissing her good-bye at the door when suddenly a bomb exploded in the hotel. He's blown down the stairs. She runs down to see if he's okay. When she sees he's dying, she screams for him to come back to her. Realizing he's dead, she leaves him and runs back up the stairs to the room they'd just made love in and starts praying. She's never prayed to anyone or anything in her life, and suddenly she throws herself at the mercy of God. She begs God to please let him live. This is the only thing that makes sense to her. So here she is, on the bed sobbing, asking God to let him live. She makes a promise with God that she will never see him again if God will just let him live.

"Suddenly, her lover appears in the doorway and asks her what she's doing. For him, it was odd he should have woken up and not found her over his body sobbing, which, of course, had already happened. The man feels betrayed and used. He accuses her of not caring. She knows she has made a promise to God, and God has obviously granted her wish, so she makes no attempt to convey her deep love for him. Instead, she puts her clothes on—she'd just been in a slip—and turns to him and says, 'Don't you believe that love can exist and last forever even if you can't see it or be with it ever again? Don't you believe in things even if you can't see them?'

"He just stares at her and says he can't live a life like that. She reminds him of all the people who believe in and love God deeply, and yet they have never seen him. She leaves. She is beyond the state of pain. She covers her mouth because she knows she is going to throw up. She keeps walking down the stairs as he yells at her. Her knees are so weak it looks as though she's drunk as she walks. She simply accepts her pain and her fate. She knows to live without him is the same as being dead. So of course, she dies, keeping her promise with God because this is how much she loved her lover. Somehow, that reminds me of you and your feelings toward Keith."

Air raised her eyebrows. "Well I, unlike her, have never had to make a promise like that to God. Nonetheless, I feel like I would do exactly the same as she did. I deeply believe that, even though Keith can't see me, touch me, hear me, or smell me, I exist; and thus, my love for him will live until the end of time, as I have told him many times. But you know how deeply I believe that life is too short and time is tricky; it's not like this is 'breaking news.' It's just a knowing, but sometimes we take 'knowings' for granted," Air said calmly.

"Air, please don't get upset with me, but Keith is a tormented soul," James said gently. "He is not capable of loving someone else. He loathes himself."

"James, I think it's important, every once in a while, to proclaim these knowings to the world—to let this immense love I have for him breathe a bit of fresh air. We have to get it out of us, out of our bodies, out of our hearts, and into the world, away from the written word and to a listening ear. It has to find, for a moment, its place in the vastness of this most amazing world we live in."

James leaned back in his chair and stretched his back. "Well, I sure hope he sends that box back to you, Air. What are you going to do with this studio?"

"Oh, Brenda will be staying here. Even though I've sold off almost everything, there's still going to be so much left that I won't be able to get rid of before I leave. She wants to move out of her apartment, so this will be perfect for both of us. I'm working on packing up my book collection now since she has a lot of books herself and will need the space. Whatever I'm not able to sell, I will pack securely and put in the back shed. She'll have plenty of room even with my stuff here. Besides, I may come back in a couple of years. Who knows? I love this place. It's like the last frontier to me. I'd love to be here with her half the year and then go back down to P—you know, be a snow bird."

"Sounds to me like you've already bought your airline ticket."

"The Mexican government has already purchased a ticket for me. I leave in a couple of weeks," Air replied.

"Well shit, maybe I'll move to New York! You know, I've been thinking about selling my little trailer. I can get a lot of money for that little trailer; it's vintage, you know. I've always wanted to live in New York City. You're so brave to take such a leap of faith, Air. I've never known anyone as courageous as you, especially knowing your background. You are an inspiration to me. I want to deal with my anger. I want to just pull up the 'taproot of James,' as you say. I know, all distilled down I am living the life I want to live. I'm about as happy as I'm going to get," he said sadly.

"I believe the most profound relationship one can have is a spiritual partnering, which furthers both partners' learning and heals them this time around. This partnering could last one hour, one week, seven weeks, or seven lifetimes! We need these lessons to understand more fully what unconditional loving, compassion, and forgiveness is really all about," Air said, looking James straight in the eyes. "You should go to New York. You'd love it."

"But what will you do if you regret selling all your shit?" he asked as he walked toward the refrigerator to get another beer.

Air stood up and followed him over to the kitchen. "I'll take another one of those, too. James, I don't believe there is such a thing as 'failure or regret.' Failure and regrets are simply impossible. There is no probable reality for them to live in. We are all experimenting. Some experiments give us the results we are looking for, and some lead us to the discovery of something brand new—something we've not thought of before. Some are simply disguised gifts we perceive as bad, but they're truly opportunities to grow and heal.

"Last night before going to sleep, I started thinking about my life. I thought about Keith and how our relationship is a spiritual relationship. It is untraditional in the sense of how Western culture perceives relationships, but we are most definitely in a profound relationship—one that has been in existence for many years and continues to expand, grow, and become trustworthy. My final thoughts were that my life is a series of continually 'just doing it, just believing.' Then, I realized I've lost the dreams part. I was totally blown away when I thought about it, but it's true.

"For almost three years now, I haven't thought about my dreams. At first, this thought made me deeply sad. To realize I'd lost my dreams made me feel empty. If one were to ask me, 'What are your dreams in life, Air?' I'd have thought I'd be able to rattle off at least five. But the truth is, at this moment, I have no dreams. I feel like my spirit is dying. I went back to sleep asking myself if I really believed that there were no mistakes in life," Air said, her voice sounding childlike. "You and Keith have been friends for a very long time. Do you think he's a control freak?"

"For sure! Besides that, Air, he's gay. You just won't accept that he prefers men over women. You think you have some magical power over him. You don't, sweetie. He cared for me, but he wasn't in love with me. That's just how it is, and I don't know how to let go either. I'll let go when I've learned what it is I am supposed to learn from him. Until then, I guess I'll keep dating guys like Gary," James said sternly.

Both James and Air stood in the kitchen drinking their beers and feeling uncomfortable with the conversation. James picked up one of her paper vases she'd made and looked at it closely. "How do you get your paints to have such a glittery look?" he asked, changing the subject.

"James, I know I've kept my heart from others. I just deal with the loss. *Relationships*. I love that word and all its meanings and all the interpretations we give it. Oh, the gift of being alive together and participating in 'test-tube experiments'—a little of this and a little of that. So far, my research has not given me the results I hoped for, but each and every attempt during life is a gift. And that's where I hold Keith and myself," she said, her voice assertive and strong.

"Listen, girly, I know you are blessed—blessed with the willingness and flexibility and adaptability given to you by your mother. I also know you are surrounded and protected by many angels. But I still have to tell you that you're doomed. I know you too well. You're going to live out your life loving Keith. You may find another guy to hang with, but you will never be totally happy," he said to her with a knowing look in his eyes.

"Forgive me for laughing. Just root me on and tell me that moving to PV is a good move!

28

The following morning, Air woke up an hour earlier than usual with severe anxiety. Her heart was pounding, and she was completely drenched in sweat. She knew all too well that she needed to get out of bed as soon as possible. She knew her dreaded demons would arrive soon and chew her to shreds. Life was like this for her. She was forever asking how her life could be so grand one moment and the next day leave her asking, "Is this all there is?" Her way of dealing with her demons, at this point in her life, was to imagine they were still busy chewing someone else to shreds a block over, and when they were finished, they would head over to her house. If she got up before they arrived, they'd loose out on their chance to do their damage.

She got out of bed thinking the demons were still at least three blocks away and wouldn't have a chance at getting her this morning. She climbed down the stairs to the loft, walked back to her private room, opened the French doors and stepped out into the cool of the early morning darkness. As she removed the cover to the tub and turned on the jets, she felt a sense of pride in all the hard work she'd done to make the patio area completely private. She took off her nightgown and slipped into the tub. The jets felt great on her lower back as she stared at the stunningly exotic purple passion flowers that were thickly intertwined with the orange blossoms of the trumpet vines she'd planted for seclusion. She tried to relax, but she couldn't stop thinking of the tasks still left to do. She needed to store her car, take anything small and of value to her safe deposit box, and pack an array of unsold small art pieces into plastic containers for storage out in a shed behind her studio. She needed to open a bank account at Citibank, since that was the only American bank in Puerto Vallarta. She was grateful that Brenda was going to sublet her studio while she was gone. Brenda would take care of the garden and maintain the Jacuzzi. There were also friends she wanted to spend time with before leaving, like James, Sandy, and Brenda.

Getting this commission was just the kick in the butt she needed to make the huge shift in her life she'd been dreaming of, and she knew it. It was a miracle. Gnawing suspicions that she was beating a dead horse with her life had plagued her long before the offer had come from Mexico. She'd tried to imagine what would make her move out of the art world and into a life without the attendant pressures—without the constant deadlines for foundation grants; the never-ending building of crates to house her work to be shipped overseas; the schmoozing with funders; the receptions, lectures, and talking with strangers about the meaning of her art; the constant travel. She was sick and tired of the routine of her life. She was grateful and knew how lucky she was, but she was worn out. The passion to create another environmental public art project was gone. If anything, she wanted to curate one last exhibit. It would feature photographs of public artists taken both before and then after they'd completed their projects. The toll it took on the artist was so apparent. Seeing the difference in the photographs would be like looking at a president before and after his term in office. She prayed that moving to Puerto Vallarta to create this project, which would continue to be successful for many years without her, would be her last public art project.

She positioned her lower back on the shooting jets and again tried to relax, taking in deep breaths. She could feel this new life that was waiting—one she couldn't exactly picture but one that would offer her the opportunity to be happy. She knew the need to create would always be knocking on her door, but she would be happy just doing "arts and crafts." Saying she was going to Mexico to create a public art project was just a story, a story that gave her the courage to board a plane and not look back.

The sun was beginning to rise, and this meant it was time to get out of the tub. She grabbed a towel and dried off. She put her robe back on, walked into the kitchen, and put some water on to boil for her morning coffee. As she was grinding the coffee beans she looked over at the empty suitcases she'd gotten out of the back shed. There was packing to add to her list. The suitcases reminded her of the first time Keith took her to Puerto Vallarta. They'd spent a week there. That trip had changed her life. She'd experienced the true state of "happiness," a state she had never known to exist. *Happy* wasn't an adjective anyone who knew her would have used to describe her. She had been so overjoyed being with Keith in PV that she'd walked around the town crying the entire time they were there. Keith couldn't understand why she was continually crying and kept wondering what he was doing wrong.

"Why would someone cry if they were so happy?" he kept asking.

Tears started to run down Air's face as she stood staring at the French press. She thought about Keith, but deep within her heart, she knew it was the undeniable sadness for the little girl inside her that she was really crying for, not Keith. She was mourning the loss of that skinny, bird-boned little girl who had been battered daily with a big black belt until her father was exhausted. For now at least, she could give herself permission to feel immense compassion for that little girl.

Air remembered that she'd planned to finish a watercolor to give to Brenda for agreeing to take her to airport, but she hadn't had any artistic passion these days and was only working on her last commission. She would find something else to give to her friend. Brenda had collected more of Air's artwork than anyone.

Will someone please point me in the direction of Princess Fairytales Lane? I must rise above this madness and find love and forgiveness for that little girl who is still in so much pain. I need to image embracing her and comforting her. I want silk thread wound around me with her since I know time waits for no one. This moment is all there is. So here I am now, in the moment, saying to you, little girl with big brown eyes of wonder and awe, I love you and will always be here for you.

Shit, Keith, I remember when you called me and asked me to have faith in your words, when you said that time would work everything out between us, that I could count on this, that this was a truth that you knew deeply.

Air put the ground coffee beans into her French press and poured in the hot water. She let it steep for four minutes and then pushed the filter down. She got out her favorite ceramic cup and filled it to the top. She took the coffee over to her computer and sat down. She paused before turning it on and thought about how she wished she could throw away her rearview mirror. Perhaps looking into the rearview mirror of her mind wasn't such a bad idea, she thought. It could reveal her progression, her regression, and even the stagnation she'd experienced in her life. Regression was acceptable, but stagnation and sin weren't.

She remembered a very romantic dinner she'd once had with Keith. He had taken her out for her birthday to one of his favorite restaurants, convinced she'd love it. Everyone knew him there, but had clearly never seen him with anyone. Air remembered how the waitresses and bartender had seemed overjoyed when Keith introduced her to them. She could sense they were very happy Keith was with someone, and the waitress had even remarked, "What a great-looking couple you two make." Keith had put his arm around Air, making her feel extraordinarily special.

They'd both dressed for each other that night. Keith wore a sensual, pink shirt with big, billowy sleeves, a shirt right out of the movie *Don Juan DeMarco*, and tight, black silk pants with black dress shoes. Air wore a vintage I. Magnin cocktail dress that was short, made of black and white satin, and had a large off-the-shoulder cowl collar. She paired it with the black, pointed high heels by Chanel she'd bought in New York. They had, indeed, look great together.

They'd sat at a table that was obviously reserved for romantic couples chatting about Keith's parents' art collection. "My favorite painter is Chagall," Air had gushed. "His pictures are incredible!" She was talking about a painting she'd just seen in an exhibit, and she pronounced the word *picture* as "pitcher."

"Air," Keith had said sternly, "the word is pronounced picture, not pitcher. If you want to be a part of my family, you have to learn how to pronounce your words correctly. Words are sacred and held with reverence in my family."

Air remembered thinking, *God forbid I should show up as a "cosmic hillbilly" who just left the barn door open at his family's dinner table.*

She turned on the computer and sipped her coffee. She went straight to her e-mail box. She was thrilled to see there was an e-mail from Keith. She opened it immediately. As she began to read, she felt a cold chill run up her spine—the opening words referred to the dinner chat she'd just recalled:

Air, I once told my Mama you said pitcher instead of picture. She said, "I love your friend Airstream. I appreciate that she's so authentic and doesn't emphasize the side of her that is an academic. I've learned to love her in spite of herself. She's like someone who still finds joy in playing with dolls."

It was great to hear my mama talking about how much she cares about you. I had no idea the two of you had become so close. I knew you had stopped by a couple of times to visit, but I didn't realize how often that was. I went to see them last night. I took them food. They didn't have the strength to get off the couch, much less eat. They seem to be heading steadily toward the end. My mama is so incredible—no major complaints and such small requests.

We hug now as never before, even my dad. I hope you can someday hug your mom. She may not need it now, but you both will one day.

Oh yes, the box, I'm looking for it and will find it. So far in my search, I have found some art pieces and old letters you gave me years ago. They are so beautiful, Air, especially my favorite print titled, "Good-bye, Joe, and Hello, Irene"!

Keith

We have an entrenched connection, Air thought. We are two ageless souls who've wandered the universe since time began. No matter what the status of our relationship is—whether we haven't talked for weeks, months, or years; whether we're angry or at ease with each other—there is no denying the non-corporal connection the two of us have.

It was not unusual for him to have the same thoughts as she was having at the same time so talking about his mother out of the blue only reaffirmed their oneness. She would miss Keith's mother, Elizabeth, very much. She thought of herself walking down the beaches of PV to watch the sunset and remembering their last visit together.

I hope you won't mind if I breathe in your strength and your smile while I am far away from you, she thought with a smile. *I am at times given to forgetting how lucky I am to know you. I will write and walk across a town that is timeless, where change does not exist. I am prone to throwing myself a "pity party" at times, and those are the moments I'll need your gaze of comfort the most. Your silence and gaze will mean so much. It took so long for me to be comfortable with no dialogue between us when I first began visiting you, and then one day I understood your gift.*

I know there's going to be beautiful sunny days and I'll be walking along the Malecon, my dress swaying in the breeze, and I will wonder what would it have been like to be in one of your dance classes, Elizabeth. I promise I will quickly remind myself, but Air, you are in a dance class with Elizabeth. It's the best dance class one could be enrolled in, "The Dance of Love and Life!"

Air turned the computer off. She did not respond to Keith's e-mail. No more thoughts of Elizabeth or Keith today. She needed to eat breakfast and finish wrapping the canvas. The painting was complete. In a couple of days, the buyer could arrange for pickup, and off the painting would go.

The next week flew by. The morning of her departure she looked around her studio. An overwhelming sense of relief engulfed her. Everything was complete. She had checked off everything on her to-do list, and her suitcases were waiting by the door. Brenda was on her way. She heard Brenda's car pull up out front. She opened the door and smiled.

"I'm headed to where I can be re-oxygenated!" she whispered to Bren when they got out onto the street.

"Air, cool out. It's four in the morning, and I'm half asleep!"

"You are my best friend, you know. I love you. Thank you so much for driving me to the airport at this godforsaken hour! Here's the print of the rabbit by the creek you've wanted for so long."

"Oh, Air, thank you so much," Brenda exclaimed, beaming. "I love this print! Oh my God, I'm going to cry, and I promised myself I wouldn't. I am going to miss you so much! Are you sure you want me to have this print. You've coveted it for as long as I've known you. I thought you were going to do a watercolor for me?"

"I know how much you love this print and I want you to have it. Bren, I've thought about this, and I want you to just drop me off in front of the airline's entrance. We'll say our good-byes as I get my bags out of your car. I can't handle you coming in and watching me leave. I know I'll start crying, and I want to be in a state of joy when I board the plane. Deal? Please?"

"Okay." Brenda smiled warmly, holding her gaze for a moment. "Deal."

29

The plane touched down in PV four hours after takeoff. Air made her way to customs. She stood in the long line and thought back to the phone conversation she'd had with Cheryl. She had offered Air her sister's house instead of the condo the government had set up for her. Staying at Cheryl's sister's place would allow Air to extend stay after the project was over.

"I just found out my sister is moving back to New York and you can live in her place while you're doing your project," Cheryl had exclaimed enthusiastically. "She owns it, so there won't be any problems. It's perfect for you. It's a medium-sized studio condo with all the amenities you need. It's right on the beach, and you'll have a view of the entire Bay of Banderas! It has a pool and a gym, and it's located in the old part of town that you love so much. It's fully furnished, and the entire front room is floor-to-ceiling windows so you have a view of the bay 24-7. It already has a TV, plus a phone, so all you'll need to do is hook up the Internet service. You're going to love it! There's a separate bedroom off the front room and dining area. You'll need to give her first and last months' rent plus a deposit up front. I suggest you sign a lease with her for at least two years."

Barely waiting for Air's reply that she'd take the place, Cheryl had gone on, gushing, "I'll go down to the ecological center tomorrow and contact whoever is paying for the condo they've set up for you while you're here and tell them you can stay at my sister's house. I know the head of the Rotary Club, which is the organization funding your housing. If you need anything done before you arrive, just let me know.

Air felt lucky to have met Cheryl. *What a great lady*, she thought with a smile as she walked toward the airport lobby. There, she saw a man holding a sign with her name on it. They exchanged greetings, and he drove her to the condo.

The condo was just as Cheryl had described, except she'd forgotten to mention the beautiful private veranda.

Air took three deep breaths. The place was traditionally decorated, and everything seemed new. The view of the bay was spectacular. Fresh cut flowers were everywhere, and a note welcomed her. It also said there was enough food in the refrigerator for two days and that the internet had been set up for her as a gift from the Rotary Club. She pulled her suitcase into the bedroom and immediately began unpacking. She put on her bathing suit and headed directly to the beach.

Air stretched out a large towel on one of the lounge chairs and ordered a fruit smoothie. The tide was out. She decided to get her feet wet. The water was warm and the waves gentle. The waves washed over her, and she instantly relaxed. Soon the beach would be packed with people for Christmas vacation. It was her favorite time of the year. She remembered all of the ceremonies and processions that would happen at the old church in town. The celebrations would last for two weeks. For now, she relaxed and watched the families and their children playing in the sand. The day passed quickly, and soon the brilliant sun sank into the bay, leaving behind a glowing red sky. She slowly walked back to her condo, kicking sand as she went.

She had set her laptop on the kitchen table. It seemed to be the most comfortable arrangement for her. She changed into a long, summery cotton dress and sat down at the table. She turned on her computer and went straight to her e-mail box. She wrote Keith a letter and kept it in draft form:

Keith,

I am finally here in PV. I suppose every mystic, every thinker, and every novice at some point concludes he or she is on a journey, or a prowl through the jungle will do—except for those poor, uneducated, disillusioned fools who think thirty virgins await them at the end of the road, instead of realizing that one lover, right now, tonight, constitutes the journey itself in part. In my perception of this sweet little town of Puerto Vallarta, harmony abounds. Peaceful spirits are playing in paradise. Laughter echoes all around. Twisting, turning energy moves in waves. Abstract thinkers are free to be. Unconditional love surrounds me, mirroring images of truthful awareness. The simple touch of sand brings grand happiness. I trust the winds of change. I'm fearless. My senses tell me to allow for the constant request for the growth of trust. I know I am a proper stranger here.

I can hardly believe I'm here. I must be having fun. Fun. Fun remains a mystery to me. Tonight, my mind is full of the universe, and my eyes see shooting stars. My heart is full of sunshine, and my dreams and wishes are of wind, rain, and lightning. Already the clouds are gathering for a full night of lightning and thunder. This will be the first time in my life I will be alone for the holidays.

Although the weather stays constant here, there is much turbulence within me. Magic. Love. Passion. Wisdom. Trust. Chaos. Now I'm amid such lushness and warmth, I am committed to stopping myself from making meaning of everything, to just noticing and being mindful. I couldn't help but notice as I was walking on the beach someone had a radio playing loudly. I chuckled to myself when I realized it was our song, "Unchained Melodies," that was playing on the radio.

I thought, *Hmm, I wonder if Keith is thinking about me right now, if he's trying to talk to me right at this very moment.* I quickly told myself to knock it off!

Today, as I was running back from the water to my chair, I looked up at the hill where we stayed. Out of the blue, as I was standing there, again our song came on another young man's radio as he walked by me. At that point, I simply started laughing out loud. I questioned whether to act on the feelings that swept over me on hearing that song, but I just told myself it was a coincidence. Then I reminded myself that I don't believe in coincidences and decided that I'd deem it a miracle when I heard the song for a third time in the same day. I tried challenging myself to knock off the "meaning crap."

The El Dorado Hotel is the same, with the same crowd hanging out for happy hour. I was walking back to my condo. Suddenly, I could hear the instrumental version of "our song" playing really loudly. I looked around and could not figure out where it was coming from. I decided it was one of two things. One, they play "our song" here as often as we play "La Bamba" in the States. Or two, you're thinking about me. I can feel it, but you aren't strong enough to reach out to me.

I plan to walk the beach most of the night. The giant female sea turtles will trundle slowly out of the waves and make their way up the beach and begin the laborious process of laying their eggs. I was told that every afternoon the humpbacks frolic with their babies and spout. What a miracle!

Tell me you're thinking about me, Keith. Tell me I'm not crazy. Tell me our gossamer silk thread that links us so deeply and has now been stretched so far will not break.

30

Air met with the officials of the environmental agency the next day. They began to plan the project. Ten volunteer artists would assist and learn from her. A major priority was to figure out how to keep the project going after Air left. The families were expecting Air and basically understood the goal of the project. Everyone was excited. They drove out to the dump to access what was needed in terms of supplies. Air was anxious to meet the families.

Air and the group of artists arrived at the site by noon and were greeted by thirty smiling families. Parents and grandparents all stood quietly waiting to shake her hand. The children ran around playing freely and giggled when they shook Air's hand.

Early on during negotiations surrounding the proposed project, Air had sent a letter to the president of the Rotary Club itemizing the needed supplies and budget, which included a generator for electricity and special papermaking machines called hydro-pulpers that would recycle paper into pulp. She also included information as to where they could order each of the items. They would also need an abundance of ordinary items, such as work tables, sponges, at least thirty large plastic utility tubs, and fine mesh painter's bags to carry the pulp to the tubs. They would need various sizes of papermaking screens, lots of special drying racks, and filing cabinets to store the newly made sheets of paper. Lastly, she'd emphasized the need for access to fresh water. There were many handmade paper mills in the States to order the materials, but Air wanted to support The Jemery Papermill since the company had donated many materials to her school projects over the years. Air was relieved to see that two large storage units had been trucked in to safely store the valuable equipment.

The first two weeks, Air trained the artist volunteers. Air taught them everything she knew about recycling paper and incorporating found objects into the matrix of the newly formed sheets of paper. The project had an environmental emphasis, but more importantly there was the goal of enabling the families to provide for themselves without having to send their children into town to beg the tourists for handouts.

The families could now learn a new, marketable skill and create art pieces—ranging from greeting cards to small sculptural cast pieces. A number of businesses in town had already agreed to take the created works on consignment. The ecological center had created lots of publicity about the project in the local papers. Tourists could read about the project on posters in the windows of the stores carrying the products of the families' newly learned skills. One of the main goals was to provide shelter for the families and to enroll the children in school for the first time.

The team worked with the families every day, except on weekends. Sometimes it was difficult to work with the stench from the garbage, but everyone kept up good spirits, which wasn't hard since they were working right on the beach and at any time could walk over to the water and splash around. The clear blue skies were full of many different varieties of birds that constantly circled the dump. The hills behind them were thick, lush jungle so the working environment was actually exhilarating. Air loved the colors of the indigenous plants. All of the colors in PV were extremely vibrant.

They taught the families how to carefully gather paper from piles of waste and put it into the recycling machines. The hydro-pulpers were large, deep plastic washtubs with ordinary sink drain holes at the bottom. Attached to the drains were industrial-strength garbage disposals that shredded the paper into pulp. A hose was attached to the garbage disposal that allowed the water and pulp to run back into the tub. It was a continuous recycling of shredding paper into a fine pulp that could be made into a new sheet of paper. From here, they dipped the papermaking screens, which were the size of standard greeting cards, into the slurry of pulp. They dried the sheets on large panels of plastic and then transferred them to drying racks.

The artists taught the families how to fold their paper into greeting cards and encouraged them to decorate each one individually. Each of the family's cards was unique. They also learned how to take the screens and create envelopes by stenciling the screen with tape. When the pulp was dry, all they had to do was fold the envelopes into shape.

It was the facial expressions of the elders when they had completed a greeting card and envelope that was especially touching and priceless to Air. She knew she'd shared skills that would change the lives of these people who had lived with despair and hopelessness long enough.

She loved watching the children squeal as they dropped their screens into the water and lifted them back out. With water being so primal, it seemed to take a week of just letting them play with the water and pulp before they were serious about making cards.

Over the next four months, the project became a huge success. The galleries and boutiques could not keep enough of the handmade recycled-paper greeting cards on their shelves. The tourists were more than willing to support the idea of helping the families. The most impressive success of the project was that fifteen young children were in school for the first time.

Each day, Air would return to the condo and turn the computer on and stare at the monitor. Her thoughts of Keith left her unsure of herself, and she found it difficult to reach out to him. She still had not heard from him—nor had she received "the box"—and she wondered if she had the will to stay strong and accept that she may never see him or the box again.

She was preoccupied with her thoughts of Keith and staring out the window, when she thought she heard Keith's voice. It seemed to be coming from her living room. Startled, Air looked around, but no one was there. She got up and walked through the condo and opened the front door, only to find no one. She went back and sat down in her favorite chair that overlooked the bay. She was reminded of D

J. and the talking Wandering Jews. Air had definitely made her own journey "over to the other side."

Back in the Bay Area, Keith was sitting out on his patio. His patio looked like a garden somewhere in Italy. He had an outdoor kitchen and a beautiful handmade wooden table that sat eight people. He loved to cook and invite people over when he felt he could handle being around people, which wasn't all that often. In the meantime, he loved to sit and feed the squirrels peanuts for hours. They would come right up to him and take the nuts from his outstretched hand. He had just finished planting a winter vegetable garden. He was a voracious reader and was almost through reading *The Star Wars Trilogy* for a second time.

Unannounced, his landlord of twenty years opened the garden gate and handed him his mail.

"How are you, Keith?" asked Roy. "I haven't seen you in a couple of days. Too much work?"

"Hey there, Roy!" Keith said warmly. "How are you? Have a seat. I've just been sitting here thinking about moving. I'm toying with the idea of moving to Puerto Vallarta. You know how much I love Mexico. Alaska Air is offering a spring clearance—round trip for only $169!"

He told Roy about Air's project in Puerto Vallarta. "I heard she signed a rental agreement for two years. Apparently, she found a sweet condo right on the beach in the old part of Vallarta," he said. "Of course, she has no idea about my wanting to join her."

"Wow! You've been talking about moving to Mexico for as long as I've known you. How good a friend is this woman? Don't tell me she's the one you say has been stalking you for all these years?" Roy asked in a disbelieving voice.

"Yeah, the same one! She's my heart, Roy. I've finally accepted the fact that we're hopelessly in love. I'm tired of fighting her off. I've just been too bullheaded to admit it. Every note, every line she's written to me either breaks my heart or fills me with memories of joy. I was the one who took her to Puerto Vallarta in the first place many years ago.

I'll never forget that trip. It was the only time in my life I've felt relaxed and okay with being around another human being for more than a day. I need to be with her, away from all the pressure of work to find out what is really going on between us. I wasn't ready for her emotionally until now. Since she's left, I've thought of her nonstop. I can't sleep. I have no desire to eat. I smell her perfume in every bookstore I go to.

"She came storming into my life over ten years ago. The moment we looked into each other's eyes we both felt the same deep connection. I know I've told you about my adventures with her over the years. Now that she's left, I feel angry, full of sorrow, and a sense of ageless emptiness. I've often wondered how I have lived without her. I've been in deep denial about my strong feelings for her ever since I was involved with her best friend. That's actually how we met. James and I had dated for a year before he finally introduced us to each other. I've had it in me to live without her, but I now question, do I want to keep on missing out on life without her? Life is incredible with her. She's like a child constantly exploring everything. I feel so alive when I'm with her. She's a wonder who I dare not speak too much of, but I can't, I won't resist her any longer."

He looked over at the squirrels patiently waiting for more nuts. Roy sat there watching the squirrels as well. He was speechless.

"Of course, there's always the possibility that we're both simply crazy. She's as manic as I am. When we're up, nothing is more delicious. But when we're down, it's unbearable to be with her. Still, I have to admit she is pure wonder, and I have a feeling it's time to surrender to something that is bigger than me. It's like someone saying, 'Excuse me, but your life is waiting.' Do you think I'm losing my mind, Roy? You've known me for many years," Keith asked, a bit of uneasiness in his voice.

Roy sat there for a few moments before replying. He didn't have answers. He wanted to support his friend but knew it was his choice. He looked over at the garden. Keith was his only tenant that actually took care of the property. "Have you made a decision about your business yet? I know you've been talking about selling it for years. Are you now serious?" he asked.

"Yeah, I've decided to sell it. I have a guy who lives out of state that has been bugging me to sell it to him for years. I've known for a long time I needed to get out from under that shop. Working eighty hours a week has deteriorated my health, and the isolation has been devastating. Many lost dark decades, Roy," Keith said sadly.

"Well, you won't hire employees. You've been doing all the work yourself for years!"

"Not really. All the long-standing companies who've ordered from me always request the same order. Maybe it will be a hundred cufflinks or five hundred tie tacks for the company's yearly banquet time. They want to acknowledge their employees for being in the business with them for twenty-five years. All I have to do is create the original dye and then send the order to the Philippines. The people in the Philippines work from the dye and do all the work for me, except if the original order has gold on it. That's a very long and tedious task and costly to farm out," Keith answered. "I do that part myself, and that's about all I do. So there's really not a lot of work. It's just been too many years now, and I'm not getting any younger."

"Last I heard you were trying to buy the building?" Roy said as he kicked some of the empty shells over toward the vegetable garden.

"Yeah, I tried. I was right in the middle of refinancing when my parents' health took a turn for the worse. They're both in their early nineties now and have cancer. I don't think they're going to be around too much longer. There will be no reason for me to stay around here anymore when they're gone. My heart is in Mexico, always has been. I've always known I would move down there. I ran away from home with some friends when I was a teenager. We went to Mexico and traveled for two years. She's the love of my life. I knew then I'd always go back," Keith said firmly.

"Well, you've been renting from me for twenty years now. I can't imagine not having you as a tenant. You pay the cheapest rent here! Wow, this is hard to believe. Well, you're right; you're not getting any younger. I honestly thought you'd live out your life alone. You're a hard nut to crack, Keith. Sometimes you're social, and sometimes I don't see you for months. I know you've struggled with your demons, Keith. Haven't we all? I really thought you and your friend James would make it."

"I did too, but he's too much into the party scene for me," Keith answered.

"How did you two meet?" asked Roy. "If you don't mind my asking?"

"I met James at a gay bar in the city."

"He seemed like a nice enough guy. Talked a lot, but he sure was funny. So, James is a friend of this gal who is in Mexico? How does he feel about you going off to be with his best friend, who happens to be a woman? What's her name?" asked Roy.

"Her name is Airstream. They went to school together. He's jealous and doesn't believe it will work."

"Isn't she the gal who has that great old '50 Studebaker?"

"Yes, that's her. And guess what? Before she left for PV, she sold it—that and about everything else she's worked so hard for all her life. She looked at her life and decided, 'To hell with all this crap. I'm out of here.' She used to refer to all her art awards and expensive stuff as 'evidence of greatness.' She hung all these letters of acknowledgment from people like President Clinton and President Bush in the bathroom, along with keeping her different awards on a special shelf in there. You know, she's very famous. She's been invited to exhibit her art all over the world. She always went along too. She's been commissioned to do public environmental art projects by many other countries besides Mexico. She's doesn't talk about her career to many people. She likes for people in her life to find out her history on their own, if they ever do," Keith said.

"So, she's been commissioned to do an environmental public art project with homeless people that live at a dump?"

"Yes, and she's using that as an excuse to leave the Bay Area and go to where her heart resides. That way, her friends won't give her any shit for giving up everything she's ever written a grant for. You know, for every grant she wrote, she was awarded the money. She's even founded two nonprofits. She almost moved to Japan a few years ago. The art form of papermaking is becoming a dying tradition, so th

University of Fukuoka offered her a teaching position. She was going to take it, but for some reason, the project she wanted to make into a nonprofit took over a year, and she lost the opportunity to teach. She's so fucking nuts. When she realized she would not be able to go back to Japan she pulled up some planks in her studio floor and put in a Japanese coy pond and built up a slate waterfall! It eased the pain of what she called, "a huge missed opportunity."

"But I'll tell you Roy, I've got the same thoughts in my head. I'm reevaluating my feelings about money and work. I've made some good investments, so financially, I'll be okay. I know I can't leave until my parents are taken care of. My mom seems to be going really fast now. She refuses to eat, which is hard to stand by and helplessly watch," Keith said sadly.

Keith stood up and walked over to his garden. He looked at the baby lettuce that was about two inches high already. He was growing snow peas along the side of the fence and spinach in front of the peas. He was an organic gardener. The harshest chemical he used was vinegar, and he believed if he put ground cinnamon and peppermint around all his plants he wouldn't have any snail or slug problems. It seemed to be working just fine.

"Funny how things work out. I thought I'd never talk to Airstream again. In fact, I have an e-mail she sent me about two years ago. It pissed me off so much that I printed it and taped it to the side of my computer just to remind myself of why I didn't want her in my life. But now, it's strange. We're so far apart and yet speak to each other in a new way. I don't like e-mails, yet I've saved every one of the e-mails she's ever sent me. I must have thousands now. You know, my mother is very fond of her. They spent a lot of time together over the last couple of years. At first, I was really pissed that she didn't ask me how I'd feel about her being friends with my mom, but now I'm happy because I see the joy in my mom's face when she talks about Air. They're very much alike," Keith said as he smiled at Roy.

Keith's landlord laughed and said, "One of those gals who'll check out with her 'inbox full,' huh? I'd sure like to see you with partner, Keith. I always felt that guy James wasn't the healthiest person for you. I think you've been alone too long. Life is meant to share experiences with another human being. Just so I'm clear about this, this is the gal who showed up here a few years back banging on your door demanding to see you, right? The time the neighbor Sarah called the police?"

"One and the same," Keith answered. "She's a hot-blooded Texan! Her mother is in her late seventies and still does online dating!"

"Get out of here!" Roy laughed.

"No, I'm not kidding. She's told me stories about her mother for years. I've always thought of her mother as not a particularly friendly person, with whom Air had nothing in common. Talk about mistaken preconceptions. Air sent me her mom's membership number so I could look her up on the net. Man, I don't know how much they have in common, but they both have that same devilish glint in their eyes, that look of careful mischief, and both look great!" Keith said with a voice of astonishment.

"Well, I'd better get going. I just stopped by to give you your mail. Looks like you got something from Mexico," Roy said with interest.

"Let's see. Yeah, it's from Airstream."

Keith left his garden and walked into his house. He set the letter on the table and picked up the phone. He called his parents' caretaker.

"Hello, Kathy, it's Keith. Just wanted to let you know I'm on my way up there. How are my parents?"

"They're about the same," Kathy told him. "Elizabeth hasn't eaten today. Maybe you can get some food into her while you're here."

His parents' home was up in the Oakland hills. It was a beautiful, Spanish style home with a view of the entire bay. He drove up the driveway and sat there, numb.

"Too many memories," he said out loud as he closed the car door.

He entered through the front door and immediately saw the mail stacked up on a table near the hallway. He started to go through the pile and found a handwritten letter from Air to Elizabeth. He opened it and started to read the letter.

While Keith read the letter, Air was talking to her mother on the phone.

"No, Mom," she said, "Keith's not here. I wish he were though. I can't help it. I've been in love with him since the first time I laid eyes on him, Mom. You tell my heart to stop loving him. That's not going to happen. I knew the moment I met him he would have my heart forever, but he's very reclusive and can't handle people. Whenever we spent time together, I wouldn't see him for weeks. It took too much of a toll on him, primarily because he says I'm too damned intense. I'm like a drink for him. He'd drink me to the last drop and wake up feeling like shit and swear he'd never touch a bottle of Air again," Air said with a hint of sorrow in her voice.

"Wh-elle, did you see his mom before you left?"

"Yes. It's hard for her to talk about Keith and me. Nothing would make her happier before she dies to see us together, but she reminds me she's not the meddling type. She says she believes Keith is in love with me. She tells me she's sorry I'm caught up in his gravity. I accept Keith will always be my 'ghostly lover,' Mom. He's my unrequited love during this lifetime."

She wasn't completely honest with her mom. She didn't tell her how depressed she was. Being alone in Mexico was taking its toll on her, even with all her time being spent working on the project.

"Mom, I'm caught in between thoughts. On the one hand, I'm lonely. On the other, I hate myself for feeling sad when there is so much horror, hunger, and suffering in the world? Listen, I'd better get going. I need to rest this weekend. This project is kicking my butt. I wish I spoke Spanish. Remember—I'm taking a break in two weeks and am coming back to the States for a week. I'll be at my old studio with Brenda. I'll call you when I get there."

"Honey, welcome to a cruel world. Ever' body's hurtin'. Sometimes ya just gotta walk away from a person who doesn't want to meet you halfway," D. J. replied. "Keep your chin up. Bye, sweetie. Stay outta the sky. I mean the sun."

❧ 31 ❧

Air boarded the plane headed back to the States with her headphones on listening to Sarah McLachlan's "Possession." She always listened to Sarah while she was flying. She knew every song by heart. She sat down and stared out the window. She took a deep breath and wondered if she would see Keith while she was in the States. He lived just four miles from her studio.

"Bye for now, PV. I'll be back," Air whispered as the plane started to taxi.

Five hours later, Air sat in her almost empty studio. *I should just call him. Now, Air, just call,* she coaxed. *There's nothing to be afraid of.*

"Hello?"

Air quickly hung up the phone as tears started to roll down her face. His voice sounded so sweet.

Why did I hang up on him? What's the mystery? I should have at least said hello. Air, there are no prayers for his return. You're just too tired.

Brenda had flown back East to see her family while Air was home. She unpacked her suitcase and had started making a grocery list when a knock on the door pulled her from her melancholic reverie.

She quietly walked up to the door and looked through the small peephole. She blinked her eyes, momentarily wondering if she was seeing things. Thoughts started to rain down on her.

Oh my God, it's Keith! My heart's pounding in my ears. My knees are starting to go weak. I'm going to faint. I can't let him see me looking like this. I look so tired. My hair's a mess, and my eyes are puffy. I've already changed my clothes, and I'm wearing a pair of flannel pajamas, not my normal vintage silk nightgowns. He's never seen me look normal. I have to open the door since this is history in the making. He'd never shown up at her door unannounced. Never.

Slowly, she opened the door in total disbelief that the love of her life was standing on her front porch. "Oh my God, Keith! What are you doing here? How did you know I was back? Oh my God! Are we on Earth or on our way back to Jupiter? Am I dying?" she said breathlessly.

Keith leaned in the doorway, raised his eyebrows, and smiled coyly at her. "Hello, sweetheart!" he said. "You do know how beautiful you look, don't you? Invite me in, sweetheart, so the neighbors don't see us making out," he added with a grin.

She opened the door wide enough for him to come in, and the two instantly fell into each other's arms. Keith held her head with both his hands and kissed her all over her face. He pushed her up to the wall, and she could feel the strength of his body against hers. She quivered uncontrollably as they kissed with wild abandon, all the while sliding slowly down the wall to the floor. Keith stopped kissing Air for a moment and looked her straight in the eyes. He slowly moved his hand from her face to her chest. He placed his hand on her heart and let it rest there for almost thirty seconds. Time stood still.

In a very loving tone of voice, he looked down at her and said, "Air, you are my heart. You always have been and always will be until the end of time." He paused. "I love you. I've loved you since I first laid eyes on you, and I am deeply sorry for all the pain I've caused you over the years."

"Keith, I love you more than you'll ever know," she responded, putting her hand on his face.

"I know. Have you forgotten what you feel, what you think is what I feel and what I think? I haven't been able to read, watch any movies, or do much of anything but stare at the ceiling since you left. I don't know who I am without you. All I know is that I love you, Airstream," Keith said, almost out of breath himself.

"I'm dead, baby. Just walk over me and make yourself at home," Air barely whispered.

"You're wondrous—you know that, right?" Keith exclaimed.

"I'm so surprised to see you. I must tell you—every time I got an e-mail from you telling me to just get on a bus and go visit blah, blah, blah little village, I felt like I was letting you down, like I was failing you and who you thought me to be. So many times, I wished I could have gotten up at the crack of dawn, gotten on a bus, and just headed out for unchartered territories, but I'm a fraud!" Air confessed. "I'm not as free as I seem to act."

"I don't care about that. I'm just so happy to see you! How's the project coming?" he asked as he helped her to stand up.

They walked hand in hand over to Air's entertaining area and sat down next to one another. Air's heart was pounding so hard, and she was having a hard time trying to act like she wasn't totally bewildered at his presence. She wondered what Keith thought about the way she looked. He didn't seem to even notice she looked tired and everyday common. She knew, ultimately, the day would come when he would see her without her façade of designer clothing. The simple truth of Air in a naked state was bound to occur at some point.

"The project is great," she said, gripping his hand more tightly. "Some of the families actually have their young kids in school for the first time ever. A very sweet thing has begun to unfold, Keith. Unbeknown to Elizabeth, and in all honestly to me as well, she gave me a gift I never would have thought could happen—a deep understanding of how to be my own best friend. I've missed her so much and can't wait to visit her."

"Both my parents are beginning to slide downhill, Air," he replied. "I don't think they're going to be around much longer, but enough of them for now. It is wonderful to see you. You look beautiful!" He stared into her eyes with a look of sincerity.

"I can't believe you're here! What the fuck are you doing here?" Air yelled as she grabbed him and started kissing him again.

"I thought you said you'd cleaned up your mouth?" he said jokingly.

"I can't help myself. Sorry. What are you doing here? In your last e-mail, you mentioned there were things I'd written that you didn't understand. Sometimes, I write too fast and just push the send button without rereading what I've written. And yes, you can send me attachments via e-mail, and no, I didn't take my printer. I had the choice of bringing along the printer or an extra suitcase full of shoes or both and paying for the extra suitcase. I chose the shoes, all seventeen pairs of them, and left the printer here! Ha, I haven't worn any of them. I am so tired at the end of the day. Actually, I take that back. There have been a couple of gala events celebrating the success of the project, and I've actually worn a couple of pairs of my designer shoes," she admitted.

"It's hard for me to imagine you like it there during the rainy season. I've always thought of you as a sunny kind of gal," he said with questioning eyes.

"The project ends in June, but I've rented the condo for two more years. I don't want to come back here."

"Hey, my sweetheart, my love, my heart, I didn't really want you to run off by yourself to San Miguel, Villa de Allende, Tasco, or anywhere without me! I was just supporting you. I know it can be lonely there, but Mexico has a way of keeping you moving. There's no time for parking violations. We'll go out in the magic rain and laugh together," he said reassuringly.

"Keith, Mexico is where I belong. I have nothing to say about it. She keeps me breathing. I'm just having a tough time adjusting. I'll never be able to thank you enough for giving me the gift of Mexico. I feel my personal power so intensely there. Sometimes I have to walk along the beach and just scream to let out all my pent up energy. My 'spidey senses' are overwhelming there. Puerto Vallarta is definitely my power spot on the planet. I had a really tough time in the beginning when I let go of all my facades. I knew I was not coming home to the States. I just stared out into a world in which I had no sense of self."

Air was careful not to make too much of Keith saying he loved her. In the past, she had misunderstood his caring for her too many times.

"Airstream, you're not listening to me. Did you hear what I just said to you? You know we're both hopeless romantics."

"Yes, I know we are! I've always known we are," Air said laughingly.

"How many seconds does it take your wondrous heart to go from manic to depressive? Air, give me a dusty old letter that is handwritten, a yellowed photograph like the one at our casa, with eyes to the sky and that look of wonder in your eyes, and I am in heaven!"

"Honestly, Keith, you and I have only existed in e-mail communication. It has been a safe place for both of us to hide out—both of us writing wonderful love lines and being fully self-expressed in the luxury of the written word. We've been the 'almost lovers' for years. There's been little exchange of eye contact and touching of souls when our bodies have been near each other. We've served as muses for each other in all reality. We've been the dearest and un-dearest of pen pals.

"Sometimes I have no idea how you can stand being on the receiving end of my voracious and endless e-mail chatter. We've experienced too much to ever let our gossamer thread break. We just have to remember e-mails suck. They lack intonation. We're both too sensitive to every written word. I admit it does bring a smile and moments of tingles and joy when you write terms of endearment to me. There have been so many nights I have gone back in time when we were here in my studio, dancing so close, to whatever song was playing on my jukebox. Any song would do those nights. Remember?" Air asked

"I will never forget those nights either. Air, you need to shut up. You've been excreting words for almost half an hour. Let me know when I can talk! I'm well aware there is an angel in the house," Keith exclaimed.

"Okay, I'll shut up. I want to share with you, though, how your mom has inspired me. In fact, while in Mexico I had an intense dream about her. She asked me to dance with her. She whispered words to me that were very sensual!"

Air began to tremble. She was on the verge of sobbing. She was afraid if she let him talk, he would probably get too nervous and say good-bye.

"Let me just say I love it when you call me sweetheart. I will make love to my bed and have luscious dreams tonight. Lately, I can

393

hear myself talking out loud in my sleep. In fact, twice I have become fully aware that I am awake talking and have allowed myself to just keep right on a talkin'," Air told him.

"Air, I need to be serious for a moment. Since you left, I've lain in my bed every night and relived that evening the plane took flight to Puerto Vallarta the first time we went down together. When we gained enough altitude, we witnessed a once-in-a-lifetime event. On one side of the plane, there was a very full moon, and on the other side of the plane, there was the full sun just starting to descend into the horizon. It was utterly astounding! I have tried to replace that memory with other images. Then, I ask myself, why would I want to do that? I will never forget that first night sensing you spooning me in bed. You were asleep, and my body started to spasm in ways I'd never known. Air, I have something to tell you."

"What is it? It isn't bad, is it?" she wailed.

"No, it's not bad at all! It's wonderful, my heart! I've realized how much I love you and want to be with you. I'm selling my business and will take care of my parents as long as they need me. Then I'm all yours, and you'll be all mine. You've been journeying toward me for many years. I've finally realized I've been journeying toward you. It's just that you always come from your heart. You have to remember I studied to be an engineer and want things proven to me. I've never easily trusted my heart the way you do. Our paths have crossed at many critical times. This time, I'm not shooting myself in my big toe!

"Air, I understand now what you mean when you say that time is tricky and life is short or life is tricky and time is short," he said in a loving and sincere tone.

Air was stunned and dazed with emotions. The voices in her head were screaming at her to tell him to leave. She felt besieged by her personalities. All of them were trying their best to overpower her weakness for Keith. As she tried to stand up, she realized she was flabbergasted at this whole bizarre scene. A voice, louder than all the others, begged her to find her anger with him. The voice pleaded with her to remember the years of agony she'd felt and to consider he was possibly drunk. It must have been Claire.

She immediately got up and went into the kitchen. She opened the refrigerator and took out a bottle of her most expensive champagne, which she kept for just such occasions as this. She reached for the two sacred champagne glasses that she kept separate from the rest. These glasses were for her and Keith only. They were magnificent. Of course, they were hand blown like the others, but these were dramatic. Intricate roses and vines were etched deeply around the tall, thin glasses. She set the bottle and the glasses on her beautiful, exquisite art-nouveau platter. She wanted Keith to do the honors of opening the bottle and pouring the champagne. She slowly walked back over to him.

I can hear the director yelling, "Action on the set!" The cameras are rolling, and I'm walking back to the man I love more than life itself, who just professed his undying love for me. Is it the beginning or the end of my movie?

She set the tray on the table and looked at him. "Oh my God! Just like when we were in the first place we stayed in PV at Playa de la Casa, my 'Playa de Spidey Senses' say you and I are at the very vortex of our relationship, Keith. What will become of us is yet to be discovered, but I am not splashing the water this time. I'm looking at the reflection of the moon, and I like what I see and how I feel. I must be dead! Tell me I am alive and not dreaming!" Air pleaded.

"Air, you are very much alive. Open your eyes as wide as you can, and look into mine. This is an overwhelming and decisive moment for us, Air. You give me pain. You give me milk and honey. I haven't really had time to read what you have written, but I will go back and reread all your e-mails. Let me have, for now, that moment flying toward the tropics with the full moon rising on one side of the plane and the sun setting on the other. For now, in our minds, let's kiss the setting sun and the full moon, which, by the way, have you looked outside? There is a full moon tonight, and I want you. No more of this life-passing-us-by stuff!" Keith exclaimed.

"My God! You're serious!"

"Oh yes, my love. You are a drug called sweetheart. Hearing your laughter makes me feel like I've discovered gold every time. We're going to have sweet, golden mornings for the rest of our lives. I'm planning to join you in Puerto Vallarta very soon. I may not be able to live there right now, but I will make lots of weekend visits when you head back."

Keith grabbed Air and twirled her around at least three times. "I keep asking are we crazy or simply hopelessly in love?" he yelled.

"Simply hopelessly in love! Oh my God, I can't believe this! This is awesome!" Air roared. "I have asked you so many times to look into your heart and ask yourself how you truly felt about us. No more hiding out for either of us. I firmly believe the gold lies in the darkness. We've finally struck gold! We now have our gold. We have each other. Forever!"

Keith opened the bottle of champagne. They looked at each other and clicked glasses. "To us!" they said in unison with grins as wide as the horizon.

"Air, I need to go back up to my parents for the night. Elizabeth asked me to spend the night. I will tell her you are back in town. She will be ecstatic. She will want to see you. I will call you tomorrow, and we'll go for a picnic at Estuary Park in Berkeley just like old times. Just like the first time I asked you to go to Mexico with me. Does that sound good? Or do you have plans?" he asked.

"No, my love. You are my plans now. I would love to have a picnic with you and yell at the pelicans like we used to do. I have so much room in my heart for you," she whispered.

"Okay, let's go kiss the moon together, and I'll call tomorrow."

❧ 32 ❧

Airstream watched Keith drive off into the moonlight. She stood there on her front porch stunned and in total disbelief still waving good night long after his car had turned the corner.

Should I go to my computer and write down this moment I just shared with Keith verbatim, just so I'll have proof I'm not dreaming? Air wondered. *Did I really hear him say he was in love with me and that we will be together for all time?*

"You've heard all his promises before," Claire yelled in an incredulous voice.

This is different. His intentions sounded so authentic, and the sincerity in his voice was so real. I'm frightened. I feel like I'm about to have a severe anxiety attack, Air replied.

"Oh good grief, you're not going to fall for his crap again, are you?" demanded Claire. "He's put us through this countless times," Claire pleaded.

"What about the time he told you the two of you were going to Paris, and you even called Elizabeth and told her what he had said!" joked Joe-Bob. "He's just in one of those moods he gets in. Tomorrow, he'll send an e-mail and apologize. Then you won't hear or see him again for months."

"How about all of us say we want this conversation left out of the book? We're getting really sick and tired of hearing about Keith this and Keith that," added Claire. "Air, we got the lessons, and it's time for us to move on."

"Shall we take a vote?" asked Veronica.

"We don't think that is necessary. Air is not in her right mind now. She knows his crap. We don't have anything to worry about. She's not going to let him take her for a ride again," Little Suzie said sadly. "God, do we fall for stupid men or what?"

"*No, we don't. We just look past the parts we can see that are not going to work and continue to believe we can change people,*" said Claire.

"*Well, our audience now knows we are courageous and strong. They'll hold us as someone who's a real survivor and very unique. Oh God, did I just say "unique"? We've actually made a difference in a lot of people's lives—differences that will live on past our own lifetimes, you know. Think of all our projects,*" said Joe-Bob.

"*Hold on, everybody,*" said Claire. "*We're forgetting Air really loves this guy and has for a very long time. I believe that, no matter what happens in her life, she would walk away in a matter of seconds and run to Keith if she had the chance. Now she has the chance. No matter what man she dates, she will never allow the relationship to get serious. Her love for Keith is so profound she feels she could never betray him. She is not capable of letting any other man get close to her. You take Keith out of the book and you take the spinal cord out of all of us.*"

Printed in the United States
By Bookmasters